CHANUR'S
HOMECOMING

CHANUR'S HOMECOMING

C. J. Cherryh

DAW BOOKS, INC.

DONALD A. WOLLHEIM, PUBLISHER

1633 Broadway, New York, NY 10019

PRINTED IN THE U.S.A.

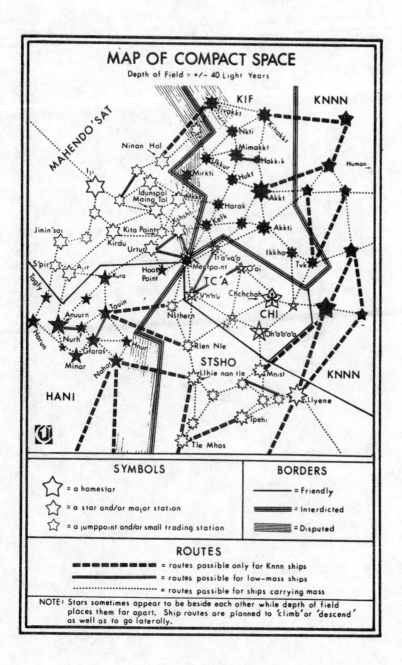

MAP OF COMPACT SPACE

Depth of Field = +/- 40 Light Years

MAHENDO'SAT

KIF

KNNN

Iyokki
Kihakkt
Nkti
Ninan Hol
Mimakkt
Ukkur
Hakkik
Mirkti
Hukt
Human
Idunspol
Maing Tol
Mkks
Harak
Kefk
Akkt
Kshti
Jinin'sai
Kita Point
Akkti
Kirdu
Urtur
Ikkho
S'pir
A'ir
Tvk
Hoas
Point
Tra'va'o
Kura
Meetpoint
O'oi
Tagty
IC'A
Touin
V'n'n'u
Cichchah
Nstheru
CHI
Anuurn
N'
Nurh
Oh'a'o'o
Harun
Gfaras
Rlen Nle
Minar
Nahor
Hnur
STSHO
KNNN
Llyene
Lihie nan tle
Mnist
HANI
Tpehi
Tle Mhos

SYMBOLS

☆ = a homestar

☆ = a star and/or major station

☆ = a jumppoint and/or small trading station

BORDERS

——— = Friendly

═══ = Interdicted

▦ = Disputed

ROUTES

▬ ▬ ▬ ▬ = routes possible only for Knnn ships

——— = routes possible for low-mass ships

········· = routes possible for ships carrying mass

NOTE: Stars sometimes appear to be beside each other while depth of field places them far apart. Ship routes are planned to 'climb' or 'descend' as well as to go laterally.

In our last episode . . .*

Two years previous, the aggressive kif, natives of Akkht, had a *hakkikt*, a leader so fearsome he united more than the usual number of kif behind him in a pirate band. This *hakkikt*, Akkukkak, had seized a ship of a hitherto unknown species, humanity; and acquired ambitions beyond the usual kifish banditry against other species. With a species to prey on which was without the protections of the Compact, he might grow powerful enough to gather the whole kifish species under his influence, sweeping down on the Compact in a wave of conquest unprecedented in history.

But his human prey escaped him. While the *hakkikt* was docked at Meetpoint starstation, the last surviving prisoner ran to shelter aboard *The Pride of Chanur*, a hani merchant ship captained by one Pyanfar Chanur, who in no wise solicited this refugee.

Still Pyanfar and her crew as a matter of policy refused to surrender the human to Akkukkak's demand. This was a two-fold calamity for the kif: first the loss of the human and all the information he held about his species; and then this defiance from a mere hani merchant—who continued to elude the great *hakkikt* in a multi-star chase. Akkukkak was suddenly fighting not only for his prey but for his life, for a kif who

---

* as told in *The Pride of Chanur, Chanur's Venture,* and *The Kif Strike Back*

loses face rapidly loses followers, and becomes the target of other kif with ambitions. Akkukkak was compelled to seek vengeance on a scale sufficient to cover this humiliation; and this humiliation involved an ambition large enough to shake worlds.

He took the unprecedented step of moving on the hani homeworld, seeking first the humiliation and removal of Pyanfar Chanur and all her clan, in what may have been a kifish misapprehension of the importance of any single hani; he was thinking as a kif, and interpreted Pyanfar's moves as aggressive ambition. He also demanded the return of his property. In all these demands he seriously misjudged the hani, for no action he could have taken would have rallied the hani against him more than this intrusion on hani home territory and the demand to surrender a living being who had taken shelter within a hani clan. Hani resisted in a battle at Gaohn station, and they received mahen help in the persons of two hunter captains, known to Pyanfar (mahendo'sat names are not easy for outsiders) as Goldtooth and Jik. This firefight would have been serious enough; but the hostilities disturbed yet another species of the Compact, the methane-breathing knnn, aliens of direst reputation and the highest technology in known space. The knnn, intervening, took Akkukkak away to a fate unguessed. And that settled that. The human Tully went home to his people. Pyanfar Chanur looked forward to a new era of trade and prosperity in which not only Clan Chanur, but all hani-kind would profit from human contact.

She reckoned, unfortunately, without the stsho, whose station at Meetpoint was the hub of all trading routes of the Compact. Total xenophobes, the stsho withdrew Chanur's trading permit. More, Akkukkak had indeed caused a profound disturbance in hani affairs by the manner of his demise. Chanur was forced to defend itself against challenge by hani enemies who took advantage of popular fears of the knnn, and though Lord Kohan Chanur held on, Chanur lost valuable allies whose support in council Pyanfar and other women of the clan very greatly missed.

To add to the difficulties, no one kept their promises. The humans did not return and the mahendo'sat withdrew into isolation.

Two impoverished years later, Pyanfar Chanur was doing all she could to keep *The Pride* running—and she was not the only Chanur captain in deep trouble.

Then by some unforeseen miracle her papers cleared and she was invited back to Meetpoint to recover her trading license.

She pulled into Meetpoint with the last cargo she could afford to buy, and fell right into the welcoming arms of Goldtooth the mahendo'sat, who handed her a courier packet with the human Tully as a secret passenger and told her to run for her life: the kif were hunting him.

Now among Pyanfar's other troubles, she had defied hani custom. Hani males were traditionally a protected class within hani society, the few who made successful challenge becoming clan lords, ceremonial heads of clans, who in fact had no meaningful authority at all, the real legal and financial power resting with the clanswomen who conducted exterior business. The rest of the males lived and died in rural exile, excluded from all society but their own; and to this pool of males a defeated clan lord must retire, to a short and wretched life among younger, ambitious males practicing their combat skills. Pyanfar's husband Khym Mahn was defeated by their son Kara, and deposed; but he postponed his exile to help her in her fight against the kif, and became one of the few hani males ever to leave the planetary surface—by interstellar agreement, they were in fact barred from doing so, since they had a reputation for berserker rages dangerous to life and property.

But Pyanfar, faced with the prospect of sending Khym downworld again to die, defied treaty and custom and took him aboard *The Pride;* more, she secured working papers for him by bribing a mahendo'sat official, and listed him as crew. Having traveled and worked with alien males, Pyanfar has begun to see in her own husband traits no hani has ever looked for in a male of her species; she conceived the idea in her heart of hearts that the berserker rages might be due more to upbringing than biology, and yet—and yet she *is* hani; and to doubt something out of all folk wisdom, something built into all language and custom and tradition, is very difficult, the more so that Khym himself doubts her theories; he is, after all, a product of his culture too, and all the complex of beliefs which encourage him to be a man also foster his aggressive impulses and his doubts about his faculties. It is not, in sum, a comfortable situation for *The Pride*'s crew either, who still cannot figure out whether they ought to treat Khym as a man or try to ignore that handicap and treat him as one of themselves—in which case modesty and custom and language are in the way: female humor and traditional curses involve sons and males; pausing to dress in shipboard emergencies is not practical; ship facilities are not designed to accommodate a man's larger stature; and male thinking is traditionally given to be hasty and imprecise, not the sort of thing anyone wants to rely on in any use of hazardous machinery.

But Khym once-lord of Mahn acquired the unprecedented (for a hani) designation of crew*man* aboard *The Pride of Chanur.*

The worst happened forthwith: Khym was involved in a riot that heavily damaged Meetpoint station. Pyanfar escaped a second loss of her license only by charging the entire bill to the mahendo'sat, who had given her a credit slip for quite different purposes—to aid her with the transport of the human, Tully.

Unfortunately this riot happened under the disapproving witness of one Rhif Ehrran, an agent of the hani government.

Now Rhif Ehrran had come to Meetpoint on quite different business. So many of the spacing clans of the hani had taken heavy damage at Gaohn that the groundling clans had seized control of the *han,* the hani senate. Meanwhile the xenophobic stsho, wealthiest species of the Compact, had bribed certain hani politicians, wanting to subvert hani politics from the inside for fear of two other species: first, humans, who had trespassed stsho borders and might do so again; second, the kif, because two of Akkukkak's erstwhile lieutenants, one Akkhtimakt and one Sikkukkut, had risen to declare themselves *hakkikktun.* These two kif were currently battling it out between themselves, but they had already polarized kifish society into a frighteningly few predatory bands. From a fragmented piratical species, kif had suddenly achieved unity to a degree Akkukkak himself never effected.

The burning issue, among kif as elsewhere, was humanity; and the persistent rumors held that humanity was coming to the Compact right through methane-breather space, to unite with the mahendo'sat, which meant trouble for the kif. The rumors happened to be true. And the stsho, who, incapable of fighting, had long relied on mahen guards for protection, suddenly suspected they could no longer trust mahendo'sat. Hence the sudden coziness with the groundling hani clans and the flood of stsho money to certain hani pockets.

The *han* had heard rumors too; and heard rumors, moreover, of one hani actively cooperating with the kif—the hani pirate Dur Tahar of *Tahar's Moon Rising.* That was the ship Rhif Ehrran had gone out there to hunt. But Ehrran was also there on secret business: negotiating with the stsho on behalf of certain of her own political patrons. Certainly Ehrran was interested when Pyanfar Chanur involved herself in a major riot aboard Meetpoint, entangled with both mahen secret agents and a high-ranking kif. So when Pyanfar paid a huge bribe to the stsho stationmaster, Stle stles stlen, and made a hasty departure from Meetpoint with the human Tully aboard, Rhif Ehrran followed, smelling political blood and seeing in this move of Pyanfar's a threat to all she stood for.

Akkhtimakt headed Pyanfar off by occupying Kita Point, strategic gateway to mahen and hani space, forcing all traffic to detour into the Disputed Zones along the kifish/mahen border. With *The Pride* damaged enroute, Pyanfar had no choice but to go to Kshshti Station in the Zones, seeking repairs and help. Her intended destination was Maing Tol, the mahen regional capital; her aim, to deliver Tully and his message from humanity into the hands of Goldtooth's superiors. But on her arrival at Kshshti, she ran into Rhif Ehrran, the kif Sikkukkut, and the hani trader *Ayhar's Prosperity,* which had lost its cargo at Meetpoint thanks to her: its captain Banny Ayhar was not pleased.

Rhif Ehrran demanded Tully's surrender to her; and her attempt to take custody of Tully resulted in a dock fight which put Tully and Pyanfar's young niece Hilfy Chanur into the hands of their enemy Sikkukkut. Sikkukkut left, leaving Pyanfar the message that she could recover the hostages at Mkks, a station right on the kifish border. It was too obviously a trap.

In the midst of all this, Goldtooth's partner Jik (whose true mahen name is Keia Nomesteturjai) showed up at Kshshti with his powerful hunter-ship *Aja Jin;* and sent the hani captain Banny Ayhar on to Maing Tol with the message Pyanfar had brought this far. He supported Pyanfar in her decision to go to Mkks: he went along and somehow argued Rhif Ehrran into joining them.

At Mkks, Sikkukkut returned Hilfy and Tully in a negotiated settlement. He also gave Pyanfar a gift of kifish esteem—a slave named Skkukuk.

And all they had agreed to do in return was to cross into kifish territory and help Sikkukkut take Kefk station, the main kifish link to . Meetpoint, in an act of outright piracy.

Jik agreed, to Pyanfar's consternation. Moreover, Rhif Ehrran did, after listening to Jik's persuasion.

They made the jump and they succeeded. Their ships occupied Kefk kifish-fashion, by superior bluff and with very little damage.

Goldtooth showed up then, furious with his partner Jik, for Goldtooth had been lying silent just off Kefk monitoring the situation. He had been off a time fighting Akkhtimakt, trying to open the way for a human fleet now enroute to Compact space, and now Jik had made a deal which would effectively bring Sikkukkut into alliance with the mahendo'sat against Akkhtimakt, emphatically not the situation Goldtooth was working toward. Humans were headed into Compact space in great number, and Goldtooth's whole plan for human-mahen alliance now was jeopardized by the taking of Kefk and its delivery to Sikkukkut, who consequently would bring the kif into unity under one *hakkikt* much faster than Goldtooth's plans called for.

Pyanfar meanwhile received a second gift of esteem from Sikkukkut, the person of her old enemy Dur Tahar the pirate, who had been a respectable hani merchant captain before she opposed Pyanfar at Gaohn and accidentally ended up in alliance with the kif, her reputation ruined. Now a prisoner of Sikkukkut, captured along with Akhtimakt's partisans on the station, Tahar had reached the nadir of her fortunes and begged Pyanfar to intercede with the kif for the lives of her cousins still in Sikkukkut's hands.

Rhif Ehrran at once stepped in to demand custody of Tahar. Pyanfar refused, having nothing but disgust for Ehrran's secret police methods and police state mentality. Tahar would go home to hani justice, but aboard *The Pride of Chanur.* It was a direct slap at Ehrran and a threat to her prestige; and a countermove against her patrons' ambitions. It served notice that Chanur, instead of bowing to political force, was going to exercise the ancient authority of a clan to take its own prisoners and administer its own justice before turning the offender over to the *han.* This effectively meant that Rhif Ehrran's superiors and political allies could not touch Tahar without dealing with Chanur as a head-of-cause in open council, and without bringing the whole foreign policy issue into debate in the *han* with Chanur as the chief spokeswoman for the opposition, precisely the situation Chanur's enemies did not want.

Then, while Pyanfar went to negotiate with Sikkukkut, Goldtooth secretly met with Ehrran. And some unknown agency started a riot on the docks, which set Akhtimakt's hitherto cowed partisans on the station to attacking Sikkukkut's forces. Pyanfar and the Tahar crew, whose freedom she had just negotiated from Sikkukkut, were caught in the middle of the firefight, as Goldtooth and Rhif Ehrran both took advantage of the confusion to break dock and run for Meetpoint—together.

The slave Skkukuk saved Pyanfar's life in the riot, to her profound distress at the debt.

But Jik, also attempting Pyanfar's rescue from the firefight, fell into the hands of Sikkukkut, who had some new and hard questions to ask of Jik regarding Goldtooth, mahen ambitions, and the whereabouts and course of human ships.

Chapter One

The Pride's small galley table was awash in data printout, paperfaxes ringed and splotched with brown gfi-stains, arrowed, circled, crossed out, and noted in red and green ink till they were beyond cryptic. The red pen made another notation and another snaking arrow; and the bronze-pelted hani fist that held it flexed claws out and in again in profoundest frustration. Pyanfar Chanur sat in this sanctuary gnawing her mustaches and drinking cup after cup of lukewarm gfi amid her scribbles on the nav and log records.

Pyanfar was not her usual meticulous self—rough blue spacer-breeches instead of the bright red silk she favored, and not a single one of the bracelets and other gold jewelry she usually wore, just the handful of spacer rings up the sweep of her tuft-tipped ears. Her best pair of red silk breeches had gone for rags, perished of the same calamity which had stiffened her joints, left several knots on her maned skull, and made small puncture wounds all over her red-brown hide. Her niece's deft fingers had tweezed out the metal splinters down in sickbay, with the help of the magnetic scanner, and patched the worst cuts with plasm and sticking-plaster. Haral, her second-in-command, had suffered the same, and limped about her duties on the bridge, running printouts and sitting watch in her turn, while the rest of the crew was in scarcely better shape, hides patched, manes and beards singed, with bandages here and there about their persons. That had been a memorable fight on the docks, indeed a memorable fracas; but Pyanfar could have recalled it with more pleasure if it had come to better success.

Scritch-scratch. Another note went down on the well-worn starchart. She studied it and restudied it, gnawed her mustaches and refigured, though all but the finest decimal exactitudes of current star-distances were in her memory. There were surely answers in that map; and she racked her wits to find them, to discover what the opposition planned and what her allies (treacherous though they be) might be figuring to do, and to juggle all the variables at once. The answer was *there,* patently there, in the possibilities of that starmap and in the self-interests of eight separate and polylogical species.

Knowing all the options, all those self-interests, and all the capabilities of the ships involved, a hani merchant might conceivably manage to think of something clever. She needed something clever. Desperately.

She sat at Kefk, inside kifish space where no hani of right mind would ever consent to be, allied to kif no hani in her right mind would ever trust; she sat in the same space station with nervous methane-breathers (tc'a and chi) who had lately been raided (reprimanded? attacked? congratulated?) by an intruding knnn ship, which had carried off a tc'a vessel. Gods knew what was in the tc'a's multipartite minds; the chi *had* no minds that any oxy breather had ever proved; and as for the knnn, no one had any least idea what they were up to. Wherever those black hair-snarls on thin black legs intruded their influence (and the power of their strange ships), things bent. Fast. But the knnn had withdrawn and Kefk occupied itself with its own affairs, like repair of its fire-ravaged docks and placating its new master, the *hakkikt* Sikkukkut, whose ships now numbered thirty-two (the count was rising). It occupied itself with the hani pirate Dur Tahar, lately at liberty by the *hakkikt's* grace; with the mahen hunter-ship *Aja Jin,* lately outside the *hakkikt's* good graces, and still at dock, sitting beside *The Pride* and not daring send a compromising query across the dockside communication lines. Kefk had a great deal to worry about, not least of which was the missing hunter-ship *Mahijiru* and its captain, one Ana Ismehananmin, aka Goldtooth, and the hani ship that had run with him.

Along with major structural damage, a breached sector, fire, disruption of the lifesupport systems, the remnants of a revolution and other nagging difficulties.

Another flurry of figures and pen-corrections. There was, number one, the mahendo'sat territory to reckon with: a wide sprawl of stars into which at least one message had gone and might have gotten through, knnn and the gods willing. Banny Ayhar would have done her best to get it through, as much as any merchant captain could do: she might have lived to get it to Maing Tol, if the knnn had not stopped her or if the kif had not been laying for her. The mahendo'sat, tall black-furred primates with enough double-turning motives involved to baffle a tc'a's multipartite brain (but antagonism toward their neighbors the kif was always high among them), *might* have made a move if that message had gotten through. Down the line via Kshshti and out to Mkks might be a good course of action for the mahendo'sat to take, if they hoped to forestall any kifish breakout along that border; but Meetpoint station or Kita Point, critical to all trade routes, was most likely the object of any major push from the mahendo'sat. That effort would have to come via Kshshti if Kita was still blocked; while Kefk, in kifish territory, was not a likely route for them. Not impossible, given the current state of borders in the Compact, just less than likely.

Also reckoning mahendo'sat moves, it was very likely there were one or more mahen hunter-ships escorting the human ships; and *they* were coming in toward Meetpoint from Tt'a'va'o and tc'a/chi space.

With human ships and human captains; still another set of motives and self-interests, on gods-knew-what orders from their own authorities. (Or lack of them—who knew what human minds were like?)

Further complication: kifish forces under the rival *hakkikt* Akkhtimakt had likely moved in to take the mahen/tc'a station at Kshshti. That might stand off any mahen flanking move to Meetpoint, if Akkhtimakt's forces still controlled Kita as well. Akkhtimakt might have Kita, Urtur, Kshshti, or all three, and advance from any or all of those points against Meetpoint and/or Kefk itself, if the report Goldtooth had brought was true and the stsho had been fools enough to invite Akkhtimakt in as hired help.

There was, lure to Akkhtimakt, his greatest enemy Sikkukkut, sitting here at Kefk gathering to his control every ship that came into port. And revenge was always high on any list of kifish motives. *Pukkukkta,* they called it. Advance retaliation was better than revenge after the fact. Having an enemy *know* his calamity before he died was best of all.

Yet another move of the pen, another arrow, lurid green: one could not exclude interference from the methane-breathers, whose motives no oxy breather could guess.

And, certainly not to be forgotten, there were the stsho who owned

Meetpoint, congenitally noncombatant, but hiring alien, aggressive help right and left and forming reckless associations.

While the *han*—gods, the hani senate was up to its nose in politics as usual, and Rhif Ehrran was on her way to Meetpoint with evidence enough to outlaw Chanur once and for all.

The Pride of Chanur sat at a kifish dock six to seven jumps from homestar, no matter which way she figured it. Six or seven jumps was a long way, a very long way, measured in stress on ship and on body; and gods knew what would follow on her heels, if she did what she would gladly do now and broke dock at Kefk and ran for their lives, withdrawing herself like a good law-abiding hani from all the affairs of kif and mahendo'sat and multifarious aliens.

But the trouble would surely follow her home; she knew beyond a doubt that it would. She had involved herself in the affairs of kifish *hakkiktun* and she had acquired their notice. She had made herself a name in kifish eyes. She had gotten *sfik*, face. And that meant that kif would never let her alone so long as she lived.

Her uneasy partner Sikkukkut an'nikktukktin would never forget her; certainly (gods forbid he should replace Sikkukkut in power) her personal enemy Akkhtimakt would not.

Pyanfar scribbled, flicked her ears, and the rings of forty years of voyages chimed in her hearing. A pearl swung from her right ear, a Llyene pearl from the oceans of the stsho homeworld; she still wore that gift, regardless of the perfidy of the giver, who was Goldtooth, friend, traitor, flatterer, and tenfold liar.

Curse him to his own deepest hell.

Goldtooth was bound for Meetpoint with Rhif Ehrran, beyond a doubt he was, the conniving bastard. He was dealing with the stsho and anyone else who offered his species an advantage, and he was betting opposite to the alliance his own partner Jik had made—to which maneuver Sikkukkut took strongest and understandable exception.

Another scribble.

A quick movement caught her eye, a black blot speeding across the floor, sinuous, small, fast.

She leapt to her feet. "Haral!" she yelled, while paper cascaded off the table and the black thing paused for one beady-eyed stare before it skittered on, faster than her limping dive to stop it.

Haral appeared, hobbling in by the short bridge-galley corridor, and did a fast skip and wince as it dived between her feet and vanished.

Pyanfar snatched up a handful of jumbled papers. "Fry that thing!"

"Sorry, captain. We're setting traps—"

"Traps be bothered, they're *breeding,* I swear they are! Get Skkukuk on it, they're his by-the-gods dinner. Let *him* find 'em. Gods-be mess. Vermin!" The hair stood up on her shoulders and she stared at her first officer in bleakest despair. No one in the crew was up to more orders, more duty, or more trouble.

"The things might get into something vital," Pyanfar said. Common sense, covering absolute revulsion. "Gods, get 'em *out!*"

"Aye," Haral said, in a voice as thin and hoarse as hers. And Haral limped away, to get their own private kif to ferret his dinner out of the *The Pride*'s nooks and crannies before something else went wrong. That took a guard, to watch Skkukuk; and gods curse the luck that had set the things free on the ship in the first place. She had heard the story, inspected the burned patch on *The Pride*'s outer airlock seal. And she blessed Tirun Araun's quick hand that had gotten that door shut— vermin and all.

Gods *knew* how those black slinking pests had gotten up from lowerdeck.

Climbed the liftshaft? The airducts?

The thought of a myriad little slinking black bodies loping along the airshafts and into lifesupport lifted the hairs at her nape.

What were the gods-be things *eating?*

She scooped up a last couple of papers with a wince and a grimace and sat down again. Rested both elbows on the table and rested her aching head in her hands.

She saw within her mind a dark kifish hall; sodium-light; and a table surrounded by insect-legged chairs—her partner Jik sitting there with one of Sikkukkut's minions holding a gun to his head, and that bastard Sikkukkut starting to ask closer and closer questions.

She had not had a way to help him. She had been lucky to get her own crew out of there alive; and to keep herself and her ship as free as it was, under kifish guns at a kifish dock.

Send another appeal to Sikkukkut to ask for Jik's release? Sikkukkut's patience with her was already frayed. Perhaps it was personal cowardice not to send another message. Perhaps it was prudence and saving what could be saved, not to push Sikkukkut into some demonstration of his power—at Jik's expense. Kifish heads adorned the stanchions of Sikkukkut's ship-ramp. That image haunted her rest and her sleep. A moment's off-guard imagining set Jik's head there beside the others.

She opened her eyes abruptly when that vision hit, focusing instead on the maps and charts and printout, where the answer had to lie, where she was convinced it was, if she could cudgel her aching skull and battered brain just a little farther through the maze.

Jik had left them another legacy: a coded microfiche which even Soje Kesurinan, in command of *Aja Jin,* might not know existed. And *The Pride*'s computers had been running on that, trying to break that code, ever since they had gotten back to the ship and had a chance to feed it in.

"Again," said Sikkukkut an'nikktukktin, *hakkikt* and *mekt-hakkikt,* lately provincial boss and currently rival for ultimate authority among his kind; while Jik, Keia Nomesteturjai, kif-hunter, captain, and what other rank among mahendo'sat this kifish pirate would earnestly like to know—focused his eyes with difficulty and managed a twisted grin. That tended to confuse hell out of the kif, who knew facial expressions were a second and well-developed language especially among mahendo'sat, and who had never quite learned to interpret all their nuances.

"Again," said Sikkukkut, "Keia, my old friend. *Where* are the human ships? Doing what? Intending what?"

"I've told you," Jik said. He said it in mahensi, being perverse. Sikkukkut understood that language, though many of his listening subordinates, standing about their table in this dim, sodium-lit hall, were not as educated. Sikkukkut, on the other hand, had a good many talents.

Interrogation was one of those. Sikkukkut had performed that office in the service of Akkukkak, of unlamented memory. All these questions, each pacing and each shift of mood Sikkukkut displayed, were calculated. It was, at the moment, the soft touch. *Have a smoke, my old friend. Sit and talk with me.* But now the frown was back, a slight drawing-down of Sikkukkut's long black snout. Hooded and inscrutable he sat, on his insect-legged chair, in the baleful light of the sodium-lamps, while Jik smoked and stared at him eye to eye. There were numerous guards about the shadowed edges of the hall, always the sycophants and the guards. In a little time the order would come to take him back to lowerdecks; and they would try the harder course again. Constant shifting of strategy, the hard approach and the soft, Sikkukkut usually the latter. Usually.

Jik kept himself mentally distant from all these changes, observed the shifts and absorbed the punishment with a professional detachment which was Sikkukkut's (surely, Jik reckoned) intention to crack. And he looked Sikkukkut in his red-rimmed eyes with the sure feeling that the kif was analyzing his every twitch and blink, looking for a telling reaction.

"Come now, Keia. You know my disposition, how patient I am, of my kind. I know that you had ample time to consult with your partner before the shooting started. We've been over these questions. They grow wearisome. Can we not resolve them?"

"My partner," Jik said, silken-slurred: Sikkukkut afforded him liquor, and he pinched out a dead smokestick and took a sip from the small round footed cup, and drew a long, long breath. Pleasures were few enough. He took what he could get. "I tell you, *hakkikt,* I wish *I* knew what my partner's up to. God, you think I'd have been out on that dock if I'd known what he was about to do?" He fumbled after his next smoke and his fingers were numb. Doubtless the drink was drugged. But there were enough of them to put the drug into him another way, so he took his medicine dosed in very fine liquor and quietly gathered his internal forces. He was deep-conditioned, immune to ordinary efforts in that regard: he knew how to self-hypnotize, and he was already focused on a series of mantras and mandalas into which he had coded what he knew, down paths of dialectic and image no kif could walk without error. He smiled blandly, in secret and bleak amusement that Sikkukkut's methods had incidentally eased the aches and the pains of previous sessions. His thoughts swayed and wove, moved in and out of focus. The docks and fire. His crew. *Aja Jin.* Friends and allied ships were just down the dock and as good as lightyears away. "Let me tell you, *mekt-hakkikt,* I know Ana's style. Think like a mahendo'sat who knows kif, *hakkikt.* If he'd asked you for leave to operate on his own you'd never have given it."

"Therefore he wrecks Kefk's docks."

Jik shrugged and drew in a puff, blinked and stared at the kif beneath heavy lids. "Well, but independence is Ana's way. I've known him for years. He's damn stubborn. He thinks he sees a way and he takes it. Agreements to this side and that—sure, he's working the mahen side. And maybe the human side too. Most of all he's gathering assets—" (Careful, Keia, the brain's fogged; stay to the narrow, the back-doubling path and lead us all round again.) Jik drew in smoke and let it out again in a shaky exhalation. "He'll negotiate with you. Eventually. But think like a mahendo'sat. He has to get something in hand to negotiate with, something to offer you, *hakkikt,* to demonstrate his worth."

"Like Meetpoint? You weigh upon my credulity, Keia." Silk, silk and soothing-soft. "Try again."

"Not Meetpoint. But some matter of substance he can come to you with. I think he means to come back to talk. But he will bring something."

Sikkukkut's snout twitched in a dry sniffing, kifish laughter, which came for many reasons, not all of which were civilized. "Like a million human ships and a great number of guns?"

"Now, that is possible, *hakkikt.*" Jik blinked and narrowed his focus still tighter on what he had resolved to say, never on what he was hiding. Find the threads of the story and stay to them, walk the narrow path, while the drug and the alcohol and the stimulants in the smoke flowed through his veins. "That is remotely possible; but the advantage would be too onesided for the humans. What good to mahendo'sat, to exchange one powerful neighbor for another of unknown potential?"

"Unknown, is it?"

"You speak excellent mahensi. Far better than I speak your language. Mechanical translators are hardly a substitute for living and fluent brains. The best human translator we know can ask for a cup of water and say he wants trade. Now, what does that tell us about human motives, human government, human minds, a? Friend, they say. You say friend, I say friend. Do we mean the same thing? What do humans mean with that word? Assuredly Ana doesn't know; and I much doubt he means to upend the Compact as long as he doesn't know." Jik held up a blunt-clawed forefinger, to maintain attention to a point. "Goldtooth, our esteemed Ana, takes orders. He also interprets them freely. This is the danger in him. The Personage who sent us both knows this. Therefore he sent me to restrain Ana from his excesses. I have failed in this. But I know Ana's limits. I am saying this to you, and you speak such excellent mahensi; but I don't know whether you know the meaning of this word *limits* in the way we do. It implies the edge of Ana's personal assumptions. Ana still obeys the Personage at Maing Tol. As I do. And I tell you that negotiation with you is in the Personage's interest and human ships running freely through Compact space is not in those interests. Therefore I make alliance with you, as I would have made it simultaneously with Akkhtimakt if he were not the fool he is."

This pleased Sikkukkut, perhaps. The dark eyes flickered. Sikkukkut picked up his cup and the thin tongue exited the v-form gap of his outer teeth and lapped delicately at the petroleum-smelling contents. "I have known mahen fools," Sikkukkut said.

"Don't number Ana among them."

"Or yourself?"

"I hope not to be."

"I have a notion what you might have been doing out on that dock-side, Keia, my friend. Ana Ismehanan-min wanted confusion behind which to depart. And *someone* fired the shot that touched off the riot."

"Rhif Ehrran."

"The hani? Come now, Keia. Hani gave no orders to the mahen-do'sat."

"It's not certain that they take them either, your pardon, *hakkikt.* Myself, I look for a fool to do a fool's work; and Ehrran is the greatest fool I know."

"Ehrran isn't sitting here at this moment."

Jik drew in a long breath of smoke and let it go again. "It did give her the diversion she needed. And indeed, she isn't sitting here at this moment. At cost to me, to Chanur—in fact, *hakkikt,* expensive as it may be to her in the long run, in the short, it served her very well. And what my partner is thinking of in her regard I wish I could tell you. I wish I knew. I think he has use for that hani he took with him, use he couldn't get out of Chanur—Chanur being no fool."

"Perhaps he has made use of all the hani. Perhaps he has secured his retreat from among us, and that is all he hoped to do—might that not be, Keia? I only wonder what you are doing here."

"Perhaps he only followed her because he saw no way to stop her."

"His ship has armaments," Sikkukkut said dryly. "He was close behind her before her ship reached velocity."

"I mean within his intentions he had no way to stop her."

"And those intentions are?"

Jik spread his hands. "I keep my agreements, *hakkikt.* And if he has abrogated our partnership—" It was his best argument, his most desperate. His brain fuzzed and the drug meandered through his veins with the force of a tidal bore. "If he has cast me off, *hakkikt,* I still keep my agreements with you. That's my job to do; and if I fare better than he does, then that will prove to my Personage which agreement is the better to keep."

"Mahen mentality."

"I tell you: it's very like *sfik.* Give me status and I'll outweigh him with the Personage at Maing Tol. It's that simple. It's not unknown that the mahendo'sat conclude conflicting treaties. And if my course looks wiser than Ana's, mine will be honored and his will be set aside. If both of us look like fools, our Personage will lean on other agencies—nor can either of us know if our Personage is not concluding a *third* treaty with the stsho. If all fail him, he will fall and another Personage's agents will be to deal with. The mahendo'sat is easy to predict and reasonable to deal with. It will always go for its greatest advantage."

"Kk-kk-t. And will this Personage of yours stir forth in action or wait for events?"

"Outcome from the subordinates is always the deciding factor."

"Where has Ismehanan-min gone? Where is this human fleet? What agreements has he made with the methane-breathers? What of your own?"

They returned to old questions, the same questions, bringing the interview in its usual circle. "Again, *mekt-hakkikt,* I don't know. They may aim at Meetpoint. It's not impossible the humans might come here. And I don't know of any agreement with the knnn. I asked the tc'a to come here to assure that there was no panic on methane-side—"

"Why did the knnn take your tc'a?"

"I don't know. Who knows the knnn? Who can make an agreement with them—"

"Except the tc'a. Except the tc'a, Keia. Tell me what dealings *you* have had with them."

"God help me, none." He held up a protesting hand. "I never deal with knnn." And carefully, with his sense in rags from drugs and drink: "That's Ana's department."

"You wish to alarm me."

"*Hakkikt,* I am alarmed. I don't know whether Ana is in control of it, or whether the knnn are doing something independent."

"In control of it."

It did sound stupid. Jik blinked slowly and took another drag at the smoke. "I mean maybe he's in consultation with them." The *hakkikt* feared the methane-breathers. Their irrationality, their technology, their vapors and tempers or whatever it was that sent them into frenzies, made the methane-folk a force no one sane wanted to stir up. "Or they approached him." That was enough to send the wind up Sikkukkut's back. "I don't know, *hakkikt.* I swear. God witness. I don't know. I did send a message to Maing Tol. So did Goldtooth. What was in his packet I don't know."

"What was in yours?"

Jik shrugged. "My deal with you. My urging they accept this treaty. I tell you, *hakkikt,* I'd urge you—all respect, *hakkikt,* you let me go back to my ship. I have a personal interest in seeing this agreement of ours flourish. It'll make me a very powerful man at home."

Give the kif something he understood, an ambition within kifish comprehension.

"You're attempting to use psychology on me," Sikkukkut said.

"Of course I am. It also happens to be true."

"What happened to *friendship?* You know I know words like this. I am not stupid, Keia; I can study up on a concept without having the—internal circuitry to process it. Friendship means that you work in concert with Ismehanan-min. Loyalty means that you might become a martyr—I learned that word of *ker* Pyanfar. An appalling concept. But there it was in the mahen dictionary. I was curious. Martyr. Martyrdom. The whole of mahen history teems with martyrs. You place value on them. Like the hani. Have you wish to become one, Keia?"

Jik lifted his brows. "Martyr is another word for fool."

"I found no such cross-reference. Tell me: Keia: I want to know this: where do the knnn fit into Ismehanan-min's arrangements? What arrangements has he made with the stsho?"

"He would betray them."

"And your opinion of them?"

"They would betray us."

"They have. Stle stles stlen is a deadly creature. For a grass-eating stsho. Is he dealing with this person?"

"I don't know. No. Yes." God help him, the drug was fuzzing up his mind again. For a panicked instant he lost all the threads and got them back again, remembering his story. "But not at depth. Ana doesn't trust the stsho. It's mutual. Of course. The humans will come to Meetpoint—eventually. I think they'll come there. And Stle stles stlen will Phase when *gtst* sees it. No sts-stsho can withstand that kind of blow to *gtst* reputation. Ana will take advantage of the confusion and seize the station. If he can."

"And Akkhtimakt will allow this."

"Ana will have to anticipate him there. Perhaps—perhaps, *hakkikt,* Ana moved so quickly because he knows something of Akkhtimakt's intentions. That there was no more time—in Ana's estimation."

"And why would he go with the hani?"

"Look for advantage." That questioning made him nervous. It was a new tack; he tried to think his way through it and in desperation went back to old answers. "I think—think he hopes to use Rhif Ehrran to get into Meetpoint itself *without* having stsho techs Phase and bring the systems down. Now you doubt this. I well know. But stsho react badly to surprises; from kif, they expect threats. Even from hani. But mahen threats unbalance them. They're *unaccustomed*. Ehrran has a treaty with them. That's all I can guess about it. She's a key. That's all. A fool and a key."

"To do what?"

"*Hakkikt,* I'm not privy to his plans."

Upon that, they were back to old matters. He sat and smoked while Sikkukkut thought that reply over once more, hunched faceless within the hooded robe, on his insect chair, the silver emblem of his princedom among kif shining on his breast stained with sodium-glow. Now and again from the shadows about them came the rustling of other robes, the restless stirring of subordinates who waited on their prince's pleasure.

In a moment Sikkukkut would negligently lift his hand and those waiting about the room would close in, to bear their prisoner back downship and belowdecks to a different sort of questioning, now that he was sufficiently muddled and drugged. Jik did not let himself doubt that. He did not let himself hope that his argument might sway the *hakkikt;* least of all did he hope that his hani allies on *The Pride of Chanur* and his own crew back on *Aja Jin* would effect a rescue. That was the core of his defense here among the kif, the hard center to his resistance that let him sit here so placidly taking his smokestick down to a stub and watching heavy-lidded while Sikkukkut an'nikktukktin meditated what next to do to him; it was the center of all secrets he held, that he counted himself already dead, from which position it was possible to be quite patient with all manner of misery, since, dead, he was enjoying a degree of sensation and occasional pleasant interlude no one dead had a right to. Even when the pain was extreme, it was better than not feeling anything at all. Ever.

Besides, he was mahendo'sat, and curiosity was second nature to him: he was still picking up information, skilled as Sikkukkut was. He had learned, for instance, that *Aja Jin, The Pride of Chanur,* and *Tahar's Moon Rising* were all at dock and all seemed free: that was very pleasant news. That Pyanfar Chanur was at hand to lend her experience to his own second in command was very good news; that Pyanfar still had credit enough with Sikkukkut to keep Dur Tahar's throat uncut was excellent news as well, and if there was still enough hani left under Tahar's red-brown hide, the pirate would adhere to her old enemy like burr to fur: hani paid their debts, if nothing else; and Tahar owed Chanur enough to stick to hell and back.

All of this he had learned in these sessions, as he knew that the human Tully was indeed safe aboard *The Pride of Chanur,* so Sikkukkut evidently valued Pyanfar more than he wanted the human to question and for other purposes, which was a mighty great deal of value for any kif to put on a non-kif. This was a double-edged benefit, of course: knowing kifish mindset, value-as-ally could turn with amazing swiftness to high-status-target. Friend in a kif's doubletoothed mouth had no overtones of loyalty or self-sacrifice at all, was in fact nearly the opposite. Ally-of-convenience, rather. Potential rival, rather. Or poor fool.

The hani knew these things; and he knew well that his second in command knew. So they would both keep one finger to the wind; and he hoped that heads would stay cool if, as seemed possible and even likely, portions of himself turned up as decoration on Sikkukkut's ship-ramp. He loathed stupidity, himself; he had sinned in that regard or he would not be here. But he truly abhorred the thought that he might single-handedly serve as trigger to the undoing of the Compact. That was the one thing even a dead man could fear, the legacy he might leave the living for generations to come. That thought was the crack in his defense: Sikkukkut, being kif, taking no thought to posterity, was not capable of reaching that chink without a strong hint.

It was very easy for species to misunderstand each other, particularly when it came to abstracts.

It was possible, for instance, that he and Pyanfar had persistently misinterpreted Sikkukkut's lack of metaphysics as a lack of emotional abstracts and irrational desires. He had come to know the kif with unwanted intimacy, and now suspected Sikkukkut of a kifish sentimentality, a preference for intimate targets for his most personal satisfaction, while Akkhtimakt was less personal in his mayhem, and more catholic in his attacks.

Akkhtimakt operates with the fist, Sikkukkut was wont to say, *and I with the knife.*

It was kifish poesy; it was also a profound statement of styles which might, if a mahendo'sat were well-educated in kifish mentality, say more than its surface content, and delve into those deep things language barriered away from translation between species.

He smoked the butt down to the last possible remnant, and carefully pinched it out instead of stubbing it, spacer's affectation. Fire never hurt if one's moves were definite and one's mind was set firmly on the extinguishing and not on the fire. Spacer's affectation, because when the fingers could bear it comfortably, it was safe to put away. He dropped the butt into the side of the pouch reserved for that and laid the pouch on the table. They never let him keep it. The pouch, with the liquor and Sikkukkut's good humor, was delivered only in this room. So he let it lie, and met Sikkukkut's eyes with lazy amusement.

Perhaps he perplexed the *hakkikt* with his attitude, a coolness between defiance and alliance and certainly not the behavior of a kif; perhaps that was what kept his head off the spikes outside. Sikkukkut gazed at him a moment in what seemed interest, then lifted his hand as he had done before, and signaled his removal.

"There it goes," someone cried down the hall, and footsteps went thundering past Chur Anify's door, disturbing her convalescence. *"Kk-kk-kt,"* something else called out, and that brought Chur's eyes open and set a little quicker pulse into her heart, so that needles jumped on the machine to which she was bound by a large skein of tubes, indicating an increase in pulse rate; in response to that, a flood of nutrients and appropriate chemicals came back into her bloodstream, automatically supplied.

Living bound to a machine-extension which thought it knew best what a body ought to feel was bad enough; lying there while riot went on in the corridor was another thing, and Chur edged her way off the bed, carefully (the spring extensions on the skein of tubings made it possible for her to reach the bathroom and saved her some indignities). In this case she gripped the various tubes in one fist to keep the extension from jerking painfully at the needles and padded over to the bureau where she had her gun, hearing the kifish clicking going on out there. Her head spun and her heart raced and the gods-cursed machine flooded her veins with sedative when it sensed her elevated pulse, but she made it to the door and pushed the button with the knuckle of her gun-hand.

The door shot open. She slumped lazy-like against the wall and stared at a kif who turned up directly opposite her and her pistol; then her eyes went strange-focussed and her mind went here and there again, so that she had difficulty recalling where she was or why there should be a kif in *The Pride*'s corridor looking as horrified as a kif could look (not extremely) and why the peripheries of her vision informed her there were her cousins and a human standing there in shock and in company with this kif. It was a great deal to ask of a drugged hani brain, but the kif had its hands up and she was not crazed enough to go firing off a gun in a ship's corridor without knowing why.

And while her brain was sorting through that crazy sequence, something small and black ran right over her foot on its way into her room. "Hyaa!" she yelled in revulsion, and the kif dived for the wall beside her as she swung to keep a bead not on the thing but on the kif. A hurtling mass of her friends overtook her from behind—not to help her, to her vast bewilderment: they grabbed her and the gun, while the kif flinched and pasted himself tight to the wall, making himself the smallest possible target.

"Chur," her sister Geran was pleading with her, and she supposed that it was Geran prying the gun loose from her fingers: she was dizzy and her vision fuzzed. She heard her cousin Tirun's voice, and human jabber, which was her friend Tully; and she dazedly let herself be dragged one step and another into the room, someone else taking the skein of tubes. A bell was going off: the infernal machine was telling off on her, that she was stressed.

"Gods rot it," she cried, remembering. "There's something in here." And then she remembered that she had seen little black things before, on the bridge, and could not remember whether they were hallucinations or not, or whether her sister took her seriously. It was embarrassing to see hallucinations. And the cursed machine kept pouring sedative into her, so that they were going to leave her alone in here and drugged, with whatever-it-was: she did not want that either.

"Look under the bed," Geran said, while Geran was putting her back into it, and she could not remember where the gun had gotten to, which was against ship's rules, which was against all the regulations, to lose track of a firearm; and there was a kif trying to crawl under her bed. A sweat broke out on her, cold on her ears and nose and fingertips. "Where's my gun?" she asked hazily, trying to sit up again; and "There it is!" someone shouted from the floor.

"My gods," Chur murmured, and her sister put her flat on her back again. She blinked, blinked again in the crazed notion that there was a kif on his hands and knees at her bedside and people were trying to get her hallucination out from under her bed.

"Sorry," Geran said fervently. "Stay down. We've got it."

"You're crazy," Chur said. "You're stark crazy, all of you." Because none of it made sense.

But something let out a squeal under her bed, and something bumped against the secure-held braces, and there was an ammonia smell to the room which was no illusion, but a kif's real presence.

"He got," said Tully's voice, and he loomed up by her bedside. "Chur, you all right?"

"Sure," Chur said. She remembered at least where she was now, tied to a machine in *na* Khym's cabin because she was, since the kif had shot her on a dock at Kshshti, too sick to be down in crew quarters; and Goldtooth had given them this fine medical equipment when he had met them here at Kefk, which was before the docks blew up in a firefight and she had been holding the bridge singlehanded when the little black things started coming and going like a nasty slinking nightmare. There *was* a kif aboard, his name was Skkukuk, he was a slave and a gift from the *hakkikt* and he stood there with his black snout atwitch and his Dinner clutched in both bony hands as he stared at her. She curled her lip and laid her ears back, head scantly lifted. "Out!"

The kif hissed and clicked and retreated in profound offense, teeth bared, and Chur bared hers, coming up on her free elbow.

"Easy," Geran said, pushing her back; and Tirun chased the kif on out, Haral's sister Tirun, big enough to make a kif think twice about any argument, and owing that slight limp to a kifish gun some years back: Chur felt herself safe if Geran was by her and Tirun was between her and the kif. She looked up at Tully's gold-bearded face and blinked placidly.

"Gods-be kif," Geran said. "Readout jumping like crazy—Tully, here, get this gun out of here."

"No," Chur said. "Drawer. Put it back in the drawer, Tully."

"Out of here," Geran said.

"Gods rot," Chur yelled, *"drawer!"* Living around Tully, a body got to thinking in pidgin and half-sentences. And the voice came out cracked. Tully hesitated, looking at Geran.

An even larger figure showed up in the doorway, filling it. Khym Mahn, male and tall and wide: "What's the trouble?"

"No trouble," Geran said. "Come on, close that door, everyone out before another of the gods-be things gets in. *Who's watching the godsforsaken kif?"*

"Put the gun in the drawer," Chur said firmly. "Tully."

"You leave it there," Geran said, getting up, as Khym vanished. She stood looking down a moment, while Tully did as he was told. Then the two of them stood there, her sister, her human friend; if there was ever truly such a thing as friendship between species. And the gods-be kif down the hall—Was *that* thing a friend, and did they have it running loose on the ship now? Had the captain authorized that?

"O gods," Chur murmured, too tired and too sick for thoughts like loose kif, and for uncharitable thoughts toward Tully, who had done his unarmed best to save all their hides more than once. But it was in her heart now that she would not see home again, and that this was her last voyage, and she wanted to go home more than anything, back to Anuurn and Chanur and to have this little selfish time with things she knew and loved, familiar things, uncomplicated by aliens and strangeness—wanted to be young again, and to have more time, and to remember what it was to have her life all in front of her and not behind.

Wanted, gods help her, to see even her home up in the hills, which was purest stupidity: she and Geran had walked out of there and come down to Chanur when they were kids as young as Hilfy, because a young fool of a new lord had gotten himself in power up there over their sept of clan Chanur, and she and her sister had pulled up roots and left for Chanur's main-sept estate with no more than the clothes on their backs.

And their pride. They had come with that intact. The two of them.

"Never looked back," she said, thinking Geran at least might understand. "Gods be, odd things were what we were looking for when we came down the hills, wasn't that it?"

Geran made a desperate motion at Tully that meant get out, quietly, and Tully went, not without a pat at Chur's blanketed leg.

Chur lay there and blinked, embarrassed at herself. She looked like something dead. She knew that. She and Geran had once looked a great deal alike, red-blond of mane and beard and with a sleekness and slimness that was the hillwoman legacy in their sept; not like their cousins Haral and Tirun Araun or their cousin Pyanfar either, who had downland Chanur's height and strength, but never their highlands beauty, their agility, their fleetness of foot. Now Geran's shoulders slumped in exhaustion, her coat was dull, her eyes unutterably weary; and Chur had seen mirrors. Her bones hurt when she lay on them. The sheets were changed daily: Geran saw to that, because she shed and shed, till the skin appeared in patches, all dull pink and horrid through her fur. That was her worst personal suffering, not the pain, not the dread of dying: it was her vanity the machine robbed her of, and her dignity; and watching Geran watch her deteriorate was worst of all.

"Sorry," Chur said. "Gods-be machine keeps pouring sedative into me. I don't always make sense."

Rotten way to die, she thought to herself, drugged out of my mind. Scaring Geran. What kind of way is that?

"Unhook me from this thing."

"You said you'd leave it be," Geran said. "For me. You told the captain you'd leave it be. Do we need to worry about you?"

"Asked, didn't I?" The voice came hoarse. The episode had exhausted her. Or it was the sedative. "We letting that gods-be kif loose now?"

"Khym's got an eye on him."

"Uhhn." There was a time that would have sounded crazy. Men did not deal with outsiders, did not take responsibility, did not have any weight of decision on their shoulders, on their berserk-prone brains. But nothing in the world was the same as it had been when she was a girl. "We left home to find strange things," Chur said, bewildered that she ended up trusting a man's good sense and an alien human's good will, a hillwoman like her. "Found 'em, didn't we?" But she saw that pained drawing about Geran's mustaches, the quivering flick of Geran's ears, well-ringed with voyages. She saw how drained Geran was, how her maundering grieved Geran, had a sure instinct that if Geran had one load on her shoulders, she had just put another there, almost unbearable for her sister. "Hey," she said, "I was pretty steady on my feet. Machine helps. Think I'll make it. Hear?"

Geran took that in and the slump left her shoulders and the grief left her eyes so earnestly and so trustingly it hurt.

Gods, Chur thought, now I've done it, I've promised her, haven't I? *Stupid to promise. Now I have to. I'll lose. It'll hurt, gods rot it. I'll die somewhere in jump, O gods, that's an awful way, to go out there, in the dark between the stars, all naked.*

"Not easy," Chur murmured, heading down to sleep. "Easier to go out, Gery. But I'll get back up there, b'gods. Don't you let the captain assign me out. Hear?"

"Chair's waiting."

"You want to fill me in, treat me like I was crew?" It was hard to stay interested in life, with the sedatives drawing a curtain between herself and the universe. She remembered her promise and fought to keep it. "What f'godssakes is going on out there?"

"Same as before. We're sitting at dock waiting for that gods-rotted kif to make up his mind to go left or right, and so far nothing's worse."

"Or better."

"Or better. Except they're still talking. And the *hakkikt*'s still real polite."

"Jik hasn't cracked."

"Hasn't cracked. Gods help him."

"How long are we going to sit here?"

"Wish we all knew. Captain's figuring like mad, Haral's laying in six, seven courses into comp. We may get home yet."

"Doublecross the kif? They'd hunt us." Her voice grew thick. "Meetpoint's the only way out of here. That's where we've got to go."

Geran said nothing. The threads grew vague, but they always came to the same point. Goldtooth had left them and his partner in the lurch and run for Meetpoint, and Tully's folk were headed into the Compact in numbers, all of which meant that a very tired hani who wanted the universe to be what it had been in her youth was doomed to see things turned upside down, doomed to see Chanur allied with kif, with a species that ate little black things and behaved badly on docksides, and did other things an honest hani preferred not to think about.

Gods-rotted luck, she thought; and thought again about the hills of home, and the sins of her youth, one of which she had left with its father; but it was only a gods-be boy, and not a marriage anyhow, and she had never written back to the man, who was no happier at getting a son than she was at birthing one (a daughter would have done him some good in his landless station), but his sisters would treat the boy all right. Rest of the family never had known much about it, except Geran knew, of course; and it was before she had joined *The Pride*. The kid would have come of age and gone off to Hermitage years ago; and probably died, the way surplus males died. Waste. Ugly waste.

Wish I'd known my son.

Maybe I could find him. If his father's still alive. If he's like na Khym, if— Maybe, maybe if I could've talked to him he'd have sense like na Khym.

Never asked that man—never much talked to him. Never occurred to me to talk to him. Isn't that funny? Now I'd wonder what he was thinking. I'd think he was thinking. I'd find me a man and make love to him and gods, I'd ask him what he was thinking and he'd—

—I'd probably confuse him all to a mahen hell, I would; aren't many men like Khym Mahn, gods-rotted nice fellow, wished I'd known him 'fore the captain got him. If he was ever for anybody but her. If a clan lord like him could've ever looked at an exile like me. I'd like to've loved a man like him. I'd have got me a daughter off him, I would've.

But what's the captain got of him? Gods-rotted son like Kara Mahn and a gods-forsaken whelp of a daughter like Tahy, no help there, gods fry 'em both, no sense, no ears to listen, no respect—doublecrossing gods-be cheats.

Want to find me a man. Not a pretty one. A smart one. Man I can sit and talk with.

If I ever get home.

She pursed her lips and spat.

"You all right?"

"Sure, I'm sleeping, get out of here. I'm trying to get my rest. What in the gods' name *are* those black things?"

"Don't ask. We don't."

The lift opened belowdecks, and Hilfy Chanur, coming back onshift, stepped back hastily as the doors whisked back and gave her Skkukuk all unexpected, Skkukuk clutching a squealing cageful of nasty black shapes, which apparition sent her ears flat; but Tirun and Tully were escorting the kif, which got Hilfy's ears back up again and laid the fur back down between her shoulderblades. She stepped aside in distaste to let the kif out and stood there staring as the door waited to her hold on the call button.

"We think we got 'em," Tirun said.

"They got," Tully said, amplifying his broken pidgin with a gesture topside. "Eat fil-ter. Lousy mess."

"Good gods, *what* filter?"

"Airfilter in number one," Tirun said. "Sent particles all over the system: we're going to have to do a washdown on the number two and the main."

"Make electric," Tully said.

"We made it real uncomfortable in that airshaft," Tirun said.

"Kkkkt," Skkukuk said, "these are Akkhtish life. They are *adaptive*. Very tough."

The creatures started fighting at the sound of his voice. He whacked the cage with his open hand and the Dinner subsided into squeals.

"Gods," Hilfy said with a shudder of disgust.

"Two of them are about to litter," Tirun said. "Watch these gods-forsaken things. They're born fighting."

"Tough," Skkukuk said conversationally, and hit the Dinner's cage again, when the squeals sharpened. There was quiet, except for a hiss.

"Kkkt. Excuse me." He clutched the cage to him and headed off down the hall with the Dinner in his arms, happy as ever a kif could be.

Hilfy's lip lifted; an involuntary shiver went through her as Tirun turned and went to keep an eye on the kif. Tully stayed, and set a hand on her shoulder, squeezed hard.

Tully knew. He had been with her in the hands of the kif, this same Sikkukkut who was their present ally; who sent them this slavish atrocity Skkukuk to haunt the corridors and leave his ammonia-stink everywhere in the air, a smell which brought back memories—

A second time Tully squeezed her shoulder with his clawless fingers. Hilfy turned and looked at him, looking up a bit; but he was not so tall, her Tully, that she could not look him in the eyes this close. Those eyes were blue and usually puzzled, but in this moment there was worry there. Two voyages and what they had been through together had taught her to read the nuances of his expressions.

"He's not bad kif," Tully said.

That was so incredible an opinion from him she blinked and could not believe she had heard it.

"He's kif," Tully said. "Same I be human. Same you hani. He be little kif, try do what captain want."

She would not have heard it from anyone else. She had her mouth open when Tully said it. But this was a man who had been twice in their hands; and seen his friends die; and killed one of them himself to save him from Sikkukkut: more, he had been there with her in that kifish prison, and if Tully was saying such an outrageous thing it might have any number of meanings, but emptyheaded and over-generous it was not. She stared at him trying to figure out if he had missed his words in hani: the translator they had rigged up to their com sputtered helpless static at his belt, constant undertone when he spoke his thickly accented hani or pidgin. Maybe he was trying to communicate some crazy human philosophy that failed to come through.

"Little kif," Tully said again. She had lived among kif long enough to know what he meant by that, that kif were nothing without status, and that kif of low status were everyone's victims.

"If he was a big kif," she said, "he'd kill us fast."

"No," Tully said. "Captain be Pyanfar. He want be big, she got be big."

"Loyalty, huh?"

"Like me," Tully said. "He one."

"You mean he's alone."

"He want be hani."

She spat. It was too much. "You might be." And not many hani in space and certainly none on homeworld would be that generous, only a maudlin and lonely young woman a long way from her own kind. "Not a kif. Ever."

"True," Tully admitted, twisting back on his own argument in that maddening way he had of getting behind a body and leaving them facing the wrong way. He held up a finger. "He kif, he same time got no friend with kif, he be little kif. They kill him, yes. He want not be kill. He lot time wrong, think we do big good to him. You watch, Hil-fy: crew be good with him, he be happy, he got face up, he be brave with us, he talk. But we don't tell truth to him, huh? What good truth? Say him, 'kif, you enemy', he got no friend, got no ship, got no *hakkikt*. He don't be hani, he die."

"I can't be sorry for him. He wouldn't understand it. He's kif, gods rot him. And I'd as soon kill him on sight."

"You don't kill same like you be kif." He patted her arm and looked earnestly at her, from the far side of a language barrier the translator never crossed. "He makes a mistake," the translator said as he changed into his own language for words he did not have. "He's lost. He thinks we like him more now. We ask him go die for help us, he go. True, he will go. And we hate him. He doesn't know this. He's kif. He can't understand why we hate him."

"Well, let's not confuse him," Hilfy snarled, and turned and stopped the lift door which had started to close on auto when she let go the button. It recoiled, held for another wait. She looked back at Tully, who looked back, aggrieved and silent. She knew his shorthand speech better than anyone else aboard: ship's com officer, linguist, translator, she had helped set up his translation system and help break through to him when they first met him. And what he was saying now made more sense than she wanted it to—that a kif, cold-blooded tormentor and killer that it was, was also a helpless innocent in their hands. If a kif saw another kif in his way, he killed; his changes of loyalty were frequent but sincere and self-serving. And if the captain's subordinates treated him better, it was because the captain had accorded him more status: it was all a kif could think, it was all a kif knew how to imagine. Pyanfar let Skkukuk loose more often, Pyanfar cared to feed him, the crew was civil to him: his place in the universe was therefore improving. Gods help them, the kif became conversational with them. Two and more centuries of contact and the kif had never let slip any casual detail about their homeworld, which no one visited but kif; and here Skkukuk, bragging on his nasty little vermin as Akkhtish and adaptive, hinted at more of kifish life and kifish values than kif had said about themselves in all of history.

And what would a man know about anything? was her gut reaction, staring into Tully's eyes. She did not think of Skkukuk as male, gods knew; hardly thought of Jik or Goldtooth as anything but female and rational, despite the male pronouns which were ordinary in pidgin and otherwise in hani: but Tully was definitively male to her, and stood there saying crazy things about an enemy, talking to *her* about self-restraint, which was a female kind of thought, or Pyanfar was right and males had a lot of hidden female about them: it was an embarrassing estimation. But the sense that it made also reached somewhere inside and found a sore spot, that Tully had found some kind of peace with the thing that had happened to them among the kif, where a sane, technically educated woman failed.

Because he's older, Hilfy thought. She had always thought of him as near her own age: and suddenly she thought that he must be, of his kind, old as Khym, whose years had burned the tempers out of him and given him self-control and lost him his lordship over Mahn. Suddenly she suspected that she had always been wrong about Tully, that he was wiser than a young man could possibly be, and cooler-headed: and there was something still he had not been able to tell her. There was something still bottled up in him, she could almost read it, but it was too alien an expectation; or too simple. She could not guess it. The lift door hit her in the shoulder again and gave up, and she reached out and gently touched Tully's face with the pads of her fingers.

"If you were hani," she said, "we'd—" But she did not say that. It sounded too foolish; and hurt too much, without an answer that resulted in anything but both of them being fools. Laughable fools.

"Friend," he said in a small voice, and touched her face. While the lift door hit her again, on shorter and shorter reminder. "Friend, Hilfy." With a peculiar stress in his voice, and a break, as it would do when he was grieved. There were things he did not commit to the translator. More and more he tried to speak hani. And to be hani. And he grew sadder and more wistful when he would look at her and say a thing like that, making fools of them both.

Gods, Hilfy Chanur, she thought, *what can you do? When did you go crazy? When did he? When we were alone and we were all we had, with kif all about? I want him.*

If he's older than me, why doesn't he have an answer for this?

Then an alarm went off. For a moment she thought she had tripped it by holding the door, and Pyanfar was going to skin her.

"Priority, priority. We've got a courier at the lock," Haral's voice said then from com, from every speaker in the hall. *"All secure below. Hilfy, Tirun, arm and stand by: looks like you're the welcoming committee, captain's compliments, and she's staying topside. Protocols. You get that?"*

"I got it," Hilfy said.

Lock up the kif, that meant. Fast.

"Tully," she said, and motioned to the lift. Panic had started a slow, hysteric beat in her heart; habit kept her face calm as she stepped aside and held the door with her arm for Tully.

I could help, that look of his said; I could be down here, I want to be here. I want to help you—

It was not the kif's feelings he had so laboriously described: *you make him part of the crew, you let him believe it, you don't know how cruel you are to let him believe you.*

He'd go out and die for you, Hilfy Chanur. Because he believes you.

No. It was not true of the kif. It was what he felt in himself.

"Up," she said. "Bridge. Haral needs you. I got enough down here."

And, gods, why put it that way? She saw the pain she caused.

He went into the lift, and turned and pushed the Close, so that the door jarred her obstructing arm and she drew it back in confusion. She opened her mouth to say something like *you can't help in this,* which was no better than she had already said; but the door closed between their faces, and left her speechless and harried in recalling that it was an emergency Haral had just sent her on—kif, and trouble, and gods knew what.

The whole situation could be unraveling. Jik might have talked, might have spilled something; it might be the beginning of the attack they had feared; it might be anything, and gods help her, she had just fouled it up with Tully and there was no time, no time, never time to straighten it out between them.

Gods, gods, gods, I hurt him. I never wanted to hurt him, we can all die here and I can't get past that gods-be translator.

Why is it all so complicated?

Chapter Two

It was not a situation Pyanfar enjoyed, sitting on the bridge and watching on the vid as a pair of armed kif headed toward her airlock. They wore no suits, only the hooded black robes universal with their kind. That meant the kif put some reliance on the jury-patches and the repressurization of this zone of the dock, more than she herself would have liked to put on it—kifish repair crews had been thumping and welding away out there, motes on vid, getting a patch on those areas the decompression had weakened.

So finally the *hakkikt* seemed to have settled accounts with the rebels inside his camp to the extent that now he could send a message to the friends of the mahen and hani traitors who had made such a large hole in his newly-acquired space station, who had disturbed the tc'a into riot on their side of the station, and incidentally sent over five hundred unsuspecting kif out into space on the wind of that decompression.

Sikkukkut had a very legitimate grievance; even a hani had to admit as much. Though the kif that had gone on that unscheduled spacewalk were many of them Sikkukkut's enemies, a good many had been partisans of his, and while no kif had ever been observed to grieve over the demise of any other kif, and while the incident might even have contributed to stopping the rebellion, still it had embarrassed him—and embarrassing a kifish leader was a very serious matter. It was not an accustomed feeling, to have a sense of wrong on her side when she was dealing with the kif; and to know, the while those black-robed figures cycled through the lock, that *The Pride* was not in a position, nose to a wrecked dock and outnumbered ten to one in ships and multiple thousands to one in personnel, to negotiate anything at all, not regarding what this mass of ships chose to do, not regarding their own position within the kifish power structure, not even regarding their safety or their lives.

So bluff was still the game, status and protocols, which was why she was sitting up here gnawing her mustaches and having her crew meet with an armed delegation that neither they nor she had power to negotiate with. She tried to use kifish manners, which kif understood, and she hoped to the gods the kif did understand the gesture she was making, which meant that Pyanfar Chanur had just abandoned her inclination to meet the *hakkikt*'s messengers on hani protocols, with hani courtesies: now she withdrew to a remoteness which to a kif (she hoped) signaled not fear (a frightened kif would show up to placate the offended party, and thrust himself right into the presence of his potential enemy to try to patch it up) but rather signaled that the captain of this hani freighter turned hunter-ship considered herself risen in the *hakkikt*'s favor, to the extent that she intended henceforth to receive her messages through subordinates. She sensed that self-promotion was the way things worked with kif: she sensed it by experience, and kifish manners, and Skkukuk's inside-out advice: their own much-bewildered kifish crewman alternately shrank and flourished in every breeze of her tempers, crushed by a moment's reprimand, bright-eyed and energetic on her next moment's better humor; and jealous and paranoid in his constant suspicions the crew would undermine him—as he tried to undermine them, of course, but less zealously of late, as if he had finally gotten it through his narrow kifish skull that that was not the way things worked on a hani ship; or that the crew was too firmly in the captain's favor to dislodge; or perhaps the crew's own increasing courtesy with him had sent his mind racing on a new stratagem down some path thoroughly mistaken and thoroughly kif: it was enough to give a sane hani a headache. But Skkukuk had shown her a vital thing: that a kif took all the ground he could get at every hour of every day, and if he made a mistake and got a reprimand, he did not, as a hani would do, cherish a grudge for that reprimand: where a hani would burn with shame and throw sanity and self-preservation to the winds, and where a hani who chastised another hani knew that she was asking for bloodfeud to the second and third generation, involving both clans and affiliate clans to the eighth degree, a kif just accepted a slap in the face with the same unflappable sense of self-preservation that would make him go for his own leader's throat the moment that leader looked vulnerable, at the very moment a reasonable hani might stand by her leader most loyally. Pyanfar had puzzled this out. In a total wrench of logic she could even understand that kif being dead as they were to any altruistic impulse, had to move to completely different tides, and the most urgent of those tides seemed to be the drive to inch their way up in status at every breath if they could get away with it.

It was a good question whether Sikkukkut understood hani half that well, despite his fluency; and upon that thought a logical gulf opened before her, whether a kif could ever truly understand the pride of the lowliest hani hillwoman, who would spend the last drop of blood she had settling accounts both of debt and bloodfeud with anyone at all, headwoman or beggar; the kif had not the internal reflexes to feel what a hani felt; and how, good gods, could a hani know the compulsion that drove a kif, lacking whatever-it-was which was as natural to kif as breathing.

Gods help us, if I had enough credit with him to get Jik loose—if anyone did—if I could crack that gods-be code of Jik's, over there in comp, if I knew what Jik was holding out against Sikkukkut, what kind of craziness he passed me at Mkks—is it his will and testament? Something for his Personage? Some gods-cursed plan of attack?

Goldtooth's plan of action?

What do the kif want down there, why come in person, why not use the com?

While the kif arrived in their fire-scarred airlock and prepared to deal with her niece and her cousin, both of whom had gotten scars before this at kifish hands.

Don't foul it, Hilfy, don't give way—Gods, I should have called her up and sent—

—Geran? With Chur shot and Geran in the mood she's in?

—not Haral, I need her.

Not a place for the menfolk down there either. Hilfy's all right, she's stable, she'll carry it off all right—she knows the kif, knows them well as anyone—knows how to hold herself—

O gods, why'd I ever let her and Chur go off the ship at Kshshti? It was my fault, my fault and she'll never be the same—

—isn't the same, no one's ever the same; I'm not, the ship isn't, Chur

isn't, none of us are, and I brought us here, every gods-be step along the way—

Haral cycled the lock and two unescorted kif walked into *The Pride*'s lowerdeck; while Geran powered the airlock camera about, tracking them, and Khym and Tully hovered over separate monitors. Haral kept cycling her own checks, keeping an eye to the whole godsforsaken dockside, screen after screen at Haral's station shifting images so that they were never blinder than they had to be.

No way they were going to be caught in distraction, even if, gods forbid, the kif tossed a grenade through the lock.

"Record," Pyanfar said. "Aye," Geran said, and flicked a switch, beginning to log the whole business into *The Pride*'s records. Then:

"Those are rifles," Geran muttered.

The kif carried heavy weapons, besides the sidearms. The dim light and poor camera pickup had obscured those black weapons against the black, unornamented robes. But the rifles were slung at the shoulder, not carried in the hand. That much was encouraging. "Polite," Pyanfar said through her teeth, while below, from the spy-eye:

"Hunter Pyanfar," one kif said as he met *The Pride*'s welcoming committee.

"Tirun Araun." Tirun identified herself—scarred old spacer with gray dusting her nose and streaking her red-gold mane. She had a way of holding herself that seemed both diffident about the gun she held (surely civilized beings ought not to hold guns on each other) and very likely to use it in the next twitch (there was not the least compunction or doubt in her eyes). *"I trust you've come from the* hakkikt," Tirun said. *"Praise to him"*—without the least flicker, kifish courtesy.

"Praise to him," the kif said. *"A message to your captain."* It took a cylinder from its belt, with never an objection to the leveled guns or Hilfy's flattened ears. *"The* hakkikt *says: the docks are secure. The matter is urgent. I say: we will stand here and wait for the Chanur captain."*

Tirun reached out and took the cylinder. And delayed one lazy moment in a gesture that could not have been wasted, especially on a kif. *"Be courteous, Hilfy."*

With fine timing, with a little flattening of the ears that might be respect and might be something else again, ambiguous even to hani eyes —Tirun delivered her signal to Hilfy and turned with authority and walked off, at a pace both deliberate and fast enough.

While Hilfy stood there with the gun in her fist and two kif to watch. *Steady, kid. For the gods' sakes, Tirun's done it right, don't wobble.*

No one said a thing on the bridge. It remained very, very quiet until the lift worked, back down the corridor from the center of the bridge. Then Pyanfar got out of her chair and went to wait for Tirun, who came down the corridor at a much faster clip than she had used below. While at the boards, Haral and Geran kept to business, monitoring everything round about the ship and inside it and everything coming from station.

"Captain," Tirun said by way of courtesy, and handed over the cylinder.

The cap stuck when she pulled at it. For one awful moment Pyanfar thought of explosives; or deadly gas. "Wait here," she said, left Tirun standing on the bridge, and stepped outside into the corridor, pushing the door switch to close it between them.

She hooked a claw into the seal then and gnawed her lip and pulled the cap. Nothing blew. Nothing came out. It was a message, a bit of gray paper.

The door shot open again in the same instant, which was Tirun; and Tirun stood there aggrieved in the tail of her eye while she fished the paper out and read it.

Hunter Pyanfar: you have made requests. I will give you my response aboard my ship at 1500, expecting that you will come with ranking personnel of allied ships.

"Captain?" Tirun said.

She passed the letter over and cast a second look up at the chrono in the bridge display: 1436.

"It's a trap," Tirun said.

On the bridge even Haral had taken one quick look around.

"Invitation from the kif," Pyanfar said. "Ranking personnel of allied ships. On his deck. Fast."

"My gods," Khym exclaimed.

"Unfortunately," Pyanfar said, and thought of Hilfy down there in the corridor with two kif alone. "Unfortunately we haven't got a real choice. Get Tahar and get Kesurinan. I'm not taking any of you—"

Mouths opened.

"It's a trap," Khym said, his deep voice quivering with outrage. "Py, Tirun's right, listen to her."

"Not taking any of you," she said carefully, "except our friend the kif. Get to it, Geran, get our friends out there."

"That dock," Geran said.

"We got worse risks than a leaky dock, cousin; one of 'em's being late and one of them's missing a signal with that kif. I'm going down there, I want Tahar and Kesurinan just the way the kif asked, and about the time I clear the lock down there I want *The Pride* powered up and held that way till I get back again. Make the point with 'em we still got teeth, hear? And that my crew's on full alert."

"Aye," Haral muttered, far from happy.

Neither was Pyanfar happy. She went and pulled one of their APs out of the locker by the bridge exit and headed back down the corridor, with the heavy sidearm and its belt in hand.

Not to the lowerdeck straightway.

First came a stop in her own quarters, for a fast exchange: for a bit of glitter, because appearances counted, a psychological weapon as essential as the gun at her side.

Sikkukkut meant to move now. In some regard.

She clenched her jaw and started cataloging things, fast, things that wanted doing. In case she had just said goodbye to her crew and her husband.

Gods, Khym had just stood there and took an answer for an answer. Her heart did a little painful thump of pride when she realized belatedly what that had cost him: he was not the gentle ignorant she had married, not the feckless man who had walked out on the docks at Meetpoint and run straight into a kifish trap. If she died today at kifish hands he would not act the male; would not rush out there like a lunatic to take the kif on hand to hand—he had grown a lot on this voyage, had Khym, when he was no longer a boy and no longer young at all. He had finally found out what lay outside his limits and what the universe was like—had found friends, b'gods, female friends and one who was even male, friends which she suddenly realized in grief that Khym had never had in all his adult life, excepting her and his other wives, and them but scarcely: clan-lord, shielded from all contact with the world by his wives and his sisters and his daughters, he had finally come out into the real world to find out what it was, and he was not just *her* Khym anymore; or even Khym lord Mahn; he was something more than that, suddenly, long after he should have gone to die in Hermitage, outworn and useless—he grew up and became what he always could have been; discovered the universe full of honest folk and scoundrels of all genders, and learned how to win respect, how to ignore the barbs and become ship-youngest and work his way out of a second youth, with utterly different rules. That was more change than most women had the fortitude to take in their lives; but by the gods he had made it complete back there; he would do his fighting from that bridge and that board, under Haral's command if something went wrong, part of the crew that drove a ship of mass enough and internal power enough to turn Kefk and Sikkukkut and all his ambitions into one briefly incandescent star.

The docks were the shambles she had expected, gray metal still supercooled under her bare feet, with a good many of the lights out—blown when the pressure went and when this dock had opened to space. Gantries loomed up down the righthand side of the docks, subtly tilting in the positive curvature of the deck, which was the torus-shaped station's outermost edge, to anyone who saw it as a wheel, from the outside. Here that rim was *down,* and floored in bare metal—Kefk had mining, metal-rich in the debris that floated around its double stars; therefore Kefk was gray and dull, except for the dirty orange of the sodium-lights kif preferred—because it never occurred to the colorblind kif to paint anything for decorative purposes, only for protective ones: they literally had to use instruments to determine what color a thing was, and gods knew whether their homeworld Akkht had ever offered them dyes other than black—though it was rumored that they had learned their color-taste from the pastel, opalescent stsho, who disparaged the riot of color which hani and mahendo'sat loved about themselves; having discovered a range of distinctions beyond their senses, having the pale example of the stsho before them, and flinching before the stsho's concept of value (such affluent consumers they set the standard for the whole Compact's economy) and further daunted by the stsho's disparagement of species who put strong color with color, the kif were all very insecure in their own dignity before the stsho and before others: above all no kif wanted to be laughed at. True black was one distinction they could make, true black and true white: so they naturally chose the dark that matched their habitat and their desire to move unseen, and became aesthetes of only one color, the blackest black. They valued silver more than gold because to their eyes it shone more; and they valued texture above other things in aesthetics, because they were more tactilely than visually stimulated in their pleasure centers: in fact they must be virtually blind to sight-beauty, and loved to touch interesting surfaces—that was what she had heard from an old stsho once upon a time, when the stsho had gotten quite giddy on a tiny cupful of Anuurn tea (it had a substance in it which reacted interestingly with stsho metabolism, which did nothing at all to a hani: such were the oddities of vice and pleasure between species). The kif in earliest days, this stsho said, had been victims of mahen practical jokes, who sold them clashing colors; and the kif did not forget this humiliation.

Kif were vastly changed, that was the truth, even from a few years ago: then they had been scattered and petty pirates, dockside thieves a hani could bluff into retreat, kif whose style was to whine and accuse and frequently to launch lawsuits in stsho courts which might make a freighter pay out of court settlement just to get the matter clear. That was the style of kifish banditry before Akkukkak.

Now she walked onto this dock in the company of a prince's escort, and had her own bodyguard—Skkukuk walking along with her, armed with the gun he had taken from a kif in the fighting, looking like every other kif in his black robe and his hood and the plainness of his gear: if she looked about and if Skkukuk and one of her escort had changed places, she would not be able to tell them apart at any casual glance. That was another effect of kifish dress: of black hoods that deeply shaded the face and left only the gray-black snout in the light; it made targets hard to pick.

And from *Aja Jin*'s berth—nothing of that ship was visible nor any of the others, only the tangle of lines and gantries that held those lines aloft to the several ports that valved through to the ship—from behind that tangle came another pair, mahen, one of them male. The other was Soje Kesurinan, Jik's second in command. Kesurinan was a tall black mahe, scarred and missing half an ear, but handsome in the way she carried herself—dour as Jik was cheerful, but she lifted her chin as she saw Pyanfar, and her diminutive mahen ears, whole and half, flicked in salutation.

"Kesurinan," Pyanfar said quietly, as Kesurinan walked up to her. And: "Kkkkt," from her kifish escort. "Tahar is on her way. An escort is going to pick her up; we can go on down."

"Got," Kesurinan said, which was agreement, economical and expressionless in a woman who had to be worried. Very worried. But they had to play everything to the kif who watched them, and give away nothing. Pyanfar nodded to the escort, and they started walking then, along the dock, the belt of the AP gun heavy about her hips, a pocket pistol thumping against her leg on the other side. Kif went armed to the teeth and so did she and so did Kesurinan, and, kifish taste and kifish eyesight notwithstanding, she had used that trip to her room to put on a pair of dress trousers, silk and not the coarse crewwoman's blues she had taken to wearing aboard; silk trousers, her best belt, the cord-ends of which were semiprecious stones and *ui*, polyp skeletons from Anuurn seas, and worth more than rubies off Anuurn: hani were not divers, as a rule, but they were traders, and knowing the substance, had suspected the stsho would prize this pale rarity—quite correctly, as it developed. In this splendor and with a couple of gold bracelets and a silver one, not mentioning the array of earrings, she headed for a meeting with the self-appointed prince of pirates, in all the arrogance a hani captain owned.

She had gotten out the door in good order, had gone down the lift, joined Hilfy in the short lock corridor and informed the kif that she was expecting her own escort, while Haral used the intercom and the central board's unlock-commands to release Skkukuk from his prison and to direct him to the lift by the farside corridor, where Tirun brought his gun to him—all managed so that it saved Skkukuk's dignity. The ammonia-smelling rascal had come strolling up on them from the direction she had come, armed and suitably arrogant with his fellow kif: after all, his captain had an appointment with the *hakkikt* and he had just been chosen over all the other crew as her escort: he was positively cheerful.

Hilfy, on the other hand—

Hilfy's ears had gone flat when she saw what was toward, and there had been starkest horror in her eyes, which the kif might well have attributed to seeing herself shunted aside for a kifish escort—correct; but for the wrong reasons.

But the kid, in fact, had kept her mouth clamped shut and taken it all in grim silence. Gods knew Hilfy would probably say something considerable when she got topside, which was probably where she had gone the moment that lock shut, topside so fast the deck would smoke.

A strobe light began to flash behind them, pulses hitting the gantries and the girders; she knew what it was, knew when Kesurinan turned, and when the kif turned in one move— "Kkkt," one said, "kkkt—"

And looked back at her again as the others did, head lifted in threat, tongue darting in nervousness: his rifle slid to his hands.

Pyanfar only stood there. Grinned at him, which was not humor in a hani as it was in a mahendo'sat or a human; but which at this moment approached it. *The Pride of Chanur* had just powered up and the sensors on the gantry-fed power lines had just shut off the flow and triggered an alarm, the same alarm that would have sounded when Goldtooth's *Mahijiru* and *Ehrran's Vigilance* had powered up to leave dock—if the station had not been too occupied for anyone to react to it. "We're not leaving," she said to the kif quite cheerfully. "It's honorific. So you know who you're dealing with—Praise to the *hakkikt.*"

Kif might be blind to a great many things: not to sarcasm and not to arrogance and not to a gesture made to the whole of Kefk station and the whole of the *hakkikt*'s power. They would not rally to their *hakkikt* in the sense that hani would rally round a leader; she bet her life on that; he was just The *Hakkikt* and there might arise another without warning. Kif would not defend him against someone of status enough to make that kind of gesture to him: such a status only made them uneasy, in the absence of orders which might have told them how the *hakkikt* would play the matter. They could anger the *hakkikt* by creating him a problem, too. She faced a pair of very uneasy kif. And grinned in something very like primate humor as she turned and walked down the dock as she had already done, with the kif at her back, with Kesurinan at her side and Skkukuk guarding her flank, armed and deadly. That was perhaps another very worried kif: his own *hakt'-mekt*, his great captain, had just defied the highest power in local space.

She had just served notice to that Power what the stakes were, by the gods; and what her life was worth to her crew.

That was power of a sort no kif wielded, of a sort no kif could easily foresee.

Martyrdom was a concept that had gotten a shiver even out of Sikkukkut.

"Word from *Harukk*," Hilfy said, coldly and calmly as she could, though her hand trembled as it hovered over the com console: "Quote: *We demand cause for this violation of regulations.*"

"Reply:" said Haral Araun, her low voice quite calm, "We have obeyed instructions from our captain."

The hair rose on Hilfy Chanur's spine. She was more fluent in mainkifish than most hani, than most communications officers far senior to her, in fact. And what Haral was telling the kif was precisely the correct response, a very kifish thing to say, whether or not the old spacer knew it: Hilfy would have bet her scant possessions that Haral had calculated it, not by book-learning, but by decades of dockside give and take with the kif. She punched in and rendered it in main-kifish to the *hakkikt's* communications officer, who let a considerable stark silence ride after it.

Click.

"*Harukk*-com just went offline," Hilfy said, still calmly, though her heart was slamming away at her ribs. Beside her, Tully and Geran and Khym sat keeping an eye on scan, on the limited view they had with their nose into station and the scan output from station. Tirun Araun ran Haral's copilot functions from her post over by the aft bulkhead, the master-alternate, acting as switcher and sequencer, Haral's usual job; and Tirun had armaments live back there too. In case.

"Haa," Khym muttered suddenly.

"We just lost station output," Geran said.

Sikkukkut's officials had just blinded them, at least insofar as station could. Doubtless someone was on the com to Sikkukkut personally, to tell him that there was a hani ship live, armed, and with its powerful nose stuck right into Kefk's gut.

Not mentioning what those engines back there could do if they cycled the jump vanes sitting at dock. Some of their particles would stay in realspace, mightily agitated; others, in their random way, would enter hyperspace, and stream for the depths of the local gravity wells, the greatest of which was Kefk's main star. Everything would part company in a rather irretrievable fashion, either turning into a bright spot or a failed attempt at a black hole, stripping its own substance down, since it had no directional potential except the station and the star's own motion through the continuum. Probably not enough to prevent implosion. Hilfy activated a keyboard in her idle moment, fed in *The Pride*'s mass and her best guess at total station mass, adding in the number of ships tied into the station, a moment of black self-amusement, filling her mind with numbers and schoolbook calculations.

It was significant that the kif had not immediately demanded that they shut down the internal power: the kif knew they had no power to enforce that until they had Pyanfar in their hands.

And Hilfy did not want to think about that at the moment. She simply ran the numbers on their own possible dissolution, and whether they would actually form the hyperspace bubble, and whether with all those ships and that station and all that mass, they might actually have a hyperspatial effect on the largest star when they plowed into it.

She sent it into Nav, since the bubble variables resided there in standard equations; and of a sudden her comp monitor blinked, beeped, and came up with output too soon to have responded to that complex query: TRLING/PR1, it read, PSWD.

Password?

Nav query?

Those were the two thoughts that hit her brain while her eyes were in motion back to the top of that screen where the program name was listed: they found that PRIORITY ONE code and the Linguistics Path Designator as the implication suddenly hit like a wash of cold water.

YN she typed, which was the shortest city name on Anuurn and the standard password for their lightly coded systems: fast keys to hit.

Syntax achieved, the screen said. *Display/Print?/Tape?/All?*

She hit *D* and *P;* the screen blinked text up, full of gaps and mangled syntax: it was running a code-cracker set in the assumption it was mahensi, but it was not mahen standard, it was some godsforsaken related language, though the computer was making some sense of it on cognates. Jik's message. The coded packet he had dropped in their laps back at Mkks.

Dialect. Which?

She punched more buttons, desperately, asking for the decoded original. It came up, vaguely recognizable as mahen phonemes. "Gods be," she muttered, "Haral, Haral, the comp just spat out Jik's message but it's still hashed up, it's got a string of words together but it's still sorting —we got a breakthrough here."

The screen blinked with a red strip across the top, which was Tirun using her keyboard to snatch information across to her board and probably to Haral's.

"Keep on it," Haral said. "Tirun, monitor com."

"Aye," Tirun said, and "Aye," Hilfy muttered, punching keys, with the hair bristling on her neck and her ears flicking in half-crazed vexation with the computer, which had thrown her a half-solved problem in her own field here on the very edge of oblivion.

Kif could call our bluff any second now.

Haral could push that button.

We could go streaming for that sun and the gods rot it what language is he using that comp hasn't got? O gods be! when's that alarm going to come? We're going to die, gods rot it, and it's giving me something to chase, and gods rot it, Haral, let me finish this gods-be silly problem before you push the godsforsaken button, it's a rotten thing to die with a question in your head, if this thing's got the whole why and wherefore of it, all Jik's conniving, all his secrets—hold off the button, Haral, tell me when we go, I don't want to die till I get this—

The computer beeped and sorted and ticked away, launched on a new hunt with a little hani shove in a certain direction for its research. It blinked away to itself and Hilfy clasped her hands in front of her mouth and stared at the screen in mindless timestretch.

Probably a letter to his wife. Gods know. Has he got a wife? Kids?

We're going to die here and this stupid machine can't go any faster and what can we do anyway? Pyanfar's already out there with the kif.

And we can't get to her. Whatever happens.

Harukk occupied a berth well around the rim, beyond the weakened section, but not beyond the damage: wreckage lay about them, walls and decks were fire-blackened and pocked with shells and laser-hits.

And the approach to the *hakkikt*'s ship was more ghastly than before, hedged with a veritable forest of poles and stanchions on which he had put the heads of enemies and rebels against his power.

Pyanfar had seen the display before; so had Kesurinan. *Hope he changes them off,* was the wisp of thought that leapt into Pyanfar's distressed mind. *M'gods, putrefaction. The things life-support has to put up with on this station—filters must be a gods-be mess.*

—in a distracted, callous mode because she had gotten used to such horrors, and only her heart flinched in a forlorn, pained recollection that there were places where such things did not happen, where naïve, precious folk went about their lives never having seen a sapient head parted from its body and hung up like a traffic warning.

This kif is going to expand beyond Kefk. Going—gods know how far. Gods help the civilized worlds.

A sneeze hit her. She stifled it, turned it into a snarl and wiped her nose. She was allergic to kif—had taken another pill when she changed clothes, but the air was thick hereabouts. Her eyes watered. Lives rode on her dignity and she was going to sneeze, the very thought that she was going to sneeze made her nose itch and the watering grow worse. But she squared her shoulders and put the itching out of her mind, eyes fixed on the ramp, on the access which lay open for them.

"It's coming, it's coming," Hilfy murmured, as the screen came up with more and more whole words, as it broke the code on a few key ones and spread the pattern wider: a makeshift job of encoding, a kind of thing one ship's computer could do and another one could unravel, if it had a decoding faculty; and *The Pride*'s did. *The Pride*'s fancy-educated communications officer had taken her papa's parting-gift in the form of the same system she had studied on by com-net back on Anuurn; it cost; and it worked, by the gods, it sorted its vast expensive dictionaries for patterns, spread its tentacles and grabbed every bit of memory it could get out of the partitionings, and sorted and cross-checked and ran phonemic sorts, linked up with the decoder-program in the fancy new comp-segment the mahendo'sat had installed in *The Pride* back at Kshshti—gods knew what all it did. While no one who wanted to keep a document in code was going to be fool enough to drop proper names through it or use telltales like *t'* or *-to,* or *-ma* extensions, it had the advantage of that mahen code program it sorted in as a crosscheck. The result was coming out in abbreviated form, truncated, dosed with antique words and code phrases no machine could break, but it was developing sense.

Prime writes haste* not * runner/courier accident* eye/see.

Events bring necessity clarify actions take* prime/audacity. . . .

She added a hani brain's opinion what the choice ought to be in two instances. The computer flicked through another change.

Number one writes hastily {?} Do not hold this courier or risk disclosure. Events compel me to clarify actions which Number One has taken—

"Haral," she said, and felt a shiver all over as she added another suggestion to comp.

. . . since {ghost?} is not holding to agreements support will go {to?} opposition all efforts supporting candidacy—

"We got some stuff here," Tirun muttered. "Jik's talking doublecross of somebody."

"Who's *Ghost?*" Hilfy said. "Goldtooth?"

"Akkhtimakt?" Tirun wondered in her turn.

"Ehrran?" Geran wondered, which possibility of double-dealing sent a chill down Hilfy's back.

"Maybe some human," Haral said, and the hair bristled all the way down.

O gods, Pyanfar needs to know this.

And may never know it.

If they lay a hand on her; if we blow this place; gods know what we're taking out—if we have to. If they make us do that.

Good gods, we're talking about conspiracy all the way to Maing Tol or wherever—Candidacy, who in creation has a candidacy anyone out here worries about—

—except the hakkikt.

The corridors of *Harukk* would haunt her dreams—ammonia-smelling and dim, with none of *The Pride*'s smooth pale paneling: conduits were in plain view, and bore bands of knots on their surfaces that, Pyanfar suddenly realized in a random flash, must be the kifish version of color-coding. The codings added alien shadows to the machinery, shadows cast in the ubiquitous and horrid orange of sodium-light and the occasional yellow-green of a coldglow. Tall robed shadows stalked ahead of them and others walked behind, as a door opened and let her and Kesurinan and Skkukuk into the *hakkikt*'s meeting-room.

Sikkukkut waited for them, in a room ringed with black kifish shadows. Two incense-globes on tall poles gave off curls of sickly spicy smoke that curled visibly in front of the sodium-lights mounted to the side of the room, while another light from overhead fell wanly on Sikkukkut's floor-hugging table, himself and his chair, the legs of which arched up about him like the legs of a crouching insect. Sikkukkut sat where the body of the insect would be, robed in black edged with silver that took the orange light, with the light falling on his long, virtually hairless snout and the glitter of his black eyes as he lifted his head.

"Hunter Pyanfar," he said. "Kkkt. Sit. And is it Kesurinan of *Aja Jin?*"

"Same, *hakkikt,*" Kesurinan said. And did not say: *where is my captain?* which was doubtless the burning question in her mind.

Pyanfar settled easily into another of the insect chairs and tucked her feet up kif-style as one of the *skkukun* brought her a cup, one of the ball-shaped, studded cups the kif favored, and another poured parini into it. Kesurinan had hesitated to sit: "You too," Sikkukkut said, and as Kesurinan took another of the chairs, next Pyanfar, he looked in Skkukuk's direction. "Kkkkt. Sokktoktki nakt, skku-Chanuru."

A moment's hesitation. It was courtesy; it was invitation to a kifish slave to sit at table with the *hakkikt* and his captain. "Huh," Pyanfar said, sensing Skkukuk's crisis; and her flesh shrank at the sudden purposeful grace with which Skkukuk came around that table and assumed the chair beside her—he *slithered,* on two feet: was, she suddenly recognized those moves, not skulking, not slinking—but moving with that fluidity very dangerous kif could use; very powerful kif; kif whose moves she instinctively kept an eye to when she saw them dockside and met them in bars. This was a fighter, among a species who were born fighting. And all hers, for the moment.

She sipped her parini. Sikkukkut sipped whatever he was drinking while a *skku* served the others in turn.

"Tahar," Sikkukkut said, "is on her way in. And your ship is *live,* hunter Pyanfar. Have you noticed this?"

"I've noticed," she said, and kept all her moves easy.

Sikkukkut's long tongue exited the v-form gap of his teeth and extended into the cup, withdrew again. "So have I. Your crew claims they're following orders. Is this so?"

"Yes."

"Kkkt." Silence a moment. "While you are on the dock."

"I hope," Pyanfar said ever so softly, "that nothing's been launched toward my ship—bearing in mind there might be agencies still on the station that would like to damage the *hakkikt's* ally. I hope the *hakkikt* will protect us against a thing like that."

Deathly stillness. At last the *hakkikt* lapped at his cup again and blinked with, for a kif, bland good humor. "You have been foolish, hunter Pyanfar. There's far too much opportunity for error. And you have delivered far too much power into the hands of subordinates. We will talk about this."

Another weighty silence, in which perhaps she was expected to reply. She simply sat still, having achieved a position in which she could sit and stare thoughtfully at the *hakkikt*.

Eggsucking bastard, she thought. *Where's Jik, you earless assassin?*

She tried not to think of what kind of demonstration Sikkukkut was capable.

"We will have a discussion on the matter," Sikkukkut said; and there was the subtle, soft whisper of arrival in the outer corridor. "Is that Tahar? Yes. Alone except for my escort. I wonder at this new tactic."

Tahar hesitated in the doorway, then ventured close—a quiet step, a quiet settling into place when the *hakkikt* gestured her to sit at the table: a rippled-maned, bronze-pelted southern hani with a black scar across her mouth that gave her a grim and raffish look.

"So all the ships in your hand," Sikkukkut said, looking at Pyanfar, "are in mine."

"*I* am in your hand," Pyanfar said, with as steady a voice as ever she faced down a dockside official bent on penalties. *But never suggest I don't control those ships, no, not to a kif. Status, Pyanfar Chanur. Status is all there is with him.* "It's a complex situation, *hakkikt*. Hani minds are not, after all, kifish. But that's my value to you."

"Godsawful gibberish," Haral said from her station. The printout was ten pages long, and full of code words that only Jik and his Personage might know. Hilfy Chanur stared at the same set of papers and flipped this way and that, trying to get some idea what they applied to.

—*Ghost is proceeding on the course suggested in her previous report.*

Pieces and bits of information depending on other information.

—reports from inconvenience/Inconvenience? are negative.

"I think Inconvenience is another codename," Hilfy said.

"We knew," said Tirun, from the end of the consoles, "that that son was in connivance up to his nose."

"Who are we?" Haral wondered. "Could we be that *Ghost?*"

"Inconvenience," Hilfy suggested. "If—"

"Priority," Geran exclaimed, atop a sound from Tully. "Priority, engine live, coming over station rim vicinity berth 23—"

Harukk's neighborhood. Kif ship.

"I am glad to know your value to me," said Sikkukkut carefully. "It's always helpful to have those things explained." His fingers moved delicately over the projections on the cup he held, restless, sensual movement. "I have held such a discussion with my friend Keia. He has tried to explain. I'm not sure with what success."

"He's very valuable," Pyanfar said, her heart thudding the harder against her ribs. *Careful, careful, don't tie the crew and all we've got to him.* "He's a force we'd miss. Against Meetpoint."

"You assume Meetpoint."

"Hakkikt, I've expected the order hourly."

"Is *that* why your ship's engines are live?"

She grinned, honest hani grin, a gentle pursing of the mouth. "I'm quite ready to go."

"Kkkt. *Skku* of mine."

"Congruent interests."

"And do your subordinates share your enthusiasm?"

"They'll follow."

"They've followed you here. Meetpoint might be far more dangerous."

"They're well aware of that."

"What is their motive, do you suppose?"

"Self-interest. Survival."

"They think then that your guidance will advance them."

"Evidently they think that. They're here."

"You see outside my ship the results of miscalculation."

"I noticed, *hakkikt.*"

"You still consider Keia Nomesteturjai a *friend,* hunter Pyanfar."

"Hakkikt, when you use that word it makes me nervous. I'm not certain we understand each other."

"When you say *subordinate* I suffer similar apprehensions. What *is* that ship of yours doing?"

"Following my orders."

"Which are?"

"Are we to *later?* I'm willing to discuss it if we are." In the *hakkikt's* stony silence she sipped at the cup. "On the other hand, we were talking about Meetpoint. That *is* where we're going."

"Do be very careful, hunter Pyanfar."

She lowered her ears and pricked them up again. But a kif might not read that hani apology; and galling as retreat was: "I retract the question then."

"Nankt." The kif waved a hand; a door opened and someone moved; it was a name he had called. It sounded like one. The hand flourished and took up the cup again from the table. "Well that you learn caution, hunter Pyanfar."

"It's holding stationary," Geran said, and Hilfy watched the development on her own number two monitor, where the limited sweep of their scan picked up a ship which had risen to station zenith, hanging where it had a free shot at everything.

"That's *Ikkhoitr,*" Haral said. "One of the *hakkikt's* oldest pets."

"If they're not talking," said Tirun, "and they're not moving, that means they're at the limit of their orders."

"Move and countermove," Haral said.

Hilfy flexed her claws out and in again with an effort at control. Her stomach hurt. She felt a shiver coming on at the thought of that button near Haral's hand. *You going to tell us before you push it? Or just surprise us all, cousin?*

With a mental effort she shifted her eyes back to the translation problem and got herself busy, leaving the ship over their heads to Haral's discretion.

From Khym and Tully, not a word; silence; Chur had not cut in her monitor: Geran had gone back to Chur's room briefly when it all started, and pushed a button on the machinery, ordering sedative, putting her sister out cold before it got to the noise of locks opening and the ship powering up. Or other things Chur might want to listen in on; and learn too much of situations that she could do nothing about. Geran quietly put her sister out, turned her back and walked back to the bridge to do her job, which she sat doing, businesslike and without a shake or a wobble in her voice or a trace of worry on her face.

Gods-be coward, Hilfy Chanur, do your own job and quit thinking about it.

It was Jik they brought into the hall—Jik, a dark, dazed figure between two kif who held him by either arm: who had to go on holding him on his feet after they brought him to the table. Jik lifted his head as if that took all his strength. Pyanfar's stomach turned over; her ears twitched against her determination not to let them flatten, and then she let them down anyway: any hani smelling that much drug-laden sweat and pain would wrinkle up the nose and lay the ears down, even if it was not a friend held there in such condition before her eyes.

"Keia," said Sikkukkut. "Your friends have come to see you."

"Damn dumb," Jik said thickly; and Kesurinan climbed slowly to her feet, stood there with her hands at her sides, a holstered pistol brushing one of them. Kesurinan had the cold good sense to go no farther than that. Tahar tensed in her seat, but she made no further move either, and Pyanfar nodded in Jik's direction.

"You don't look too good."

"Lot drug," Jik said, head wobbling. "You damn fool. Go ship. Private, huh?"

"It is the drug," said Sikkukkut. "I forgive his discourtesies. Do you want to cede him your place in our council, Kesurinan? Or not, as you please."

Do you repudiate your captain? Do you want his post?

Perhaps Kesurinan had no idea what was being asked. She moved and took Jik's arm from the kif who held it, flung her arm about him and gently eased him down onto the chair.

"Kkkt. Mahen behaviors." Sikkukkut lapped at his drink while Jik leaned on one of the upraised insect-legs of the chair his first officer had yielded him and stared through a pair of them at Pyanfar.

"H'lo," he said. "Damn mess."

"Godsrotted mess for sure. What've you been telling the *hakkikt,* huh? You going to go with us to Meetpoint?"

"I dunno," he said. He shut his eyes as if he had gone away a moment and opened them again. They shone dark and desperate in the orange light, spilling water onto his black skin and black fur. His nostrils widened and sucked in air. "Go ship, Pyanfar."

"You see," said Sikkukkut, "we *are* moving at some deliberate speed. Kesurinan, Tahar, I tell you what I have told my other captains: follow your orders. You came here, which is very well. Now you will go to another room; and you will stay there. Until I release you. Tell them they will do this, hunter Pyanfar; and dismiss this *skku* of your own ship."

"Do it," Pyanfar said. It was protocols. Or a demonstration of power. There was no choice, not even with all of them armed. She looked at Tahar as the scar-nosed pirate got up and stared back at her with that expressionless calm that had carried her through two years of close dealing with kif. Skkukuk got to his feet on the same order.

And:

"You go," Jik murmured on his own, speaking to Kesurinan.

"A," Kesurinan agreed.

"Kkkt," Sikkukkut said, not missing that little distinction, it seemed, of control in that exchange. He waved his hand: kif cleared a way and one of the ranking *skkukun* motioned to Tahar and to Kesurinan and Skkukuk. There was, Pyanfar noted with some relief, no question about the weapons they wore, and Skkukuk had not signaled any warning. If he had not changed sides altogether when he sat down at that table.

"Would you," Sikkukkut said, when the others had gone, "like something to drink, Keia?"

"No," Jik said thickly.

"He still has his wits," Sikkukkut said, turning his head slightly to Pyanfar. "And he still has all else he was born with, by my strict order. In consideration of an old friendship, kkkt, Keia? But you don't then order *Aja Jin,* hunter Pyanfar. Nor order this one. He makes that quite clear, doesn't he?"

"He'll do what I ask him. As an ally."

"If he does what you ask, as an ally, do you then do what he asks?"

"I have in past. I think he owes me one."

"Merchants. But Keia professes not to be a merchant at all. I don't think he will trade. Will you, Keia?"

Silence. Long silence.

"Stubborn. He is very stubborn." Another lap at the cup. "Tell me, *Chanur-skku,* what am I to think about that ship of yours?"

"That we're ready to go to Meetpoint, *hakkikt.*"

Sikkukkut's long jaw lifted. It was not a friendly gesture, that shift of the head that stared more nearly nose-on: that was threat, the eyes glittering cold black with the sulfurous highlights of the lighting. "Ismehanan-min went to Meetpoint, *skku* of mine: now, I am not patient of this. By now there is a ship of mine over the station axis with its guns aimed at your ship. And we are at impasse."

"Hakkikt, when I go back to my ship I'll power down. My crew has its orders until then."

"That's a very stupid bluff, hunter Pyanfar."

"I'm not bluffing. We can all die here. You're not dealing with a kif, *hakkikt.* I'm hani. Remember?"

There was a stir all about the hall. Clicks and subsequent red gleams of weapons ready-lights. And Jik pushed his hands against the insect-leg and lifted his head slightly.

"Your ship isn't moving on mine," Pyanfar said, "since you don't want your station damaged. And mine won't move. Leaving dock isn't what I ordered them to do. I told them if I die here, or if they're attacked from your side, to cycle the jump vanes."

Chapter Three

There was stark silence in the hall.

"Cycle the vanes," Sikkukkut repeated, and rested his hands on the legs of the insect-chair. "That would be a curiously futile gesture for them."

"What should I care," Pyanfar said, "if I were dead? But never doubt that my crew is prepared to do that."

"Martyr," Jik said in his hoarse voice, and hauled himself by his arms on the chair to face Sikkukkut: he rested there leaning on the upraised arch of the chair legs, head on forearms and a grin on his face. "She *hani*. She tell crew blow us all to hell, they do it. You deal with damn fine hani crew. Same be lot brave for you. You got use right."

More profound silence. Then Sikkukkut lifted his cup and lapped at it delicately. "*Bravery*. This is another of those words which sounds kifish until one looks more deeply at the mindset. I distrust it. I distrust it profoundly."

"Just consider it," said Pyanfar, "a longrange survival plan. But *don't* consider it." She waved her hand. "What I'm truly interested in, what I'm sure we're all interested in, is what we do about Meetpoint, *hakkikt*. You want Jik's cooperation: I can get it for you."

"I remind you that you failed miserably with Goldtooth. We *assume* that you failed there. In certain moments I wonder."

"In certain moments *I* wonder, *hakkikt;* and I still don't know what he's up to. I'm more concerned what the humans are up to; and I can tell you plainly—" she held up a forefinger, claw extended,—"Tully doesn't know. I've questioned him closely on it, and I know when that son is lying and when he isn't. He was a courier who didn't know his own message; Goldtooth used him and dumped him, which is a little habit of Goldtooth's that I want to talk to him about. Goldtooth doublecrossed Tully, doublecrossed Jik. Doublecrossed me. And to confuse it all he gave me help, in the form of medical supplies we needed. *I* don't know how to read his signals. I'm being perfectly frank with you. I can tell you that Ehrran and I aren't friendly; and she's dealing with the stsho, which I trust even less. That's where I stand. I want Jik back. Under *my* command, *hakkikt."*

"Damn," Jik said. "Hani—"

"He's honest," Pyanfar said. "If you do that favor to him, at my request, he'll be caught in a moral tangle his government won't like at all. But we don't need to tell them that, do we? And we don't need to leave Goldtooth alone to represent the mahendo'sat. *Jik* supports your side. And if you lose him, *hakkikt,* you'll have no chance in a mahen hell of getting the mahendo'sat to make any treaty. Give him to me. I can handle him."

"Prove it now. Get the truth from him. Have him say where the humans are going, what Ismehanan-min said to him before he left, and what agreements he knows of with the methane-folk."

Pyanfar let go her breath slowly. Her laboring heart found a new level of panic.

Fool. Now you get what you bargained for. Don't you, Pyanfar?

But what else is there to do? How do we win anything without this kif?

She looked toward Jik as he shifted his hold on the chair to face her direction. A fine dew of perspiration had broken out around his eyes, running down into his black fur; his eyes glittered in the orange light and the darkness, and there were lines about them she was not accustomed to see there. "Jik," she said. "You heard him. You know what he wants."

"I know," Jik said, with no intimation he was going to say a thing.

"Listen." She reached out and took hold of his arm where it rested on the chair; she smelled the sweat and there was the stink of drugs in it; drugs and raw terror. "Jik. I need you. Hear? Hear me?"

Jik's face twisted, showed teeth, settled again in exhaustion. His eyes shut and he got them open again. "Get hell out. Hear?" And he meant more than get out of *Harukk:* she read that plainly.

"If the *hakkikt* fails," she said, "what does that leave us with? Jik. Jik—" *There's a reason I can't tell you.* She tried to send that with her eyes, with the sudden force of her hand; and with her thumb-claw, dug in so hard he winced.

"Damn!" he cried, jerking back; she held on.

"Listen to me. If the *hakkikt* fails, where are we? That bastard Akkhtimakt—" She tensed the thumb-claw again. *J-i-k.* In the blink-code. "Do you hear me? Do you hear?"

He no longer pulled back. His hand twitched. "I hear," he said in a hoarse, distracted voice. "But—"

"You'll take my orders. Hear?" And: h-u-m-a-n-t-r-e-a-c-h-e-r-y she spelled into his flesh. The sweat ran in rivulets past his eyes, in the thin areas of his facial hair. "Jik. Tell him everything."

A long moment he hesitated. She felt the tremor of muscles in his arm. The fear-smell grew stronger. The look on his face was a thing to haunt the sleep: he poured all his questions into it, and there was nothing she knew how to send back—let one kif note that hidden move of her thumb on the underside of his hand and they were both in it. But:

T-r-u-s-t, she signaled him. *D-o.*

He broke away from her eyes. He leaned himself on the other side of the chair, facing Sikkukkut. "Ana say—humans come Meetpoint. Truth. They go fight Akkhtimakt. Gather hani, make fight 'gainst kif. Then got—" His voice broke. "Got—hani, stsho, human, mahendo'sat, all fight kif."

"And it's your task," Sikkukkut said quietly, "to see that I reach Meetpoint to engage my rival Akkhtimakt—all while being attacked by all the others. Is *that* what your partner told you to do?"

Prolonged silence.

"Answer," Sikkukkut said.

"He not tell me what he do. He say—say I got go Meetpoint, wait orders."

"To turn on me at the opportune moment. Kkkt. And now what will you do?"

"I think he damn fool, *hakkikt.*" Again Jik's voice cracked. "I think I first time got better idea, help you take out Akkhtimakt."

"And then to turn on me."

"Not. Not. I think Ana got wrong. I damn scared, *hakkikt,* he got number one bad mistake. I don't think he do what he do, damn, I come on dock, try get Pyanfar out lousy mess, I don't know my damn partner going to blow the damn dock, I don't know he going outsystem, I don't know he got deal with Ehrran and the damn stsho—What happen? I get shoot at, I get caught, I get lousy drug and beat up, you think I be damn fool, *hakkikt,* come outside if I know what he do? Hell, no. Maybe Ana same time got smart idea, but he don't know I be out there, I don't know he be going to leave the dock—lousy mess. Ehrran be the one break dock, she be the one kill you people; I don't think he know what she do."

"They met. They talked. We know this."

Jik's head dropped, his shoulders slumped. He looked up again, leaning on his arms. "I think they talk stsho deal. I think Ana not know, not know what she do—He just got move fast. He plan go, yes. Not then. No so fast. He think got time. Ehrran make him move. Maybe he think I be dead, I don't know; maybe he think we all be on that dock, maybe he think *The Pride* crew be gone, maybe think ever'thing be gone to hell—I don't know, *hakkikt.* I don't know."

"You contradict yourself."

"Not lie. Don't know. I don't know."

"And the methane-folk? What dealings with them?"

Jik's head dropped again onto his arms. For a moment he was utterly still, and a kif moved closer at his side. Pyanfar sat quietly, forcing a calm over her nerves from the outside in, till it got to the depth of her mind.

We're talking about the whole gods-be Compact going up in smoke.

We can take him, at any time, we can take this kif bastard, if we're willing to die—and we're both dead now, Jik and I. It doesn't matter. Doesn't matter that he's in pain, it's nothing, nothing in the balance, nothing that really matters. I'm sorry, Jik; I can't care, can't afford to care, can't stink of fear, I daren't. Not if we've got a chance. And I'll take it wide and high, Jik, if I have to. You're a professional, you know what I'm doing, you know I can't do anything else, drug-drunk as you are. We can settle it later.

"Answer him, Jik." *And gods, come up with a good one.*

I need you, Jik.

I can't play this throw alone.

He moved. He lifted his head again. "Tc'a," he said thickly.

"What about the tc'a?" Sikkukkut asked.

"I talk with. Lot scare'." His hands slipped. He caught himself and lifted his head with an effort. "Knnn lot disturb. Humans come through knnn space. Maybe shoot at knnn ship."

"Kkkkt."

"Damn fool. Tc'a want keep knnn quiet. They want mahendo'sat make all quiet, quick. Tc'a lot mad with Ana. Talk me—talk me—want make knnn be quiet. I say tc'a—tc'a, you got help Sikkukkut. Fine fellow, Sikkukkut. So tc'a come with us to Kefk. But knnn—"

"The knnn took it."

"Took. Don't know why. Maybe want ask why come with us. Maybe want ask what we do. Knnn lot crazy. No know knnn mind. I tell Ana —he be crazy want talk to knnn. Make quiet, I tell Ana, you got make quiet. Knnn be disturb, I don't know, don't know, don't know—"

Both hands went. He hit the arch of the chairlegs and hung there.

Pyanfar carefully took up her cup and sipped at it. *Don't think, don't react, he's not in pain now. Be cold and careful and don't care. There's no guarantee what the bastard's going to do with either of us now he has what he wants.* "That, I think, was the truth. It jibes with other things he's said. Mahendo'sat have their own ways. And it's very likely that Goldtooth is pursuing some contrary course, giving his Personage a second option. Unfortunately that course seems to involve helping Ehrran ruin me—friendship is worth something, *hakkikt,* but species-interest in Goldtooth's case is a great deal more potent. He'll be sorry to see me ruined and my influence broken—I was useful to him once; we even had a personal debt. But sorry is as far as it goes. Ehrran seems to him to have what he wants right now: influence in the *han.* Jik is pursuing a totally different course for the Personage they both serve—so Goldtooth wouldn't work directly against Jik, in the interest of giving the Personage that double choice; but he'll by the gods cut Jik's throat when he thinks it's come to crisis. And it will be crisis at Meetpoint, when we all go in there. That's how Goldtooth will deal with the methane-folk: kill Jik and remove the one person who can deal with the tc'a —because Jik does work with them." She took a second sip. "You told me back at Meetpoint, that one day I'd want revenge on my enemies. *Pukkukkta.* I had to look that word up. I know now what you offered me. You said at the same time that if I didn't want it then, I'd want it later. That was before I knew my enemy was a bastard of a hani who was out to get me from the start. I'll give you a hani word. *Haura.* Bloodfeud. Ehrran's got that now, with me, with Chanur, with Geran and Chur Anify; and Haral and Tirun Araun have a grudge or two themselves. And I'll get Rhif Ehrran if I have to go through Goldtooth and the stsho and the mahendo'sat and the humans to do it. *Puk-kukkta*'s a cold emotion; *haura*'s a hot one; but that doesn't mean it can't last years. Am I making clear sense? However long it takes, I'll get her."

"You make sense, hunter Pyanfar."

"Tahar also has a bloodfeud with Ehrran. And Tahar interests are linked to mine. I'm her only hope of recovering her reputation. And her power."

"That also makes sense."

"I also have a certain matter to settle with Goldtooth. A personal matter. And Jik is the best leverage on that. That's why I want him."

"No kif would be as forward."

"No kif can offer you what I do."

There was a soft clicking about her, a stirring; and the guns were still live.

"What do you offer?"

"An alliance with non-kif."

"Kkkt." Sikkukkut placed his hands on the chair, lifting his jaw. "Where is it?"

"Lying in that chair; and sitting in this one. And neither's inconsequential. Neither's without ties that go far beyond one ship and a small authority. Give me Jik and give me *Aja Jin,* and I'll use him to settle with Goldtooth *and* Rhif Ehrran. A weapon in my hand is a weapon in yours."

"Is it?"

"Since we have common interests. A hani is very easy to understand. Look for clan interest. And Rhif Ehrran is out to destroy my clan, with Goldtooth's help. I told you I'd go through all the others to get her. And that's exactly what I'll do."

Sikkukkut leaned his long chin on his fist, the silver-bordered sleeve fallen back from a thin and muscular arm, the light gleaming on his eyes. "I well tell you, hunter Pyanfar, you will have the chance to make good what you say." The forefinger lifted. "You will have everything you ask."

O gods, the thought hit her then. *Too easy. Too fast. Too complete.*

"You will take *Aja Jin* and *Moon Rising* and you will take Meetpoint."

"*Hakkikt—*"

"You claim a great deal for yourself. Can you deliver more than words? Or perhaps—will you defect to my enemies?"

"To Ehrran?" Her ears went flat. It took no acting at all. "No."

"You encourage me." A second finger lifted beside the first. "So I will give you Keia. On condition."

"That being, *hakkikt?*"

"He will go aboard *The Pride*. In your charge."

"He's the best pilot—"

"I know his skill. I know Kesurinan's, which is considerable. But she has less recklessness. I tell you how I will arrange things and you will accept them for your own good, hunter Pyanfar. Keia would betray your interests, left free to follow those he serves. Instead I give him to you, and you will use him wherever it profits you, but most of all where it profits me. I insist on this point. Do you understand me?"

Her ears twitched again, and it was not acting either. "You're very clear. And you may be absolutely right. I agree."

"I *may* be right. How generous of you. Is that the word—generous?"

"I'm taking your orders. Those who know me would be shocked to hear that. I'm a bastard, *hakkikt*, and a graynosed old bastard at that, and I'm not in the habit of taking orders, but I'm taking yours." *You don't back me up, son. You don't treat me like one of your rag-eared lot.* "You impress me and your opinions make absolute sense to me. You give me Jik here, I'll keep Kesurinan in line. And him. I know what you're saying, and yes, you're right. You want me to take Meetpoint, I can't do that. Even with Jik for a wedge. But if you're coming in behind me and want the stsho all dithered—" *Which is what you plan, isn't it, you son?* "—I can by the gods keep them busy."

Sikkukkut sipped at his drink. "You'll have to be more than that, *skku* of mine. I have a ship to spare. Do you know what a single hunter-ship can do to an inhabited world?"

O my gods.

"No warning would travel faster than that ship. It would strike and go. And hani would be removed from the question. The power I give you would be removed, *skku* of mine. Always remember I can take it away. I can remove Anuurn from consideration as an inhabited world. Do you understand me?"

"Entirely." *Bastard. Thanks for the warning. Haura, bastard. You know how long Akkht itself would survive a move like that? Let's talk about life in the Compact. Let's talk about wiping out species.* "When do I go?"

"I have a packet for you. You'll have it. With the person of my friend Keia. Treat him gently." Sikkukkut's nose twitched. "And under no circumstances set him free. I have uses for him myself: he's a loan, not a gift." Another lap at the cup. And a wave of Sikkukkut's hand, at which several kif near him stirred forth from the shadows, passing in front of one of the lights and casting long shadow over the table.

The shadow enveloped her, enveloped Jik as they laid hands on him and gathered him up with soft clickings and chatter among themselves. Jik lolled limp, in a way that said he was not shamming: his arm swung down, his head fell back when they lifted him, and there was no muscle tone in the arm they grasped—kifish fingers bit deep when they swung him up to carry him.

"Your leave," Pyanfar murmured, set her drink down, and stood up. She bowed, as carefully and formally as ever before the leadership in the *han*. She kept her ears up and her face calm as she glanced aside to their handling of Jik, and looked again to Sikkukkut for instruction.

He waved his hand again. A second time she bowed, and walked out the door, into the dim corridor outside, into the presence of lesser kif who gave way to someone of her evident status, who edged out of her path, lowered their faces and made themselves shadows against the walls and the conduits.

Her knees were going to be weak. The ammonia smell dizzied her: she had not sneezed, thank the gods, she had snuffled once or twice and covered it; but of a sudden her stomach felt queasy and her heart which had exhausted itself in terror, labored away in slow, painful beats.

The nightmare was not going away. They were bringing Jik, she had to pick up her three companions, mahe, hani, and kif, on her way out; and she had to get down that dock and observe whatever the kif sent her in the way of instructions.

Had to.

"I got him," she said curtly to Kesurinan when the kif brought her companions to her in the exit corridor. "He's staying in my custody."

And it hurt, somewhere dimly and at the bottom of her soul where she had put all her sensibilities—the quick lift of Kesurinan's ears, the dismay, the instant smothering of all reaction, because Kesurinan was not a fool, and knew where they were and who was listening, and then that they would have to do everything the kif insisted on to get her captain out of *Harukk*. Kesurinan thought she was talking to an ally.

Sikkukkut was absolutely right: the mahendo'sat would be an ally right down to the point their own species-interest took over. And then Jik would save his own kind.

So, she discovered, would she.

* * *

They made slow progress down the unstable docks—a gang of kifish *skkukun* carrying a stretcher with Jik strapped tightly to it; Jik's First Officer walking along by him, anger and concern in every line of her back: and with a gun on her hip. Pyanfar walked to the side and a little behind, with Dur Tahar on her right and Skkukuk at her left, Tahar inscrutable as Tahar had become in her life among kif, while Skkukuk gave few signals either—except in squared shoulders, except in less nervousness than he had ever shown; except in every subtle move that said here was a kif whose status was no longer that of an outright slave, a kif whose captain had just dealt with the *hakkikt* and won. He carried a weapon beneath his outer robes and gods knew what ambitions in his narrow skull. If ever a kif was pleased, this one positively basked in his change of fortunes, inhaled the chance in the air, savored the sight of the *hakkikt*'s slaughtered enemies, his dreadful signposts—and the sight of his captain rising in that service.

Cold in all the warm places and fever-warm in all the cold ones, gods, a hundred eighty degrees skewed. Alien. *The kif are that thing in doubles and triples.*

Stay cold, Pyanfar Chanur. Save it. Jik's a piece of meat. Tahar an ally-of-fortune, Kesurinan's potential trouble, and this gods-be son of a kif is a convenience.

Kesurinan's not going to make trouble, not yet. She'll let us take Jik aboard.

Gods, don't let Jik come to out here.

Slowly, slowly they walked up the dock past the section seal, into that area where there were no pedestrians. Where there was no traffic at all but themselves.

And there was *The Pride*'s berth ahead, still flashing with those warning lights. She took her pocket com out, within range of the pickup now: "This is the captain. I'm coming in."

"Aye," Haral's voice came back to her, thin with static: that formality she had used was warning, and Haral took it: *I've got company, Haral; don't get easy with me.*

Another eternity, walking that fragile dock: and gods help them, Tahar and Kesurinan had farther still to go. "Skkukkuk," Pyanfar said, and the kif beside her was all attention. "Tell the *skkukun-hakkiktu* I want Tahar escorted to her ship by the quickest and safest route. Through the central corridors if they can."

"Hakt'," Skkukuk said, acknowledging the order; and walked up with the litter-bearers and gave that instruction with all the kifish modulations of a superior's relayed instructions and his own high status with that superior. Then he fell back a step or two and lifted his face in satisfaction.

She said not a word to Tahar, and Tahar offered not a word to her; that was the way of things.

Toward *The Pride*'s open accessway, then. "Wait here," Pyanfar said to Tahar and Kesurinan, and with a special coldness in Kesurinan's direction, when they reached that gateway: her flesh crawled in that earnest look of Kesurinan's scar-crossed face. "Aye, captain," Kesurinan said, all unknowing.

And betrayed her own captain into foreign hands.

"Chanur-hakto," the foremost kif said, when they had deposited Jik on his litter in *The Pride*'s airlock. That kif took a packet from within his robes and offered it.

Skkukuk intercepted it in one smooth move. And waved his hand, dismissing the other kif out the airlock.

"Seal us up," Pyanfar said to the air and the crew watching on monitor.

The lock shot closed, hissed and thumped into electronic seal.

"Power down," Pyanfar said.

"Aye," Haral's voice came to her. All business, even yet. Pyanfar took the packet Skkukuk offered her officiously, with the stretcher lying on its supports at her feet. Now the shivers wanted to come, but she kept her ears up and looked her own kif in his watery, red-rimmed eyes.

"Good job," she said to Skkukuk.

"Kkkkt," the kif said. "You need me, hakt'. Who else of your crew has manners?"

Her gorge rose. She swallowed and tucked the small packet into her pocket, squatted down by Jik's stretcher and patted his face gently. It was cold and there was no reaction.

"This is an ally?" Skkukuk asked.

"This is a complicated situation," she said, trying to tell a kif the truth; and then a second thought ruffled the hair down her back. *Gods, this is a killer I'm talking to. With hairtrigger reflexes.* "Yes. An ally." She moved her hand down to Jik's neck and felt the pulse there. "Haral. Get Khym down here. We got Jik to move. He's still out."

"On his way, captain. You all right?"

"Fine. I'm fine. We got out in good shape. Open that door." She patted Jik's face again. "Hey. Friend. Come out of it. You hear me? You're all right."

Friend.

He was under. Deep. She heard the lift work: Khym had either been on his way or he had run that topside corridor. And *The Pride* was proceeding with power-down, a series of subtle noises that her ear knew in every nuance. "Skkukuk. You'll help Khym. You'll do what he says."

"Kkkt. This is your mate."

She stood up and looked flat-eared at Skkukuk, with the ammonia-stink in her nostrils and the antiallergents drying her mouth. Something about the asking crawled along her nerves. This alien, this unutterable alien, was feeling out who was to consider among the crew, who he could displace, who he could get around and who not.

That's one job you can't work your way into, you slithering earless bastard. You keep your mouth off my husband's name. You better figure that, fast.

A thousand thousands of years of hani instinct ran up her spine. And Skkukuk read that look and took on one of his own.

Caution.

Footsteps in the lowerdecks corridor. Rapid ones, more than one set.

Don't run, Khym. Dignity, Khym. In front of the kif, gods rot it, Khym.

She was still standing squared off with Skkukuk when Khym showed up in the doorway with Tully close behind.

"You're all right," Khym said.

"I'm just fine. Take Jik to sickbay. Get Tirun onto it. Skkukuk—"

The kif was still waiting. Armed. Their ex-prisoner, possessing a gun that could blow a hole in armor plate. And expecting in his aggressive little kifish soul that he had just won his freedom.

"You're offduty," she told Skkukuk. "You'll keep that gun in your quarters. You've got a lowerdecks clearance. You understand me."

"Kkkt. Absolutely."

"Move."

Everyone moved. Skkukuk got himself out of her sight, correctly reading her temper. Khym and Tully got to either end of the stretcher, got it lifted with its not inconsiderable dead weight of tall mahendo'sat, and maneuvered it out the hatch.

"Tirun's on her way to sickbay, captain." That from her niece. While the powerdown proceeded.

"Understood," Pyanfar said calmly. And stood there a moment staring at the wall. With a kif's orders in her pocket. She fished them out and broke open the brittle seal to look at the written portion.

"*Departure at 2315,*" was the center of that detail. It was, at the moment, all she was interested in. The kif gave them time enough to get organized. Barely. With precise course instructions, aborting one that they had laid in.

"Hilfy."

"*Aye,*" the subdued voice reached her.

"Message to Kesurinan and Tahar: stand by departure; they'll have a bit over six hours. So will we."

A pause. "*Aye.*"

Silence after. *The Pride* was at rest again. The crew on the bridge could see her, where she stood. The camera was live. She looked up at it. "Things could be worse," she said glumly. "I can think of one way right off. But we got Jik in our custody, we got Tahar and *Aja Jin* with us, and we've got the *hakkikt*'s orders: it's Meetpoint. His way."

A longer pause.

"*Aye,*" Haral said simply, as if she had given a routine order.

The largest space station in the Compact.

And a forewarned one.

"Clear the boards, stand offduty; I got Jik to see to."

"Aye, captain."

She walked out of the airlock. And only then it occurred to her, like the ghost of an old habit that no longer meant anything, that she had just packed her husband and another crewman off to tend another man, knowing beyond the last twitch of instinct, if it was ever instinct, that Jik was safe with them, safe as that kif was safe to send down the corridor in the other direction, because even the kif was a rational mind and sane and sensible, while the universe quaked and tottered on all sides of them.

She walked down the corridor and into the open door of sickbay, their little closet of a facility. Tirun had beaten her there. Khym and Tully were taking Jif off the stretcher and laying him on the table.

"He'll have some bruises," Pyanfar said. "You'd better run a scan on him. He may have more than that." She went to the med cabinet, keyed the lock with a button-sequence and sorted through a tray of bottles— hani-specific; hani drugs did strange things with some mahendo'sat. No telling what the kif had given him even if she ran a query into Library, and it was better to stick to the simple things. She pulled out an old-fashioned bottle of ammonia salts and brought that over to hold under Jik's nose.

Not a twitch.

"Gods-be." She capped the stinking bottle and slapped Jik's chill face. "Wake up. Hear me?"

"What did they give him?" Tirun asked, lifting Jik's eyelid, peering close. "He smells like a dopeden."

"He's a hunter-captain, gods rot it, his own precious government's got him mind-blocked, gods know how far down he's gone." She turned around, shoved her way past Khym and got to the intercom. "Bridge! Get *Harukk* on, tell 'em I want to know what they dosed Jik with, fast."

"*Aye,*" Haral's voice came back.

Tirun was counting pulsebeats. And frowning.

"Gods, he doesn't know where he is." Pyanfar crossed the deck again, shoving roughly past both the men, to grab at Jik's shoulders. "*Jik, gods fry you, it's Pyanfar, Pyanfar Chanur, you hear me? Emergency, Jik, wake up?*"

Jik's mouth opened. His chest moved in a larger breath.

"*Come on, Jik—for the gods' sake, wake up!*" She yelled it into his ear. She shook at him. "*Jik! Help!*"

Tension began to come back to his musculature. His face acquired familiar lines. "Come on," she said. "It's me, it's Pyanfar."

Help, she said. And the great fool came back to her. He hauled himself out of whatever mental pit his own people had prepared for him, the way he had run out onto that dock to fight for her and her crew, when an absolute species-loyalty had dictated he save himself. *Help.* More strangers handled him, dumped him from stretcher to table, gods, not unlike what the kif must have done to him, and he went away from them, deeper and deeper, only knowing at some far level that he was being touched.

Knowing now that there was a hani cursing him deaf in one ear and asking something of him, but nothing more than that.

O gods. Gods, Jik.

His eyes slitted open. He was still far away.

"Hey," she said. "You're all right. You're on *The Pride.* I got you out. Kesurinan's gone back to *Aja Jin,* you hear me, Jik, you're not with the kif anymore. You're on my ship."

He blinked. His mouth worked, the movement of a dry tongue. He heard her, she thought, at some level. He was exploring consciousness and trying to decide if he wanted it.

"It's me," she said again. "Jik," She patted his arm and stooped with a sick feeling at the gut when he flinched from her touch. "Friend."

"Where?" he said, at least it sounded like that.

"On *The Pride*. You're safe. You understand me?"

"Understand," he said. His lids drifted down over the pupils. He was gone again, but not so deeply gone. She hesitated a moment, then turned in a blind rage at two fool men who had not sense enough to clear out of sickbay's narrow space and give them room to work.

She found herself staring eye to eye with Tully—with Tully who had been twice where Jik had been, and whose face was stsho-white and his eyes white round the edges. She had been about to shout. The look on Tully's face strangled the sound in her throat.

"Out," she said, and choked on the word. "Clear out of here, you're not doing anything useful."

Khym flattened his ears, thrust out an arm and herded Tully away; Tully went without seeming to notice it was Khym who had touched him. The human was a shaken man.

So was she, shaken. The hair was standing up all down her back.

"Captain," Haral's voice came, *"it's sothosi. Library's sending to labcomp right now."*

"We're on it."

Tirun was on it, a quick move for the comp unit; a glance at the screen and a dive for the medicine cabinet. She broke open a packet, grabbed an ampule and an astringent pad and made herself a clean spot on Jik's arm.

The stimulant went in. In another moment Jik made another gasp after air, and another, a healthier darkness returning to his nose and lips. "There we go," Tirun said, monitoring his heartbeat. "There we go."

Pyanfar found herself a chair and sat down, before her knees went. She bent over and raked her hands through her mane, conscious of the uncomfortable weight of the AP at her hip and the prodding of the gun in her opposite pocket. She stank. She wanted a bath.

She wanted not to have done what she had done. Not to have made the mistakes she had made. Not to be Pyanfar Chanur at all, who was responsible for too much and too many mistakes. And who had now to think the unthinkable.

"You all right?" Tirun asked.

She looked up at her cousin, her old friend. At a crewwoman who had been with her from her youth. "Tirun." She lapsed into a provincial hani language and kept her voice down. "He'll stay here. I want this room safed, I want him left under restraint—"

She tried to keep the cold distance she had had on *Harukk*. It was hard when she looked into an old friend's eyes and saw that natural reaction, that dropping of Tirun's ears.

"Tirun," she said, though she had meant to justify nothing; she found herself pleading, found a shiver going through her limbs. "We got a problem. I'll talk about it later. Do it. Can you? Stay with him till he wakes up and make sure he's breathing all right. And for godssakes leave those restraints on him. Can you do that?"

"Yes," Tirun said. No doubt. No question, from an honest hani who handed her captain every scruple she had and expected her captain was going to explain it all. Eventually.

"Tell him I'm going to come back down. Tell him it's because we've got a few hours, I want him to rest and I can't think of any other way to make sure he does." She still spoke in chaura, a language no mahendo'sat was going to understand; and that was statement enough how much truth she was handing out. Tirun stared at her and asked no questions. Not even with a flick of her ears. Lock up a friend who had saved their lives and come back in this condition from doing it. Lie to him.

If she could knock him cold again without risking his life she would do that too.

She got up and walked out, raked a hand through her mane and felt the stinging pain of exhaustion between her shoulders, the burn of cold decking on her feet. Kif-stink was still in her nostrils.

She flung the kifish packet onto the counter by her own station on the bridge.

No one had left post; or if Geran had left to check on Chur she had come back again in a hurry. Solemn faces stared at her: Hilfy, Geran, Khym and Tully; Haral kept operations going.

"Leave it, Haral," Pyanfar said.

Haral swung her chair about, same as the others.

"You know the way we came in here," Pyanfar said, "and took Kefk. We got orders to do it again. At Meetpoint."

Ears sank. Tully sat there, the human question, hearing what he could pick up on his own and what garbled version whispered to him over the translator plug he kept in one ear.

"You've heard bits and pieces of it," she said, and sat down on the armrest of her own cushion, facing all of them. "We've got to follow orders the way they're given. Or we've got to blow ourselves to particles here at dock. And that takes out only one kif faction. It leaves the other one the undisputed winner. And by the gods, I'd rather they chewed on each other a while and gave the Compact a chance. That's one consideration. But there's another one. Sikkukkut's threatened Anuurn."

"How—threatened?" Haral asked.

"Just that. One ship—if he thinks we're getting out of line. He's not talking about an attack at Gaohn. Nothing like it. He means an attack directly on the world. That's the kind of kif we're dealing with. One large *C*-charged rock, hitting Anuurn, before Anuurn can see it coming, gods know. It was a threat. I hope it was a remote threat. We're dealing with a kif who knows too gods-be much about hani and too gods-be little: he was a fool to tell me that and maybe he doesn't imagine what we'd do to stop him—before or after the event. But I don't think he's the only kif who'd think of it. I hope they chew each other to bloody rags. We arrange that if we can—but we've got to do what we're told right now or we find ourselves looking the wrong way at one of Sikkukkut's guns, and we don't get the chance to warn anybody, or work our way around this, or save a gods-be thing."

"Captain," Haral said, "we got a kif up there at zenith. He's got position on us."

"I know about it. We're not going to take 'em on. We just get out of here. We've got six hours, we're dropping into a Situation at Meetpoint, and the Compact may not survive it in any form we understand it. *That's* what we've got. That's what we're up against. I don't know what we're going to find at Meetpoint. Tully—are you following this? Do you understand me?"

"I understand," he said in a faint voice. "I crew, captain."

"Are you? Will you be, at Meetpoint?"

"You want me sit with Hilfy at com, speak human if humans be there." His voice grew steadier. "Yes. I do."

With all he could and could not understand. She gazed on him in a paralysis of will, as if putting off deciding anything at all could stop time and give them choices they did not have.

Jik, they had locked up below. A kif and a human were loose among them. The human sat in their most critical councils.

But Tully had given them the warning she had passed to Jik, a warning blurted out in one overcharged moment that Tully had stood between her and Hilfy and she had questioned his motives.

Don't trust humans, Pyanfar.

On one sentence, one frightened, treasonous sentence in mangled hani, they bet everything.

Gods, risk my world on him? Billions of lives? My whole people? My gods, what right have I got?

"I'll think on it," she said. "I haven't got any answers." She picked up the packet and flung it down again. "We've got our instructions. We've got Tahar with us. We've got Jik's ship. And we've got orders to keep Jik with us and keep that ship of his under tight watch."

"There's something else," Hilfy said. And took up a piece of paper and got up and brought it to her. It trembled in Hilfy's hand. "Comp broke the code. Maybe he meant us to break it. I don't know."

She hesitated in the dim doorway of sickbay, with that paper in her pocket; Jik was awake, Tirun had said.

He was. She saw the slitted glitter of Jik's eyes, saw them open full as she walked in, quiet as she was. She went and laid her hand on his shoulder, above the restraint webbing. Tirun had put a pillow under his head and a blanket over his lower body.

His eyes tracked on her quite clearly now, gazed up at her sane and lucid. "Come let me go, a? Damn stubborn, you crew."

But she did not hear the edge of annoyance that might have been there. It was all too quiet for Jik, too wary, too washed of strength. It was—gods knew what it was.

Apprehension, comprehension—that he might not be among friends?

That for some reason she might be truly siding with the kif—or that she was operating under some other driving motive, in which they were no longer allies?

He had for one moment, in that kifish place, drugged and on the fading edge of his resources, answered questions he had held out against for days, answered because she got through his defenses with a warning his mind had been in no shape to deal with, and because she had signaled him that he had to do this.

Now he was clear-headed. Now he knew where he was, and perhaps he recalled, too late, what he had done. That was what came through that faint voice, that failing attempt at good humor.

"Hey," she said, and tightened her hand. "You got nowhere to go, do you?"

"Aja Jin."

"Told you about that. Kif'll shoot your head off. We're clear. Got it all patched up with Sikkukkut. You passed out on me. Missed the good part. I need to talk to you."

"I got talk to my ship."

"That can wait. You'll fall on your nose if you try to get up. Don't want you trying it, hear? Tirun fill you in?"

"Not say."

"Your ship's fine; the dock's patched; I got you clear and got everything fixed up with Sikkukkut: he's a gods-be bastard, but he does listen. He's still suspicious, but he's put you aboard *The Pride,* says you've got to ride out the next move aboard my ship and let Kesurinan handle *Aja Jin.* That was all I could get. We've got to live with that."

"I got damn itch on nose, Pyanfar."

She reached and rubbed the bridge of it. "Got it?"

"Let me go. I walk fine."

"Haven't got time. We're moving. Going to Meetpoint. You're going to have to ride it out where you are. I'm sorry about that, but we haven't got another cabin we can reach till we undock. And then things are going to go pretty fast."

He was quiet a heartbeat or two. Then: "Pyanfar—"

"I got a question for you. I want to know what we're headed into. What did Goldtooth tell you before he left us, huh?"

A silent panic crept into his eyes. He lifted his head and let it fall back against the pillow, still staring at her. "Not funny."

"I need to know, friend. For your sake, for that ship of yours, gods know, for mine. What are we headed for? What's he doing?"

"We talk on bridge."

Bluff called. She stared at him and he at her and there was a knot at her gut. "You know how it is," she said.

"A," he said. "Sure."

"I got this thing to ask you. I want to know the truth. You understand me."

He ran his tongue over his lips. "What this deal with humans?"

"Tully told me—told me flatly not to trust them. You know Tully; he's not too clear. But what he said, the way he said it—I think they're going to doublecross your partner. I think they're not the fools Goldtooth thinks they are. And they're not taking his orders."

"Maybe you do better talk to Tully."

"I have. We've got a problem. Sikkukkut wants Meetpoint. He wants us three to go in first, *The Pride, Aja Jin,* and *Moon Rising.* You see how much he trusts us. He wants us to go in there and shake things up and crack Meetpoint so he can walk right in easy."

"Akkhtimakt maybe be there."

"So's everyone else. Aren't they? I got one more question. What about the methane-folk? What's the real truth?"

"Lot—lot mad." Another pass of Jik's tongue across his lips. "I try talk to tc'a. They want keep like before. Knnn—different question. Goldtooth said—said got maybe trouble."

"Who's *Ghost?*"

Jik blinked. His eyes locked on hers, pupils dilated.

"When you were in trouble," Pyanfar said, "I hauled out that little packet you gave me at Mkks and started it through comp. We got a number one good linguistics rig. The best. *Mahen* make, a? Why'd you ever give me that packet, huh?—to carry on for you. In case something happened here at Kef'k? So I could get through to Kshshti or Meetpoint? Gods-be careless job of encoding if we could break it—but then, then it might have had to go to a mahen ship way out from your Personage, mightn't it? Someone like Goldtooth, maybe? And the real code's in the language—*isn't it?*"

"Maybe same—want you to have."

"You knew gods-be well we'd have to go to mahen authority to read it? You by the gods knew we'd have to run to your side when it got hot —we'd be held to being your courier again, that's what you knew, that's what you set us up for, rot your conniving, doublecrossing hide?"

He lay there and blinked at her.

"*Was* it because you thought something might happen to you, Jik? Or did you already plan to do what Goldtooth did for you here at Kef'k? Blow the docks and run and leave me to get anywhere I gods-blessed could, with your confounded message? *Was it you who gave Goldtooth the orders to break dock?*"

"Hani, you got damn nasty mind."

"I'm dead serious, Jik."

"You crazy." He gave a wrench at the restraints. "Damn, Pyanfar? I walk fine."

"Answer me."

"What you think, I run out on you, leave you talk to kif? *I on that damn dock myself!*"

"You weren't in the zone that blew! That's by the gods close timing, Jik!"

"I not do!"

"Didn't you? I think you knew with Chur sick I wasn't free to run for it. That it'd kill her and I wouldn't move if I had a chance in your coldest hell. *Goldtooth* gave us that med unit—fine, so I could run. *You* gave me that gods-be packet back at Mkks before we knew we'd find him here—you gave it *in case* something happened to you, a packet we'd *have* to take to mahen authorities. And what does it talk about? People reneging on agreements, that's what; it talks about contingencies, talks about supporting some candidacy—*whose?* Sikkukkut's? What agreements?"

"Sikkukkut. Same. You know agreement."

"You're lying, Jik. By the gods, you show up at Kshshti and help me out of one mess, then you help me all the way here, deeper and deeper you helped me, you and your godsforsaken partner, you and your gods-be deals—"

"I come out on that dock save you damn neck!"

"Where were you planning to ditch us? *Where,* huh? Here? Or later, at Meetpoint? Where was it I was supposed to find this gods-be packet was the only currency I had, where was I supposed to go? Kshshti? Back through kif territory, get my ship and my crew shot up one more time, end up on mahen charity because there's no gods-be help else when you've got through using me and mine for every gods-be gods-rotted piece of mahen politics you've got going? Or maybe I get to Meetpoint and find you'll drop me to politic with the stsho to save them from the kif—some mahen squeeze play, throw one kif at them from Kefk, another from Kita and Kshshti, catch them between your ships and the humans and haul the whole gods-be Compact into your lap, with me and the *han* left the way you left us the last time, out in the cold with our ships shot up, our station in ruins, and nothing this time to do but come crawling to your gods-be charity! Is that the way your favors go? Am I what you think you're buying with this little packet that tells your authorities how to deal with me?"

"I not do!" Jik fell back from a convulsive shout, breathing hard, and they stared at each other for a moment.

"Then who's this Ghost? What's the rest of it?"

Silence. Jik only stared and breathed.

"It's another doublecross. Isn't it? *They've threatened my world, you hear me?"*

He blinked. That was all.

"Gods rot you—" She snatched the paper from her pocket and waved it in his face. "What's this thing mean? What's this gods-be message worth if the humans doublecross you?" And when his mouth only clamped the tighter: "Jik—"

"My nose itch, Pyanfar." Quietly. With full self-possession. And when she lost the breath to shout with: "Damn miserable, Pyanfar, damn ridic'lous situation, you and me. You come get me. Now what we do? What you think do?"

She took the paper and folded it, absorbed in that meticulous task.

"You got too good heart deal with kif," Jik said.

"What's our choice? What gods-be choice have we got? Your whole plan's blown up, we've got the Compact coming apart around our ears—"

"Same you, me, a?" He made a grimace, blinked sweat and strained to see her. "What we do, a? How far we want go, you, me?"

"I don't know." She shoved the message into her pocket and leaned into his view, close, ears flat and a shaking in her knees. "How far *do* I go, huh, Jik? How far'd you go? This mess you put in motion is threatening to take my *world* out. We talk about friendship now? We talk about what you'd do in mahendo'sat interests? About two mahen bastards who'd doublecross every friend they got, all for the Personage?"

"You want try drug next?"

"Don't push me."

"What *we* got, huh? Damn Anuurn hani sit and wait, good friend? You longtime got mind like rock, Pyanfar, whole damn *han* got own interest, let mahendo'sat fight kif pirate, let mahe do, hani too damn busy make politic—"

"Why blame us? You created the *han,* take the poor hani bastards, teach 'em spaceflight, shove 'em into your own gods-rotted politics with the stsho, and to a mahen hell with the clans—"

"What you want? Sit on world, be sit there when politic in the Compact roll over you heads like wave in the sea? Be sit there when kif eat our heart and come find hani? Maybe all time you like sit on world, Pyanfar, maybe you get old, want go sit in damn dirt and wait for kif?"

"So what d'we get? The kif or you?"

"You got choice."

"Gods blast you!"

"If we want you damn world, Pyanfar, we one time got, first time we land on Anuurn you got nothing but point' sticks. You forget? You ask us leave, we go."

"Sure, you went. You never turned loose of us. Manipulate our trade, shape our government, let us here and let us there and *don't* let us get beyond ourselves—"

"Fine. You make fine deal. Maybe you like kif lot better. Wish you luck, Pyanfar. Or you got trust me—"

"*Trust* you!"

"Damn, you come, I crazy drunk, *talk kif,* you say; I do, I *do,* Pyanfar, I got so much trust in you, I *do.* All diff'rent, you say; got human louse things up, got bad trouble—*'Talk, Jik: tell the kif what he want, I get you out—'* God! what kind fool I be with trust?"

"I should let you loose on my ship? Let you loose with my crew? Jik, I got you out of there. I did that for you. If you trusted me you'd tell me what's in this paper, but you won't do that. You can't do that, and I know why, like you know why I don't dare let you go. I've got to survive. I have to stay alive in this gods-rotted mess you handed me. I've got to hold a position where I can still do something. You under- stand me? I'm *going* to do something."

"I tell you paper." Jik's voice came faintly, almost inaudible. "You know mahendo'sat—know I got power to make agreement for my Per- sonage. I make now—with you. With hani."

"Same as you make with Sikkukkut, huh? Same as you make with Akkhtimakt and set them at each other's throats."

"Same I keep. Same I give him Kefk, same I fight with. You same know mahendo'sat. I keep agreement. I don't say Personage keep. But—" Jik blinked again and licked his lips, eyes lively as if he had already won his point. "—if you get this kif, we got deal with you fair, a?"

"Tell me the paper."

"Let go first."

"Oh, no, friend. You listen to me. You listen good. We're going out of here, going to come kiting blind into whatever you set up over at Meet- point, and Kesurinan's going in there on my directions. It's your ship. Your crew. I'd think you'd be a little concerned."

"Damn kif heart, you got kif heart, Pyanfar."

"I got a hani one, same as you're working for your own." She laid her hand on his shoulder, even knowing it was unwelcome. "Listen, you bastard, you and I had rather deal with each other. I take your agree- ment. I'll *sleep* with your gods-be Personage if it gets us out of this, but the first thing I got to do is get us into Meetpoint in one piece. And I want those code names and I want every godsrotted thing you've been holding out on me. Right up front, I want to know what's in that message, and what kind of a deal you and Goldtooth have already made."

He shut his eyes, blinked at the sweat. "Paper say—most this you got to know already: the stsho betray us; the human maybe ally; hani—hani not reliable; I make deal with Sikkukkut to make him *hakkikt,* I got also deal with tc'a—Pyanfar, you say this wrong ear, you blow Compact to hell."

"That's real fine. What of it we've got left. Keep talking."

"Tc'a long time take knnn orders: why they change now, I don't know. Got some crazy input from chi, damn lunatic chi got notion want go out from Chchchcho, want expand—"

"You mean the *chi* are pushing the knnn? Good gods, those—"

"Not sure. Maybe tc'a idea. Methane-breather be lot crazy. But knnn —we not be sure, think maybe knnn got eye on chi. Also human got lot planetaries, got lot thing knnn want, maybe; also got human-ity, number one problem. Long time problem. Stir up kif. Stir up methane-folk. Big trouble. You not know."

"The Akkukkak business?"

"Before Akkukkak." Jik explored a cut on his lip with his tongue and drew a deep breath. "Old *hakkikktun* be small stuff; lot little *hakkikktun* be lousy neighbor, lot trouble, steal you cargo, do little pirate stuff, easy we keep lanes clear—few hunter-ship take care these bastard number one good. Then we get fellow name Af'kkek, nasty lot trouble. He go down, we get 'nother, name Gotukkun. He got own authority, take what belong Af'kkek too. After Gotukkun be Sakkfikktin. Kasotuk. Nifekekkin. Each more big."

"Each adding his own followers to what he'd taken."

"You got. Long time kif be fight at Akkht, lot internal stuff. Long time we know kif got more big and more big *hakkikt.* So we try—try push *hakkikktun* make difficulty with methane-folk. Sometime work good. Now—we got mistake. Big mistake. We been get human signal, longtime."

"You *asked* them in? Gods blast—!"

"Not ask. We try take quiet look, see what be this kind. Lose ship. Lose two ship, we think be knnn, maybe kif take those ship. Maybe knnn same time got curiosity 'bout humanity. I think, me, I think

Akkukkak set up trap, bring human, take. But we not know this: he be dead; maybe no one know."

"Of course you didn't share this information with anyone."

"Who we tell? Stsho? *Han?* You got Tully. We don't know what else you got. We don't know what he tell you—I tell you, Pyanfar, you come mahen station, bring human—you trust us damn too much. 'Cept we be friend, a? We don't tell you all thing we know. But we fight with you keep kif off Anuurn. Lot thing then we don't know. We got find out. You know when Tully 'scape kif? Lot time kif operate at Meetpoint, make trade with stsho. They got Akkukkak, got couple kif be rival—lot trouble with kif. Ana try—not know what that ship got; he know one kif ship chase 'nother, Akkukkak come there 'cause he got no safe route else. Then he not be real happy find my partner Ana come in port. He 'fraid stay, got other kif; 'fraid go, 'fraid Ana get on his tail, he got tail in vise number one good. So he sit at dock. He so damn busy watch Ana he forget watch other kif. One kif inside ship make snatch Tully; Tully run like hell down dock—you got rest. Now Ana lot worry, not know what this be, not know if this be species we know about, or be something lot different. He try find Tully. Kif try find. Tully go *you* ship and start damn lot trouble. Now you got stsho go crazy, all scare' 'bout knnn, scare' 'bout humans come, damn mad 'bout you damage station —Mahendo'sat work hard, bribe lot stsho, make so hani come back to Meetpoint. We *need* hani. Need balance with kif, damn sure stsho no good, tc'a and knnn lot disturb. We get hani back to Meetpoint, go try make careful new contact with humanity, try find out what they be, how big, what they minds be like—find out what knnn want."

"And the kif took offense at it."

"Kif damn busy big fight on Akkht. We know we got worry 'nother *hakkikt* grow up; so we got make opposition, hit here, hit there, try make lot little *hakkiktun.* Then we got Sikkukkut. My mistake. Sikkukkut."

"Who already had his hands into Akkhtimakt's organization. He got that ring, Jik, that ring Tully has on his hand. He got it from a human prisoner in Akkhtimakt's hands—Sikkukkut was already poised with his spies and his organization before we ever got to Kshshti, before you dealt with him at Mkks. This wasn't a little provincial boss we were dealing with, this was a kif already on his way to being what he is. Sikkukkut knows humans. He was Akkukkak's interrogator, he killed all of Tully's crew except the one Tully killed himself, when it got that bad, Jik, and you know better than I do what it could get to. This is the gods-be kifish *expert* on humanity we're dealing with, and if kif have anything like a security organization, I'm guessing some of Akkukkak's old staff that got swept up into Akkhtimakt's organization—never were Akkhtimakt's. They were Sikkukkut's partisans all along. Am I wrong?"

Jik stared at her. "You got damn good ears."

"I'm an old trader and I know how to add. You knew this. You knew some of it; and you went right ahead and you promoted this kif of yours at every step. The wrong gods-be kif. I didn't see it. You didn't see it till Kefk. Jik, I could take this dock out. I could stop this one. And that still leaves Akkhtimakt—"

"Same damn bastard. I be right, Pyanfar, still be right 'bout that one. Akkhtimakt got no bottom. Swallow everything. Sikkukkut—want *use* everything. Ana—Ana got this idea he use human for break the kif. But if *they* got motive—"

"Tully's got no reason to lie. They're *big*, Jik. You're not dealing with one human government. There's their homeworld, but there's two other powers. Tully's from their homeworld. It's fighting the other two and it wants to beat them—you tell me how. They've shot at the knnn. The knnn are putting up with it for reasons the gods and the knnn only know; we've got one human planet out there at odds with every other human in space, and there's gods know how many worlds the other side of their homestar from us. Their homeworld is cut off, isolate, having bloodfeud with its own outposts—what in the gods' name can you imagine we're dealing with? What's this lot after, when they've got a dozen worlds in the other direction and all of them are shooting at each other?"

"Tully say this?"

"By bits and pieces. Yes. That's what he's told me. We've just got the tail of the creature. When it turns around—"

"God."

"If you and your earless Personage had told the same truth twice in a day we might not be in this mess. You understand me?"

"If we not got damn hani traitor, if we not got the *han* screw up—we both got damn fools, Pyanfar, both kind. We got be fools too? Let me go. You got one of you crew sick. You want damn good pilot, you want me sit boards, you got. You want chain me to damn chair, you got. Pyanfar. I don't want lie down here in dark!"

She stood there on yea and nay, reached as far as the release and took her hand back. "Agreement?"

"You got."

She pulled the first release; and the second.

And stood there remembering the power there was in a mahen arm. And the wit there was in this mahendo'sat, and all his twists and turns: make a simple move against her he would not—until it was profitable.

Fool, a small voice said, while Jik slowly lifted his hands to his face and wiped the sweat, while he groped for the edge of the table and gave every indication of weakness and disorientation. He looked apt to pitch onto his face. She made a grab for him and steadied him as he got his feet over the edge and sat there blinking and grimacing as if his head hurt considerably. He put a hand up to his brow, wiped his eyes and looked at her.

As well admit Skkukuk to the bridge during jump. Much rather admit Skkukuk—who *was* on their side.

Of all the things I've done, she thought to herself, staring into Jik's alien eyes, *this is the one I'll deserve to die for. I know I'm making a mistake. I'm wrong. I'm going to foul up and the kif'll launch that ship, that ship no one can stop and no one can catch, and there won't be hani left except those of us who happen to be in space, that the kif will hunt down one by one. All because there's this chance that we need him, and Tully, and that gods-be kif who thinks I'm his ticket to kifish glory; because I'm an old fool of a hani who's been out in the dark too long and I can't shake it off and think clear of it any longer.*

"Pyanfar," he said gently, "you be damn bastard."

"Got you out, didn't I?"

"You got."

"You know you're not sitting a post on this ship."

"What you want?" He held out his hands together. "Chain to chair? Do! I want be on bridge. Want talk to my ship. Want hear my ship."

"Hear them, I'll give you."

Fool, Pyanfar. This isn't Anuurn. He isn't hani. Parole means nothing to him weighed against his orders.

And how do I treat him like this and trust him again, ever?

"Agreement, Jik. You put this one in my hands. You stay on the bridge, but you keep your mouth shut and you keep your hands off controls."

He turned his hands, showed blunt mahen claws which nature had never made retractable, or fine enough for the smaller controls on hani boards; and they were broken and bloody, the fingertips swollen and coated with plasm from Tirun's caretaking: it was sure the kif had done no good for them.

She felt a cold shiver inside, a sympathetic twitch of her own claws in their retractile sheaths. But she set her face all the same. "Is that all the answer I get? Or do you give me those codewords and give us some honest help?"

He looked at her straight from under his dark brow, a hard glitter in his eyes. "I do, Pyanfar. Now you got believe what I say, a?"

Chapter Four

I am writing this in haste at Mkks. Do not hold or compromise this courier. Present crisis compels me to clarify the actions which I have taken in support of Ismehanan-min, since his lines of operation have crossed mine. I trust his report has reached you, but have placed a duplicate in the care of the Personage at Kshshti should the courier have failed. Since Stle stles stlen is not holding to treaty agreements both Ismehanan-min and I are taking measures to support other candidates and to prevent replacement of mahen personnel with hani. Here at Mkks we have retrieved all hostages and have suffered no damage at present. We are requested by Sikkukkut to add support to his candidacy by moving on Kefk. I am not apprised of Ismehanan-min's whereabouts and do not speculate. I advance on Meetpoint by that route. All reports from tc'a sources indicate that Stle stles stlen is proceeding as in the previous report, and reports from our contact inside stsho space are not encouraging. . . .

Tc'a contacts report knnn agitation in urgent terms. . . .

I have given Ehrran a false packet. Evidently this is a stsho agent and I dispense only disinformation into this outlet. Her willingness to participate I am certain is only a means to gather information on our activities which I am sure she has gained through stsho contacts of her own and which she has twice attempted to relay through furtive contact with stsho agents, some of which have eluded the net. Our movements are reported through an efficient system of couriers and I maintain a close watch over Ehrran's transmissions.

Thus far Chanur remains reliable. Support for this agent must be managed with extreme discretion on all levels. I would send her on to Maing Tol but I see no means to do this over Sikkukkut's objections and considering Ehrran's present state of mind. Therefore Chanur remains with us, under utmost priority of protection. Particularly alarming is Sikkukkut's courting of Chanur. Leverage will have to be arranged to counter this. . . .

Pyanfar looked away from the translation on screen, and Jik, sitting in a ring of Chanur at the bridge com station, gave a pained shrug as she flattened her ears. "What kind of leverage?"

"Money," Jik said faintly. "Debt. Like maybe—a, Pyanfar, I not arrange these thing. This *gover'ment* stuff. They also help. Who repair you ship, a? Who bribe Stle stles stlen get you license back?" He looked around him, at face after face, looked again as Khym leaned a huge hand on the back of the cushion, and gazed up at Khym's glowering countenance before he thought otherwise and turned back to Pyanfar. "No good this read message," Jik said. "Damn, you read mail you going find stuff don't got all the truth. Truth, truth I can't say in letter— What you want, I write to Personage say I want help friend, I say I want them do good to you? No. I do quiet. I push make Personage you friend, I push keep you out trouble, I down on knee ask Personage treat Chanur right—" He reached and made a backhanded gesture toward the screen. "This, this be *evidence* in law. You know what I mean say. You don't write down some thing. No want enemies get, not kif enemy, not hani enemy, not mahe, not stsho. God, Pyanfar, you know what I try say."

She stared at him bleakly, saw the tremor in his hand and the pain etched around his eyes and his mouth, saw—maybe she *wanted* to see past the damning words on the screen.

"I know," she said, and saw the tremor grow worse in his arm before he let it down. Proud Jik, vain Jik, pressed to give accounts he would not have given, not for any threat, except for hope of help from the friends he had doublecrossed, with his ship held hostage and more than his freedom and his reputation at stake. What she saw hurt. And rang clearer than any protestations. "I know, gods rot it, we both got a mess. Haral, what's status on our allies out there?"

"*Aja Jin* and *Moon Rising* both report on schedule. I reported ourselves the same, all well aboard."

"So we've told Kesurinan you're fine," Pyanfar muttered to Jik. "So what was the hope—send me off sideways about the time you made the jump with Sikkukkut to Meetpoint?"

"We not want lose you," Jik said.

"I ought to be flattered," she said in her throat, and looked up at the others. Tully was on the bridge with them. Everyone but Skkukuk. Tully as usual lost all of it. He looked confused. So did the crew, confused and on the edge of anger. "We got a value to the mahendo'sat," she said. "They like their friends to survive. Gods know what else they want. It's fair, I guess. We have certain mahendo'sat we favor more than others. No great wrong in that, as far as it goes. You're offshift. Whole crew. Get a good meal in your stomachs: we got gods know what coming up. We got more than Meetpoint laid into Nav. If we have to."

She looked toward Jik. Jik leaned back in his chair, folded his hands across his stomach with something more like his usual ease. His eyes were tired. But the gesture at least looked like Jik, bedraggled as he was and lacking his usual finery.

"You too," she said. And for a moment the lids half-lowered on his eyes, the faintest of warnings.

Don't give me orders, that was to say. *I've had enough.*

Well, it was Jik, and he was only trying to recover a bit of his dignity. She let her ears dip: *all right.*

Then he unfolded his arms, pried his stiffening frame out of the chair and gave himself up to Tirun Araun, who indicated the galleyward corridor.

Fool, she told herself again. It was not just Jik she was trusting. It was a mahe the mahendo'sat put ultimate confidence in, one of a few who were turned loose in the field to make decisions across lightyears too many for the central government to be consulted on every twitch and adjustment of policy—places where agents had no time to consult, and a hunter-captain like Jik had to make up his own law and make treaties and direct local ships with the authority of the whole mahen government behind him.

Personage was more than an individual back in Maing Tol and another at Iji. It was the whole concept on which the mahendo'sat concluded anything: when a mahe was right he was right as law, and when he made a mistake he fell from power. His superiors would disown him. And if he made too great a mistake the superior who appointed him might fall: so there might be more than one agent in the field making contradictory arrangements.

The most viable would be acknowledged, the agents who stood too visibly for the nonviable policies would fall from power, and the mahen government went smoothly on.

Doublecross was the standard order of business. Betrayal of each other, of everyone but the superior. That he protected his own agents was Jik's saving honesty, and Goldtooth's, who had run and left Jik because he had to. It took this many years in space for an old hani to understand how it worked and to understand *that* it worked.

And there was still the question whether Jik might turn back on an agreement he had made, and repudiate it himself.

He had made a hard one, gods knew, with Sikkukkut.

And a contradictory one with her.

She frowned, and walked on the way others had gone, into the galley, where Tirun had gotten Jik seated at table and where Haral and Hilfy and Khym and Tully were all delving into the cabinets and the freezer hunting quick-fix edibles. There was the bitter odor of dry gfi in the air: Tirun was filling a pot. There was the rattle of plastic: disposables. Pyanfar leaned on the table with both hands and looked Jik in the eyes.

"Got a question for you. Say you got two agreements, you, yourself. And the people you made them with—get at odds. How do you resolve that?"

Jik frowned. His eyes still wept. His sweat smelled of ammonia and drug even yet. "You, Sikkukkut?"

"Me and Sikkukkut."

"I keep best agreement."

"The one that serves the mahendo'sat best."

"A." He blinked and gazed at her like a tired child. "Always."

"Just wondered," she said. "In case."

Something else occurred to her, when she turned to the cabinet and took a packet of dried meat out of the storage.

Jik had just, for whatever reason, told the truth. Against his own Personage and all those interests. Which made him, in mahen terms, a dishonest man.

Gods, what's gotten into us on this ship? We got nobody aboard who hasn't gone to the wrong side of her own species' business—Tully, Skkukuk, all us of Chanur and Mahn: now Jik's sliding too.

Treason's catching, that's what it is.

She got a cup, wrinkled her nose as Khym dosed his gfi with tofi. She poured her own from the fastbrewer, looked back at their unlikely crew crowded into the galley. At Jik sitting disconsolate and hurting and trying his best to choke down a sandwich and a cup of reconstituted milk; no one in Chanur put off any temper on him, not Hilfy and not Khym either.

So. Crew was going to give him a chance. For their own reasons, which might include latitude for the captain's judgment; but maybe because of past debts.

It was hard, being hani, not to think like one. There were times they had been as glad to see Jik as he had surely been to see her come after him on *Harukk*. Even if on his side it was all policy and politics. He had saved their skins many a time.

Even if it was always to bet them again.

Chur slitted open her eyes, wrinkled her nose and blinked sleepily at her sister. Her heart sped a bit. She had dreamed of black things in the corridors, had dreamed of something loose on the ship. Noise in the corridors. It felt as if some time had passed.

And Geran had noted that little increase in pulse rate. Geran had this disconcerting habit of taking glances at the monitors while she talked, and whenever she reacted to anything. Geran's be-ringed ears flicked at what she saw now; and it was a further annoyance that the screen was hard to see from flat on one's back.

"We got Jik out," Geran said.

Chur blinked again. So much that came and went was illusion and it was the good things she most distrusted, the things she really wanted to believe. "He all right?"

"Knocks and bruises and the like. Told Tirun he'd run into a wall trying to leave. Likely story. You know you never get the same thing twice out of him. How are you feeling?"

"Like I ran into the same wall. What'd you do to that gods-be machine? You put me out?"

"Got pretty noisy around here. I thought you might need the sleep."

"In a mahen hell you did!" Chur lifted her head and shoved her free elbow under her. "You want my heartbeat up?"

"Lie down. You want mine up?"

"What happened out there?" She sank back, her head swimming, and tried to focus. "Gods, I still got that stuff in me. Cut it out, Geran. F'gods sakes, I'm tired enough, hard enough to go against the wind—"

"Hey." Geran took her by the shoulder.

"I'm awake, I'm awake."

"You want to try to eat something?"

"Gods, not more of that stuff."

Foil rustled. A sickly aroma hit the air, which was otherwise sterile and medicated. Food, any food was a trial. Chur nerved herself and cooperated as Geran lifted her head on her arm and squirted something thin and salty into her mouth. She licked her mouth and took a second one, not because she wanted it. It was enough.

"Not so bad," she said. It was so. She had missed salt. It did something more pleasant in her mouth than the last thing Geran had brought her. She cautiously estimated its course to her stomach and felt it hit bottom and lie there gratefully inert. She looked up at Geran, who had a desperately hopeful look on her face. "You worried about something, Gery?"

The ears flicked. "We're doing all right."

Lie.

"Where's those gods-be black things?"

"Got 'em all penned up again." Change of subject. Geran looked instantly relieved. And the traitor machine beeped with an increased heartbeat. Geran looked back at it and the facade fell in one agonized glance.

"We under attack?" Chur asked.

"We're prepping for jump," Geran said.

Scared. Gods, Gery, you'd send a monitor off the scale—

"Huhn," Chur said. "What're you thinking? That I won't make it?"

"Sure, you'll make it."

"How far're we going?"

Geran's ears went flat and lifted again. There was a drawing round her nose, like pain. "Home, one of these days."

"Multiple jump?"

"Don't think so."

"Maybe, huh?"

"Gods rot it, Chur—"

I haven't got the strength. I can't last it out. Look at her. Gods, look at her. "Listen. You mind your business up for'ard, f'godssakes, what d'you want, me make it fine and you marry this ship up with a rock? You pull it together. Me, I'm fine back here. Back here feeding me—" The monitor started going off again. She let it. "When'd *you* eat, huh? Take care of yourself. I got to worry whether you're doing your job up there?"

"No," Geran said. She gave a furtive glance at the monitor and composed herself sober as an old lord. "I just want to make sure you get anything into your stomach you can."

"Don't trust this machine, do you? I make you a deal. You cut that gods-be sedative out of the works and I'll try to eat. Hear me?"

"Stays the way they set it."

The monitor beeped again.

"Gods fry that rotted thing!" Chur cried, and the beep became a steady pulse. Geran reached and hit the interrupt; and it prevented the flood of sedative.

"Quiet," Geran said.

She subsided. Her temples ached. The room came and went. But in the center of it Geran stayed in unnatural focus, like hunter-vision, hazed around the edges.

I can think my way home, she thought, which was rankest insanity, the maundering of a weakened brain. *Just got to hold onto the ship and get there with it.*

That was crazy. But for a moment she seemed to pass outside the walls, know activity in the ship, feel the rotation of Kefk station, the whirling of the sun, a hyperextension like the timestretch of jump, where time and space redefined themselves. An old spacer could take that route home. She could not have explained it to a groundling, never to anyone who had not flown free in that great dark—she stopped being afraid. It was very dangerous. She could see the currents between the stars, knew the dimplings and the holes, the shallows and the chasms planets and stars made. She smiled, having mindstretched that far, and still being on her ship.

I can think the way home. Bring us all home.

"Chur?"

"I'll be with you," she said. "No worry. Wish they could move this godsrotted rig onto the bridge." She shut her eyes a moment, shut that inward eye that beckoned to all infinity, then looked at Geran quite soberly. "When?"

"Bring *him,* captain?" It was not Tirun Araun's way to question orders; but there was reason enough, and Pyanfar let her ears down and up again in a kind of shrug that got a diffident flattening from Tirun's ears and put a little stammer in Tirun's mouth. "That is to say—"

"Skkukuk's not the one I'm worried about," Pyanfar said quietly. They were outside the lift, in upper main, and the ship hummed and thumped with tests and closures, autorigging for a run. And if there was a place Tirun ought to be it was at her boards down on lowerdeck, in their cargo bridge; and *The Pride* ought to have a cargo to carry, and a trader's honest business. But those days were past for them. There was only something dreadful ahead; and she went from one to another of the crew and spoke with them, quietly, of things that had to be done, and never of the situation they were in. With Tirun it was just a matter of giving her orders, and of telling her, obliquely, in that way they had talked for forty years and more, that she knew that she asked a great deal; and Tirun's worried look settled and became quiet again, still as deep water. "How many rings you got, cousin?"

"Oh, I don't know." Tirun flicked her ears and set the ones she wore to swinging. " 'Bout many as proves I've got good sense, captain."

"We get out of this one, cousin, I'll buy you a dozen more."

"Huh," Tirun said. "Well, I got enough. We get out of this one, captain, you and I'll both be surprised, and that son Sikkukkut no more than most."

"All of our allies will," Pyanfar said. "Skkukuk's safe. He's *on* this ship, isn't he? Kif don't understand that kind of suicide. You know Jik had to explain to Sikkukkut we'd really blow the ship? Couldn't figure why you'd do that. You can tell a kif about it all you like. He'll think it's a lie. A bluff. Skkukuk's no different, I think. Tell the son I'm going to give him a job to do: he'll handle kif-com. I'm putting him under Hilfy's orders."

"My gods, cap'n."

"Tully's sitting com too, this jump. No choice, is there? You've got to handle armaments—this time for real, I'm very much afraid; and back up Haral, and keep an eye on scan: I'm putting Jik in Chur's seat, but his board stays locked, whatever condition his hands are in; and sure as rain falls down I'm not giving him com. While we're at Kefk we've got one excuse; at Meetpoint we may have to contrive another. But I don't want to put him between his ethics and our survival. Gods know, maybe it'll take something off his shoulders, in some bizarre turn of the mahen mind. He *wants* to help us; he *wants* to carry out his own orders; he probably *wants* to save Goldtooth's neck in spite of what the bastard did to him, he *wants* a whole lot of things that are mutually exclusive. Or that may turn that way in a hurry. And gods know I don't want him in reach of your board and the guns."

"He won't like Skkukuk there."

"He'll know why, though. I figure he'll know inside and out why that is."

"Him knowing the kif and all, yes."

"Him knowing the kif and knowing what his own side wants from him, gods save him—gods save us from mahendo'sat and all their connivances. And watch Goldtooth, cousin, for the gods' own sakes, if we do spot him, keep us a line of fire there. I don't like the rules in this game either, but we didn't make them up. They're his, they're that bastard Sikkukkut's, and gods know who else has a finger in it. Watch them all."

"Aye," Tirun said in a hoarse, faint voice. "Them and Ehrran."

"Everyone else for that matter. I don't know a friend we've got."

"Tahar," Tirun said.

"Tahar," she recalled.

A pirate and an outlaw.

And: "I've got *Skkukuk?*" Hilfy said. Her jaw had dropped, her ears were flat.

Pyanfar nodded. They stood where she had caught up with Hilfy, in the galley. And Tully sat sipping a cup of gfi, his blue eyes following their moves and his human, immobile ears taking in the whole of it. His com-translator would whisper it to him.

"Luck of the draw. He's sitting down by Tirun on the jumpseat, but he'll be working off your board. Just keep your finger by the cutoff. If we have to. And get your wits about you when we come out of the drop. I have to ask you this: how good are you on kifish nuance?"

"I'm good."

"Objective assessment: good enough to pick up the subtleties in a kif's transmissions?"

Hilfy paused, and gathered her cup off the counter. She glanced Tully's way and back again. There was clearest sanity in her golden eyes. "I know what you're saying. No. But Skkukuk can do it. What I've got to do is watch what *he's* saying. And be fast on the cutoff."

"You tell me this: is a kif going to damage a ship he's on?"

Hilfy thought about that one too. Her ears dropped and lifted again. "No," she said. "Not when you put it that way. But there is a point he'd turn on us."

"He'd be alone. Crew wouldn't go along with him the way it might on a kifish ship. Kifish crew'd turn on their captain and mutiny. Hani won't. I think maybe Skkukuk's got a glimmering of that. It'll make him behave."

Again a dip of Hilfy's ears. One ring swung there. But the eyes were not that young any longer. "I tell you what that son's thinking. He's thinking the crew's conserving its own position and it's rallied around you out of fear of him. That's what he's thinking. He's thinking if we got into trouble we'd do a real stupid thing, standing by you just for fear of him. He thinks if we prove tough enough other hani will join us on Sikkukkut's side. It's all very simple to him. One thing I've found the kif astonishingly free of is species-prejudice."

"I think you're right."

That seemed to soothe some raw spot in Hilfy. The ears came up again, pricked in an expression that made her look young again. And they flagged when she looked at Tully.

So you're not a fool, Pyanfar thought. *Thank the gods great and lesser.* And did not miss that distracted look that passed between those two. No species-prejudice there either. Too little species prejudice. *O Hilfy, you're a long way from home and gods-be if I care if you're two outright fools in that regard. I ought to be shocked. I can't even find it anymore. Gods save you both, I hope you've done what I don't even want to think about. I hope you've had a little bit of what I've had forty years of.*

And what kind of thinking's that?

Khym was sleeping when she came into their quarters. She dropped the trousers on the floor, quietly, pocket-gun and all; and came and got into the bowl-shaped bed, down in the middle of it where he was, a huge warm lump all hard with muscle and tucked up like a child. She put her arms around his back, buried her head against his shoulder. He turned over and nuzzled her shoulder.

Sleep, she wished him, with a bit of regret. Among pleasures in life a warm bed and a nap in her husband's arms was not the least. She had not the heart to wake him, not when he was this far gone.

"Py," he murmured, in that breathy rumble of his voice at whisper. And bestirred himself, perhaps for his own sake, perhaps just in that way a man would who knew he was wanted: matter of kindness, for a tired wife who came to him for refuge. What they did had nothing to do with time of year. That would have shocked the old graywhiskers back home. Wives and husbands were a seasonal matter: men were always in and wives got around to it when they were home, by ones and twos and, in spring, a confounded houseful of women with hairtrigger tempers and demands on a single, harried man; then the house lord got round to driving out all the young men who had overstayed their childhood, before some scandal happened: young women went to roving, older sisters heaved out any near-adult brother the lord happened not to take exception to. It was housecleaning, annual as the spring rains.

A spacer missed the seasons. She just came home when she got the chance, and tried to make it coincide with spring, a little visit to her brother Kohan, who was glassy-eyed and distracted with affairs in Chanur at such a time, she paid a little courtesy to his wives and any sister or cousin who lived in the house or just happened to be home—

—then it was up in decent leisure to Mahn in the hills, where Khym and his groundling wives held court. His other wives had never much gotten in her way: they were outfought and knew it, and hated her cordially in that way of rivals who knew she would be gone within a week or two, back to her ship and her gadding about again: if one had to have a rival one could not shove out, best at least she be the sort who was seldom home.

Now where were those wives? Hating her still, because she had him to herself at last and he was not decently dead, in his defeat? They would pity him and hate her, and call it all indecent, as if he himself had not had a choice in the world about being snagged up onto a Chanur ship and carried away to a prolonged and unnatural preservation. It ruined his reputation. It touched on their honor. Likely they imagined just such lascivious and libertine unseasonal things as she had led him into, or worse, that he was the prize of all the crew.

She thought about that. "What do you think," she said into his ear, "do you think you'd object to one of the crew now and again? How do you feel about that?"

"I don't know," he said. "I mean—they're—" He was quiet a long time. "They're friends."

"I don't mean you should." She brushed his mane straight, dragged a clawtip along beside his ear. "I never meant that. I was asking if you ever wanted to."

"They're your friends."

She felt his heart beating faster. Like panic. And cursed herself for bringing it up at all. "They never asked. Gods, what a mess. Don't even think about it. I'm sorry I said it. I just felt sorry for them."

"So do I. I'd do it. Tell them that if you want to. Like friends. I think they'd be sensible about it. I think I could be."

Ask *sensible* of a man. Trust him. *Gods, that's what's changed, isn't it?*

He's steady as a rock. He wouldn't play games about it. They wouldn't, with him. They respect him. They'd treat him like a sister—in crew matters. Not one of them is petty and not one is the sort that has to prove a point in bed or after. You know that about women you work with for forty years; and they'd know he was a loan. I'd take that risk for them.

But what's good for him, that matters; that, they'd never question. Gods know I wouldn't.

"I think you could trust them," she said. "It's all of them if it's one, you understand that. I'm just telling you it's all right with me. Won't make me happy or unhappy. I just thought—well, if it ever does happen, you don't have to slip around about it."

"I never—!"

"I know that. I'm just telling you how I feel. If it's ever one, it's all. Remember it. Gods, back home I'd drop in on you for a hand of days and shove your other wives out; been the longest five days yet, hasn't it? I'm feeling guilty about hanging onto you so long. It's getting obsessive. I thought maybe, if things settle down again—" Thoughts crowded in that made it all remote and hopeless and stupid even to talk about it; but it was peace that she had come here for: she shoved Meetpoint aside and pretended. "Well, I thought I ought to give you a little breathing room. I shove you into my room, I don't give you much choice, do I? I want you to know you've got a berth on this ship. On your own. As much as you want to be. Or where you want to be. You want not to share my bed a while, that's fine. I'd miss you. But I don't want you ever to think that's what you're aboard for."

"I'm aboard because I'm a total fool." A frown was on his face, rumpling up his brow. "The rest came later. Py, don't talk like this."

"Gods, you don't understand."

"I don't own this ship. It's Kohan's. I can't come here, bed his kin—"

Male thinking, hindend-foremost and illusionary. Downworld thinking. It infuriated her in him, when so much else was extraordinary. "This ship is *mine,* gods rot it, Kohan's got nothing to do with it. And if you want to bed down with Skkukuk, he's mine, too. I'll also shred your ears."

That struck him funny. And wrinkled his nose in disgust.

"I didn't consult with Kohan," she said. "I don't consult. You know gods-be well how the System works, how it always worked, your sweat and your blood and you never *owned* a gods-be thing. Now you really do. Something you can't lose. You can do as you godsblessed please, and you *do* it, husband. Forty years I've been out here. You've been here two and already your thinking's skewed. You at least listen to my craziness. All those years in Mahn, you used to ask me what the stars were like. Now you know what I come from, why I didn't get along with the rest of the women . . . why I never could make our daughter understand me. Tahy thinks I'm crazy. Some kind of pervert, probably. Kara knows I am. I just can't get excited about what they think down there. I don't have those kind of nerves anymore. Their little laws don't seem important to me. That's dangerous, I think. I don't know how to get back to where I was. None of us do. Haral's got a bastard daughter off in Faha; Tirun's got a son somewhere still alive, left him in Gorun. Gods know they usually take precautions. But they've never married; they never will; they just take their liberties down in Hermitage with whatever takes their fancy, and I don't ask. You know why they do that? I was lucky. My sister Rhean—one spring that we coincided down in Chanur I asked her how her husband was, you know, not a loaded question. But she got this look like she was dying by inches: 'Pyanfar,' she said, 'the man doesn't know where Meetpoint is. He doesn't know *what* it is. That's how my husband is.' And I never asked her. That's lord Fora she was talking about."

"He's not stupid, I knew him in Hermitage."

"No, he's not stupid. Rhean just can't talk to him. Her world isn't where he lives. His isn't where she lives. Nowadays she comes home as little as she can. If she could go to Hermitage and do her planettime there, I think she would far rather. A man you pick up in the hills, he'll pretend you're all his dreams, won't he?"

"You ever do it?"

She hesitated. Which was as good as yes. She shrugged. "Not after we were married."

"A Morhun found me like that; and left me a week later. Me, a kid out in the bush, hoping for an ally. Playing games with a boy like that—that's cruel."

"I was honest about it. I said I was down on leave. When I was. When I was younger than that I was honestly looking."

"No boy of that age'd know you meant gone in the morning. No boy would know that that ship's worth more to you than he ever could be. No boy would know he couldn't follow you where you'd go, that the territory you want isn't—isn't something he could take for you. And he'd want to lay the whole world in your lap, Py, any man would want to, and he'd try to talk to you and maybe learn by morning he couldn't give you anything you cared about. That's a hard thing, Py. It was hard for me."

"You were lord of Mahn!"

"I was lord of the place you used to go hunting, the house you lived in when you wanted a rest. I was a recreation. I never could give you anything. And I wanted to give you everything."

"O gods, Khym. I said I was lucky."

"But I could never give you anything. And I wanted to. When I went up to Gaohn to fight for you, gods, it was the first time I ever felt I was worth anything. When you wanted me to go with you—well, I followed you off like some boy out of Hermitage, didn't I? Go off and fight our way up in the world like two teenaged kids? Didn't know then the size of the farm you had picked out for me to take. Gods, what an ambition you've got! Give you a spacestation or two, shall I?"

"Gods, I wish you could." For a moment Meetpoint was back in bed with them. The room felt cold. His arms tightened. He gave her what he had, and she still did not know whether it was out of duty or out of his own need; but at least it was a free gift, not something she demanded by being there. That was what she hoped they had won, after all these years, and this far removed from all the rules.

"You never were a recreation," she said. "You were my sanctuary. The place I could go, the ear that would listen."

"Gods help me, my other wives always knew who I was waiting for. Who I was always waiting for. They took it out on Tahy and Kara. I tried to stop that. Py, I spent thirty-odd years buying my other wives off our kids' backs and it didn't work."

It was like a light going on, illuminating shadow-spots. Corners of the old house at Mahn she had never seen. The reason of so many things, so evident, and so elusive. "You never told me, rot it."

"The times you were home—were too good. And you couldn't stay. I knew that. I did what I could."

Gods, I poisoned the whole house. All the other marriages. Ruined my kids—hurt Chanur in the long run, when my daughter turned on Khym and took our staunchest ally out. My doing. All of it mine.

He sighed, a motion of his huge frame against her. "I didn't mean to say that. Gods blast, Py, I just fouled it up, is all."

That was his life. That was why he walked on eggshells round those women, lost the kids. O gods. Lost Mahn alone, finally. And came back to Chanur like a beggar when I finally came home. Alienated his sisters.

Everything. His sisters—for an outsider. They couldn't forgive that. And the wives' clans too. All for one wife. That's crazy.

But, gods, what I've done—for a husband. I think I love this great fool. Isn't that something? Love him like he was clan and kin. Like he was some part of me. It's gotten all too close. He needs someone else for balance. Some sense of perspective. So do I. And I'm not interested. Handsomest man on Anuurn could walk in stark naked, I'd rather Khym. Always would. And he'd rather me. I never saw that part of it. I never saw that that was always what was wrong with us, and look what it did. We did so much damage, never meaning to; I did so much to him. Gods, I wish I could turn him over to the others.

They wouldn't know how to treat him but they'd try. Even Tirun.

He wants so much to be one of them. That's what he really wants. And they'd forget that. They'd forget because I can't tell them any way I could make them understand what goes on in him.

Haral would. Haral might make a dent in Tirun, the old reprobate: gods, Khym, if you knew what good behavior Tirun's been on—not laid a hand on you, has she? Because you're mine. She'd go off and get drunk with you and take you home nice as milk, she would, because she's onship and you're offlimits and gods know she likes you, thinks you're something special. I don't know. She might be the real lady with you, you're so much the gentleman. Funny what a crooked line we walk.

No, if you knew either side of Tirun, really knew her, you'd like her.

Geran and Chur—Gods. I wish you'd known them before this mess. So pretty. But deep water, both of them. And dark. You don't ever pick a fight with either. But they've got a godsrotted broad sense of humor . . . never told you those stories. Not planetside. They don't go down so much. Not comfortable around groundlings. That's the awful thing: sometimes you want the land under your feet and the sun on your back, and then you've got to deal with the people that live there.

And Hilfy—you see what's going on, her and Tully? My poor, conservative, ex-groundling man—not a flicker. We're too well-bred. We don't see. We don't know what to do about it, so we don't see; and we wish them by the gods well, because you and I, Khym, we're on the downside of our years and we've got enough to do just to do for ourselves, in the mess we're in.

You couldn't sleep with Hilfy; never her. She's the odd one out. Species she can get across. But the generations she can't bridge. Can't figure me out; gods, she can't figure herself out. You'd confuse everything. And you're uncle to her, you always will be, even if you haven't a corpuscle in common. You're her substitute for Kohan. She loves her father so much. That's why she fusses over you like a little grandmother.

Bring her out here, never give her a stopover at home, and her in the growing years—She takes what she can. It was all so pat for us. And we wasted so much time. Good for her, I think. Good for Hilfy.

Thank the gods you're here.

2342 and *The Pride* was stretching muscles, electronic impulses sending tests down to systems aft and bringing internal support up full, while lights on the bridge flickered and instruments blipped, routine departure-prep.

Given a kifish ship still stationary over station axis, bow-down so that its guns were constantly in line with every ship on the rotating station, but most notably the ones whose systems were now live, the ones full of non-kif who thought non-kifish and unpredictable thoughts.

But they kept com flowing naturally between *The Pride* and station central, which was partly *Harukk* personnel. And com operations went on likewise between *The Pride* and *Aja Jin* and *Tahar's Moon Rising*, nothing compromising in any fashion, just the necessary coordination of three ships which planned to put out close together. There was still the coder they might have used. There were languages the kif might not understand.

There was also that ship over their heads, and mindful of that and of the firepower here gathered, they refrained from all such options.

"Hilfy," Pyanfar said, "take message on your three: first thing at Meetpoint, auto that escape course out to both our partners."

"Aye," Hilfy said. "Understood."

Hilfy and Haral and Tully were all settled in, Khym was settling. Haral was still running Geran's station from the co-pilot's board, but that was all perfunctory: there was not one gods-be thing scan could tell them at this point. If the kif decided to fire, they fired. That was all. And lost part of their station doing it.

"Geran come," Tully said, doing—gods witness, the service Hilfy had drilled him on at that board: he had a pick to use where his poor clawless fingers had not a chance, he stuck it into the right holes in the right sequence, and he was at least adequate to keep an ear to internal operations. Even trusting him with that was taking a chance: Tirun was downside with Skkukuk and Jik was loose, but Pyanfar got a firm grip on her nerves and figured that (gods save them from such insanity)

Tirun and Skkukuk between them could handle Jik if he had something inventive in mind.

While Tully, in a good moment and with the gods' own luck on his side, might handle an emergency call down there: *The Pride*'s autorecognition was set on the word *Priority,* which no one let past their teeth during ops if it was not precisely that: *Priority* got flashed to Hilfy's board and Haral's simultaneously, and Tully would have to make an unlikely sequence of mistakes to take the lower corridors off wide open monitor.

Geran arrived, she saw that in the conveniently reflective monitor, a shadow arriving from the main topside corridor, larger and larger until the bridge lights picked out Geran's red-brown coloring and the glint of the gold in her ear-rims. "H'lo," Geran said. After putting Chur to bed, and walking out of that room. With all the chance of finality. *H'lo,* to Hilfy, when Geran normally said nothing at all when she walked on-shift. *I'm all right,* that meant. *Don't doubt I'm on.*

"We're routine right now," Hilfy said quietly. Which was the right tack to take with Geran. No fuss. No emotional load. Pyanfar kept an ear to it all and keyed an acknowledgment to dockside's advisement they were about to withdraw power.

"Tirun," Tully said.

"I've got it," Khym said, second-com, picking that up; and: "Right. I'll tell him. *Na* Jik, you'll come topside now; Tirun's on her way."

"Geran," Pyanfar said on bridge-com, "Jik's in your charge. Best I can do." There was the matter of Jik's hands, which would heal of injuries in the several day subjective transit before systemfall; but recuperation and jump was not a matter she wanted to open up with Geran at the moment. "I don't much want him on your elbow, but I haven't got a place else to put him."

"I'll watch him."

Enough said, then. If Geran buckled there was still Tirun on Jik's other side. And that left Tully down at that end of the boards with Skkukuk. She might have put Khym in that seat. But Khym was getting used to the com board; he was actually worth something with it in a pinch. Putting Khym at Tirun's confusing second-switcher post handed him a system that had a completely different set of access commands. Tully could learn a sequence from scratch; Khym, jump-muzzy and in emergency, might touch a control he thought he knew. Disastrously.

"Yes, *Harukk*-com," Hilfy said. "That data is current. Captain, they're inquiring again on departure time and routing."

"It stands as instructed."

Uncoupling began, a series of crashes as *The Pride* disengaged itself from dock under Haral's signal to the other side of that station wall, and Haral's touch at the controls of her board. There was the low drone of Khym's voice, making routine advisements to the dockers and station com, and Hilfy's voice talking quietly to *Aja Jin* and *Moon Rising*.

"Captain," Tully said, "Tirun come."

"Got that," Pyanfar murmured.

If Tirun was on her way, that was the last and they were going to make schedule easily. So much the better with nervous kif all about. Pyanfar flicked her ears and settled her nerves, while *The Pride*'s operating systems made noise enough to mask the lift and rob them of other cues to movement in the ship. There were the telltales on the board—if she chose to key the matrix over to access-monitor. Her nose twitched at the mere thought of Skkukuk in proximity. She dared not take the allergy pills. She needed her reflexes. She rubbed her itching nose fiercely with the back of her hand, curled her lip, and looked up at the convenient reflection in a dead monitor as the gleam of the lift's internal light reflected a motley assortment of silhouettes in the distance down the corridor at her back.

Her eyes flicked to the chrono.

2304.

"Moon Rising reports all ready," Hilfy said.

"Got that," Haral said.

Tahar was showing off. Flouting the schedule on the short side. Which took work.

Tahar clan was Tahar clan, even when it owed Chanur its mortgaged hide.

The lift door had closed back there. The shadows in the reflective glass had come closer. Pyanfar slowly rotated her chair to face the last-comers. Courtesy. Tirun walked beside Jik, Jik beside Skkukuk's dark-robed shape. They had washed Jik's clothes for him, had not even dared have clean ones couriered over from *Aja Jin*, for fear of rousing kifish suspicions. And someone of the crew must have lent him the bracelet on his arm. The kif had robbed him of the gaudy lot of chain he usually wore.

"This person," Skkukuk said the moment he got through the door, "this *person* refuses your order, *hakt'*."

"He means the gun," Tirun said.

"We don't carry firearms up here," Pyanfar said patiently. With spectacular patience, she thought. "Nor do we change captains under fire." With an internal shudder and a thought toward Jik: *I hope.* "Tirun will give you instructions. If you're that good, *prove it.*"

So much for kifish psych.

But the son moved. Jik was still looking at her.

"How my ship?" he asked, very quiet, very civilized. She would not have been that restrained, under similar circumstances.

"Hilfy, give his station that comflow on receiving only."

"Aye," Hilfy said. "It's in."

"That's scan two," Pyanfar said, meaning seat assignment; and he gave a short, more than decent nod of his dark head and went to belt in, wincing a bit as he sat down. He spoke quietly to Geran; and Pyanfar found her claws clenched in the upholstery: she released her grip, carefully; and turned her seat around again.

"We're on count," Haral said. "*Aja Jin* reports ready. We're on."

"Stand by."

"We going to show the *hakkikt* punctuality?"

She considered the potential for provocation. Considered the kif. And considered another possibility as she put their engines live. There was another set of switches by her hand, safety-locked by a whole string of precautions which they had a program now to bypass. Input three little codes and that set of key-slots would light. And *The Pride* would have a last chance to take out a space station full of kif, a handful of innocent methane-breathers; a doublecrossing allied ship that held one of two plans for a mahen hegemony over the Compact; a kif who was very close to having a kifish hegemony, and who with cold intent, threatened the whole hani species. Half the whole problem in the Compact was sitting right here at this station, with the solution within reach of her hand; and for one ship to take out half the problems in the immediate universe was not a bad trade, as trades went.

It also assured by default the immediate success of their rivals, whose intentions were also mahen and kifish hegemonies, maybe a human one, a methane-breather action, and the immediate collapse of the stsho and then the *han* into the control of one or the other hegemonies. Which meant years of bloody fighting. Not taking into account humanity, which was already at odds within its own compact, and whose ships they knew were armed.

Take out one set of contenders here or make Jik's throw for him and play power against power.

She was not even panicked in contemplating that sequence of by-passes. She felt only a numb detachment: she could give it, and only Haral would know; Haral would look her way with a slight flattening of the ears and never pass the warning to the crew. Just a look that said: *I know. Here we go.*

Perhaps Haral was thinking the same thing about now, that it was one last chance, while their nose was still into the station's gut and they were an indisputable part of station mass. Haral went on flicking switches, the shut-down of certain systems no longer necessary, along with the check of systems-synchronization and docking jets.

2314.

"We break on the mark," Pyanfar said in the same tone in which they threw those checkout sequences back and forth. "Advise them down the line. Advise station."

"Aye," Haral said. "Hilfy."

"I got it," Hilfy said.

The minute ticked down.

2314.46.

"On mark," Pyanfar said. "Grapple."

Clang. The station withdrew its grip.

Thump. They withdrew their own as the chrono hit 2315; and Pyanfar hit the docking jets. Precisely. And hard. *G* shifted, momentum carrying them in a skew the jets corrected, and more so, as *The Pride* left the boom and the hazard of collision with the kifish ship down-wheel from them.

Another *G* shift, no provision for groundling stomachs, as she sent *The Pride* axis-rolling on a continual shove of the docking jets.

"Show those bastards," Haral muttered beside her. As *The Pride* finished her roll with never a wasted motion, precisely angled the jets and underwent outbound impulse.

"*Aja Jin's* cleared on mark," Geran said. "Precisely."

Pyanfar flicked her ears, rings jingling, and her heart picked up.

Show these bastards indeed. That was a fancy new engine rig *The Pride* carried, the ratio of those broad jump vanes to her unladen mass was way up since Kshshti; and any kif who saw *The Pride* and *Aja Jin* move out in close tandem, would remark the peculiar similarity between their outlines, give or take the cargo holds which were firmly part of *The Pride* and which were stripped off the hunter-ship's lean gut and spine.

"Tahar's away."

Routine out to startup. The mains cut in on mark; *Aja Jin* was on the same instant, and Tahar, playing the same insolent game.

It was quiet on the bridge. No chatter, none of the talking back and forth between stations that was normal, all of them kin and all of them knowing their jobs well enough to get them done through all the back-and-forth. They were not all kin on this trip. And none of them were in the mood. Only she looked over at Haral, the way she had looked a thousand times in *The Pride*'s voyages; it was reflex.

Haral caught it and looked back, a little dip of one ear and a lift of her jaw, a cheerfulness unlike Haral's dour business-only blank.

Same face she might have turned her way if she had decided to blow the ship. Pyanfar made a wry pursing of her mouth and gave the old scoundrel the high sign they had once, in their wilder days, passed each other in bars.

They had a word for it. Old in-joke. *Meet you at the door.*

She drew a wider breath and flexed her hands, reached across and put the arm-brace up, when they would need it.

She had never been so outright scared in her life.

"Coming up," Haral said finally. But she knew that. The numbers kept ticking off to jump. They took the outbound run with less haste than they could use, on the mark the kif gave them. There was a little leisure, a little chance for crew to stand up and stretch and flex minds as well as bodies; but no one left the bridge. Not even Geran.

She's asleep, Geran had said when Pyanfar offered her the chance to leave scan and take a fast walk back to Chur's cabin while they were inertial and under ordinary rotation. So that was that. Pyanfar gnawed her mustaches and offered no comforts; Geran was not one to want two words on a topic where one had said it, and she was focussed down tight; took her little stretch by standing up beside her chair, and kept her eye still to her proper business; answered Jik's rare comments with a word or two.

"Tully," Pyanfar said, "get ready."

"I do," he said. He had his drugs with him, the drugs that a human or a stsho needed in jump. He prepared to go half to sleep in his chair, sedated so heavily he could hardly stay upright.

Interesting to contemplate—a horde of human ships, all of them that automated. Like facing that many machines.

Set to do what? React to buoys and accept course without a pilot's intervention?

Defend themselves? Attack? A horde of relentless machines whose crews had committed themselves to metal decisions and a computer's morality, because their kind had no choice?

Stsho did that, because stsho minds also had trouble in jumpspace; but stsho were nonviolent.

Gods, so gods-be little he says, so little he's got the words for.

"Tully. Are human ships set to fire when they leave jump?"

He did not answer at once.

"Tully. You understand the question?"

"Human fire?"

"Gods save us. Do their machines—fire after jump? Can they?"

"Can," Tully said in a small voice. "Ship be ##."

Translation-sputter.

"Captain," Hilfy said, "he's got to go out now. Got to."

His mind was at risk. "Go to sleep," Pyanfar said, never looking around; his back would be mostly to her anyway, the bulk of the seat in the way.

"Not trust human," Tully said suddenly.

"Go *out,*" Hilfy said sharply. "You want me to put that into you? *Do it.*"

While the chronometer got closer and closer to jump.

"Tully," Pyanfar said. "Good night."

"I go," he said.

"He's got it," Tirun said. "He's all right."

"We're on count," Haral said.

"You give me com we come through," Jik said.

"*Aja Jin* has its orders." They had talked through that matter already. Jik made a last try.

And: "You got anything last minute you want to own up to?" she asked. "Jik?"

"I damn fool," he said.

"Count to ten," Haral said, and the numbers on the corner of the number-one monitor started ticking away.

"Take her through," Pyanfar said. They did that, traded off; and she suddenly decided on the stint at exit.

"Got it," Haral said. That section of the board that pertained to jump was live. "Referent on, we got our lock."

Star-fixed and dead-on. It was a single-jump to Meetpoint from dusty Kefk, with its armed guardstations and its grim gray station—

—to the white light and opal subtleties of a stsho-run station.

If that was what was still there.

"Going," Haral said.

Down. . . .

They stopped being at Kefk.

. . . . *Gods save us,* Pyanfar thought, which thought went on for a long long timestretch.

She dreamed of ships in conflict in their hundreds, burning like suns.

Of strange gangling beings that had walked the dock once at Gaohn, sinister in their numbers and their resemblance to a creature she had befriended (but too many of them, and too sudden, and with their Tully-like eyes all blue and strange and malevolent). They carried weapons, these strangers; they talked among themselves in their chattering, abrupt speech, and laughed their harsh alien laughter out loud, which echoed up and down the docks.

What do they want? she asked Tully then, in that dream.

Look out for them, he said to her. *And one of them drew a gun and aimed it at them both.*

What does it say? Pyanfar asked when it spoke.

But the gun went off and Tully went sprawling without a sound; in slow motion the tall figure turned the weapon toward her—

Chapter Five

. . . .it went off.

The Pride made the drop into realspace and Pyanfar blinked, gasped a breath, and felt an acute pain about the heart which confused her entirely as her eyes cleared on *The Pride*'s boards and blinking lights and her ears received the warning beeps from com: *Wake up, wake up, wake up*—

Meetpoint?

Her eyes found the data on the screen, blurred and focussed again with a mortal effort. "We're on," she said around the pounding of her heart, "Haral, we're on."

And from elsewhere, distant and echoing in and out of space: *"Chur, do you hear me? Do you hear?"*

From still another: *"We've got passive signal. Captain! We're not getting buoy here. They've got Meetpoint image blanked!"*

"Gods and thunders. Geran!"

"I'm on it, I'm already on it, captain."

—Hunting their partners, who could make a fatal mistake in a jump this close, looking for the first sign of signal, and themselves rushing in hard toward Meetpoint, into crowded space, where the scan's bounce-back could only tell them things too late and passive reception might not have all the data. They were blind. Meetpoint wanted them that way. It was somebody's trap.

"Priority," Hilfy said. "Buoy warning: *dump immediately.*"

"Belay that," Pyanfar said. With two ships charging up behind them out of hyperspace, she had no wish to have herself slowing down in their path. Collision to fore was an astronomical possibility; behind was a statistical probability.

And the kif who gave them orders meant business.

"Acquisition," Geran said, "your one, Haral."

"Your two," Haral said; and id chased the image to Pyanfar's number two monitor. *Aja Jin* was in.

"What've we got here? Geran—"

"I'm working on it. We got stuff all over the place on passive, nobody outputting image, lot of noise, *lot* of noise, we got ships here—"

"Mark," Haral said, "less twenty seconds."

"That's it, that's it, brace for dump."

She sent it to auto; *The Pride* lurched half into hyperspace again and fell out with less energy—

—*gods, gods, sick as a novice—What in a mahen hell's in this system? Come on, Geran. Get it sorted. O gods—* At forty-five percent of Light. With the system rushing up in their faces. Their own signal going out from that traitor buoy at full Light. Themselves about to become a target for someone. She fumbled after the foil containers at her elbow, bit through one and let the salt flood chase down the nausea. There was a meeting of unpleasant tides somewhere behind the pit of her throat and her nose and hands and the folds of her body broke out in sickly sweat. "Geran. *Get me id.*"

"Working, I'm working."

Dump fouling up the scan; nothing where it ought to be, the comp overloaded with input and trying to make positional sense out of it before it got around to analyzing ship IDs.

"Multiple signal," Hilfy said. "Nothing clear yet. Multispecies."

"Arrival," Jik said. *"Moon Rising* is in."

"On the mark," Haral said. "Second dump, stand by."

Taking it down fast. The pain in her chest refused to leave. The nausea all but overcame her; but she hit the control anyway—

—down again.

—Gangling figures against white light. *Captain,* a voice said, and Chur was there with the light shining about her, in the midst of a long black hallway, and shafts of light spearing past her as she moved in the slightest. She turned her shoulder and looked back into the light—

—*"Chur—"*

—they cycled through again, back in realspace. And the weakness that ran through her was all-enveloping. She fought it back and groped after another of the packets. Bit into it and drank the noisome stuff down in a half dozen convulsive gulps.

"We got signal on *Moon Rising,"* Geran's voice reached her, indistinct; she heard Tully talking, some half-drunken babble.

"Chur," he was saying. "Chur, you answer. Please you answer."

No sound out of Chur, then. It might still be the sedative. The machine would knock her out in stress. They had plenty of it. Pyanfar blinked again, flexed her right arm in the brace, withdrew it and shoved the mechanism aside, out of her way. Her hands shook. She heard the quiet, desperate drone of Tully's alien voice: *"Chur, Chur, you hear?"*

While Geran battled the comp for ID they desperately needed. Mind on business.

"We got recept on Meetpoint," Hilfy said. "Lot of output. Busy in there. I'm trying to link up with our partners, get a fix on those ships—"

"We've got to keep going," she muttered. "Got to. No gods-be choice. Blind. We got our instructions, we got—"

"Kif," Skkukuk said suddenly. "Kifish output!"

"Audio two," Hilfy said.

It was. Some kifish ship was transmitting in code. Unaware of them yet, it might be. Or close enough to have picked them up, inbound from Kefk. "Going to have an intercept down our necks any minute," she muttered, and sweated. "Akkhtimakt. He's on guard here. Or he's running the whole gods-be station—"

"Image, *priority,"* Geran said. "My gods."

Passive scan came up with resolution, a haze to this side, to that, all in differing colors indicating different vectors and slow, virtually null-movement, relative. Big hazy ball where Meetpoint ought to be. Haze to zero-ninety-minus sixty. Haze to minus seventy-thirty-sixty. Another ball out to one ten. The only thing that made sense was the Given in the system, the Meetpoint Mass itself, big and dark and dead from its eons-old formation. And the station itself. The rest—

"Khym," Pyanfar snapped. "Interior com. Tully! audio one. Listen sharp. We don't know what we've got here. Could be humans, could be anything. Whatever we got, it's a lot of it."

"Got it," Khym said; and: "Got," from Tully.

The comp main panel between Haral and Hilfy was a steady flicker of inter-partition queries and action from this and that side of its complex time-sharing lobes. Like the lunatic tc'a: it had several minds to make up, and they were all busy.

She rubbed her chest where the pain had settled and swiped the back of the same hand across an itch on her nose.

And listened to Khym trying over and over again to raise Chur on the com.

"Chur," he cried suddenly. "Geran—I got her, she's answering! Chur, how are you?"

She was alive back there. Someone switched Chur's answer through. It was scatologically obscene.

Pyanfar drew one painful breath and another.

"Thank the gods," Haral murmured in a low voice. And from Khym: *"Ker* Chur, we have a problem just now—"

"That's stsho," Hilfy said. "I'm picking up something near the station. Stsho. And hani. More than one. You got data coming, Geran, Jik. —I hear that." To someone on com. And Geran:

"Gods rot it, I'm working." Then: "Yeah, just take it easy, hear?"

"I got," Jik said quietly. "They be here they don't—"

"Ten minutes station AOS," Haral said. "Mark."

Pyanfar drew another breath and flexed her hands. "Hilfy, output to Meetpoint traffic control: coming in on standard approach."

"Aye, done, standard approach data in transmission."

"Aja Jin make dump," Jik said.

"Stand by our final."

The wavefront of their arrival had not yet gotten to Meetpoint central. The robotic beacon in the jump range knew as much as its AI brain was capable of knowing anything; but the buoy was not communicating data back to them even after it had had time to receive their ID squeal.

It was certain that it was a trap. Stsho had no nerve sufficient to antagonize an armed enemy, blinding them as they came in. It was what they hired guards to do.

"No telling where Sikkukkut is," Pyanfar muttered. "It'd take him maybe another hour to get that lot away from Kefk. But he's fast."

"Kkkkt," Skkukuk said, which sound sent the hair up on her back. Not a comment except that click which meant a thousand things. "You all right back there: Skkukuk, you all right?" she asked the kif. And deliberately pleased the bastard. It was a genuine question; nourishment for him was a problem. *No gods-be little vermin on my bridge,* was her ultimatum; and Skkukuk had come up with his own answer. Straight simple-sugars and water, into a vein.

"Kkkkt," he said again. "Yes, hakt'." Doubtless coming to a whole array of mistaken kifish conclusions about his status, the crew's, Jik's and Tully's; that elongate, predatory brain was set up to process that kind of information constantly, inexorable as a star in its course. Claw and crawl and climb. With a sense of humor only when it was in the ascendancy and demonstrating its power.

Creator Gods, if You made that, You must've had something in mind. But what?

"Imaging," Tirun said; "priority channel four."

"Your two," Haral said; but that change was already there, the hazy ball of Meetpoint separating into a whole globe of points. So did one of the other patches of haze. Another remained indistinct.

"We got a lot of company," Haral said.

It was a swarm for sure. A monstrous swarm sitting around Meetpoint station, like insects around a corpse.

"Migods," she murmured.

Another blur materialized. About ten minutes Light off station nadir. Unresolved yet, and small. It could get a lot wider.

"There's another one," Haral said; on the second Geran and Jik both came in on com.

"Got that," Pyanfar muttered, her mind half there, half on what the comp was bringing up, color-code spotted into the station-mass that said *stsho/hani ID.*

More IDs. There were stsho and hani in the station imaging, there were mahendo'sat and kif outlying. But not a single methane-breather in the output, which could mean that imaging had ignored them; or that no methane-breather was outputting; or that the methane-breathers had gotten the wind up them at some time earlier in events and lit out for their own territories.

"Captain," Geran said.

"I got it, I got it."

"Not a methane-breather anywhere," Haral muttered. "I don't like this."

"Got to be Akkhtimakt out there," Tirun said. "Looks like we got a real standoff here."

"Mahen ships out there," Pyanfar said. "Goldtooth, I'll bet you that, eggs to pearls. And too many ships. Gods, *look* at that."

"Humans," Haral said in a low voice. *Not* on bridge-com; voice-only.
"Yeah."

Tully knows it. Got to know it. He's not deaf. Not blind either.

"Pyanfar," Jik said. "Give com."

"In your own hell I will. Sit still."

Stsho and hani sitting there dead at dock with kif in full view, kifish ships with the advantage of position and startup time and the mass of Meetpoint's dark dwarf to pull them in?

But so had those other blotches on scan, mahen and alien. Standoff for sure.

We got troubles, gods, we got troubles.

"Hilfy: to both our partners; stand by hard dump, at the 2 unit mark; gods-be if we're going into that. Hard dump and brake. We're going to sit."

"You got damn kif come in here behind us, upset ever'thing!" Jik cried. "Give com, dammit, I talk!"

"Sit still while you got ears!"

"*Aja Jin's* outputting," Hilfy said. "Jik. Translate."

Faster than the mechanical translation.

"They make ID. Say hello to Ana. Say got kif coming behind us."

"Gods rot them." Monitors flicked and shifted. They were being inundated with com input, faster than their operators could handle it. Transcriptions were coming over. Kifish com. Hani ships were standing out from station. Stsho were in panic. Their wavefront had gotten to the station but not to the outliers they had seen on passive. Three more minutes for Akkhtimakt's kif to notice them. Seven for the unidentifieds that might be mahendo'sat. Eight for the ones farthest out, who might be human. And double that for response time. "We're going to have kif up our backsides."

"You going have damn kif break through system, they don't stop, you hear? Pyanfar! Give com!"

"Shut it up. Haral! Dump us down."

Haral hit the switches. *The Pride* shed V in a single lurch to a lower state; space went inside out—

   . . . another lurch. The universe spun once about. . . .

      . . . .revised itself.

Instruments cleared. Broke up again with a heartstopping jolt and cleared, some ship too near them and themselves displaced off their nav-fix as the field popped them down the gravity-slope.

The rate was far less. Easy from here. Two more blips reappeared:

Moon Rising and *Aja Jin* matched them and came *down* again widely spaced from them and a little to the rear.

"Reacquire," Geran said.

"Com output to my board," Pyanfar said; and when the light went on: "All ships: this is Pyanfar Chanur, *The Pride of Chanur.* Take precautions; all station personnel, go to innermost secure areas. Maintain order. All ships drop to low-*V* for your own protection.—We have limited time. This is *The Pride of Chanur* and allied ships urging all ships to maintain position and take no action. The *hakkikt* Sikkukkut is inbound with a large number of ships. Take precautions—"

"Sheshe sheshei-to!" Jik cried. And Geran:

"Priority, Priority!" Geran cried, as the scan-monitor went red all across the top, with a breakout behind them like plague in the jump-range.

"Gods-*be!*" Pyanfar cried; and hit the alarm.

Useless. With ships coming up their backsides and under their bellies at *V* that could cross a planetary diameter in seconds. The informational wavefront was on them at *C* and the ships a fraction behind it—

Instruments jumped and went crazy. Her heart slammed in her chest, and the first firing of panicked neurons said they were dying—the second, that they had not died and the encounter was over in nanoseconds.

It passed like a storm. It was inbound to Meetpoint with a dopplered flare of output, like devils screaming down on the damned, Meetpoint with minutes left and mortal reflexes hopeless of mounting any response—

"O gods," she said for the third time. It came out with what felt like the last of her breath.

"Give com," Jik yelled. *"Give—"*

"Stay in your seat!" Tirun snarled back.

"Priority, com," Hilfy snapped. "Tully!"

And hard on that a stream of alien language, Tully's voice, rapid-paced: ". . . to all ships," the words turned up on monitor, translator-function. "This is # Tully ###, ask you # stay #####—"

Total breakup. Whatever he was speaking, it was not in the comp-dictionary.

"Damn," Jik said. "Ana!"

While a mass of kifish output raced ahead of them, *Sikkukkut,* howling down on the station, nadir-bound, past a stationful of stsho who could not fight; and a cluster of hani ships who might try. And die doing it.

"Gods curse that bastard," Pyanfar muttered, and something hurt deep in her gut, diminishing that pain about her heart. "Gods curse him. Haral. To my boards. Hilfy: tell our partners stand by. Haral: course to Urtur."

"Aye," Hilfy said.

"Do it," Pyanfar said, "Haral."

A code flashed to her screen. *Priority four. Personnel emergency.* From Tirun's hand.

"Pyanfar!" Jik's voice. She spun the chair, saw Jik unbuckled and rising to his feet as Khym scrambled for his and Skkukuk moved faster still.

But Jik stopped. Stopped still. So did everything else when she held up a hand. "Pyanfar, you got give me com—"

"*Aja Jin's* outputting code," Hilfy said. "Inputting to code faculty, Haral."

"Jik," Pyanfar said, "I don't want my crew hurt. Don't want you hurt. You're about to give me no choice. You hear me?"

"Damn fool hani, that be *Mahijiru*, Ana be wait signal—he get your message, he go from here. He got go from here. I give you message. You send: say *Sheni*. He understand, give you same co-operation. *I tell truth, Pyanfar.*"

"Directive to that ship can't go out from here," she said, ears flat. All but deaf. Her heart was pounding. "You trying to fry us good, Jik? Mahen ships are dead-stopped out there. They're caught, same as hani are. We haven't got a choice here and Sikkukkut isn't just real pleased with us to start with. Khym. Skkukuk. I think you better get Jik off the bridge."

"No! Pyanfar! Damn fool, you need me. Need me here. *You send message!*"

"I can't trust you. I'm going to ask you to leave. Quietly. Right now. Or you sit in that chair."

Jik's hand tightened on the chair back. Not going to move, she thought; it seemed forever. Khym would never delay so long. Time spooled itself out the way it did in jump. She had to think of her own ship; and of the gun in her pocket. *I'll use it, Jik; I'd use it if you made me, for godsakes, don't, don't make me, I've got my ship to protect—*

He moved to put himself in the chair. And she let go the breath she had forgotten, and spun her chair back again.

The translations were multiplying on the screen. *Aja Jin* was spilling out everything, a flood of com-sent explanations, coded and headed out toward the mahen ships. Tully was still sending on their com, never having stopped. It was a guess what he was sending. Saying everything they could not, dared not, in a code no one could crack.

Treason against the *hakkikt*. Perhaps against them.

Or against humankind itself.

But what did the *hakkikt* expect, sending them in first, to paralyze the system—when his own arrival hard upon their own would send ships running like leaves in the wind?

She switched that to Jik's monitor. Silent comment.

It's getting done, Jik. And it may kill all of us.

Tully's output made no sense at all, misapplications or coded applications of vocabulary driving the translator to lunacy. What came out of *Aja Jin* achieved syntax. It made no sense in some of its parts. But did in others. They were onto those codewords. If Kesurinan over there had truly suspected something she might have used some alternate; it was a guess that the mahendo'sat *had* alternates. But Kesurinan did not suspect. That was the best guess: Kesurinan did not suspect that they had those words at least; or that Jik would have given them out against his will, to a ship that had a mahen-given translation program.

While the ship hurtled on at its reduced *V* and duty stations talked back and forth to each other in muted voices and the blip and click of instruments and boards.

For Jik it was already past. And there was the kif in front of him, and hani who had kept him from his ship at a moment that might prove decisive in all history.

She found not a thing to say either.

Sikkukkut's kif hurtled on toward attack on Akkhtimakt and on Goldtooth and the humans, if that was what that mass was out there. While the stsho and any other non-combatants on that station abided the outcome in helpless terror.

"Priority," Geran said. Scan went red-bordered, a group of outlier ships went from stationary blue to blinking blue of a low-*V* ship from which passive-recept had picked up some activity. Like engine-firing.

Akkhtimakt.

Her claws dug into the upholstery. "What AOS are they on?"

"That's our message," Tirun said. "They don't know Sikkukkut's here yet. That AOS is coming up minus three. I've got ID on some of those hani ships at station. Negative on Ehrran. That's *Harun's Industry* and *The Star of Tauran,* stsho ship *Meotnis;* hani vessel *Vrossauru's Outbounder; Pauraun's Lightweaver; Shaurnurn's Hope—*"

Old names. Spacer names. The clans of Araun. Pyanfar heard them and clenched her hands on the arms of the chair.

As the color-shift on Akkhtimakt's kif went over from blue to blinking green. To purple, like the image on Sikkukkut's ships. But a double hand of Sikkukkut's ships were shifting down, going brighter bluegreen, and two brighter still. Different assignments. Stopping in midsystem. Where they could shift vector and strike at Meetpoint Station. Or at the mahendo'sat.

"Priority," Geran said.

"I got that," she said. "Sikkukkut's got his tail guarded, he does."

"AOS on our message," Tirun said, monotone. "Akkhtimakt's present position."

"Gods." *Vector, gods rot it, Geran. What's Akkhtimakt's vector?* "Geran, can you get me a—"

The projection took shape. "Priority, priority," Geran said. And her answer came up two-vectored, one part of Akkhtimakt's group bound nadir, twenty ships for Urtur and ten for Kshshti. Her heart seized up and beat painfully against the stress.

"Gods and thunders."

"Sikkukkut may just chase 'em," Haral said. "Gods send he chases 'em clear to Urtur, get him by the gods out of here."

"Give me com," Jik said in a low voice. As if he had no hope of it already. "Give me com. I talk to Ana—"

But suddenly Goldtooth's image was blinking too. Imminent motion, as yet undefined in the comp. The doppler shift could tell it what it had, and comp was working on the precise figure.

"Pyanfar."

"No, gods rot it. Gods-*be,* that bastard's just AOS on that move of Akkhtimakt's and he's losing no time taking out of here. Whatever *Aja Jin* sent may not reach him before he goes. Running. Where? How far's he going?"

"Not know," Jik said.

"Outsystem? Turn around and come in?"

"Give com. I tell him, he do! Code. God! Kif not break fast enough! Give com."

"You might not catch him. And he might not listen. And that leaves us with the kif, doesn't it? *All* alone; and us transmitting to his enemies in code. No thanks."

While, beside them and behind, *Aja Jin* kept quiet. Perhaps

Kesurinan believed that that order for silence came from Jik, relayed because he was not on the bridge; or Kesurinan still trusted. Perhaps.

"Mahen ships are AOS of our number-two message," Tirun droned placidly, their relativity-timekeeper, while disaster went on shaping up around them. "Going to be a while on Kesurinan's. It may not make it."

The Goldtooth-human aggregate went green. Retreating. Faster and faster.

Jik swore. In mahensi. "All way doublecross. Pyanfar. You, me, Ana. Damn, *damn!*"

"Shut it down."

"Kif—damn, kif do this thing, you don't go in fight, don't go in, Pyanfar."

"That, you got. No way are we going into that."

While the recent past unfolded on the screen, the computer struggling to make sense of it and sending out image that had two shades of the same kifish color on the ID monitor.

"Gods-be fool kif've hardly dumped," Haral muttered at her side. "Carrying sixty-five of light. Gods, *look* at that."

"I'd rather not," she said back. And felt sick at the stomach. Felt a tremor in all her limbs. "Bastard's got enough V to hyper out of here, right up Akkhtimakt's tail."

"Dangerous," Haral said. Meaning collisions on the other side, where they would drop down into the well at Urtur not knowing the trim and the precise capacity on the ships ahead of them. It was asking for it.

And the godscursed mahendo'sat were leaving system. *Abandoning* them. There were other conclusions, but none of them were enough to pin hope on. Knowing Goldtooth, whose priorities were all mahendo'sat.

That's one more I owe you, Goldtooth, you bastard.

We got hani ships at station. We got three hundred thousand stsho who can't defend themselves.

She reached after the last of the food packets by her chair and got it down; her mouth tasted of dry fuzz and copper. She was aware of loose fur rubbing between her skin and the chair leather; of hair sticking to the console-rim where it had rubbed from her arm; sweat had soaked her trousers and made the leather of the seat moist wherever she touched it.

Once at Urtur Akkhtimakt might turn about and come back with V

on his side. Even if it took four months. But beyond Urtur was hani territory; the conflict might keep going.

Four months out and back, again and again and again. Years of maneuvering as the ground-bound saw it. Mere weeks in the time-stretch of ships that made virtually no system-time at all. Years of fighting, with ship-crews caught in virtual stasis, unaged.

How does anything survive in that kind of lunacy? What have we got at the end of it?

Gods fry him, what game is Goldtooth playing now? Him and the humans. All running. What in a mahen hell good are they?

What doublecross are the humans planning?

What did Tully tell them?

"Priority," Hilfy said. "Message from Sikkukkut: quote: Dock and hold the station."

Got our orders, do we? Kiss the hakkikt's *feet, do his work, move at his order. Go in there like a bunch of gods-be pirates?*

I wish I were dead before this.

"Advise *Aja Jin* and Tahar," she said.

"Aye," Hilfy said. And a moment later: "They acknowledge: final message: *Going on your signal.*"

We're worrying about what Goldtooth's doing. What Akkhtimakt's doing. We forget one important thing: Sikkukkut's no fool. He's had time to think this thing through. He's got something planned. He's thinking ahead of Akkhtimakt. Gods, what's the next move?

"Put us in," she said.

"Aye," said Haral. And began to lay course. They were moving in approximately the right vector. Haral hit the directionals and they started hammering off the *V,* turning, bringing the mains to bear on it. *Those* cut in, a one-*G* push, sudden and solid against the downward *G* they had from the rotation, a steady discomfort.

"Chur all right back there?" she asked. "Khym?"

"Chur's asked," Khym said, "What we're doing. I've tried to explain. I think she's drugged. She says she wants free of the machine. I said no, we had enough trouble."

"We got enough trouble," she muttered, and punched in all-ship. "Chur, we're all right. We got our hands full up here, huh? Just don't worry your sister."

"Aye," Chur's voice came back to her. She had been Geran's partner at that board. Now she lay listening while scan tried to track a Situation multiplied by fives and worse. "Geran, I'm . . . going to sleep . . . gods-be machine."

"*G*-stress," Pyanfar said.

Is it? Gods, cousin, hang on.

"We're headed into station," Geran said. "Hear that, sister of mine?"

"Got it," Chur murmured. It sounded like that. But she was far from the pickup.

The mains cut in, hard acceleration. And cut out again.

"We're on," Haral said. "We're going to be inertial. Take our time getting in there."

Preserve our options. Haral was reading her mind again. And inertial-time was rest-time.

She dropped her hand from the boards and sat there a moment while her muscles went weak and she was not at all certain that she could stand up. The interval between the two groups of kif narrowed further and further, changes perceptible only in the data-tags, but definitive. That would go on for the better part of an hour till someone got in position to do something. Jump and shoot, respectively. Then it remained to see what Sikkukkut would do.

Leave us to hold onto Meetpoint while he chases that bastard down?

Us to hold Meetpoint with Goldtooth loose? Goldtooth's taking his options. He won't jump till he has to, he wants to know what Sikkukkut's doing; and Sikkukkut's going to give him no options, going to follow right on his tail till he jumps. There's some small chance that Sikkukkut might leave if he can get Goldtooth out. He might rip loose everything he can pirate here and go for Akkhtimakt at Urtur. Akkhtimakt's got to go slow on the turn-around there, all that gods-be dust. Got to. Then Sikkukkut could catch him up and hammer him good.

If we knew Goldtooth's mind. Kifish ships are going to run up his backside, make him jump for Tt'av'a'o, they got V on him, he's got no choice either.

And once Goldtooth goes, he and the humans've got a three, four month turnaround to get back here. Gods, think, *Pyanfar! What* are *the options?*

"Tirun. Take watch. All the rest of you, you're off. Get something to eat. Geran, you're cleared aft; Skkukuk, belowdecks. Take what you can get. Jik. You I want to talk to."

Seats moved, restraints clicked open. Everyone was in motion, Haral as well. Pyanfar turned her own chair and stopped. Jik still sat in his place, staring at the screens. Tirun was beside him, keeping her station.

And Tully, though Hilfy had him by the elbow, lingered with a confused and sorrowful look toward the boards. Toward—gods knew, his own people starting off in retreat with Goldtooth, leaving him behind, perhaps forever, who knew? It was not a time to say anything. Pyanfar stared their way till Hilfy prevailed and they went out the door.

"Haral," she said. "Take the long break. Tirun, board to you, you go off when we get to final. Sorry about it."

"Got it," Tirun said hoarsely. "I'm fine, captain."

That left Jik to deal with. Khym had lingered in the corridor. She saw him standing down near Chur's door, looking back toward the bridge.

In case.

"Haral," she said in deepest and most impenetrable hani: "You want to bring me up a sedative. Something our guest can take. If we have to do that."

"Aye, captain," Haral said.

"I'll be in galley."

She wanted to be clean. She wanted to go back to her cabin and run herself under the shower. The whole bridge smelled like ammonia and hani and human and mahen sweat, an aroma even the fans did not totally disperse. But there was no time for that. It was far from over.

Even on this deck.

"Get me up," Chur said, with a move of an aching arm. "O gods, prop this gods-be bed up. I'm a mess."

"That's all right." Geran sat down on the bedside and checked the implanted tubes with a quick glance, bit a hole in the packet she had brought and offered it to Chur. "Take this and you get the bed propped up."

"Unnhhn." The very thought hit her stomach and lay there indigestible. "Prop it first."

"You promise."

"Gods rot you, I'll rip your ears."

Geran touched a control and the bed inclined upward. Chur flexed her legs and shifted her weight and grimaced in pain as the arm with the implants shifted down. But Geran, relentless, got an arm behind Chur's head and held the packet where she could drink.

It hit her stomach the way she had feared. "Enough," she said, "enough." And Geran had the sense to quit and just let her lie there drifting a moment, in that place she had discovered where the pain was not so bad. "Where's the shooting?" she asked finally.

"Hey, we ducked out of it."

Chur lay there a moment adding that up and rolled her head over where she could look at her sister, one long stare. "Where'd we duck to? Huh?"

"Kif are about to chew each other to rags about fifteen minutes off. We're headed to station for R & R. Maybe I'll buy you a drink, huh?"

"We take damage?" She recalled a lurch, like the thrust of the mains from the wrong angle . . . impossible to happen. Recalled a long hard acceleration, till the machine put her out cold. "Geran, what's the straight of it?"

"That is the straight of it. We're in one piece, we're going into station while the kif work it out. That's all."

Too gods-be cheerful, Geran. Whole lot too cheerful.

"Give me the truth," Chur said. "That's a gods-be dumb move. Sit at dock. Who knows what could come in? Huh? What's going on?"

"You want to try something solid?"

"No," she said flatly. And lay there breathing a moment, and turned her face toward Geran's stricken silence. Gods, the pain in Geran's face. "But I have to, don't I?" Her stomach rebelled at the thought. "Bit of soup, maybe. Nothing heavy. Don't push me, huh?"

"Sure," Geran said. Her ears had pricked up at once. Her eyes shone like a grateful child's. "You want the rest of this?"

O gods. Don't let me be sick. "Soup," she said, and clamped her jaws and tried not to think about it. "I rest, huh?"

"You rest," Geran said.

She shut her eyes, turning it all off.

You're still lying, Geran. But she did not have strength to face whatever it was Geran was lying about. She hoped not to discover. Her world limited itself to the pains in her joints and the misery of her arm and her back. The world could be right again if she could keep her stomach quiet and ease the pain a little. She just wanted not to throw up her guts again, and any problem more than that was more than she could carry.

It was impossible not to ask. But in a dim, weary way, with the data that came over the com all muddling in her head and promising nothing good at all, she thanked the gods Geran held back the answers.

* * *

"Jik," Pyanfar said.

Jik pushed himself back in his chair and looked at the board in front of him, its screens all dark and dead. And turned his chair then and stared at her across the width of the bridge.

A word was too much. Till she had something to offer him from her side. Time seemed to stretch further and further like the eeriness of jump. And there was no rescue and no way out of the impasse they were in. Him on *The Pride*'s bridge. *Aja Jin* ignorant and silent beside them.

His allies outbound. Unless by some monumentally unexpected turn the kif all went after their enemies and left them alone.

And none of them believed that.

Down the corridor the lift worked, and opened, and let Haral out. Pyanfar got up and went to the door of the bridge and out it, to intercept her in the hall; and Haral slipped her a couple of pills. "Thanks," she said; "you sure about this stuff."

"This'll make it sure," Haral said, and fished a flask out of her capacious pocket. Parini. Pyanfar took it and gestured with a move of her jaw back the way Haral had come. Haral went.

And Pyanfar turned back toward the bridge, where Jik sat quietly in his chair, caring not to turn it when she came up on him. She walked back to the fore of the bridge, and stood there looking back. "I want to talk to you. Private." Only Tirun was left with the boards; and she herself was not up to a hand-to-hand with a taller, heavier mahendo'sat, even if he was jump-wobbly too. *Fool,* she thought. But some courses had to be steered. Even at risk to the ship.

"Come on," she said again. "Jik."

He got to his feet. She walked away, deliberately taking her eyes off him, though it was sure Tirun was alert to sudden moves.

But he came docilely after her, and followed her through the short corridor to the galley.

Tirun being Tirun, she would both monitor it all on the intercom and pass the word to all aboard that the galley had just gone offlimits.

She turned when she had gotten as far as the counter and the cabinet with the gfi-cups.

"*Captain,*" Tirun said via com. "*Pardon. Goldtooth's group has started shifting out, first one just went. Before AOS on Kesurinan's message. Close, but they're not going to get it. Thought you'd want to know.*"

"Huh," she said. "Pass that to the crew."

"Aye." The audio cut out. The com stayed live, its telltale still glowing on the wall-unit.

And Jik stood there, just stood, with a slump in his shoulders and a set like stone to his face. "Sit down," she said, and he did that, on the long bench against the wall, elbows on the table. She got a glass from the cabinet, the flask from her pocket, poured a shot of it and set it in front of him.

"No," he said.

"That's prescriptive. You drink. Hear?"

He took it then, and took a sip and shuddered visibly. Sat there looking nowhere. Thinking of friends, maybe. Of Goldtooth, outbound and not to return for months.

Of his ship, so close and himself helpless to reach them.

"Take another," she said. He did, shuddering after that one too, and that shudder did not stop. Liquor spilled out onto his hand, pooled on the table as he set the glass down. He put the hand to his mouth and sucked at the knuckle where it had spilled. His eyes glared at her.

She sat down, opposite him. If Tirun wanted her, there was the alarm. Her own aches could wait. She was prepared to wait. For whatever it took.

It was a long time before he moved at all, and that was to lift the glass and take it all down in one long stinging draught. He shuddered a third time, set the glass down empty and she filled it.

Got a crate of the stuff in storage. Pour it all down him if we have to.

"Hao'ashtie-na ma visini-ma'arno shishini-to nes mura'ani hes." Whoever he was talking to, she did not follow it. Something about dark and cold. It was that dialect he spoke with Kesurinan. "Muiri nai, Pyanfar."

"Mishio-ne." *I'm sorry.*

"Hao. Mishi'sa." —*Yes. Sorry.* "Neshighot-me pau taiga?" *What the hell good is it?*

"None. I know that. Species-interest, Jik. I warned you of that. Now you can try to break my neck. It won't get you our access codes. What it will get you is a lot of grief. You don't want it; I don't want it. We're old friends. And you know down that one way's a lot of trouble and no good at all and down the other's a hani whose interests might be a lot the same as yours in the long run."

For a while he said nothing. After a while he picked up the glass again and took a tiny sip. "Merus'an-to he neishima kif, he?"

Something about damned kif, himself, and bargains.

"I want my people safe, Jik."

"You damn fool!" His hand came down on the table, jarring the liquid. "Give me com."

"So you can doublecross me again? No. Not this time. Too many lives here."

While pacifist stsho ran in gibbering terror in the corridors of their station and discovered there were species which could neither be hired nor bribed nor prevented from being predators.

"Humans," she said; "and mahendo'sat. If Tully's right, if Tully's telling the truth, and I think he is—there's one more doublecross in the works. The humans will betray Goldtooth. Hear? And you know and I know Sikkukkut's got to do something here. Your partner's going to push and herd the kif into fighting. He thinks. But in the meanwhile who does the bleeding? They'll herd him right away from mahen space. Right? Where does that leave? Stsho? Tc'a? Goldtooth's defending that. That leaves hani space—*friend.* You don't push me right now. My people have got *me* between them and *that,* and don't push me, Jik!"

"You—" Jik fell silent a moment, coughed and rested there with his mouth against his hand as if he had lost his way and his argument. "Merus'an-to he neishima kif. Shai."

Bargains and the kif again. Then: *I.* Or something like that. He spoke mahensi. As if he had forgotten that he was not on his own ship. Or as if, exhausted as he was and wrung out, he lacked the strength to translate. He had that glassy look. Jump healed, but it took it out of a body too. And he had gone into it hurt, in body and spirit.

He was still reasonable. Still the professional, getting what he could get. She counted on that.

"I have to go in there to Meetpoint," she said. "I got to get what I can get. I won't doublecross you. Won't do any hurt to the mahendo'sat. I swear that, haur na ahur. But I don't want you against me either. I don't want you trying to get at controls, I don't want you trying to get at my crew. And everything you tell me's going to be a lie. Isn't it? Con the hani again." She fished her pocket and laid the two pills on the table. "You take those when you want 'em. Nothing but sleeping pills. I got enough troubles. You got enough. You're strung. You know it. I want you to go out of here, mind your manners with my crew, get some sleep. That's all you can do. All I can do for you. Like a friend, Jik. But first I want to ask you: have you held out on me? Conned me? You got anything you think I better know? 'Cause we are going in there. And we're going to get blown to a mahen hell if this is a trap. And Sikkukkut just might not go with us, which would be a real shame."

He shoved the glass up against her hand. "You want talk? Take bit."

She had no business taking anything of the sort, straight out of jump, with a ship to handle in what was going on out there. But it was cheaper than argument. She picked up the glass and took a sip that hit her dehydrated throat and nasal passages like fire, and her stomach like an incandescence. She set the glass down and slid it across the table to touch his hand again. He sipped a bit more and blinked. Sweat moistened trails down his face and glistened on black fur; the dusky rim around his eyes was suffused with blood and they watered when he blinked. And after all that liquor on an empty stomach and straight from injuries and jump, he showed no sign of passing out.

"I want stay on bridge," he said. "Py-an-far. Same you don't trust me, this know. All same ask."

"I can't shut you up. I can't have you distracting my crew. I can't risk it. I'm telling you. I can't risk it. You want your ship to survive this? You help me, gods rot you, *cooperate.*"

He lifted his face then, his eyes burning.

"Survival, Jik. Is there anything we'd better know? Because we've got two kif out there fighting over everything we've got, and gods rot it, I *hate* this, Jik, but we got no gods-be *choice,* Jik!"

His mouth went to a hard line. He picked up the glass and drank half the remainder. Shoved it across to her. "I deal with that damn kif, set up whole damn thing." His hand shook where it rested on the table. *"Drink,* damn you, I don't drink without drink *with."*

She picked it up and drank the rest. It hit bottom with the rest and stung her eyes to tears.

"We got make friend this damn kif," he said, all hoarse. "I don't know where Ana go, don't know what he do. We, we got go make good friend this kif. This be *job,* a? Got go be polite." A tic contorted his face and turned into a dreadful expression. "Pyanfar. You, I, old friend. You, I. How much you pay him, a?"

A chill went up her back and lifted the hair between her shoulderblades. "I won't give you up to him. Not again."

"No." He reached across and stabbed a blunt-clawed finger at her arm. "I mean truth. We got to, we *deal* with this damn kif. You got to, you give him me, you give him you sister, we got make surround—" His finger moved to describe a half-circle in the spilled liquor. "Maybe

CHANUR'S HOMECOMING • 127

Ana damn fool. Maybe human lot trouble. We be con-tin-gency. Con-tin-gency for whole damn Compact. We be inside. Understand?"

"I don't turn you over to him again."

"You do. Yes. I do job. Same my ship. Same we got make deal." His mouth jerked. "Got go bed this damn kif maybe. I do. Long time I work round this bastard." He shoved the glass at her again. "Fill."

"I'm not drinking with you. I got a—" —*ship to run.* She swallowed that down before it got out. "Gods rot. You got to get something real on your stomach." She filled the glass and got up, jerked a packet of soup out of the cabinet and tore the foil, poured it into a cup and shoved it under the brewer. Steam curled up. It smelled of salt and broth, promised comfort to a stomach after the raw assault of the parini. She took a sip herself and turned around to find him lying head on arms. "Come on," she said. "I'll drink this one with you, turn about. Hear? You take the pills."

He hauled himself off the table and took a sip of the cup. Made a face and offered it back.

One and one. She gave him the next sip. "Just keep going," she said. "I got a sick crewwoman to see about back there." Her stomach moiled. She still tasted the parini and she never wanted to taste it again in her life. But it was to a point of locking a friend into a cubbyhole of a prison and letting a kif loose as crew to walk the corridors where he liked. That was the way of things.

He was right. He was utterly right, and thinking, past all the rest of it.

They might have no choice at all.

"Come on," she said. "While you can walk. Going to put you to bed myself. Pills in the mouth, huh?"

"No." He picked them up and closed his fist on them. "I keep. Maybe need. Now I sleep. Safe, a? With *friend.*"

He gathered himself up from the table. Staggered. And gained his balance again.

She motioned toward the number two corridor. The back way toward the lift, that did not pass through the bridge, past delicate controls.

He cooperated. He went with her quietly, when he had every chance to try something. But that would be stupid, and gain him nothing, in a ship he could not control.

He had also told her nothing, for all his talking.

That in itself said something worrisome.

They went down to the lift; and down to the lower level; and as far as Tully's cabin, far forward. Next to Skkukuk's.

Tully was not there. That meant he was in crew quarters. That did not surprise her.

"Get some sleep," she said.

"A," he said. And parked his wide shoulders against the door frame, leaned there reeking of parini and looking as if he might fall on his face before he reached the bed.

"And don't forget the safety, huh?"

The next door opened. Skkukuk was there, bright-eyed and anxious to serve.

"You don't be fool," Jik said to her. *"Friend."*

And spun aside into the room and shut the door between them.

She locked it. And turned and looked at Skkukuk. "This man is valuable," she said. Kifish logic.

"Dangerous," Skkukuk said.

She walked off and left him there. Took out the pocket-com and used it and not the intercom-stations along the way. "Tirun, we got it all secure down here."

"Kif are pounding each other hard. We got approach contact from Meetpoint. Stsho are being extra polite, we got no trouble if the poor bastards don't Phase on us in mid-dock. I got no confidence I'm talking to the same stsho from minute to minute. Scared. Real scared. I got the feeling kif-com isn't being polite at all. Ships inbound are Ikkhoitr and Khafukkin."

"Gods. Wonderful. Sikkukkut's chief axe. You could figure."

"You going on break?"

"I'm coming up there." No way to rest. Not till they had an answer. Even if her knees were wobbling under her. She envied Jik the pills. But not the rest of his situation.

Tirun caught her eye as she walked onto the bridge and looked a further worried question at her. Tirun, who looked deathly tired herself. "No change," Tirun said. "Except bad news. Goldtooth's bunch had two chasers on his tail when he went out. Akkhtimakt's got to jump any minute now. Got to. He's getting his tail shot up. Some of those ships may not make it otherside. They got to clear out of here." Pyanfar looked. Everyone was still running for jump. The last of Goldtooth's company was gone. And a flock of stsho, fortunate in being out of range of all disasters and *not* being tied up dead-*V* at station. Not a sign of a methane-breather. Anywhere.

No hani was moving. They were caught at dock. And there was not a way in a mahen hell to get out vectored for hani space with the angle and the *V* Sikkukkut's two station-aimed ships had on them. *Ikkhoitr* and *Khafukkin* were going to make it in before their own three ships. Kif were going to have control of that dock, and gods help the hani who took exception to it.

"We got one more ship ID: a Faha. *Starwind.*"

"Munur." That was a youngish captain. A very small ship. And a distant cousin of Hilfy's on her mother's side. Ehrran?"

"Not a sign."

"With Goldtooth or kited out of here home a long time ago. Want to lay odds which?" Exhaustion and nerves added up on her. She shivered, and a great deal of it was depletion. "Yeah. Stay on it." She indicated the direction of the galley and marshaled a steady voice. "Jik's going to rest a bit. He's plenty mad. And crazy-tired. I hope to the gods he takes those pills and settles down, but I don't think he'll do it. Pass out awhile, maybe. Maybe come to with a clearer head. Right now he's real trouble. He's not thinking real clear. Me, I'm not, either. We put his quarters on ops-com when he wakes up. *Maybe* let him up here, I don't know yet. It's *my* judgment I don't trust. I'm going to clean up, pass out a few minutes. How are you holding?"

"I'm all right," Tirun said. It was usual sequence: Haral first on the cleanup; Haral first to snatch a little rest, Haral the one whose wits had to be sharpest and reflexes quickest, their switcher; and Haral generally shorted herself on rest-time to pay her sister for it. " 'Bout time, though." And before she could leave the chair she was leaning on: "Captain, Chur's wanting a bit of something hot. Geran went to the lowerdecks to fix it."

That was the best news since the drop. "Huh," she said. "Huh." With a little relaxation in tensed muscles. She shoved off and walked on down the corridor. She wanted food. Wanted a bath. Wanted, gods knew, to be lightyears away from all of this. But they did not have that choice. They could run for it and get out of Meetpoint system while Sikkukkut was busy. But he would find them; and anyone they were attached to. Their world was held hostage. Not mentioning the immediate threat to three hundred thousand gods-be stsho and a handful of hani ships.

A kif could not forget an insult.
No more than a hani forgot harm to her friends.

It was a quiet gathering down in crew quarters, in the central area where they had a microwave, and a little store of instant food: one of those amenities they had installed along with the high-V braces and the AP weapons they had acquired on the black market. A couple of little couches and a table or two in a lounge, and a common-room for sleeping, in which they could have installed partitions, but they had never gotten around to that—never much wanted it, truth be known. A body learned to sleep with cousins trekking in and out, and there was never any urgent reason to change, even in the days when they had had wealth.

Right now, Hilfy thought, it was the best reason of all; a body wanted company in this crisis. Geran came kiting in and out again with two cups of soup, gods only hope she got one into her own stomach on the way topside; Chur was evidently awake and willing to try it eating, which was one heart-lightening event among all the bad news. Haral was sitting on the couch opposite with a bit of jerky in one hand and her mouth full, while she raked her damp mane into order with the other. Her eyes had that distracted, glassy weariness jump left in a body. Tully came out of the common bath with a towel over his shoulders, wearing a pair of Khym's trousers, a rust silk pair which he had had to pin at the waist, but Haral was out of spares and the other pair was going through the laundry. He staggered over to the cabinet and got a cup and poured soupmix and water into it, shoved it in the microwave and sat down to towel his head and beard dry. Pale, old scars stood out on white-skinned shoulders; and pinker, recent ones.

"Akkhtimakt's jumped out," came the bulletin from the bridge. And: *"We got a general slow-down on Sikkukkut's side, sure enough, 'cept for two of 'em it looks like Sikkukkut's sending out to keep 'em worried, same as he did with Goldtooth's lot. Looks for good and sure like Sikkukkut's going to stay with us. Thought you'd like to know."*

"No surprise," Haral muttered. *"Couldn't* be that lucky. Couldn't be lucky enough to get help out of Goldtooth. Sikkukkut's going to have this place stripped to the deckplates before he gets back."

"Going to do whatever he wants," Hilfy said, "that's sure."

"Lousy mess."

Tully had lifted his face from the towel and looked at them, yellow hair tousled, eyes showing lines of strain about the edges. Sometimes he seemed too tired even to make the effort of speech. Or to listen for the translator's sputtering whisper giving him its mangled version of things around him. The things hardest to get across were the delicate topics, like: *How's Chur—honestly?* Or: *What do you think Jik will do?* And: *What are we going to do when the kif move into the station?* He seemed to go away at times. At others he seemed desperate to say something of too much difficulty to attempt it.

Things like: *My people are going. I talked to them. Even if the message didn't get there. I was that close.*

I didn't betray you.

I swear I didn't try.

The microwave bleeped Finished; and Tully got up and got his soup, with a package of shredded meat and a packet of mahen fuyas, which he and Haral thought edible and everyone else aboard loathed. He offered one of the grain-meat sticks to Haral: she took it and stirred her soup with it, and he settled down with the other packets in his agile fingers, cup in both hands and elbows on his knees, to drink a sip and sigh in profoundest weariness.

"I figure," Hilfy said, to fill the quiet, and to answer questions Tully did not ask, "Goldtooth rendezvoused here with the human fleet. *That's* why he kited out on us at Kefk. He and Ehrran came in here, *he* got stuck here, in a standoff with Akkhtimakt. Maybe he got Akkhtimakt pried loose from the station. He did that much for the stsho. But Ehrran's on her way to Anuurn. Bet."

"Godsrotted well has to be," Haral muttered. "But with Goldtooth in it we got to wonder, don't we?"

"Like what happened here?" That bothered her. The whole arrangement of things bothered her. The lack of methane-breathers. And Akkhtimakt and Sikkukkut, if they both wanted to be fools, could go on trading that position till the suns all froze. Every few shipboard days, every few ground-bound months, one side could do a turnaround at Urtur or Tt'av'a'o or Kefk or wherever, and come in and strafe the other who had taken possession of Meetpoint. Or Kefk. Or wherever. If ships got to trading positions like that, time-dilation got to stretching lives wider and wider; no in-system passages. No slow-time. Just run and run and run as long as a ship could take it and a body could take the depletion. A merchant ship did its jumps with a lot of slowtime and dock-time in between; and a tradeoff like that could do as much time-stretch in a month of their own perception as a trader did in a decade.

Before flesh and bone and steel had gone their limits. "Wonder is he didn't come in on Kefk."

"Kefk's got two guardstations. Kefk's got position on him."

Tully stared at them both. He had lost that, probably. But of a sudden the problem had found itself a cold spot in Hilfy's gut. She took a sip of her cup to warm that cold and licked the soup off her mustaches.

"Sikkukkut's got something in mind. He's sure not going to sit here."

"There *are* fools in the universe," Haral said.

"What if he isn't? What if he's not sitting still here? What if he's got something else in mind?"

But Goldtooth was out on the Tt'av'a'o vector. Methane-breather territory. Logical choice: the stsho feared the humans like plague. Stsho would deal with Ehrran; they would deal with the kif before they dealt with Goldtooth and his human allies. They would go with the known villains.

Stsho had no armaments. No capability for that kind of stress. Stsho would run if they could. Evade it all.

Tc'a and chi and—gods save us—knnn—they're not here, they're always here. Where are they? Knnn aren't afraid of anything. They won't run. Avoid, maybe; run in panic—not the knnn. Ever.

"Methane-breathers," Hilfy said. "Gods rot it, Haral. It's a trap. Sikkukkut's and Goldtooth's both."

Haral's ears flagged and lifted again, and a thinking look got through the exhaustion in Haral's eyes.

"Hilfy." Tully held his cup between his knees and his brow furrowed with worry under its fringe of pale wet hair. "Goldtooth not go Tt'av'a'o."

"You mean you *know* that?"

"I think. He come—turn, go *whhhsss,* like Tt'av'a'o. Not."

"You mean he faked a jump? Stopped out there in deep space? You think he can *do* that?"

Tully might or might not have gotten all of that. "Mahe," he said. "Human do."

"Stop a jump short?"

"Same."

"Good gods."

"Makes sense," Haral said. "If they've got the stuff to do that. If they got it from humans— He waits here to fake a run."

"And Ehrran runs for good and real and leaves hani here to catch it when Sikkukkut came through? Gods-be, she's got a *treaty* with the stsho!"

"Give her credit. What could she do—if Akkhtimakt was here first. Goldtooth *wanted* Akkhtimakt intact. He's shoving the two kif into a fight, by the gods, that's what he's doing!" Haral rubbed her graying nose and it wrinkled up again. "Let them weaken each other before he throws the humans at them and before the mahen forces come in here. That's what he's up to. Let Jik hang; let Jik keep at least one gods-be kif halfway tame if he can while Goldtooth sets it up so he can take out both kif. That's what the mahendo'sat would really like. Throw the humans at 'em. Let the humans get shot up. That's why he left Jik behind at Kefk."

"No mahen workers left here onstation, I'll bet on that."

"Gods-rotted sure. Goldtooth could have had the word out long before this. Routed everything out of here. Cleared it all out when the stsho broke that treaty."

"Eggs to pearls Goldtooth's left a spotter here."

"No contest."

"*It's* still insystem," Hilfy said. "*It's* still in position to get whatever happened here, maybe there's more than one of them, huh? Maybe a couple of spotters, one drifting out slow, going to fire up when it's outside normal pickup, just sneak out of here. And if Goldtooth's out there in the deep and those fool kif that were tailing him jump all the way to Tt'av'a'o—"

Haral's ears lifted. The exhaustion melted from her eyes and replaced itself with a hard, hard look. "Keep going."

"Goldtooth might wait for news. Before his turnaround. If he makes one. He may have put more than one or two spotters on the outside of this system. He's used up all his credit with Sikkukkut himself, he's out there in the dark with the humans, with the tc'a that Jik was working with, he's got some credit with the *han,* maybe some with the knnn. What if he decided there wasn't any choice and he just lets the kif fight it out?"

"Maybe that's the safest thing we could all do."

"But—"

"I'm listening."

"But—you know the mahendo'sat are going to save their own hides. Ehrran's left him. We can't speak for the *han.* We got kif going to go head-on against each other with the humans on their backside. If both of them get busy, if the mahendo'sat hit them in the back—neither

Akkhtimakt nor Sikkukkut can stand for that chance. They're in a mess. They can't leave the mahendo'sat armed at their backs. They're *kif,* and Goldtooth's going to attack and they know it. My gods, we got one kif making a threat against Anuurn. What's *Akkhtimakt* going to threaten, huh? Or is he just going to turn around and send a ship apiece at every mahen world and station?"

Haral's ears were all but flat. She was still listening.

"Ask Skkukuk," Tully said suddenly.

"Ask him *what?*" Hilfy asked.

"He kif. Ask what kif do."

"He's not on Sikkukkut's level. If he'd outthought him, we'd have Skkukuk to worry about."

"Kif mind. Lot dark. *I* go ask."

"Man's got a point," Haral said. "But no way we talk to the kif. Better we talk to the captain. Py-an-far, you understand me, Tully?"

"You think I'm right?"

"I been in space forty some years, kid, I never been real close to kif on their terms. You have. And you speak main-kifish. Which I still don't, not real well. But I've had a look at our passenger, 'bout enough to get an idea or two. And between the mahendo'sat and that kif, I'm real anxious. We got that other bomb aboard. And sorry as I am for him, he scares me worse'n Skkukuk."

"Jik," Hilfy murmured. And took another sip that failed to warm her gut.

"He's got a lot on him," Haral said, "and much as we owe him and he owes us—first, he's hurting; second, he's *been* hurt, by the kif *and* by his own partner and by us on top of it all; and thirdly, he's mahendo'sat and seeing his whole species in danger, and *maybe* he's got more information than we've gotten out of him. What's he going to do?"

The cold got worse. For one uneasy moment Hilfy could not even look at Tully. For one uneasy moment he was like Jik, alien and full of strange motives and unpredictabilities. And she was female and he was not, with all the craziness on that score. *No place for him to be sitting. Listening to us. Gods, what if he was only waiting, all this time? He's alien. Isn't he? Same as Jik. And we've been through so gods-be much— and I don't know what's in his mind right now. My friend. My—* She gave a mental shiver, looked at the time. "Gods," she said, "we better get topside. Tirun—"

"Yeah," Haral said. And: "You want me to talk to the captain?"

"She listens to you more than me."

"Hey," Haral said. And fixed her with a lazy, flat-eared stare. Reprimand for that small remark. Hilfy dipped her ears.

"Kif," Tully said.

"No," Haral said. "We let that son sleep. You stay here. Rest. Understand. You go down that hall to talk to that kif, I'll skin you. Hear?"

"I understand," Tully said. His mouth had that set it got in unhappiness. "Not right, Haral. I sit here."

"Argues," Haral said. "Huh."

"He wasn't juniormost on his ship," Hilfy said. "I know that. He's not a kid, Haral."

"Who is, on this ship? Tully. You want to come? Talk to the captain?"

He had a few bites left. He made it one, drank the cup dry and got to his feet, still trying to swallow what he had.

"How's it going?" Pyanfar asked quietly, leaning shower-damp and exhausted over Tirun's chairback. Khym had come back to his post, far from skilled enough to relieve Tirun, but there, at least for support. Tirun looked back at her with flagging ears and a desperate weariness. Tirun had not had a chance at the showers. That was evident.

"No answers yet," Tirun said. "*Na* Jik's asleep, I think. Stopped stirring around down there after I heard the safety-web go." She tilted an ear generally downships and down below. "We got our routine instructions, I just fed it into auto. All the kif are on schedule, Sikkukkut's pair's in final just now and the stsho're sweating it."

"Huhhhh." Pyanfar had an eye on the scan from her vantage; ships proceeding sedately on course. No one out there had done anything definitive. And she leaned closer to Tirun's ear, her elbow on the chairback. "Get out of here, huh? I'll take it."

"Haral'll be here." The voice came out hoarse. "You want to go catch a bite? I c'n take a little longer, 'm not doing anything but sit."

"Neither am I. Get. I'll hold the boards." She shoved off from the chairback and paused half a heartbeat considering her husband, who had never looked away from the screen in all this time. Covering, while she distracted Tirun, though the board was audio-alarmed, and her own eye had automatically held on that screen the minute Tirun looked her way. Tirun had known where she was looking—experience, decades of it. Bridge rules. But Khym covered. That was bridge rules too. She gave Khym's chairback a pat, approval, with a little unwinding of something at her gut. Closer and closer to reliable. On the standard of the best crew going. An impulse came to her; she unclipped one of her earrings.

"Hey," she said, and leaned next to him where her breath stirred the inner tuftings of his ear. "Huh," he said, as if it were some intimacy.

"Hold still. Don't flinch." She nipped right through the edge of his ear. *"Owwh!"* he grunted, and did flinch, turning half about in indignation and then—perhaps he thought it was some bizarre test of his concentration—jerked his gaze right back to the boards.

She slipped the ring right into the wound and clipped it.

"Uhhhn," he said, and felt of what she had done. Never looked around.

"Good." She patted his shoulder, remembered then that he had once upon a time reacted with temper over that gesture of shoulder-patting. But maybe it felt different somehow. He did not object. And she went off to her own station, sat down and brought in the scan images and the com.

Sikkukkut was still on course. *Ikkhoitr* and its partner were docking ahead of them, and *The Pride* was on a course right down lane-center, neat and precise.

They were going to have some specific docking instructions very soon. *The Pride* and *Aja Jin* and *Moon Rising* were about to put themselves where the kif could get at them.

And where Sikkukkut could make demands of them. Jik, for instance. Jik, for a very large instance. Or even Tully. Or Dur Tahar. All of which items Sikkukkut might want back. She sat and gnawed her mustaches, wishing she dared talk back and forth with Dur Tahar over there, who assuredly knew something about kifish mentality. But absolute com silence seemed the best policy at the moment. Gods knew she wanted no questions out of *Aja Jin,* where Kesurinan still followed her orders. And did not ask, as Kesurinan might well have asked: How is my captain? Is he recovered? Why do I have no instructions from him?

Kesurinan believed she knew the answers to all these things, perhaps. And stayed patient. So far.

But on that dockside Kesurinan was bound to ask questions that needed direct lies. And inventive ones.

Goldtooth, gods curse you, what have you set up here?

Made an agreement *with someone, have you?*

Or have we got something else lurking out there, outsystem, that we're going to find out about when our wavefront gets to them and they get themselves run up to attack speed?

Gods, gods, this is no situation to be in. What's Sikkukkut doing? Is that son really depending on us, for godssakes? Are we the backup he thinks he has?

Fool, Sikkukkut. Can a kif mind be that tangled, to trust us now?

Or are you no fool at all?

Com beeped. "Py," Khym said, and cut it in from his board.

"I got it." It was station, talking to them in effusive jabber. A stsho told them that they could, if they wished, have any free berth, but suggested numbers twenty-seven, twenty-eight, twenty-nine. Which the lord captain of *Ikkhoitr* had suggested, praise to the *hakkikt.*

"Affirm," she said, and with a flattening of her ears: "Praise to the *hakkikt.*"

"No real choice, do we?" Khym asked.

"Life and not. We got that."

"What are we going to do?" There was the faintest note of despair there. A man asking his wife for reassurance. *Tell me there's something you can do. Tell me it's not that bad, not that hopeless.* A man lived within the small borders of his estate—never tell a man a thing: never worry him with problems he had no capacity to deal with. And no power. *Old habits, Khym, gods rot it, grow up!*

No. It's crew talking to captain. That's all. Get off him, Pyanfar.

"Feathered if I know what we're going to do," she muttered. *No mercy, Khym.* "Got an idea?"

"He's going to ask for Jik."

"I'm afraid he is."

"What are we going to do?"

"I'll make something up."

Nothing to do but watch it unfold. Obey instructions, take the berth. *You got it, husband. There isn't an answer. I haven't got a miracle to pull off. I don't know what in a mahen hell we're going to do and most of all I don't know how we're going to get out of here.*

Thank gods Ehrran's headed home to warn the han. *Even if she goes for Chanur in the process. Better the clan goes down than the whole world. Better a whole lot of things than that.*

But, gods, Ehrran's a fool. What's a fool going to tell them? What's a fool going to persuade those fools to do?

Gods, give her good sense just once and I'll go religious, I swear I will. I'll reform. I'll—

Haral startled her, settling ghostlike into place beside her.

"Captain," Haral said. "What we got?"

She turned the chair half-about, saw Tirun out of her place and Tully and Hilfy settling into theirs, ghostlike silent under the noise of operating systems. "We got our docking instructions. Give Tirun time to get herself down to quarters. We can brake a little late. Meetpoint sure as rain isn't going to file any protest on us for violations." She swung the chair about again and punched in com. Two veteran crewwomen in their places and two novices. But it was a routine docking, whatever else was proceeding. "Geran," she said. "Five minutes."

"I'm on my way," Geran answered back from somewhere.

"Captain," Haral said, "Hilfy's got this idea—"

"Tahar acknowledges recept on docking instructions," Hilfy said. "They're on our lead."

"—Akkhtimakt's just lost any reason he had for restraint," Haral said. "He's losing. *Mahendo'sat* aren't dealing with him. He's gone off toward Urtur; there's two moves he could make. One's us. One's the mahendo'sat. Things could get ugly. Real ugly. That's what we been thinking."

"Huhhhn." Another body hit the cushions, hard. She heard the click of restraints. Geran was in. Heard a wild high chittering coming down the corridor, which was a kif in full career, headed for his station and trying to tell them to wait for him: a shove of *The Pride*'s mains would send him smashing back into the lift door with the same force as if he had fallen off a building roof.

"We hear you," she said over general com. "You got time, Skkukuk."

And thought about the web of jump-corridors around Meetpoint and where they led.

Gods know what's already been launched at us. "Mahendo'sat aren't going to sit still for it," she said. "It's not their style."

"If they push back," Haral said, "it's going to shove that bastard right into hani space. We figure there's a push coming here. Cap'n, Tully says human ships can drop out of hype in deep space. Do a turn. Says he thinks the mahendo'sat can do it too."

She shot Haral a look. It was a knnn maneuver, that stop-and-turn. Or tc'a. "Friends turning up in odd places."

"From here, cap'n, it's a real pocket out Kura-way."

It was: hani space was an appendix of reachable space, right on the mahendo'sat underbelly, near the mahen homestar. But the accesses in that direction were few and defensible.

"Yeah," she said, thinking of that geometry, which thought suddenly shaped itself into coherent form, in full light. "Yeah. It might work. If they can do that kind of thing. But that'd mean those human ships aren't freighters in any sense of the word—wouldn't it? What's a ship with holds need with that kind of rig, huh?"

"Sure seems like not. And a strike coming in here rams it right down hani throats. Again."

"It does that, too. If they can do that." Another and worse thought. "If mahendo'sat can pull this—wouldn't be the first time they had some new rig they didn't tell us about. Wouldn't be the first time the kif turned up with it too. Before we did. Praise to the mahendo'sat. More gods-be careful of what their allies learn than what gets to their enemies."

Gods, don't let Ehrran be a fool.

Then, down the boards: "Priority," Geran said. "Priority, we got a shift going on, we got a vector change on some of Sikkukkut's lot. That's *Noikkhru* and *Shuffikkt*—"

It came up on the monitor, part of the image changing color again as kifish ships finished their braking and began to slew off on new headings.

Headings at angles to Sikkukkut's.

Chapter Six

Color-shifts multiplied on the scan.

"Gods," Pyanfar muttered, and put in the general take-hold. Alarm rang up and down the corridors. In case. "Message to our partners: hold steady, keep course; Khym, advisement to Chur: Take precautions, we got kif moving gods know where. Tirun, feed scan down to Jik's monitor; tell him we're all right, we're still on course, we just got something going here."

Acknowledgments came back.

"Tahar acknowledges," Hilfy said. "They're on our lead. Aye—we got that, *Aja Jin.* Thanks—"

"—Akkhtimakt's got bad troubles," Haral said. "I think we got 'em too."

She waited. Waited till she heard Tirun report all personnel accounted for; Tirun had made it onto the bridge. A last safety snicked into place.

They were secure for running. If they had to.

On the screens the flares continued as the doppler recept sorted it out and got information trued again.

And one and another of Sikkukkut's ships flaring green and going into maneuvers.

Not all on the same vector. They were headed out like thistledown scattering from a pod. Everywhere.

In every direction open to them, mahen space and hani and stsho and tc'a.

"They go," Jik exclaimed over the open com. And something else profane in mahensi. He was monitoring the situation, down there in his sealed cabin. *"Damn, they go, they go—"*

To every star within reach. To strafe every station and every system where there might be a hostile presence.

"Priority, priority," Hilfy said, overriding something Geran was saying: *"Harukk*-com says: *Pride of Chanur,* proceed on course."

"They go hit ever' damn target in Compact," Jik cried. There was the sound of explosion. Or of a mahen fist hitting something. *"Damn! Let me out!"*

"She was right," Haral muttered. "Gods-be right. They're going to do it anyhow and we got kif every which way. Captain, they're going to push Akkhtimakt right down that open corridor, to *Anuurn,* captain, by the gods they are."

"We got problems," Pyanfar muttered.

While a stream of mahen profanity warred with Chur's insistent question on the com.

"Kkkkt." From a forgotten source behind them.

And station was ahead. Meetpoint, with three hundred thousand stsho and a handful of hani citizens. With kif closing in on them with declared intent to dock.

"Transmit:" Pyanfar said. *"The Pride of Chanur* to all hani on station: prepare to assist in docking for incoming ships. Join us. This is your greatest hope of immediate safety."

Offer a hani an overlord, a master, a foreign hegemony—

They would spit in Sikkukkut's face. And die for it. That, beyond doubt.

But if they heard the reservation in that message, if they keyed on the nuances of safe-shelter-in-storm and all the baggage that went with it— even if the kif did, it was no more than kif expected, even if it was something no kif dared say: *until we find a better.*

"Repeat?" Hilfy queried.

"Repeat."

"Still braking," Geran said.

And the brightness on the amber lines that was their own position crept closer and closer to their own brake-point for station approach.

"Harun's Industry responds," Hilfy said, "quote: We take your offer enthusiastically."

It took awhile, for ships to reduce *V*.

It took awhile for outbound kifish ships to go their way, leaping out into the dark, toward Hoas Point and Urtur System, toward Kshshti and Kef'k and Tt'av'a'o and V'n'n'u and Nsthen. Seven ships, to follow right down Akkhtimakt's tail in a second strike after the first one; and right down the throats of Goldtooth and humans and mahendo'sat and whoever else might be coming in if they could find them.

It was, Pyanfar reckoned bleakly, both ruthless and effective.

"Kkkkt," was Skkukuk's comment. "Kkkkt."

"Kkkt," said Skkukuk. "He is challenging you all. Kkkkt. But his throat is unprotected. *You* are here. He thinks to daunt you. Surprise him, hakt'."

She spun her chair about to face the kif who sat at the aft of the bridge. And there was not a hair on her unbristled. "What has he in mind for us?"

"You are part of his *sfik*. You increase him. Kkkkt. His move is very good. He has penned you all in with his main force. Any attempt to exit toward your territories of resource are blocked first by his enemy and then by his own ships, whose capacities you do not know. It is a fine move, hakt'. But I have faith in you."

"Faith."

"Inappropriate word? *Sgotkkis.*"

"Call it faith." She laid her ears back and stared at her private curse with coldest, clearest threat. "Since you don't have an idea in a mahen hell what I'm likely to do about it. But *I* am still here. And my resources have not diminished."

"Kkkkt, kkkt, skthot skku-nak'haktu."

Your slave, captain.

"Captain," Hilfy said. "Communication from *Harukk.* Quote: *You have made a proposal to hani ships. You will gather these captains for my inspection on-station. End message."*

Second move. It's going too fast. O gods.

"Acknowledge," she said, cold as routine. While they slogged their way at a sedate pace through a system laced with kif, toward a station which was going to be under kifish occupation. "Sikkukkut's going into dock. Cocky son's going to bring that ship in."

If Goldtooth and the humans have stopped short and the kif pass them by in hyperspace, we could get hit here.

Hilfy and Haral have got it figured. All of us do.

If Akkhtimakt's set up to dive in here again—an attack could be poised at system's edge right now. Or already inbound. Not saying whether the kif are onto that trick of stopping a jump. They could well have it. Maybe and maybe. It's not saying all their ships can do it.

"Transmit," she said. "Honor to the *hakkikt:* beware system edges. I fear more than spotters."

"Done," Hilfy said.

We help the bastard we're with. While we're with him.

We take whatever they want to do. And maintain our options. Ehrran's lost all hers. We got hani on that station and gods know how many fluttering stsho. Keep a cool head, Pyanfar Chanur. It's by the gods all the chance you've got.

"We're getting docking instructions," Hilfy murmured finally. They turned up on screen, where kifish ships were already well toward touch with station.

And from Chur, plaintively over com:

"What in a mahen hell's going on?"

"Easy," Geran said. "It's all all right."

"Got crew falling on their noses tired," Pyanfar muttered. "Haral, keep it steady, standard dock. Tirun, get yourself below, take the rest of your break."

"Aye," Tirun said. Old spacer. *And* falling-down tired. A belt snicked. Tirun went away in silence, to food, sleep, anything she could get.

"Jik's requesting to be out," Khym said. So that voice had vanished off com. Khym had silenced him. A mahen hunter captain, locked in a lowerdecks cabin and probably trying to think how to shortcircuit the latch or take the door apart.

"Jik," she said, cutting in on that blinking light on her com section. "We're all right. F'godssakes, be patient, get some rest, we've got our hands full, you got our scan image. We're moving in on dock and that's all that's going on for a while."

"Pyanfar." The voice was calm, quiet, reasoning. *"I understand. I make problem, a? You got protect you crew. I make 'pology. I lot embarrass', Pyanfar. Long time with kif make me crazy. Now I got time think —I know what you do. We be long time ally. We be friends, Pyanfar. Same interest. You unlock door, a?"*

"I tell you there's nothing you can do up here. You got awhile to rest, Jik. Take it. You may need it."

"*Pyanfar.*" Thump. Impact of a hand near the pickup. Hard. So much for patience. "*You in damn deep water. Hear? Deep water!*"

"We got another expression." She flattened her ears, lifted them again. "Told you. After we dock. We got enough troubles, friend. I want your advice, but I got enough to deal with right now."

"*It be war,*" Jik said, and sent a chill up her back. War was a groundling word. "*Fool hani! The ships go, they go ever' damn place, not got stop, not got stop!*"

"F'godssake, this is open *space!* This is the Compact, we're not talking about some backwater land-quarrel!"

"*No. No harus. New kind thing. Not with rule. We talk 'bout make fight all kif, all hani, all mahendo'sat, make ally, make strike here, strike there. This new kind word. Not like clan and clan. Not like go council. Here we got no council. War, Pyanfar, all devils in hell got no word this thing I see.*"

Colder and colder.

"I see it too. So what are the mahendo'sat going to do about it? What *have* they done about it? Play games with the kif til we got 'em all at each others' throats? Shove Akkhtimakt off toward hani space? My world? How'm I supposed to be worried about you and yours, rot your conniving hide, when you doublecrossed my whole *species!* You doublecrossed the stsho, f'godssakes, and *that* takes fast dealing! You doublecrossed the tc'a, gods help us, you doublecrossed them and the chi and maybe the knnn!"

"*We got humans. We got humans, Pyanfar. Same got hunter-ships, got way shove these bastard* back *from out hani territory, you got listen, Pyanfar. Pyanfar, I got timetable!*"

Her finger was on the cutoff, claw half-extruded. She retracted it.

"*Do* you? Way I hear, you got something else too. Like a fancy new maneuver your ships do, just like humans."

Silence from belowdecks then. Profound silence. Then: "*Open this door, Pyanfar.*"

"At dock."

"*Soshethi-sa! Soshethi-ma hase mafeu!*"

Thump.

She cut him off. Looked Haral's way. Haral studiously lowered her ears. "Not too happy," Haral said. "*Timetable.* What's he mean?"

"By the gods I bet there's one. At our expense. Mahen gifts. 'Got a present for you.' Jik, turning up at Kshshti. Us, miraculously getting our papers cleared so we could turn up back here."

"I'd sure like to know what was in that packet Banny took on, I tell you that."

"Eggs to pearls that Jik slipped something into it. Goldtooth's version, I got a copy on. The stuff that didn't take a translator to dupe, at least. Which won't be the sensitive stuff. But anything might be helpful. Downgrade the nav functions: we'll run that packet of his with the decoder."

"I'll start it," Hilfy said. "My four."

She keyed the access up and sent the packet over, while *The Pride* started freeing up computer space.

Jik had held out on Sikkukkut. And on her. It was certain that he had. He had been dead silent on that gibe about mahen ship capabilities.

The archive in question blinked into Hilfy's reach.

And they slipped closer and closer to dock.

"Might have some lurker outsystem," Hilfy said. "I've been thinking about that. Might have a strike here most any time."

"Cheerful," Geran said. That sounded almost normal, crew bickering and muttering from station to station.

"Station's on," Hilfy said. "Docking calc."

"That's got it," Haral said, and sucked them into nav. "Auto?"

"Might as well. Nothing problematical here." Pyanfar sat and gnawed her mustaches, gnawed a hangnail on her third finger. Spat. "Hilfy: send to all hani at dock, hani-language, quote: *The Pride of Chanur* to all hani at dock: we are coming in at berths 27, 28, 29 consecutive. Salutations to all allies: by hearth and blood we take your parole to assure your security. *Industry,* salutations to your captain in Ruharun's name: we share an ancestor. Let's keep it quiet, shall we? End."

"Got that," Hilfy said.

Haral gave her a look steady and sober, ears back-canted. "Think the kif read poetry?"

"Gods, I hope not."

Five decades ago. Dayschool and literature. When she had ten times rather be at her math. *Stand and recite, Pyanfar.*

"I hope to the gods this younger generation does."

> *On a winter's eve came Ruharan to her gates*
> *beneath black flight of birds in snowy court.*

*White scarf flutters in the wind, red feather
the fletch of arrows standing still in posts
about the yard and the holy shrine where stands
among a hundred enemies her own lord,
no prisoner but of her enemies foremost
seeming. But Ruharun knew her husband
a man with woman's wit and woman's
    staunchness.
So she cast down her bow and spilled out the
    arrows,
on blood-spattered snow cast down defense,
bowed her head to enemies and to fortune. . . .*

"*Industry* answers," Hilfy said. "Quote: *We got that. 27, 28, 29. We have another kinswoman here in Munur Faha. Greetings from her. We are at your orders.*"

"Gods look on them." Pyanfar drew a large breath. Message received, covered and tossed back again under kifish noses. Munur Faha of *Starwind* was kin to Chanur. But not to Harun. Harun had no ties of any kind.

And Faha had a bloodfeud with Tahar of *Moon Rising*.

A small chill went down her back. It was response to her own coded hail. It was just as likely subtle warning and question, singling out Faha for salutations: strange company you keep, Pyanfar Chanur, a mahen hunter, a kifish prince, and a pirate. The Faha-Tahar feud was famous and bitter.

At your orders, smooth and silky. It was kifish subservience, never hani; it was humor, bleak and black and thoroughly spacer. *Let's play the game, hani. You and your odd friends. Let's see where it leads.*

It took a mental shift, gods help her, to think hani-fashion again, and to know the motives of her own kind. Like crossing a gulf she had been on the other side of so long that hani were as strange as the stsho.

"Reply: See you on my deck immediately."

Grapples took. *The Pride*'s G-sense shifted, readjusted itself. Other connections clanged and thumped into seal. They were not the first ship in. *Ikkhoitr* and *Chakkuf* crews were already on the docks. *Harukk* was in final. But no kif came to help non-kif ships dock. Pointedly, they handled their own and no others. They were *Industry* crewwomen risking their necks out there on the other side of that wall.

"I've got business," Pyanfar said, and unclipped the safeties.

"Aye," Haral said. "Routine shutdowns, captain. Go."

She got out of the chair and saw worried looks come her way. Tully's pale face was thin-lipped and large about the eyes, the way it got in Situations.

Thinking, O gods, yes, that this might be the end of his own journey, on a station where the kif had won everything that he had set out to take; and where humans were still a question of interest to Sikkukkut an'nikktukktin. He had reason to worry. The same as Jik did.

Queries were coming in, com from *Moon Rising* as it docked, operational chatter. *Aja Jin* was a minute away from touch.

Still playing the game, Kesurinan trusting that her captain was consenting to this long silence.

"Stay to stations," she said to all and sundry. "Khym, monitor lowerdecks."

"You going down there with him?" He looked at her with his ears down, the one with its brand new ring.

She flattened her own. He turned around again without a word. "Tirun's down there," she said to his back and Tully's face and Skkukuk's earnest attention.

I would go, hakt', that kifish stare said. *Tear the throat out of this mahendo'sat, I would, most eagerly, mekt'hakt'.*

"Huh." She made sure of the gun in her pocket and walked on out, wobbly in the knees and still with the sensation that *G* was shifting. She felt down in her pocket, remembering a packet of concentrates, and drank it in the lift, downbound.

The salty flood hit her stomach and gave it some comfort. Panic killed an appetite. Even when panic had gotten to be a lifestyle and a body was straight out of jump. She ate because the body said so. And tried not to think about the aftertaste.

Or the ships around them, or the situation out there on the docks.

Jik was on the bed, lying back with his head on his arms. He propped himself up as the door opened, his small ears flat, a scowl on his face.

" 'Bout time."

"I'm here to talk with you." She walked in and let the door close behind her. His ears flicked and he gathered himself up to sit on the edge of the bed, with a careful hitch at his kilt.

"You been listening to ops?"

"A." Stupid question. But an opening one. He drew a large breath.

"You do damn fine job, Pyanfar. We sit at station, same like stsho. We got kif go blow Compact to hell. *Now* what do?"

"What do you want? Run out of here? I got hani ships here, I got ten thousand kif on their way to Urtur, right where you wanted 'em, gods rot you."

"Listen me. Better you listen me now."

"Down the Kura corridor. Isn't that the idea?"

"He be kif, not make connection you with these hani. They got be smart, save neck all themselves—Better you do own business. You don't panic, Pyanfar. Don't think like damn groundling! Don't risk you life save these hani. You get them killed, you make damn mess!"

She laid her ears back. "I got kifish ships headed at my homeworld, Jik. What am I supposed to do, huh? Ignore that?"

"Same me." Muscles stood out on Jik's shoulders, his fists clenched. "You let kif make you plan for you? They shove, you go predict-able direction? Damn stupid, damn *stupid,* Pyanfar! You lock me up, take kif advice now? You let be pushed where this bastard want?"

"And where does that leave my world, huh? I got one world, Jik. I got one place where there's enough of my species to survive. Hani men don't go to space, they're all on Anuurn. What in a mahen hell am I supposed to do, play your side and lose my whole species? They got us, Jik, they got us cornered, don't talk to me about casualties, don't talk to me about any world and any lot of lives being equal, they're not. We're talking about my whole by the gods species, Jik, and if I had to blow every hani out there and three hundred thousand stsho to do something about it, I'd do it, and throw the mahendo'sat onto the pile while it burned, by the gods I would!"

The whites showed at the corners of his eyes. Ears were still back, the hands still clenched.

"Why you here?"

"Because," she said, "two freighters and a hunter can't stop it. Because there's a chance I can turn Sikkukkut to do what I can't. Now you tell me about timetables. You tell me about it, Jik, and you tell me all of it, your ship caps included!"

He sat silent a moment. "You got trust."

"Trust. In a mahen hell, Jik. Tell me the truth. I'm out of trust."

"I got interests I protect."

"No." She walked closer, held up a forefinger and kept the claw sheathed with greatest restraint. "This time you trust *me.* This time you give me everything you've got. You tell me. Everything."

"Pyanfar. Kif going to take you 'board *Harukk.* They try question me, I don't talk. My gover'ment, they make fix—" He tapped the side of his head. "I can't talk. Can't be force'. You whole 'nother deal. They shred you fast. Know ever'thing. They know you got me 'board, a? Know you got chance make me talk. Maybe they give me to you for same reason—they can't, maybe Pyanfar can do, a? Maybe block don't work when you ask, I tell you ever'thing like damn fool."

"*Can* you tell me? Can what they did to you, can what your Personage did to you—make you lie to me, even when you don't want to?"

A visible shiver came over him. Hands jerked. "I ask not do."

"Jik—you got to trust me. However they messed you up. Jik, if it kills you, I got to ask. *What timetable?*"

The tremor went through all his limbs. He hugged his arms against himself as if the room had gone freezing. And stared her in the eyes. "Fourteen," he said past chattering teeth. "Eighteen. Twenty. Twenty-four—First. Seventh." Another spasm. "This month. Next. Next. We g-got maneuver—make jump coordinate with same."

"You mean your moves are aimed at certain points at certain dates?"

"Where got th-threat. Don't fight. Move back. Make 'nother jump-point on focus date."

"So that somewhere, tracking the kif, your hunters are going to coincide and home in on them."

"Co-in-cide. A." He made a gesture with shaking hands. "More complicate', Pyanfar. We push. We pull. We make kif fight kif. We make kif go toward Urtur, toward Kita."

"Toward Anuurn!"

"Got—got help go there. Back side. We not betray you, Pyanfar!"

Her legs went weak. She sank down where she was, on her haunches, looking up at a shaken mahendo'sat on the edge of the bed. "You swear that."

"God witness. Truth, Pyanfar. You got help." The hands clenched again. "Ana—me *Aja Jin.* He got chance. Got *chance,* damn! and he run out from this place, leave us in damn mess! Got 'nother plan. He got 'nother plan, got way push kif on kif, damn conservative."

"Or he suspects deep down his human allies aren't to be trusted. What if he knows that? What would he do?"

"He be damn worried. Same got worry with tc'a." Another convulsive shiver. Jik wiped his face, where it glistened with sweat. "He maybe listen to me too much. Take my advice. I come into his section of space. He damn surprise' see me at Kefk. I tell him—I tell him we got save this kif, make number one. True. He be confuse', he pull out." He slammed his hand onto the bed beside him. "I don't send code. You understand. I not on *Aja Jin,* I don't send code, he don't attack!"

"Kesurinan doesn't know all this."

"I not dead. She got file to read if I be dead, but I be on friendly ship, a? She take you instruction, she think I be on bridge—She not know. She don't send the damn code and Ana don't move on this kif!"

There was sickness at her stomach all over again. She stared up at him. *And have you told me the truth even yet, old friend, my true friend? Or have you only found a lie that'll keep me moving in the direction you want? Or are you giving me the only truth you've been brainwashed into believing? Would they do that to you, your own people?*

Would they stick at that, when they got into your mind to do other things?

Gods save us, I almost trust the kif more.

"The kif would have blown us, Jik, before we could help anybody. We could've lost it all. I don't think it would've worked. We still got a chance, don't we? Where's our next rendezvous point? When?"

"Kita. Eighteenth next month."

"Can't make it. Give me the next *we* could reach. Or is it *here?* Is Goldtooth just waiting a signal?"

"Two month. Twenty-fourth. Urtur. You got. Maybe be there. Maybe not. We got now six, seven ship go out from here."

And a single incoming ship at extremely high *V* had a killing advantage. If it turned out to have position as well, its high velocity fire could rip slower ships to ribbons.

"When's Goldtooth come back?"

"I not say he come back. Don't know what he do. *Not get damn signal!*"

"Gods-be *lie,* Jik, you got to coordinate this somehow. You know what he's going to do. My information says he can short-jump and turn. That maybe all those ships can. Is it *here,* Jik? Is Meetpoint the place we have to be? Was that message he didn't get from Kesurinan—aimed to catch him a few days, a few hours out from this system, was *that* it?"

Terror. Never before in Jik. Raw fear.

"Scared I'll tell the *hakkikt?* Scared I guess too much?" She was sitting vulnerable and too close. She stood up and looked down at him, mindful of the gun in her pocket. "Scared they'll get it out of me?"

"You damn fool."

"I want your help. You want mine. You want to figure your chances without the hani? If it was you and nothing else, alone with the kif, with three human governments all doublecrossing each other, and the tc'a and the chi, gods help us, running lunatic? You refigure it, Jik, hear? You got some authority of your own. You got authority to take up a Situation and settle it, I got that figured. And I'm giving you a Situation. I'm giving you the fact we got this bastard going to take my species out, going to kill all of us, which loses you an ally, which loses you a major market, doesn't it, which loses you *friends,* about the time you need 'em most, you and your Personage. Humans aren't half your trouble. *I* am. The *han* is. And you don't give me orders. *I* got the influence, *I* got the thing in hand, and all of a sudden I'm dealing with a threat to my *planet,* Jik, which means I'll do any gods-be thing I got to and I'm not kiting off in any gods-be direction you want. I got *one* direction. And you got no choice but my choice, because I'll shoot you down before I let you do something that'll stop me. I love you like kin and I'll shoot you with my own hand, you hear me, mahe? Or you help me and give me the truth at all the right spots and maybe you still got an ally left."

Muscles were still clenched. Hard. He took a long time. "Got," he said finally. "You open door, a?"

"No deal. *Not* your terms, you hear?"

He stood up, gave the kilt a hitch, and stared down at her. Made a sudden move of his hand, a strike. She skipped back, ears flat.

"First thing," he said, "you got learn not trust ever' bastard got deal. You damn fine trader. But kif not be merchant."

"Neither are you. I'm proposing something else. I'm telling you you're not going to break my neck because you got more sense."

"You got right," he said, and sniffed and drew a large breath. The fine wrinkles round his eyes drew and relaxed and drew again in an expression very like Tully's. "Love you like kin. Same. Got tell you you going to bleed." He touched his heart. "Same you win, same you lose. You number one fine woman. Got lot haoti-ma. Lot. I make deal, honest. You get me smoke, I give you whole timetable."

"You gods-be lunatic."

"Sikkukkut not only source. You got whole station. You got ask *Aja Jin.* Same bring."

"Drug's scrambled your brains."

A little light danced in his eyes. "You want me stay 'board, you got find me smoke. I be number one fine pilot. Same better when I got relax. You maybe need. You, Haral, you number one too. Not too many."

"What are you talking about?"

"Same you." He gave another hitch at the kilt. He had lost weight. "You got deal." More wrinkles round the eyes, a grimace. "My Personage damn me to hell. Same be old territory for me. You want me, you got. Long as Sikkukkut not got us all. You got trade sharp, hani. Number one sharp. This be hard deal. Maybe he take me. Maybe take you: you got no knowledge. You want plan you got get me back. Safe."

"He hasn't asked for you."

"He do. You wait, see. *Know* this kif."

"How's your nerves?"

"You not forget get smoke, a? Same time you get me out."

"Captain," Hilfy said over com. *"Harukk's coming in right now. They're insisting to pick up all the captains. With appropriate escorts. They want Jik and Tully too."*

Jik lifted his brows. "See?"

"Gods rot that kif." But she thought: *He could strip every ship here of its senior command. Couldn't he? Me. Dur Tahar. That'd leave Haral Araun, but he doesn't know her that well.*

I need an escort. Not Haral. Gods, I can't take Haral off this ship.

Not one of my crew. Just my translator.

"Hilfy. Tell Skkukuk he's going with us. No other but the ones they asked for. Send my gear down here. Send an AP for Jik too. We got a point to prove."

Gods send the rest of the captains have got some sense.

Gods send they understand old epics.

"Aye," Hilfy said after a second. *"Captain. Tahar's here. We got others coming. Haral asks: let 'em through?"*

Not happy. No. Sikkukkut's not going to like this.

And, no, niece, I'm not crazy.

I just got no choice.

The lift worked. That was Tully coming down. Or the kif. She walked along the corridor with Jik for company, spotted Tirun coming the other way about the time the lock cycled with its characteristic whine and thump and let someone into the ship.

That and a cold lot of air with the smell of Meetpoint about it. Nostalgia hit, and left an ache after it. Old times and rotten ones, but that smell was familiar in a mundane way that made the present only worse by comparison.

Tully and Skkukuk arrived together, Skkukuk a-clatter with weapons, his own and what he had gathered on Kef'k dock: maybe, she reflected dourly, it was sentiment.

Tully had her gun slung over his shoulder, and an AP at his hip: that took no claws to operate—shove in the shells and pull the trigger. He was steady and able to use it. He had proved that at Kef'k.

And from the airlock corridor, Dur Tahar arrived with Soje Kesurinan.

Pyanfar drew in a large breath.

So how stop her? If hani were going to hold a meeting under the *hakkikt*'s nose, what stopped Kesurinan from joining it?

And what stopped Jik now from joining her?

"We got a problem here," she muttered. "Jik, don't you do it."

"Lo," he said, "Soje. Shoshe-mi."

"Shoshe," Kesurinan said. And something else, in dialect.

While other figures came down the white corridor, several hani-bright and equipped with weapons. And one dark and tall—as a foreign kif walked right into *The Pride*'s lowerdecks.

Countermove.

Do what, Pyanfar? Throw it out? This is a friendly *conference we're going to, that's likely Ikkhoitr crew, and that bastard's one of Sikkuk-kut's own special pets.*

Her heart set to beating doubletime. *Fool. Twice a fool. Do what? Do what now?*

"Gods be," Hilfy muttered, "we got Kesurinan and a kif past that lock. Gods *rot!* Haral—"

"I'm on it, I'm on it." Haral's voice rumbled with vexation. They were observing from the bridge. It was all they could do.

"I'll go down there," Khym said, a deeper, more ominous rumble.

"Easy, easy, stay put, the captain's handling this. Let's don't make it worse."

And from the com: "Pride of Chanur, *this is* Vrossauru's Out-bounder, *our captain should be arriving at your lock. Please confirm.*"

"Affirm that, *Outbounder.* No difficulties." With more confidence than she felt.

"I've got the lift under bridge control," Haral said. "We're sealed up here. They're not going to try anything on us, I don't think."

"Faha's going to be gnawing sticks with Tahar in reach," Hilfy said.

"At least they're not siding with Ehrran," Geran said.

"Spacers," Haral said. "You want to bet young black-breeches stopped to consult these crews before she kited on out of here? They've had their backsides to the fire here, and it's sure she didn't help their case."

It made sense. That the hani insystem had not fled meant that they had not had the chance; there was, gods knew, no profit in this crisis for a trader.

Now the resident hani had a further insanity to contemplate: kif in control of the station; and with those kif a mahen hunter-ship, and with them, Tahar and Chanur, who were blood enemies to each other.

But if these ships had been stuck at Meetpoint through all the troubles, they must be used to lunacies.

"Pride of Chanur," com said, *"this is* Faha's Starwind. *Request explanation at your leisure. Standby signal for tight-beam."*

Cagy old spacer, playing it very careful. Lifetime of experience with the kif. And taking a bigger risk than she knew.

"Starwind, this is *The Pride,* stand by your query." The board signaled acquisition of the impulse against *The Pride's* receptor-dish, and confirmed their own pulse sent back; all discreet and hope to the gods the kif did not pick up that furtive exchange. "Haral, we got a ship-to-ship—"

"Break it," Haral said, and Hilfy shut down at once, thwarting the contact. Then over a station-system relay Haral appropriated: "This is Haral Araun, duty officer, *The Pride of Chanur:* all com will go on station relay. The *mekt-hakkikt* Sikkukkut an'nikktukktin is an ally, and beyond that we aren't authorized to say anything—is that Junury I'm talking to?"

"Gods-be right it is. Haral, what in a mahen hell is going on between you and Ehrran? Can you at least answer me that one?"

"Bloodfeud, that's what's going on. Which is no part of anything going on in this system, excepting some deals with the stsho. Excepting deals in the *han.* I'll fill you in on it later. Junury, anyone else who's listening: we've been doubledealt in the *han,* every spacer clan's been done up inside and out by a few gods-be graynosed groundling bastards with full pockets. We had bloodfeud with Tahar; we paid that out; gods know Tahar's paid in blood. Right now I got a cousin lying gut-shot from back at Kshshti thanks to Ehrran and thanks to that bastard Akkhtimakt, and we got trouble loose that we got to settle—we got *hani* interests at stake, like we never had. And thank the gods you stayed, Junury. Thank the gods, is what I say: we can use the help, and

I don't know if you'd have gotten through the way you were headed. Hear me?"

A long pause. *"I hear. I hear you, Haral Araun."*

For Haral it was outright eloquence. Hilfy drew a long breath when Haral did; and tried to think whether Haral had shot any messages into it between the lines—nothing but *caution, caution, caution, we're being monitored,* was what she heard.

"Starwind," Transmission came from another source, *"this is* Moon Rising. *Our captain's gone same as yours. We're under parole to Chanur. We'll stand trial. Araun's too polite. We're coming in for that. We haven't got a choice. So we surrendered. We're still armed and we're under Chanur's direction. End statement."*

Transmissions ceased. Discreetly.

Hilfy switched back in on the intercom channel Khym was on, leaned back in her chair and tried not to think at all. She worked her hand and extended claws and tried to keep her ears up and her expression matter-of-fact as Tirun's down the row, while Khym *nef* Mahn sat there beside her with a new-won ring in his ear—a man, with a spacer's ring; with his scarred face grim and glowering at the trouble belowdecks, and the certainty Pyanfar was bound for the kif.

What kept him in that chair and what kept the pressure-seal on that temper of his gods alone knew; Hilfy felt his presence at her right like boding storm, like something ready to erupt, but which never did.

"Fry Ehrran," Khym muttered to himself. "Gods-be Immune. I *want* a few of them."

Khym *nef* Mahn was not a swearing man. Hilfy turned a second misgiving look his way and saw the set of his face and his ears, which was a male on the edge. With not an enemy in reach.

"Health," Pyanfar murmured—other salutations had loaded connotations in main-kifish. As more of the captains walked in on *The Pride*'s lower deck and joined the conference. With one of Sikkukkut's kif to witness. Her own kif took up a wary stance with rifle in hands. Prudent; and ignorant and naive in his own kifish way, gods knew. "It's all right," she said in pidgin, and in hani: "Kerin, hau mauru." *Clanswomen, there's no worry.* "Haaru sasfynurhy aur?" *Everyone understand the pidgin?* She gave a meaningful glance up and about the edges of the ceiling. *We're being monitored. So you know.* "This is Tully. And *na* Jik. Nomesteturjai. And his first officer Kesurinan." No need for more than that. Since Gaohn, *Aja Jin* was famous among hani. Ears were up in respect, among these armed and vari-shaded hani, who came from every continent of Anuurn, mostly graynoses like Kaurufy Harun with younger escorts; Munur Faha being the exception, a red-gold smallish young woman with a graynosed and scarred old cargo officer beside her: that was Sura Faha, and a good and a steady old hand she was.

She knew most of them from docksides from one side of the Compact to the other, and the sight of familiar faces ought to have been a comfort. It was a mortal jolt, that sense of disconnection, how far she had come from civilization; it was like looking at it all through a window.

And Dur Tahar stood there to complicate it all, in a company that had individually and severally sworn to have her piratical hide, and carrying a heavier complement of weaponry than the rest of the captains, whose sidearms were all legal in the Compact.

"This is Skkukuk," she had to say atop everything else, smooth and never stopping, with a gesture to her left hand. "He's mine. *Sha mhifÿ- shau.*"

My vassal-man. She bent the language to make a word that had never existed: and called a kif a man, into the bargain, because so far as she could figure, he was not female. *Mhifÿ* was a word for a woman who came to link herself to a more powerful clan. Women could do that. Men just fought their way in, with their lives at risk and in the greatest likelihood of being driven off by the clanswomen before they ever got as far as challenging their lord for his place. Male vassal, indeed. Ears flicked and flattened all around the room; and frowns grew darker.

"He was a present," she said. "The *hakkikt,* praise to him—" Another glance aloft: *we're not alone, friends—* "I couldn't explain anything when I sent that message out; but we've got a delicate situation in progress here. I'll be honest with you: the *han* has signed some kind of treaty with the stsho; Rhif Ehrran may have been carrying it—she came through here. She may not have stopped."

"Didn't," said Kauryfy, and drew a large breath, setting her hands in her belt. "But she blasted out a warning." Kauryfy's ears went all but flat, lifted, flattened again nervously. "Said there were kif coming; and us up to our ears in aliens. Godsrotted late news. We got caught here—I gather this *hakkikt* isn't friendly with the other one."

"You might say." She flicked her own ears. *Careful, Kauryfy. You're no fool; don't begin now. Watch the mouth.* "Glad to see us, were you?"

"Crazy around here. Gods-be aliens. Mahendo'sat feuding with the kif. Stsho Phasing all over the place. Never know who you're dealing with from one hour to the next. Gods know who's maintaining station's lifesupport. This Akkhtimakt—not a friend of yours?"

"No."

"Well, none of ours either. A rotted mess, that's what we've had here. Got stuck here with Urtur shut down, just kept running up dock charges and mortgaging our hides with the gods-be stsho, and everything going crazy—Five months, five *months* we've been stuck in this godsforedoomed lunatic port, Chanur! Then we get the kif. Came in all peaceful, and us knowing, by the gods, *knowing* what he'd done over by Urtur, and these godsrotted fool stsho putting it out over the com that they'd asked him in, that it was all treaty—"

"It was. Treaty with the *han* and faceabout, treaty with Akkhtimakt. All to save them from humanity."

"Well, they got a gods-be poor bargain."

"You got stuck here."

"We got stuck here. That son moved in and interdicted traffic, got himself onto the station and did about what you'd figure. We went along with him while it looked like everything was going to be blown to a mahen hell and then the mahendo'sat showed and the humans came in and the kif cleared the station, we just sat still and hoped to all the gods it wasn't our problem. Now it is, I'm figuring."

Kauryfy's face underwent subtle changes, the tightening of her nose, the slight and timely tightening of a muscle by one ear—a wealth of signals a kif might miss. *I'm trusting you only halfway; and there's a lot I'm not going to say out loud.*

"Yes," Pyanfar said, with a like set of signals back again, and thrust her hands into her belt. *So humans arrived here out of the dark. Couldn't be a coincidence of timing. They were short-jumped and parked out there. By the gods they were waiting. Goldtooth knew they would be.* "It *is* our problem. The whole Compact's coming apart, and the *han's* policy has got us in a mess. I need you. Hear? Never mind the aliens. The *hakkikt* is going to ask you where you stand. And I'm telling you: we've never been worse off than we are right now. You can believe me or you can believe Ehrran; that's the sum of it. I'm trusting she messaged you more than just the news. Must've had plenty to say about us."

There was prolonged silence. Ears moved, flattened, halfway lifted.

"It got here," Munur Faha said. "We got it from the Stsho and we got it when she kited through. Urtur-bound."

"Gods fry her," Tirun said.

"There's a real strong reason," Pyanfar said, "she doesn't want to see us again. That's a *han* matter. Meanwhile we've our own business to tend to. Yours and ours. Very critical business."

"Specifically?" Kauryfy said.

"Settling things among ourselves. This isn't over. Far from it. I want you to take my orders."

Kauryfy's pupils did a quick tightening and re-dilating. Her mustaches drew down. "Known each other a few years, haven't we?"

"There was Hoas."

Kif dust-up, back in the small-time pirate days. Another flicker of Kauryfy's eyes.

"Yeah," Kauryfy said, and looked from her to the kifish shadow that stood at her back; and back again. "Well, we got along then."

"I'll go with it," said Haurnar Vrossaru, in her deep northlands accent.

"Same," said Haroury Pauran, dark as some mahendo'sat, and with one blue eye and one gold. She thrust her hands into her belt and scowled, looked aside at young Munur Faha, who sullenly lowered and lifted her ears: "Aye," said Munur. She was Hilfy's cousin, remote. "I'm with you."

That left two. Vaury Shaurnurn gnawed at her mustaches and turned her shoulder to the lot of them: the other (that would be Tauran, by elimination, of *The Star of Tauran*) turned and looked Shaurnurn's way. And then Tahar's.

"Kin of ours died at Gaohn," said Tauran.

"Here is here," Tahar said.

And: "Kkkkt," from Skkukuk, who had antennae for trouble. That long jaw lifted. So did the gun. And the other kif stiffened.

"Pasiry died at Gaohn. Your allies shot her in the gut. She bled to death while we were pinned down."

"Here is here," Pyanfar said. "Argue it later. For godsake, *ker* Vaury. I'll tell it to you later, where we got Tahar. Right now we've got an appointment. An important one. In Ruharun's name, cousin."

They were not kin either. Far from it. Vaury Shaurnurn looked her way with ears flat. *Cousin. Listen to me,* ker *Vaury. Believe nothing I say, do everything I say, make no false moves. Cousin.*

She stared Vaury Shaurnurn dead in the eyes and thought that thought as hard as she could. Vaury's ears lowered and lifted again. "Cousin," Vaury said ever so deliberately. "We've been in and out of the same places, haven't we? Never been other than courteous with me; all right. That's all I'll say. All right." Vaury gave a glance at Tully, up and down. "This the same one?" The glance lingered at the AP at Tully's hip and traveled up again to his face. "Same human as at Gaohn?"

"Tully," Pyanfar said. "Yes." She looked aside to the stranger-kif. "Who this visitor of ours is, is another matter. *Ikkhoitr* crew, I'm thinking."

"Ikkhoitru-hakt'."

"Captain." The hair bristled down her back. "Honored, we are. I'll trust your people are going to escort us over to *Harukk.*"

Ikkhoitr's captain turned and stalked down the hall in that direction, kifish-economical. And without hani courtesy.

"Kkkkt," Skkukuk said, warning.

It was not friendly, that captain's move. He was, kifish-like, on the push, looking for chinks and advantages; and one little lapse into hani courtesies had achieved unintended irony. She had ordered him.

She had invoked the *hakkikt.* And being kif, he dared not demur or hesitate. She had scored on him, who had come in here looking for fault, fluent and deadly dangerous.

Gods hope he had failed to find it. Or that kif did not have the habit of lying in certain regards.

"Skkukuk says watch him," she muttered to the others. "Tirun, you stay aboard. Hear?"

Tirun did not like it. But crew did not argue these days. Not in front of kif, even their own.

The personnel lock cycled, letting the party out. And closed again, audible from the bridge over the steady bleep and tick of incoming telemetry and com. "That's seal," Haral said to Tirun belowdecks. "Get up here."

"Station com's still gibbering," Hilfy said. "Gods-be stsho're going crazy. I can't make out anything except how glad they are to have the noble *hakkikt* back a—" She blinked, as Geran suddenly turned her head, and blinked again, seeing Chur wobbling into the bridge, Chur without her rings and dressed in a towel, the implant still in her arm and secured with tape. Her mane and beard were dull, her fur thin in pink spots where skin showed through, and her ribs showed prominent above a hollowed belly.

"Geran—" Hilfy said, but Geran had already grabbed her.

Haral turned her chair and took a look. "Geran, for godssakes—"

"Got to walk a bit," Chur said, the merest ghost of Chur's voice, but she passed a glance around at monitors and displays. "Got a mess, do we? Lock working down there—Y'don't expect a body to sleep. Geran, set me down, I've got to sit. Who's covering you?"

"He is." Meaning Khym. "Sit."

"You're an emergency," Haral said. "Gods rot it, *sit down."* As Chur wilted onto Skkukuk's seat. "We're up to our noses. Could have an attack from gods know who come screaming through here any minute, we got to be able to move, how do we move with you wandering around?"

Chur gave a ghastly grin. "Hal, cousin, if we've got to move without the captain, I'm sitting a chair, no way I'm not. What in a mahen hell is going on out there?"

"The captain aboard *Harukk* is what's going on out there. We got kifish guns to our heads and gods know what else about to come in here for a piece of stsho hide."

"Figured." Chur drew a large breath as if breathing was hard. "Gods take 'em. What's our cousin up to?"

"Sfik," Hilfy said. "She's got three species for an escort and a half-dozen hani captains following her moves. She's running the biggest gods-be bluff of our lives, that's what she's doing. Trying to buy us time."

"If we got two hani walking sequential it'll be the first time since we went on two feet." Chur leaned her head back on the headrest and rolled it aside to look at the displays. "Not mentioning the mahen-do'sat." Her breath was coming harder, and for a moment Hilfy tensed in her chair, thinking she might go unconscious; but Geran had Chur's shoulder, and Chur got her head up again. "Haral, I want a pocket com and I want ops-com run back there to my cabin. All right?"

"You got it," Haral said. "Geran, get her out of here."

"Hilfy," Khym said, "you want to cover me?" —preparing to get out of his seat and help. But: "I'm doing all right," Chur said, and caught hold of the arm and levered herself up like an old woman, where Geran could steady her. Then she walked, slowly, slowly, back the way she had come, past a startled Tirun Araun, just arrived up from lowerdecks.

"What's that?" Tirun asked when she and Geran were out and down the corridor. With a look backward. "She all right?"

"Wants to know what's going on," Khym said. "She's fighting."

"She's got her way again," Haral said in the same low tone. "Too." And swung her chair back around.

"Priority," Khym said suddenly, which set a lurch into Hilfy's pulse.

"Scan-blocking," Tirun said, slipping into place while Hilfy cast an anxious look at the scan display on her number-two monitor. A vanished ship reestablished itself in the red of projected-position. One by one other ships went red, the blight spreading in an orderly way. Then:

"That's friendly of them," Haral murmured as their own position at station vanished from the other display. "At least they're catholic when they blank the scan."

The ramp access doors opened, above the once-teeming docks: deserted now, mostly. Bits of paper. Trash. Abandoned machinery. Burn-scars on the paints. And cold, which the Meetpoint docks always were, too much size and too little free heat from the dull, dead Mass about which the station orbited. There were abundant kif—not far away, black shapes in robes. *Skkukun*, likely, quasi-slaves on *Ikkhoitr*. Expendables and dangerous as a charged cable.

And there were stsho, fragile-looking pale figures huddled over against the far side of their own docks, scurrying like pale ghosts, out of doorways and shelter, the dispossessed owners of Meetpoint. A mass of them surged toward the foot of the ramp, indecisively retreated, bolted again toward them in utter chaos, a crowd all spindle-limbed and gossa-mer-robed in opalescent whites and pearl, stsho of rank, with their feathery, augmented brows, their moonstone eyes struck with panic. They gibbered and wailed their plaints, their effusive pleas for protection—

And they came to one collective and horrified halt, and gasped and chittered for dread. Of the kif, perhaps.

Or perhaps it was the first sight of Tully that did it.

"Stay close," Pyanfar muttered to Tully. "Not friends."

"Got," he said under his breath. And kept close at her elbow as they descended, Jik trailing behind her; and Tahar; and Harun and all the rest. Kif waiting below formed a black wedge as they went down into that mass of stsho, and the stsho gave way before that like leaves before a wind, gibbering as they went, down a dock on which many of the lighted signs, indicating ships at dock, showed stsho names. Too timid to break dock, helpless in the advent of armed ships sweeping in out of Kefk inbound vector, which was unhappily also the outbound vector for the nearest stsho port, at Nsthen—they could do nothing in their unweaponed state but cower and wait, while their appointed kifish defenders did the smart thing and ran like the devils of a mahen hell were on their heels.

"Lousy mess," Pyanfar said; and hitched the rifle she carried to a more conspicuous attitude, while they walked along an aisle of kif with *Ikkhoitr*'s black-robed captain, and stsho retreated and stared at them from concealment with terrified, moonstone eyes.

Then a kifish name showed in lights above a berth: and the ramp of *Harukk* gaped for them.

She hitched her gunbelt up and tried to calm her stomach. Her nose had begun to prickle and she searched after another pill in her pocket, never minding the timelapse. Metabolism did peculiar things after jump. She was strung tight and getting tighter, on the raw edge of fatigue.

Walking up that ramp was very much not what she wanted to do, if her body had had its choice in the matter; but brain began to assert itself as cold terror ebbed down to a different kind of wariness.

Gods, we got to think, Pyanfar Chanur, we got to think about all those stationfolk, dithering stsho though they be, and gods help any hani and any mahendo'sat—the hakkikt's just taken himself another spacestation, and this time he's got his blood up and he's got a point to make. Gods help 'em all, think, *think, get the mind wide awake.*

Gods-be pills make you sleepy, curse 'em.

I haven't got the strength for this. I'm not any kid anymore. The knees are going to go. I'm going to fall down right on this godsforsaken rampway, and if I do it's all unraveled, we're all going to die and the gods-blessed Compact is going to go all to pieces because I can't keep my knees from wobbling and my gut from hurting and my eyes from fuzzing.

Ten more steps, Pyanfar Chanur, and then ten more, and we get to rest a while, we can lean on that lift wall, can't we? They won't notice.

Down the corridor, the bleak, black, ammonia-reeking corridor past *Harrukk*'s airlock; and Jik and Kesurinan walking side by side behind her— *No knowing what signals they've passed, gods rot the luck—*

Tully, where's Tully, f'godssakes—

She caught sight of him, shouldered back by Skkukuk as she entered the lift with *Ikkhoitr*'s captain and Jik and Kesurinan and Tahar. "Tully!" she snarled, and he dived forward and made the door before it closed on the first group, leaving the others for a second lift, and gods only hope they ended up in the same place.

Herself and Jik and Tully and Skkukuk, with Tahar and the kifish captain and his lot: the lift let them out in *Harukk*'s upper corridor, in a chill, damp closeness and the stink of ammonia and incense.

They'll die if we foul it up. All these people on Meetpoint. My crew. Us on this ship. How do you reason with a kif?

Kif waited for her at the other end, kif dressed in skintight suits and robes modified for freefall work. Sodium-light glared and tinted gray-black skins, the glitter of weapons, of wet-surfaced eyes as they waited to welcome the *hakkikt*'s guests.

In a hospitality both Jik and Tully had abundant cause to remember.

Chapter Seven

The *hakkikt* waited for them in his audience-chamber, deep within *Harukk*'s well-shielded ring, and, thank all the gods, there was a place to sit, a chair at a low table, the captains and Jik and Tully all offered chairs at the table with Sikkukkut, and the captains' escorts left with the *skkukun,* standing about in the dim sodium light and the smoke of incense. Pyanfar took the little cup of parini they offered her as she sat: her hand shook when she did it, and if the cup was not drugged, it was as dangerous on her queasy and pill-shocked stomach as if it had been. She had rather food, she had far rather food at the moment.

But not on a kifish ship.

And: "Tully," she said. "Be careful of that. *Hakkikt,* I don't know if he can drink."

"Kkkt. Indeed. *Can* you, *na* Tully?"

"Yes," Tully said in perfect hani. And answered the *hakkikt* face to face, after all his evasions and his stratagems. He sipped a bit from his cup, and what went on behind those strange, shyly down-glancing eyes was anyone's guess.

So with Jik, who drank his own cup, carefully. And if there was raw hate inside him, if there was shock and a still-raw wound, it did not surface. Kesurinan sat beside him, at this different, jointed table with the hollow center, in which a kifish servant squatted ungainly with a serving-flask and waited for someone's cup to empty. Harun and Tauran, Vrossaru and Pauran and Shaurnurn, Faha and Kesurinan and Jik and scar-faced Dur Tahar; Tully and Skkukuk side by side; and the captain of *Ikkhoitr,* if she had not lost track of the kif in the shuffle, sitting by his (her?) prince's elbow.

Gods save them all from the *Ikkhoitr* captain's talebearing. The long-snouted bastard had indeed been whispering and clicking away, nose to Sikkukkut's hooded ear.

"Kkkkt," Sikkukkut said then, and looked at his senior captain with —it might be—curiosity. "Indeed." He turned then and extended a thin tongue briefly into the metal-studded cup which rested like a silver ball in his black hand. "Is there unanimity among you?"

"Enough," Pyanfar said; and in coldest blood: "Hani methods, *hak-kikt.* Hani will always dispute. Even when they agree. A *sfik*-thing. Mine and theirs. It's satisfied and they're here. In fact they're glad to see you."

"Kkkkt. *Are* they?"

"We weren't fond of Akkhtimakt," Harun said in a low voice, before Pyanfar could mull it over.

Gods, be careful. Speak for yourself and you become a Power, Harun. He may ask what you don't know how to answer. Watch it, for godssakes watch it, you don't know what that sounds like in kifish.

"Hani understatement," Pyanfar said. "Akkhtimakt, a curse on his name, moved in here and dealt with the stsho. That was one thing. He disturbed hani interests. That was another."

"There were, of course, the mahendo'sat. And this other group of ships. Humans? Were those humans?"

"Yes," Harun said.

"Interesting." Another sip at the cup, a glance Tully's way and back again. "Close but not close enough. The mahendo'sat have pulled off, doubtless to try again. Hence my watchers about the system. A fool would linger on these docks. We might have another Kefk here. In an emergency. There might even be sabotage, kkkt? Did the mahendo'sat touch here?"

"No," Harun said.

"Who is this captain?"

"Harun of *Harun's Industry,"* Pyanfar said.

"Ah. Your cousin."

Cold went through her nerves. "Distant," Pyanfar said. "Our clans have a distant tie." *O gods, I hope he doesn't have our kinships in library.*

"Ceremonial." The lie wove itself wider and wider. "Hani place *sfik* on kinships. And blood-debts. Harun has ties to some of these. I have ties to Harun and Faha, there. It's really quite simple. And blood-debt to Jik and Kesurinan." *Not to forget that business. Add it in. Secure Jik much as I can.* "We can have that even to non-hani." *Change the subject. Hold out possibilities to the bastard.* "There's *sfik*-value on that too."

And if hani around the table did not know now that every other word she said to the kif was a lie, they were deaf and blind.

"Has he talked to you?"

"Somewhat." She took a chance, reached and took a sip of parini. "I'm going to keep him on my ship as advisor. I'm sure Kesurinan understands, ummn? But he misses the smokes, *hakkikt.* He truly does."

"The smokes," Sikkukkut repeated in a flat tone, as if she had gone quite mad. "Do we still have such a thing?"

The *skku* in the center of the tables searched anxiously among its robes. Efficient, by the gods. Foresight covering all sorts of hospitality. It brought out the little sack, eyes aglitter with triumph.

"Your *skku* is amazing," Pyanfar murmured, making a low-status kif very happy in its neurotic zeal; and took another minuscule sip of parini.

"I might bestow you another gift," Sikkukkut said. And scared two kif and a hani at the same time.

"Huh." She kept her calm. With difficulty. "We hardly have formalities enough to keep another *skku* occupied. Nothing so splendid, *hakkikt.*"

"But you want another gift."

Bluff called. She looked up, lowered her ears and got them up again, heart hammering. "Is the *hakkikt* disposed to talk policy?"

"Ah." Sikkukkut set down his cup, hands in his lap as he sat cross-legged in the insect-chair. "Shikki," he said sharply; and the *skku* eeled its way over to lay the smoke-pouch on the table in front of Jik.

Jik picked it up carefully, felt of it and carefully extracted a smoke-stick and a lighter. "You mind?"

Sikkukkut gave a wave of his hand and Jik put the stick in his mouth and carefully lit it. His hands were shaking, but only a little, limned in the fire that lit his face. The light died. He drew a long breath of smoke in as if it was life itself.

"Foul habit," Sikkukkut said as the smoke went up to mingle with the ammonia-stink and the incense. He rested an elbow on the raised insect-leg of his chair and leaned his chin on that hand. "But you and I remain friends. Kkkt. Good. That is very well. Kotgokkt kotok shotok-kiffik ngik thakkur."

—prisoners?

All round the table backs stiffened. Except Jik's, to look at him; he sat there concentrating on his smoke, with a cloud of it round his head.

"Sit still," Pyanfar said in hani; and Haunar Vrossaru and Vaury Shaurnurn turned their heads to look toward their escorts, the only two who did.

But maybe they knew their crew.

"Is the *hakkikt* disposed?" Pyanfar repeated.

"The hani captain may push too far," *Ikkhoitr*'s captain said out of his silence. "Be careful of it."

"Makes me nervous," Pyanfar said. "This place. We're exposed sitting here at station. If I were Akkhtimakt—" She rested her elbow on her knee, easy pose, though her heart was hammering away fit to take her breath: thank gods for the incense that masked the sweat. Her nose itched and ran. She ignored it. "This place smells of trap, *hakkikt.*"

"In what way?"

"I'm an old trader, *hakkikt.* And stsho may cheat you one way and five more, but I never knew them to plot violence." *Phrase it so the bastard has salve for his pride. A trader can know merchant-things. He isn't expected to understand grasseaters, is he?* "But they'll buy violence, without understanding what they've bought. They've made mistakes before. This is a big one. They've involved the *han.* Technically, hani are allied with Akkhtimakt, because of the stsho treaty, which gave him what he never would have had. Support on the far side of the Compact. All of a sudden you don't hold the majority of Akkhtimakt's territory. He's just quadrupled his holdings. And he's on the other side of an uncrossable gulf. No jump points, *hakkikt,* no bridge between hani space and here. It's a narrow neck and one where he can interdict you if hani abide by that treaty."

There was deathly quiet in the room. No kif moved. Then a nervous shift from the Faha. Ears were flat, all in that section of the table.

And Jik shot her a carefully frowning glance. Sucked in a great deal of smoke and let it go. "A." Drawing Sikkukkut's attention to himself.

"Is it so."

"He go Urtur. Damn sure not go Kita."

"You have ships at Kita."

Another slow draw at the smoke. "I don't swear. Good guess. We send message Maing Tol. My Personage make move on Kita. Where he go? Here? Got no cross-jump but Tt'av'a'o, damn bad choice. Methane-breather, human, lot mahendo'sat. Damn bad choice. You no do. He no do."

"Should I wonder that that is then precisely what I should do?"

Go off toward Tt'av'a'o and possible ambush, and involve himself with everything Jik had listed? Go home to Akkht and consolidate his hold? Or to Llyene and terrorize the stsho in a raid every kifish pirate must have dreamed of?

They were all good choices for the Compact as a whole. If they cast themselves totally on hope of rescue from the mahendo'sat.

Who had their hands full already, saving their own hides.

"Masheo-to," Jik said. And something more involving Akkhtimakt and ship IDs, rapidly. While Sikkukkut's black eyes fixed on him.

"Kkkt," Sikkukkut said. "Interesting thought. Do you follow that? No? Keia proposes that Akkhtimakt may have faked identification in his ship ID. That he may not be among that group we dispersed, but already at Urtur. We will both have taken precautions: my ships will reach all the jump-points that lead out from here in time to prevent escape from insystem or to prevent any ships not already launched from arriving here. But Keia favors us with another interesting proposal. I tell you I value you both."

Gods, he means it. The absolute, thorough-going bastard. He's dead inside. He doesn't know what he's done. He doesn't know Jik's his enemy. Or if he knows it he doesn't know *it, from the gut. He hasn't got the equipment. He theorizes. You can revise a theory, but never gut-knowledge, never instinct.*

He's naïve as Skkukuk in some ways. He mimics our ways. Even friendship. And he can't feel it. He can't ever understand us: just logic his way through our motives; and that won't always work for him.

"Not know where he be," Jik said. Another puff of smoke. "Maybe even hani space."

Hani bodies all about the table stiffened.

"Maybe already there, a?"

Gods look on us all. Let it go. Let him think his way into it. Slowly, slowly.

"Kkkkt. Kkkkt." Sikkukkut's tongue flicked in the gap of his teeth. *Can we go too far? Make him lose* sfik *in front of his servants?*

And beside the *hakkikt* the captain of *Ikkhoitr* leaned over and spoke rapidly and quietly. Sikkukkut answered a word or two back.

Gods rot him. That one's no good news.

Worse and worse.

Ikkhoitr's captain got up from table. And left. While Sikkukkut looked their way again. "You will have noticed the dispatch of certain ships. They are not the first. From Meetpoint, from Kshshti, from Mkks and Kefk. Continually my messengers have gone to inform my ships. And ships have moved. You have never seen all I have. Nor is this all of Akkhtimakt's company. You are quite correct. Kkkkt. From you, Keia, I expect a certain astuteness in such matters. But the hani are also hunters. And you've talked to them, have you, Keia?"

Jik frowned. And said nothing at all.

"Not quite by his wish," Pyanfar said. "Say that friendship has other uses. He was confused when we got him. He talked rather too much to us. That simple." *We're lying, Kesurinan. Trust me. Sit still.* "It's what I said. Nothing *Jik* wants. He knows something Goldtooth doesn't. *That* made the difference. Tully doesn't know what the humans are up to, but a thought occurs to me that I don't like, *hakkikt.* That the trouble inside the Compact is weakening us as a whole. That the humans may not wait until the trouble's settled. Just delay their attack till the most advantageous moment. Because they will push at us."

"Is this so, Tully?"

Tully made an uncomfortable shift of position. A shrug. Turned a worried look Sikkukkut's direction, hers.

"He has trouble understanding sometimes. Tully. The *hakkikt* asked: will the humans fight the mahendo'sat?"

"Not know." Tully's eyes fixed on hers, shifting minutely as if they hoped to read a clue.

"You told me. Tell him what you told me. *Do* it, Tully."

"Human—" He looked back toward Sikkukkut. Toward this kif who was more than all others his personal enemy. "Come. Got three—" He held up fingers. "Three human—"

"Governments," Pyanfar said.

"Three," Tully said. "Fight. Push one humanity to here."

"Kkkkt."

"I belong *The Pride.* Crew-man!"

Keep your hands off me, you bastard.

And implicit in a glance her way: *Captain, don't let them take me.*

"He doesn't know much more than he's said, *mekt-hakkikt.* But he understands methane-breathers. I don't think the rest of his people do. He had no importance among his people. They got what information from him they wanted to hear and they shoved him aside without listening to the rest of what he had to say. They didn't *want* him to say the rest. We think. Gods know *he* might not understand as much as I think. We might not understand him. I think he's tried to tell the truth, but I don't think he was in on the planning. Just a crewman. That's all he ever was. That's what he still is." Her hands wanted to shake. If the kif took him, there was nothing she could do to stop it. *I got their attention on him. Gods, get it off!*

"But," Sikkukkut said, "we have other sources to question. The stsho will not hold back information. They bend to any wind. And I have sufficient of them to gain an excellent picture of what happened here—they will lie to a mahendo'sat, they will lie to a hani, but they will not lie to a kif. And they have very large eyes. Two of my least *skkukun* are on the station at this moment; and so are three hundred thousand stsho." Again Sikkukkut lifted the cup and drank, a quick dart of his dark tongue. "They are apprised of the possibility that I will decide to remove this station. And that they will not be allowed to leave—"

My gods.

"I have told my *skkukun* the same. They will find information. They will cause the stsho to find it. We have already identified responsible individuals. My enemy destroyed the station datafiles. After doubtless sucking them into his own records. So there is nothing to learn there: I expected as much. But we have direct resources. Ksksi kakt."

A servant moved. Fast. Hani shifted anxiously as an inner door opened, as kif rearranged themselves, arustle like leaves in a midnight forest.

"Sit still," Pyanfar said again. In case any of them forgot. Her ears were flat, her muscles had a chill like fever in them that was going to start her shivering. She reached, ears flat and scowling, and picked up her cup and drank.

The parini went down like fire. And held her caught in that minor, eye-watering misery when a gibbering outcry rang out from the opened door.

A gleam of white showed in the doorway, where kif parted, where dark-robed kif shoved stsho forward, through the shadowed rows of their own kind. Stsho white, stained with sodium-light, marked with darker smears, their pitiful, spindly limbs all bruised from kifish handling.

So fragile. A breath could break such limbs.

Jik turned his face in that direction, slowly. The smoke curled up from the stick in his hand. He did not move, himself, beyond that; the other captains turned in their chairs; and Tully—on her other side—she had no way to observe. She guessed.

"Now," said Sikkukkut, "let us ask some questions."

"Translator's not making sense of it," Hilfy murmured, gnawing her mustaches and monitoring kifish transmissions. *Harukk* was talking to its minions off-station. Talking a great deal. "I don't like it, gods, I don't like this."

"Takes a decision somewhere," Geran said, "to get that ship that talkative. You'd think Sikkukkut'd be busy. You'd hope he'd be."

"Calling more of them in?" Khym said.

"They got a worry about something," Geran said. "No. They won't pull ships in while there's a chance of something coming in and catching them nose to station. That's some kind of bulletin. Instruction. Gods know what."

"Still talking," Hilfy muttered. And remembered *Harukk*'s dark bowels. The transmission went on at some length.

Likely Haral remembered *Harukk,* too. She had seen it, when they pulled the Tahar crew out of there.

"Hostages," Hilfy said. "That's what he's got Gods-*be,* Haral, I could make a routine query over there, take the temperature."

"Just sit still," Haral said. "Captain's got enough trouble. Let it be."

They flung the larger of the two stsho at the table, between Pyanfar's chair and Haroury Pauran's. *Gtst* collapsed all in a nodding huddle of white, delicate limbs, of swirling pearlescent draperies at the table edge. *Gtst* shuddered and shivered and bubbled.

While Pyanfar looked at the designs of pastel paints on *gtst* brow and her heart thudded in shock.

It was Stle stles stlen. Or it had been. Gods knew what personality the wretch had fragmented to when the second wave of kif invaded *gtst* station.

"You recognize this creature?" Sikkukkut asked. "Or do they still look alike to you?"

"I know *gtst.*"

Gtst—or *gstisi:* it might well be Phasing—wrung *gtst* hands and wailed something about noble kif and noble hani. Moonstone eyes looked her way, liquid with pleading, and Pyanfar's stomach turned over. *Gtst* stank of oil and perfume and something indefinable, doubled when the kif flung the other stsho down beside it.

"Talk," Sikkukkut said to the stsho. "Or we begin to hurt something, perhaps one of these others; perhaps your translator. And then if you don't, we will hurt *you.* Do you understand, creature?"

The stsho bubbled and babbled at each other; the one clung to the person which had been Stle stles stlen, fingers locked in *gtst* robes. *Do it, do it,* the translator was crying, and the erstwhile Stle stles stlen poured out a sudden flood of wails and words.

"—The Director is not responsible," the translator cried then. "*Gtst* was another person—"

"That's very well. We don't care which of you we skin."

"—*But!* But! noble, esteemed friend—this wretch Akkhtimakt—"

"You begin already to make a lie. Tell us about the treaty and about what happened here."

More babble. The translator turned *gtst* face about again, moonstone eyes wide, *gtst* mouth a tiny, trembling *o.* "It was a mistake, it was—"

"Report what you did!"

"We are not a violent people, we had need—"

"This translator is useless. We can send for another."

"—*but!* but! in our foolishness we listened to agents of the other *hakkikt,* we had need of ships to defend us and in our foolishness—"

"What of your bargains with mahendo'sat; with hani; with the methane-folk; with *humans?*"

"Mahendo'sat are with these creatures, these—" The translator looked Tully's way with a visible shiver that made all *gtst* plumes tremble. "Creatures! We ejected them. We sought accommodation with the hani. But hani have no great ships. What can we do now but shelter with the most powerful? We were fools to think this was Akkhtimakt: we see very well now: we will make treaty with you, at once, at once, estimable! Defend us!"

"Kkkkt. What an offer! And what will you do for me, little grass-eater?"

"We have science! We have—unique objects—"

The whole of stsho culture—open to kifish piracy.

Pyanfar coughed, and the stsho mistook it and trembled the more, lifting *gtst* hands to the kif.

"Save us! Estimable!"

"This thing is a fool," said Sikkukkut. "Where is Ismehanan-min? What bargains have you made with him and with his Personage?"

Jik, Jik, for godssakes don't make a move, gtst'll talk, O gods, we can't help it and we don't need craziness right now, we need wits, we need the sharpest gods-be dealing any trader ever made.

The stsho once Stle stles stlen waved *gtst* hands and babbled.

"Hakkikt," the translator lisped. *"Hakkikt,* Ismehanan-min dealt with us, he is the other side of a conspiracy, pernicious, pernicious, most honorable *hakkikt*—" The stsho waved *gtst* hands, rocking and tearing with nervous fingers at *gtst* robes; *gtst* cast an anxious look back where the kif stood with guns all about them; toward Jik, who had no restraint on him. "We are not a violent people. What are we to do? Mahendo'sat crowd upon us, they force their way into our offices—we need guards to secure our privacy, but we are not a violent people—"

"And we are not a patient kind," Sikkukkut said, and Stle stles stlen said something lengthy and urgent.

"—The mahendo'sat left us. They left these few they said must close out certain business, menials, functionaries, persons of no import— Lies. They attempted bribery—"

"To which you surely listened."

"—Akkhtimakt had betrayed our agreements!"

"What are the mahendo'sat up to?"

"—They are making you fight each other, *hakkikt.* One mahe aids you; the other dare not aid your enemy, but he leads and lures him."

O thank gods.

"Kkkkt, is this so, Keia?"

Jik was relighting his smoke, which looked to be reluctant to stay lit. He capped the fire. "Sure. Same we always like you best. You win, *hakkikt,* we glad deal with you. I think maybe you do win. Right now I not much happy 'bout humans. So same I convince Ana, he switch tactic fast. Maybe come you side, a? Meanwhile got this hani problem."

"A ship of mine has gone to Kshshti. If it finds no resistance it may find other sympathetic kif and send them out from there. I tell you that we will cover all of space. We are already close to encounter with your partner. At Tt'av'a'o. Or wherever he is."

Pyanfar sat still, forced herself to sit still. *O gods, gods, how much does he know? How much can these hunter-ships do? If kif can match the mahendo'sat, all bets are off, what Akkhtimakt may be doing, what he's doing—Would the kif ever have started this mess, with inferior ships?*

"We sit here," Sikkukkut said, "attempting to preserve three hundred thousand fools. Why this is, I wonder. Perhaps I shall lose patience with it. In a very little time any outsystem spotter will be receiving our early movements down his timeline. Once he knows *Harukk* has docked, he will know it is too late: I will not have stayed here overlong. Or if he is a fool and does not know that, still I will not be here, kkkkt?" Sikkukkut took a sip from his cup. "As for incursions from system-edge in general, that is all anticipated. *If* some of Akkhtimakt's ships exist out there, which I still doubt. Only a fool would annoy me and pen himself into the system with me, a fool or a very formidable enemy. Or my friends Keia and Pyanfar, kkkkt? But I am not vastly worried. On the one hand I am not anxious to lose the station itself; on the other anything that brought Akkhtimakt's ships within my reach would please me, and likewise," Sikkukkut said, and turned a glance on the two stsho before which they wilted like grass in the fire. "Likewise anything that brought the perfidious Ismehanan-min to an interview with me. Do you understand me, kkkt?"

"Yes. Yes, honorable."

"He dislodged Akkhtimakt. And the hani ship with him?"

"—Yes, yes. He hung off and waited, the hani went to Urtur. Discovering Akkhtimakt here, these perfidious scoundrels abandoned us, each, yes, honorable."

"And sent you nothing?"

"—Nothing, nothing, O, Honorable, we would tell you. They waited and then these *creatures* came out of hiding! Waiting at the limits of our system! We were shocked, we were dismayed, we cannot understand how they penetrated our net—"

"Akkhtimakt here," Jik said lazily. "Ana know you come. He do thing I say. He wait. Wait you come. Maybe you fight these bastard kif, he come in. He got these human on short chain."

"And you?"

Jik drew a mouthful of smoke and let it out. "What I do, a? What do my ship? My First, she don't fire. We make quiet, wait. I be you friend, *mekt-hakkikt.* Not po-li-cy fight you. Po-li-cy my side want you win. What we got, we come in, hit both you *hakkiktun,* a? Damn mess. Ten, fifteen week got new *hakkikt,* whole different game." There was a stirring in the hall, ominous movement against the lights. Jik lifted a hand. "I not dis-courteous, a? Long time neighbor, you, me. We do fine. I know these thing, same Pyanfar know these thing. Same time I got big worry what we see here not real honest. Maybe bait. Maybe Akkhtimakt sudden smart, want bring us here, hold us here, make us fight Ana while he go do what he want."

Safeties had gone off weapons. "Kkkkt," Skkukuk said anxiously, with a furtive wave of his hand.

"No. Long time the *mekt-hakkikt* been patient with truth. He ask question, he still be patient."

"I am still patient, Keia." Long jaw rested on black, retractile-clawed fist. "Pay no attention to them. I am listening."

"This got big danger. Tully say don't trust human. What happen, a? You got fight Ana, fight human, fight maybe other mahen ship, few; then come some bastard out from Akkht, want make self *hakkikt*— same all time happen, you know you people real good: first time you got trouble you got some bastard want make suicide. All same take time, take ship, take you attention. Same time got Akkhtimakt settle in real good in hani space, same time far from methane-breather—*you* got methane-breather trouble, a? You be real close over here. But Akkh-timakt not got. Maybe he make good friend with mahendo'sat over by Iji—same join with them, come fight human when human make trouble —now where we be, a?"

"That is an elaborate possibility. Very elaborate."

"Same. But two kif want fight, my people always help." Another lifting of a finger. "This time you got luck. Akkhtimakt damn fool, all time push mahendo'sat, mahendo'sat never like help that bastard. A? So you got *no* mahen help to you enemy. Maybe change. That bastard get rule in hani space, he be whole different bastard."

"Can it be you're trying to maneuver me, Keia? Or do you agree in this move, hunter Pyanfar?"

"I think it a real possibility, *mekt-hakkikt.*" While hani captains and Tully sat and listened to this; while kifish hands rested near weapons and the two stsho retreated into a small, soiled ball, glad to be forgotten. Her heart beat to the point of hurting. Her stomach ached and weakness came and went in tides. "I see one way Akkhtimakt could go from here. One path. Mahendo'sat occupy Tt'av'a'o; you have Meet-point. Either you've got Kshshti or the mahendo'sat have, by now; or they'll be headed there like chi to a hot spot; on that, I wouldn't predict. The third path Akkhtimakt assuredly has, open all the way behind him." *Do you see, sister captains, do you see yet what we're dealing with, what we're trying to do? For godssakes don't twitch, don't distract this kif, don't make a slip.*

"Kkkkt. One path. Yes. Why do you think I've favored you as I have? That area of space which lies like a peninsula amid a gulf without jump points. That unfortunate circumstance which has made hani isolate. And kept them pinned between that gulf and mahen ambitions. Do you understand me, hunter Pyanfar? Do you know now why I have given you so much?"

"Hani space." The pain was back in her chest. She found breathing difficult. "A pocket in which Akkhtimakt can be contained. Uncrossable space on two sides, unfriendly mahendo'sat on the third, yourself on the narrow fourth."

"Mahendo'sat will be quite busy. I want Akkhtimakt kept busy. I know you have self-interest in that. Do you recall our debate on self-interest?"

"I have one there. Yes. A considerable interest."

"Name what you need."

So easy? My gods. So easy. "These captains. All these in my company. Their ships."

"Do you include *Aja Jin?*"

Gods, gods. Be calm, Pyanfar. Don't lose it all. Don't let the voice wobble. Her nose was running. She sniffed and tried to focus. Ignored the itch. "I wouldn't put Jik to a choice between you and Goldtooth. Not twice. With *me* he's got clear reason to cooperate. With me he'll be fighting something that's clearly his enemy, and a threat to that whole border. Self-interest. He won't bolt and go home till he knows hani aren't going to collapse. I *know* the mahendo'sat, and everything he's done is perfectly reasonable. So is his going with us now. You want hani ships to fight against Akkhtimakt, they will, and a lot safer with *Aja Jin*'s guns with us."

"Kkkkt. Merchants. Against hunters. I will give you reliable ships of my own. *They* will give you that chance."

"And Jik, *mekt-hakkikt.* I'm going to have to make a show of power with both the mahendo'sat and the *han:* call it hani psychology, call it *sfik,* but it works that way. You need no ornaments. I do, to prove what I've got. I need Jik and *Aja Jin;* I need my human; I need your ships—"

All right, I accept them. Worry about my motives, bastard.

Sikkukkut's jaw lifted ominously. And sank again. Dark eyes glittered in the sodium-light, beneath the hood.

"*Skku* of mine, you look to make yourself a *hakkikt.*"

"I look to hold hani space, *mekt-hakkikt.* I'm securing my agreements."

There was profound silence. Her heart beat hard, every thump a pain in her chest; her limbs went cold and hot and the edges of the room went in and out of focus around the one darkness that was the kif; and life or death, then and there, if the kif took suspicion, if one of the hani captains reached her tolerance, if someone moved or sneezed, they could all die.

And worlds would.

O gods, O gods of my mothers, gods greater and lesser, littlest and far away, gods of my world—hear an old reprobate: can you move a kif . . . even a little bit?

"Kkkkt. Take all you have named. Dispose of Keia as you will. On his ship or in your hands. Now. Go. You are dismissed, *skku-hakkikt.*"

She drew in a breath; a second one. Not *skku-hakkiktu* but *skku-hakkikt.* Not *vassal of mine* but *vassal-prince.* Her heart beat and skipped. Then she gulped air, grabbed the insect-leg of the chair and thrust herself to her feet. "Up," she said. "Move. The *hakkikt*'s order, gods rot it, don't sit and think about it!"

Hani moved as if galvanized; Jik was slower, but only to put out his smoke and to pocket the pouch.

And the stsho huddled there at her feet gibbering and wailing in pain. A chill went over her. She hesitated, turned back toward Sikkukkut, opened her mouth.

"If the *hakkikt* has no use for these—"

"Enough!"

She stepped past the stsho. One caught at her trouser-leg. "Help," it cried. "Esteemed hani, help, intercede—"

She walked past. She had to. The kif had made an aisle, directing everyone out.

No further risk, I can't, I daren't, gods, don't let me fall on my face here and now.

I can't do more than I've done.

"That's another," Hilfy said. "*Harukk*'s talking again. Encoded. Names—that's orders to ships. *Chakkuf. Sukk. Nekkekt.* I can't make anything out of it, but they could be moving-orders."

"I don't like this." From Tirun.

"What's going on?" From Chur's channel, over the main speakers.

"You know everything we know," Khym said.

Which summed it up well enough.

If there was a spotter, something they had constantly to worry about, it would lie more than a lighthour out, maybe three or four. And it would move when it felt like it. When its own criteria had been met. One of Goldtooth's ships, maybe. Maybe one of Akkhtimakt's. Or more than one. They sat here with nose to station with the chance, however remote, that some attack might come in, some mass of ships might be sitting out there dead silent and so lost in the immensity of the spherical search-zone that they were virtually invisible. Like the spotters. There was no way to find that kind of lurker either, except by that same blind luck, or its own error. The entire perimeter of Meetpoint's dark-mass influence, at a spherical radius of one to four lighthours—was an impossible area to search for any single ship. Station obscured part of their sweep and rotation complicated matters, with station not sending, the buoys on but erratic, and the kif deliberately censoring their own scan output. There was not even a star close enough to light an object, little help that that was: the dark-mass radiated, but with a sullen, dying heat, a spot their instruments regularly scanned, looking for any anomaly that might be a ship trying to mask itself; Meetpoint's own mass gave off a quiet white noise to their most sensitive instruments, the several system navigational buoys screamed their false information into the dark, emissions of a vast number of ships churned and dispersed in a maelstrom generated by other traffic; while their best chance of seeing a hidden ship lay in the computer's memory of the starfield continually overlaid on its present reception. Any star occulted, anywhere about the sweep, might signal that presence, and they had had two such occultations, which buoy-information called planetesimals—

"—Library," Haral had said on the first such: "does the Meetpoint buoy correlate its input with archives?"

Meaning did the buoy-system ever check itself to see if a cold, silent object it spotted was a known planetesimal? Affirmative. It did. But it reported it out as a planetesimal even while it was relaying a query: it was defaulted that way. The AI of the buoy *knew* nothing else to call it. The stsho who built it built no contingencies into it: or they had made them and did not put that information into the navigational ephemeris.

If something was out there hours out it had not *seen* recent developments in any of its timelagged reception: depending on its line of sight, it might only now be watching *Harukk* arriving at station . . . in the confused, digital way of distance-scattered passive. It might not know what ship; or be sure how many were out here.

And gods only knew what would trigger it.

Hilfy wiped her eyes, shifted the com plug and kept focused. For their very lives.

"Abort linguistics search," Haral said suddenly, out of profound silence. "We need the room in nav."

Hilfy hesitated. And did it. Haral started running calc and never saying what it was for; but if Haral aborted one of Pyanfar's orders it was desperate. She pulled out the print she had, which was all gibberish. Lost. Utterly.

Then com beeped:

"Harukk-*com to all ships at dock: praise to the* hakkikt, *stand by departure.*"

"What are they doing?" Khym exclaimed. "They can't be putting out!"

"We're going live," Haral said sharply. And started throwing switches. Systems thunked and started coming up.

"We keep those connectors?" Tirun asked, businesslike, while Hilfy sweated in panic and punched buttons on her own: "*Harukk*-com, this is *The Pride of Chanur.*"

"*This is* Harukk-*com, praise to the* hakkikt, *report your status.*"

Her mind blanked. She sorted wildly, found the standard reports, shot them over. "Praise to the *hakkikt,*" she muttered, "status on our personnel."

"*Returning,*" the kif said. "*We are in receipt of your data, Chanur-com. Provide data on your subordinates.*"

She shut the channel down to hold. Kifish courtesies, abrupt and rude by any other standard. She punched in on Haral, whose information-request light was flashing priority. "They say they're coming back. *Harukk* wants stats from the rest."

"Subordinates," Haral said. "Get the stats on *all* those ships."

Haral was right, gods, entirely right: it was kifish, it was a matter of protocols, claim everything the captain claimed, have all those stats in hand, permit no ship they claimed to report on its own. Her fingers stabbed at buttons, opened com to the mahendo'sat, to Tahar, to every other hani berth.

Claim it or lose it.

Down to the docks again, herself and all her company, and no kif but Skkukuk with them. Pyanfar drew one great breath of burn-tainted air and drew a second, and ventured a glance about her as others overtook her at the bottom of *Harukk*'s ramp. Jik and Tully, Harun, Tauran, Vrossaru, Faha— The faces blurred and hazed: she went lightheaded in the change of air. "Did what we could," she muttered. "We got a chance. Whatever we got to argue among ourselves we do it on the way. Jik, Jik, my gods—" She bit it off, with the sight of the kif in the tail of her vision and remembering Skkukuk's interested ears. "Come on. Let's move it. We got to clear this dock." The departure light was flashing on the wall over their heads, *Harukk* preparing to move out. Across the dock, stsho huddled in forlorn panic—foolhardy of their kind. The prudent were locked in other levels, hidden deep in station interiors.

Where kifish crews searched for records and raided central in search of names and data.

"We're ready to move," Harun said. "We've been ready, waiting the chance for months. And we've got questions, but I'm not going to ask any. Any way we can get out of this godsforsaken place I'll take the ticket."

With an ears-down, troubled look. No fools in this group. Oldest to youngest.

Though Munur Faha looked at her with her anxieties plain and the whites showing round her eyes.

What are you doing? What kind of deal are you making? You were lying but how often and where and for whose sake?

As for Dur Tahar, she walked along in her own world, her scarred face grim, never looking at other hani. Scars were everywhere about her. Inside and out.

Skkukuk brought up the side and clicked and muttered to himself; Tully walked along with his hand on his gun the same as the kif.

And Jik asked Kesurinan quiet, rapid questions, the two of them talking dialect as they walked.

Do what about it? Jeopardize his life and everything else? Pyanfar fretted and gnawed her mustaches, and walked along near the pair, her heart speeding as she saw other departure lights start flashing all down the row. Their own ships.

"Word's out," she said, and glanced at the hani walking on the other side of her. "We do it the way you heard it. Adjustments and amendments when we clear Urtur. We've *got* to clear Urtur. We'll be thanking the gods for that kifish escort and I hope to gods Urtur is as far as Akkhtimakt gets, but I doubt it. We have a long run and a hard one ahead of us. We're fast enough to keep pace with the hunters. We've had some modifications: say we've been running courier for the mahendo'sat and we've got a hunter-rig. There's a *lot* been happening, but you heard some of it in there. What I'm worried about is getting us through systems fast enough and holding together long enough to get home in time.

I can slow down; so can *Aja Jin;* and I can argue the kif into it; but nothing's going to slow Akkhtimakt down, and they're all hunters. Days can count in this. We're bypassing Hoas Point. What're your unladed caps on the Urtur jump and what on the brake and cross to Kura vector? Who's low?"

A low mutter of stats and capacities. *Industry* was far and away the strongest; little *Starwind* was fast enough, engines large enough with its light mass to send her right up into *Industry's* rating. *Shaurnurn's Hope* put them only a little down, and *Pauran's Lightweaver* only a shade under that. But *The Star of Tauran* was far under. Likewise *Vrossaru's Outbounder.*

"You know," Pyanfar said, "Tauran, Vrossaru. We can slow down and make your rate; it'll cost us. You understand what we're facing. I'm going to ask you—I got to ask—"

"We'll get there," Sirany Tauran said. "Our own way."

"No. Power down. Mothball at dock. I know it's risking your ships; so's the trip home. Listen. My crew's blind tired, strung out. Tahar's little better. I can take Tahar on *The Pride*—" Instant glower from Dur Tahar, but no word. "Or one crew can go with me and work alternate; other with Tahar. Get us all there alive and precious days faster."

Work alternate with a pirate? Bloodfeud and outlawry. She all but heard the scream. But:

"You can keep an eye on us," Tahar said in a low voice. "Split shift or whole. Whatever suits you."

"All right," Vrossaru said. *"We'll* take you on."

Tauran looked at Pyanfar's direction. Thoughts went through her eyes. *Aliens. Gods know what.* And maybe on the other side: *That Chanur ship's got priority protection from the kif. And it's fast. It'll get us there alive. And we'll be sitting where we can do some good if they're lying, won't we?*

"All right," Sirany Tauran said. "Soon as I can get my crew off. We got seven. You got berths?"

"We'll find 'em." *Does she know about Khym?* Pyanfar's muscles clenched up and let go again. *Gods be, we got worse problems than hani prejudices.* "Thanks." They had reached *Moon Rising's* berth. And *Aja Jin* and *The Pride* beyond, all with departure warnings blinking urgently above. "We get those stats relayed ship to ship, right down the line, direct transmission. We have to share specifics with our kifish escort, no choice. Let's get ourselves out of this port, we don't want anything intervening and we got gods know what going we don't know where."

"Understood," Harun said. "Luck to us."

"Luck," Faha said. "Gods look on us." And with the appearance of a shudder, she looked at Tully and his dark-robed partner. Perhaps in that instant of afterthought she wanted to take that pious wish back. But that would have been an embarrassment. "Hearth and home," she added, and with monumental charity: "and whatever." With a physical effort.

Then Munur Faha started on ahead, her own ship farther on; other captains followed, Harun and Vrossaru with a backward look, Vrossaru's ears flat in dismay.

"Tahar," Pyanfar said; and Tahar stopped there at her own dock. So did Tully and Skkukuk. "Jik," she said. Jik and Kesurinan stopped, too, within an easy sprint of *Aja Jin*'s berth. "We got it worked out," Pyanfar said. Which Jik and Kesurinan might not have heard, they had been talking too intensely and too urgently all the way back. Passing instructions, fomenting conspiracy. Gods knew what.

But Jik left his First and came back to her, his dark face all sober. "Where I go, a?" He held up both hands. "Want back? Or you tell me go?"

"Gods rot you, what are you likely to do? Leave us? Get us all skinned? Kill my world with your conniving?" Sikkukkut's kifish ignorance had let this hazard loose: *Dispose of Keia as you will.*

Now it came to a bluff she could not call, force she could not use, persuasion she knew would not work. To haul him aboard *The Pride* even by strong pressure now would set Kesurinan off, trigger gods knew what contingency orders.

"I do number one good back there."

"I got no way to trust you!"

"I got interest like I say." He reached out and laid his hands on her shoulders. Stared into her eyes, and she stared up at him, looking for something to rely on. *Liar. Ten times a liar. Your gods-be government won't let you tell the truth once a day.* "Hani got importance, Pyanfar. I swear. God witness."

"More than your own? Don't tell me that!" Her knees felt weak. The face looming over her was alien, the eyes as unreadable as Tully at his most obscure.

"We be neighbor to hani more than kif, a? That be backside whole mahen space, I don't doublecross you."

"Gods be, we're reasoning like the kif. Self-interest!"

"Politic all time reason like kif. Damn mess. I best pilot you got, hani. You want lock me up? Or you want trust?"

"When did it ever work?" Panic rushed over her. "No, gods rot it, I don't want to trust you."

"Work in there number one good. You get me out, got me smokes, a?"

"Same time we got Sikkukkut going to come in behind us! You know he is! He's appointed *me* to do his work for him, you think he's not going to follow up on it?"

"Damn sure. You be no fool, Pyanfar." He waved a hand toward *Aja Jin*'s berth. "Number one fine ship in whole Compact, you got. Got number one fine pilot. Me. We go keep promise, a?"

"Get! Go! Give your orders! And get your rotted carcass back aboard my ship and give me that data before we undock. I want it, Jik, I want it in plain language and plain charts!"

"You beautiful." A touch at her face. She flinched and spat; and he gave one of his maddening humor-grins, then turned and sprinted for his own access-ramp, Kesurinan running with him stride for stride.

For their own ship. Their own choice. Gods knew if he *would* come back. The docks were dangerous. Kif might intercept him even on that short a crossing between ships. Sikkukkut might discover something in his questioning of stsho to change his mind. Stle stles stlen might have secreted damning records, being a trader through and through.

She looked at Dur Tahar. And had no doubt at all of the pirate, of her enemy, of a hani she had been willing to kill.

"That may have been a mistake," Pyanfar said.

"Could be."

"Tahar, if we get through this, anything between us. . . ."

Tahar's face went hard, her ears flat. "Yeah. I know."

"You don't know, gods rot it! There *is* no bloodfeud, between you and Chanur. You've paid it."

The ears came up. "Paid it on your side too," Tahar said with Tahar's own surly arrogance. And stood there a breath longer before she turned abruptly and headed for *Moon Rising*'s ramp.

It left her Tully and Skkukuk. A bewildered and nonplussed Skkukuk, Tully close at her side and the kif standing there as if his orderly world were all disarranged.

The great captain let his enemy lay hands on her. The great captain believes she has these for subordinate. The captain is wrong. Can the great captain be such a fool? Beware these hani. They are not subordinate either.

She lifted her chin. Come-hither. And Skkukuk came, all anxious, not without a suspicious glance toward the vanishing mahendo'sat. "Hakt', that is dangerous."

"Friend," she said. And in perversity reached out and laid a hand on Skkukuk's hard arm, from which touch he flinched out of reach.

"Kkkt!" As if she had attacked him. Very like her own gut reaction with Jik. And she had not perceived Jik's touch as lifethreatening.

"I teach you a thing, Skkukuk. You're traveling with hani. You'll hear things that may disturb you." A second time she reached, and this time caught him. The arm was thin, hard as metal. She felt a tremor there. *"Scare* you, *skku* of mine? Power among hani is a different matter. Power among hani is a handful of clans that just decided to go along with me because I handed them the only way out of here they're ever going to get. And because as long as there've been clans on Anuurn, there's been Chanur, and our roots go deep and our connections are complicated, and we're calling in debts they have to pay for *sfik* reasons and self-protection. We're connected to Faha; Faha's got ties of its own. Gods know I'd have to look up library to see where the others run. That's the way we are. Clan is *one entity.* You're *skku* to Chanur. Do you see? You behave yourself with these strangers aboard. And they won't gain a bit on you. Their relation is all with Chanur as a clan, do you follow that?"

Dark eyes glittered. She stared at a kif's face a handspan from hers, closer than she ever wanted to be. He made her nose run. And she made him shiver.

"Yes, hakt'." he said. "Power."

She let him go. And wanted a bath. Wanted clean air. Wanted—gods, never to have tried to reason with a kif. Or to have dealt with one.

"Come on," she said, shoved him and then Tully into motion and turned and hurried to *The Pride,* faster and faster, Skkukuk close after her, Tully panting along beside her, his breath hollow and hoarse from the thin air and the chill. *Get you out of this, lad, before you catch a cough. Get me out of this. Gods, I'm too old for this kind of stuff.* She took the pocketcom from her belt. "This is Pyanfar. Open up, hear me? We're coming in."

"Aye," Haral's voice came back.

Up the ramp. Into the chill ribbed yellow of the passageway. Around the bend and toward the white light, the safety of the airlock. She came across that threshold weak-kneed and with her side one mass of pain.

"Lock it up," she yelled at com. "We're all in."

"Aye," Haral said. *"Everyone all right?"* The hatch whined and hissed shut; and they were as free of the kif as they were able to be.

She shut her eyes and hung there, bent over then to get her breath while Tully did the same.

"Captain?"

"Fools, fools!" Skkukuk cried, and an alien grip closed on her arm. "The *mekt-hakt'* is starved, is fainting for your incompetence!"

Tully snarled something at him. Pyanfar rescued her own arm, blinking dazedly as it became almost a matter of keeping two men apart. Neither one hers. And both being hers, in a way which had nothing to do with being male. She had never seen that look on Tully's face. Tully's teeth bared without humor at all, teeth no match for Skkukuk's, which were all too close. She straight-armed them apart, hard. "Manners, gods-be, *shut it down!"*

"Captain?"

"I'm all right," she said, and shook her head, dazed, dizzy, and with a rush of fight-impulse going through her veins that turned her giddy. Human sweat and kifish mingled in her nostrils with her own. *So much for human/kifish cooperation.*

Gods, no time, we got our orders, I got no time to go away like this.

"I'm coming down there," Khym said.

"No need." She felt totally disconnected, blinked back and forth between Skkukuk and Tully. Her husband in it was the last thing she wanted. "We got more coming. Tauran's crew is boarding as soon as they can get locked up and back here. Working alternate with us. They tell you? We got a trip to make."

The door to the inside corridor opened. *"Where, cap'n?"* Haral's voice took over com again. *"Where are we going?"*

They had not known. "Home," she said; and felt a momentary rush of triumph for her own cleverness.

Until she thought again of Chur, and the cost it might be to them all in more terms than one. The triumph faded, left only an ache and a vast and mortal terror. "They've turned us loose. We're going home."

Chapter Eight

"Go," she said to Skkukuk outside the airlock. "If you want to get to quarters for any reason, get to it. You're going to be standing watch out by the ramp in ten minutes. We got too much traffic coming in here to take any chances. *And be polite!* Hear?"

"Yes, hakt'!"

"Get!"

He ran, a flurry of black robes and rattle of weapons, down the corridor toward his own quarters.

That left her and Tully; and Tirun coming to meet them, welcome sight. "You all right, captain?"

"We got Tauran coming in, we got nowhere to put them, we got data up to our ears to process into nav, but things could be worse—" Another figure turned the corner, tall and wide-shouldered and hani: her husband was coming her way in a hurry, and she flinched to the very bones. "Haral, you listening up there?"

"Aye, captain."

"Lay us course for Urtur on our old capacity: we got some slower ships to take with us. Have Hilfy line up our direct transmission with *Aja Jin,* we got specifics to get. Then relay the result to Tahar. Have *Aja Jin* run our backup check."

"Won't take long; I got us course plot already on our present cap. I got

*their caps. We got this fancy mahen computer and I figured we were
going somewhere. We doing the sequencing for the whole convoy?"*

"You got it." Miracles from the harried bridge. She did not even
question them. "Do it, cousin. And get kif stats out of *Harukk,* we got
an escort."

Khym intercepted them and fell in to walk with her and Tirun and
Tully. "You all right?" he asked. That was all.

"I'm a whole lot better." She discovered she could breathe again. The
tightness in her chest let up a bit, and a sneeze startled her. "Gods-be
kif." Her eyes watered. She wiped her nose. "Khym, you and Tully
want to go up there and get us some sandwiches and get us rigged for a
run? We're getting out of here."

"They're letting us go?" Khym asked, ears half-back. Worried-look-
ing.

"You're right, we got troubles. Even the kif are worried. We got to get
through Urtur, remember? We got to get past Akkhtimakt to get home.
Got to clear out the opposition all the way to Anuurn, that's what
we've got. Go do the galley. And give Tully a chance to get off his feet,
he's exhausted."

*Me, I got to take this ship through jump. We got to move, I got no time
to be resting—*

"Tully," Khym said. "Galley."

"Aye," Tully said, and quickened his pace and got through to join
him; the two of them went off up ahead at a fair walk, Tully staggering
a little as he went, muscles undone by fatigue and exertion and cold.
Her own felt like rubber.

"Tirun, we got seven of Tauran clan coming in. We got to bed 'em
somewhere. Run protocols for me. My brain's mush. Got to figure out
where to put Tully and their captain. No, b'gods, put Sirany Tauran in
Jik's cabin. Tully—"

"He's with us."

"They're not going to like sharing sheets with 'im on offshift. Gods-
be. Our attitudes. We got the world going down and we got to worry
about sheets and our godscursed prejudices."

"Let 'em gripe. He's crew, captain."

She gnawed her mustaches and heaved a breath. "Let 'em howl, then.
We're going to split-shift with a couple of them if I can get it out of
Sirany. Do the best we can and hang their sensibilities. If Khym doesn't
send them into frothing fits—"

"Aye," Tirun said.

"Let's get at it, then." She waved Tirun into faster motion as they came to the turn for the lift. "We don't know what's going to break loose here. I want us out of here. Fast. We could have a hundred ships all round us."

Three hundred thousand stsho, Pyanfar. Vulnerable and helpless, whatever breaks around them.

Ask the kif to let them go?

What reason? What reason can I think of?

"Better restock that downside freezer, huh? How close are we to full tanks?"

"Three quarters, last I looked. Haral's running checks on systems. She had to cancel that linguistics run in favor of the course plot, cap'n; sorry about that."

"Sorry. My gods. Get. Go. Out of here is all we got time for; tell her I want that course sequence as tight as she can shave it down, no waste time, everything up to cap. Time's what we can't buy."

"Here, here, here," Jik said, using a light-pen to mark the moves on the computer monitor, and the 3-d rotating model obligingly paced itself through its level-changes: he had brought both fiche and software key aboard when he came, and the mahen-installed comp suddenly displayed unguessed virtuosities. "Same come in maybe Tt'a'va'o, maybe V'n'n'u."

Geran made a sound deep in her throat, slow and full of omen. "We got the whole mess shoved off into hani space is what we got."

Jik said nothing at all to that. He had a mouthful of sandwich. He had not stopped for food on *Aja Jin* and arrived opportunely for a handout from *The Pride*'s galley. Pyanfar gulped a mouthful of gfi and blinked with the heat of it while she watched the display run its paces.

Tauran clan was on their way down the docks, with everything they could carry. Tirun was down there in the airlock with Skkukuk on guard at the foot of the ramp, preparing to receive them with their baggage. An eerie quiet hung all about them, *Harukk* and its chosen few bound out from dock on whatever business it chose, the station itself subject to kifish piracies she had no wish to think of; and saw every time she shut her eyes—the wretches on *Harukk,* pale and fragile and physiologically incapable of violence, not even to save their minds or their lives.

A destruct mechanism on the station might be set to blow on a signal sent from outsystem. That was possible too, if someone were totally ruthless: if someone like Akkhtimakt, with no sympathy for three hundred thousand stsho, had mined the station exterior, the whisper of a transmission arriving at lightspeed to some receptor could blow the station's vulnerable skin. On certain vectors they would never know it till it blew, even if they were listening. Gods knew she had no wish to give Sikkukkut any ideas he did not conceive of on his own, by warning him of the possibility. Neither did she want to stay connected to the station any longer than she had to.

In the meanwhile she sat drinking gfi and watching a wobbly-tired mahe trying to reconstruct diagrams out of his memory and a computer's help, and listening to him make mis-identifications once and twice and catch himself.

They both needed help. Food was no substitute for rest. And they had soon to move out and start ops for a long, risky jump. Pumps were filling the tanks to capacity. Khym was wandering about readying all the duty stations, setting up everything they had to have to keep them going.

Thank gods for a backup crew on this one.

We're laying ourselves wide open, Tahar and Chanur both—to mutiny and murder. You'll understand us at close range or you'll kill us on the way home.

That was what she implied in that offer. And all the captains knew it; while presumably Sikkukkut and even Skkukuk just thought she had all her compatriots sufficiently bluffed.

Gods hoped they understood, because one hani ship would not be able to talk anything but ops with another of their ships so long as they had their kifish escort; and that meant all the way home.

She watched the red and green marks grow on the screen as Jik built the patterns, and sipped her drink and ate her sandwich.

And slowly the wider implications of what Jik was constructing dawned on her.

Longtime moves. Very longtime moves.

The kif had not lied: the mahendo'sat scheme had been aimed at the kif from the start, a series of operations stretching back to the days when Akkukkak had been the threat. And even before that. Mahendo'sat owned far more than the few hunter-ships they were supposed to have, which meant shipbuilding and secrecy—heavy secrecy, to have kept the whisper of that construction out of the rumor mill.

Gods knew what the kif had been doing during that time. Or what the mahendo'sat knew and what the kif knew about their own intentions that they were not telling and that even Jik might not know the truth of.

Gods knew too, what both kif and mahendo'sat knew about humanity; or how long ago they had known it; and how much truth anyone was telling in that department.

And right now and to this hour, if Jik could get his hands on Tully, she feared, in some dark corner of *The Pride,* Jik would ask him some very hard questions; and perhaps Goldtooth had done that, when he had had Tully aboard *Mahijiru,* and, irony of ironies, gotten distrust. Likely Tully had done his don't-understand-you act. He was very good at it. And gods knew—perhaps Tully's instincts about when to use that silence were better than any of them believed.

Tully had asked her once, with distress wrinkling up his smooth brow, whether Goldtooth was on their side or not. She had not suspected the full implications of it then, or the extent of the pressure Goldtooth might have been putting on him. Or why Goldtooth had jerked him alone away from the human crew that was traveling on the mahen ship *Ijir,* before it fell into Akkhtimakt's grasp.

Being taken off that foredoomed ship was Tully's good fortune; indisputable. But she remembered his face when he had seen her aboard *Mahijiru,* remembered an expression she could read a little better now in retrospect, the terrible stress and the relief with which he had flung himself toward her and wrapped his arms around her, shivering and smelling of fear.

Friend, he had said over and over, said it repeatedly, with a worried look, during that early part of the voyage; but he had kept what he had known behind his teeth. . . . while dissension among them, the normal stresses of the crew, any hint of violence—had sent Tully into a panic that was not at all reasonable in their old friend. He had become afraid of them, in the isolation of his translator-interpreted environment, missing virtually all the nuances and the subtleties of what was said around him. He had lived in doubt of them right down to the moment he betrayed his own kind with a warning not to trust humanity.

Tully's was a treason unlike Jik's complicated diagrams. But not simple at all. She watched Tully sitting at scan-monitor, his face—gods, she had even gotten used to it—intent on that screen, seeming lost in his autistic world while the alien babble went on. He *was* listening; she would bet a great deal on it. He was a great deal *like* Jik on some levels. That was the anomaly. He did his work. He came with her time and again onto a kifish ship, which had to be terrible to him. But kif were not his greatest fear. She sensed that in a thousand little moves, little twitches of expression, the way his face and his whole body reacted when there was some momentary false alarm.

It's something not here present. Akkhtimakt's only another kif. He hates Sikkukkut but Sikkukkut doesn't panic him. There's Goldtooth and the mahendo'sat for him to worry about. There's his own kind.

We might end up in a fire-or-die case of mistaken identity: that's certainly to fear, if humanity comes breaking in here.

Or is it something he knows they'll do? Or that he'll have to do?

Or does he see a day—no matter who wins—that someone might take him into that dark corner and start asking questions he won't want to answer?

Gods, why'd he do it? Why'd he help us, even when he's afraid of us, over his own kind? He knows loyalty. He knows friendship. He commits himself to us like kin. It doesn't make sense. What kind of people could create him, and still make him betray them?

A people varied as we are. A people in internal conflict.

A chill went through her. A bit of sandwich went down hard. She washed it down with gfi and focused on Jik's dark, red-rimmed eyes. He had asked her something. *Got?* she realized belatedly. She glanced at the diagrams, at the instructions inbuilt to the comp. She had followed him, followed maybe more than Jik thought. The data and the model were both in their library now, and connected to Nav, the probability of mahen ships being anywhere in this zone.

"Backside," she said. Meaning the hinder side of hani-mahen space. "Where's the stats on that, huh?"

"Not got. Not mine."

A fool would believe this mahendo'sat. But he had shown her too much, confirmed too much, admitted too much. And he knew she could put it together.

The whole mahen-hani treaty was in rags with what he had handed over. And as much as she could ever believe him, it had harm enough in it to be most of the truth he had.

"No way we can make that rendezvous with your ships at Urtur," she said. "And remember, we got two of Sikkukkut's ships running hours in front—days, with these merchant rigs dragging at us, if they don't keep the pace we tell them."

"Cost us five day. We got five day?" A weary blink. "World can die in five hour. I got crew shoot message out."

"You mean when we go through there? You got a beeper?"

"Silent till got mahen ID. 'Spensive. I try. Mahen ship come through there, they get, if we don't get kif notice."

Truth, something said again. "Jik. Truth about those short-jumps. Can you do it? Can the kif do it?"

"Got limit like maybe two day light, precise. You try farther you don't come down ever."

"Two days. Then Goldtooth is short of that. Out there turning around."

"Same." A flicker of dark eyes, a little withholding of truth. "We try fix other end, a?"

"You going to run on me?"

"No," he said, and looked her in the eyes when he said it. Reached and grasped her wrist where it lay on the counter. "You, me do lot work get inside this business. We got high priority stay there. You understand? Ana be outside. We be inside. He *use* us way we want to be use', number one good deal. Best. I tell you I damn smart." Ghost of a grin. His hand squeezed her hand. She tolerated it. Gods-be mahendo'sat never figured what pressure did to retractile claws. Same as Tully. "I tell you. You valu'ble. Damn valu'ble. You don't take chance. Hear. All spacer hani be precious stuff."

She retrieved her hand. "You better get back. While you can. Before I change my mind."

"You got good nerve," he said. "Mahendo'sat got no better."

"Same you, gods rot you." Mawkish sentiment overcame her. She laid her ears down. They burned. Crew was witness. But it occurred to her she might never have the chance. "That was quick thinking in there, on *Harukk.*"

"A." He tapped his head. "Number one stuff." He levered himself blearily to his feet and caught himself on the cabinet. "See you otherside, a?"

"Get. Geran, walk him down."

She watched him go, tall black mahe and smallish red-maned hani, off the bridge and down the corridor. A shiver came over her. She drank the last of the gfi and got up to toss the cup. Haral got it from her. They treated her as if she were glass.

"Captain," Haral said, "you want to go lie down, catch a nap, I'll get Tauran settled. I've had my off-shift, you're—"

"I'll take you up on that," she murmured, and wandered off, toward the corridor. There was a thump from below. That was the airlock cycling, too soon to be Jik. Tauran was arriving. They were about to take boarders. They had about time to get them settled in and then they started their outsystem run. It was discourtesy to Tauran, not to be there to meet them.

But to dump her ship into system at Urtur, into kifish fire and Urtur's dust, herself helplessly groggy, she could not do that either.

Neither could she trust a strange pilot at Urtur. It had to be her or Haral. Tirun at a pinch. No one else. *Not with The Pride's new rig, either. O gods. I've got to brief Tauran on systems, she's not used to that much power. Haral's got course auto'ed in, gods know all we have to do is persuade Tauran's pilots to keep hands off the autos and ride with it, o gods, I hope they take orders.*

She turned and trekked the weary, staggering way back to the bridge, over to com, leaned there, over Hilfy's shoulder. "Give me lowerdecks main." And when the light lit: "Tauran. *Ker* Sirany?"

"I'm here," the answer came back.

"Pyanfar Chanur here. Welcome aboard. I'm about to go offshift awhile. I'd do briefing myself but I'll be taking us through jump. I want you to sit topside during undocks; Meetpoint system is the best chance we have for you to check out our boards, on the run out. Appreciate it if you'd make a quick settle-in and come up to bridge, let my onshift crew show you the rig."

"Understood."

"We're running wobbly, *ker* Sirany. Out on my feet. Profoundest apologies."

"We'll be up there directly, ker *Pyanfar."*

"Thanks." She clicked them out. Shoved back from the board and wandered off with the sour, distressed feeling of proprieties slighted and gods know what she had just said or how it sounded or whether it did any good or not. And no one had explained to Tauran clan about Khym's crew status.

No. They would have heard. Everyone at Meetpoint would have heard plenty about Khym and the riot and the kif. *The Pride* and Chanur had become notorious. They would have heard about Khym, about Tully, even before they saw him. Only Skkukuk had startled them.

They were spacers, not groundlings. Not Immunes, black-breeched and arrogant with power like Ehrran and her ilk.

She stopped by Chur's cabin, shot the door open a moment. Chur was awake, there in her bed with the silver machinery there by the wall and all the tubes going into her arm and out. "You doing all right?" she asked as Chur lifted her head. "We're going home, you hear that? Got crew from *The Star of Tauran* coming on board. You're going to hear strange voices on the bridge. Didn't want you to worry."

"Aye," Chur said. "Been keeping up with things, captain." A difficult wrinkling of her nose. "You look like you could 'bout as well trade places with me."

"Hey, we're all right, we got Jik out. Got his charts and some cooperation for a change. He's back on his ship. We got the whole lot of kif backing us. We're going back home, to make sure nothing of Akhtimakt's gets that far. Minor matter to the kif, but it may be just our size, huh? We got this one turn at Urtur. Then easier. How are you doing?"

"They threw me back in here. I was up walking, captain."

Her ears pricked up. "Want you to think about that one double-jump, about getting to the other side of it. It's all easy after that. Home. You hear me?"

"Promised my sister," Chur said. The voice grew strained with the effort of lifting her head. "Gods-be machine trying to put me out again. No sense of proportion. No sense."

"Cousin." She shut the door and went on, next door to her own cabin, leaned on it and pushed the open button. It let her in. She left it on autoclose, crossed the floor to her bed and flung herself onto it facedown and fully clothed. She reached blind and fumbled after the safety net. It hummed across.

Chur.

Jik could still be setting us up.

Tauran—got to make them understand.

We got Skkukuk down there lunching on little animals, we got Tully stark scared and sitting next Armaments, if he could read the keys; we got Urtur—

—o gods, Urtur.

"Py. Py." A gentle shake at her shoulder. She gasped air and blanket fluff and came out of it with a swimming-motion, a wild flailing of her arm for the bed-edge. It would be an emergency. Everything was an emergency.

She clawed her way to the edge and a hand helped her upright, two hands held her there by the shoulders. She flicked her ears with a chiming of rings she had not taken off; and blinked into her husband's face.

"They need you," he said. "It's all done, we're inertial. I'm one of the ones going offshift. Haral said they need every experienced hand they have up front for this one. They got two Tauran-clan at the boards. I'm just going to have a nap myself. All right?"

He was so calm. She stared at him stupidly. She had slept through undock? Slept through all the clank and thump and the shift of gravity? Haral had handled the ship gentle as eggshells.

Then Haral had evidently told her husband to give up his post and get off the bridge: more, to shut himself up alone in here and wait out the worst jump they had ever made; so her Khym just came back and explained it all calmly? He was terrified. He had to be. *She* was.

Of a sudden she felt a great tenderness toward him; she reached up and touched his face, nosed him in the ear. "Huh. Good job. Real good job." Nothing more than that, no compliment for following orders; he deserved having that part taken for granted.

Going home. If they lived to get there it was no good place for him. If they lived past Urtur.

"Don't do that," he said in his lowest voice. "You don't want to be late."

"Uhhn." She scrambled past him.

She came onto the bridge still raking her mane into order, still with sleep fogging her brain.

Everything done, the man said. Haral had let her sleep, that was what; Haral had gone and run everything her own way, the competency of which she trusted with her life, high and wide and inside out. But there was more than a handful of lives riding on it this time. And she had wanted her hand on it.

There was Tauran crew in Chur's seat. Skkukuk was in place. Another young Tauran sat at the com, in Tully's place. Haral and Tirun, Geran and Hilfy; and strangers. Sirany Tauran rose from her seat, forward. Her gut knotted in spite of everything.

"Tauran," she murmured, offering a dip of the ears by courtesy to the tawny-hided westerner. "Sorry, dreadfully sorry. I meant to be up here long before this."

"Your First told me you'd run without sleep." Tauran lowered her own ears; they stayed half-down, an attitude of reservation, jaw jutting.

She swept an arm about. "My cousin Fiar Aurhen at com. Sifeny Tauran at scan: call her Sif. I'll be heading down."

"Haral explained—"

"As well as she could." Tauran gave a hitch at her breeches. "I took you on credit, *ker* Pyanfar. I'm still doing that. I'd better get moving. We're coming up on our jump."

"Right," she murmured. "*Ker* Sirany." At Sirany Tauran's departing back. The Tauran went off in some haste. The whole bridge crackled with necessity.

"Entering count," Haral's voice said over the intercom. "That's five minutes."

Pyanfar went to her chair and settled into it. The food and the water was in the appropriate clip. She powered the frame into position, adjusted the restraints, swung the arm-brace up and locked it.

"Four," Haral said, flicking switches. They were by the book on this one: too many strangers aboard. "You want it, captain?"

"You got it, do it." She was checking displays. Tirun was switching at the moment, Haral having her hands full with the count and the last-minute power-ups. *The Pride* upped her rotations a bit, a little more *G* dragging them into the seats, for comfort's sake when they made drop at Urtur.

"We got our escort," Haral said. "That's *Chakkuf, Nekekkt, Sukk.* None I know."

"Me neither."

"Message sent," Hilfy said. "They're on final to jump, on schedule."

"My captain's secure," said a strange voice from across the bridge.

"Clear to go," Tirun said.

"Mark," Geran said. "We got everyone on the mark back there."

They were moving, a field of blips going with them, while another field, stationary, shifted color downward. They were leaving Sikkukkut and company behind. Gods help the station and the stsho.

"Steady on," Haral said. "How're you doing, captain?"

"You going to take it amiss if I ask what in a mahen hell we got set up?"

A dip of Haral's ears. "Same as you planned, captain. I got a check-list, your four." Haral pushed a button and two screens flashed and changed displays. "Tauran asked questions, I answered as I could, no apparent problems. We're shift on and off with Tauran down in crew quarters; sent Tully down to ride it out in ops. Tauran was going to get upset about him. He said it was all right. And *na* Khym, by your leave. I figured we needed senior crew up here on this one—"

Haral let her voice trail off. *And men and aliens were an issue,* was the unspoken part.

"Did right," Pyanfar said. Gods rot them, Tully all by himself down there, contrary to her orders, because a priggish lot of hani balked at having him in in crew quarters even with opposite shifts. Same sheets and blankets. Gods rot them all.

Couldn't put him with Khym. Or in Skkukuk's stinking quarters. Sirany Tauran got Jik's, captain's privilege, private cabin.

No room with Chur. Except in the same bed. Gods, and the protection might be worth it. Chur—.

Gods, let her make it. This is the hard one, gods. Get her through it.

Let me get her home. She's so small a matter in the balance. One hani. While You're doing all the rest, gods of my mothers—can't you just keep her with us?

You want my cooperation, gods?

No, no, not the way to go about it. The gods traded too sharp.

She scanned the list, flicked a glance over at number three monitor on her board, where augmented scan showed nine ships moving with them. Five hani, *Aja Jin,* and three kifish ships. The list showed tests run, checkout made, Tauran's agreement to crew assignment and quarters, status on Chur, and the fact that ops-com was open all over the ship for anyone who wanted to access it.

Course plot: affirm.

She affirmed. Plotting came up, splitscreen with data.

It was an illegal course, skipping to Urtur's zenith, braking hard, and jumping again from the incoming range. No passage through the dust-and-gas soup of the accretion disc at the ecliptic. No high-V passage through *that.*

It was also where trouble would be waiting. Best of all if they could have skipped directly nadir; but few stars had such a relative axial tilt that made that maneuver possible. The Meetpoint Mass and Urtur were not two of them; and trying it would probably pull them at high-V right into the worst of the disc.

If it did not drop them instead right into the heart of the well, into the bosom of Urtur's sullen yellow sun.

"We running calc on our collective?" she asked, while the chronometer ticked down. "Where is it?"

"We got it," Haral said. "It's going. We're sequenced two minutes apart, you want it closer?"

"Gods, no." They were going to make one long streamer through hyperspace as it was, which was going to put some additional push on all of them, and that meant being very careful on the braking capacity. There was fuel-mass to worry about. They could not afford wastage. Little *Starwind* had particular trouble in that regard. *The Pride* had large fuel cap, but also a larger mass with that new engine pack; and as for the rest, freighters were designed to haul, not do stop-and-turns under fire, even if the super-sized tanks and small unladed mass were in their favor on this run. *All* tanks and engines and hollow holds. But no extra shielding. It was going to be touchy. In all departments. She pulled the figures up—telemetry was flowing between ships now, fast and furious, catching up on status advisements. Their weakest was *Lightweaver,* with *Star of Tauran* and *Vrossaru's Outbounder* both left behind at dock. *Lightweaver* had to trail them; no other position for a ship with that mass/engine ratio.

The three kif ran ahead, indubitably with live armaments and kifishly intent on the business in front of them. A chance for distinction. For advancement. A proof of the *hakkikt's* favor.

And doubtless having their own instructions: the ops log had a separate note from Hilfy: a great deal of kifish chatter had gone on between *Harukk* and the ships of the escort.

Coded, to be sure.

"Give me Jik's map."

"Your three," Haral said, and it displaced the display on that screen.

She studied it, watched it flick through its dated changes, the moving and spreading of kifish power over decades; and mahen actions; and the sudden intrusion of humanity. . . .

. . . the slow ebb of hani influence.

Gods rot you, Jik—

Her pulse quickened, watching it through again. It was truth, unpalatable, plain, and simple. Jik had made a political statement, telling her more than she asked, more than timetables: the information went into history as well as the imminent future.

"*Ker* Fiar. *Ker* Sifeny." Her mind had two spare moments, amid the scramble to catch up. "This is Pyanfar Chanur; welcome aboard."

"Captain," a double murmur came back. Gods knew *what* their captain had instructed them—before she abandoned *The Star* and they boarded. Things like: keep an eye on the bastards? Wait my orders? Keep your heads down and be polite?

We'll take the ship if we have to, and mahen devils take the kif and all foreigners?

"We're not a by-the-book ship," she said. "You can guess that, the way things have been running. The second you get something my First better know about, you sing out *Priority-priority* and you get it; interstation com's usually free for crew chatter, meanwhile, station-station or all-stations, same as my own crew, no differences on this deck. We got non-hani aboard, same rules, and men on this ship get no special courtesy, no discourtesy either. We got a long trip and a hard one and Chanur's grateful for all the help we got; we need it at the other end too. You want to know anything, you ask, we'll answer; you have any trouble, you come to me same as your own captain. You won't have any trouble. If you do, I want to know about it. Hear?"

"Aye," the double voices came back.

Probably unconvinced.

"There's *Chakkuf* jumped," Sif Tauran said.

"Got that," Haral said.

"Priority," Geran snapped, and scan flashed to monitor one. "We got movement incoming, bearing 05, 35, 19, point zero zero 3 by 5 *G*s—"

An object was out there, coming out of concealment and accelerating as if devils were behind it.

"Time we got out of here," Pyanfar muttered. "Gods and thunders, it *had* to be on our side of the system—"

"Priority," Geran said, "Sikkukkut's moving."

Scan showed the color-shift.

"Tirun—" Pyanfar said. "Intercept calc, all along that vector."

"I'm on it," Tirun said, "coming up. They can't do it, can't do it, nowhere along our line, beam or missile, b'gods, the incomer's lost us, but it's gods-be close."

Close for intercepting fire, pegged anywhere along their track; sweat broke out all over her.

"Priority." Geran's voice, booming out over the com on override. *"We got another incoming—"*

Pyanfar overrode with a priority master and a button on intercom. "Priority, priority," from Sifeny. "That's two more."

"Got that," Pyanfar said. "Tirun: recalc."

"They're farther down, we're all right, I'm checking it anyhow, cap'n."

"Priority!" The monitor screen blinked alarm: space was blossoming with ships.

"Kkkkt!" Skkukuk cried over station-to-station. "Priority, this pattern is *gktokik!* This is methane-breather, this is tc'a and chi! Avoid output!"

"F'godssakes—" —*Shut up on my bridge, you gods-be lunatic!*

"Clear on our vector," Tirun said, "we got it, we got it clear, go, go."

"Sikkukkut's got visitors and we're not waiting for this to unfold around us. *Out* of here, as the schedule goes. Stay by it!"

"Priority," Hilfy said.

Comflow was coming over from Tahar, hani and obscene. Her heart lurched. "Hilfy, I got it, I got it. Send. Tahar! This is Pyanfar, what's happened back there?"

"Chanur," the answer came back, *"we got a glitch in final-check. We're trying to fix it. You got to go, go. We'll come in as we can."*

A sick feeling hit her stomach. Irony, maybe. It was a jump-lost ship that had started the Faha-Tahar feud. And it was a Faha-kinship crew and Tahar riding together on a ship that might not make it this time.

"Yeah, I hear that, Dur. How much lag?"

"Feathered if I know. We're tracing it. Give us a quarter hour down if we're lucky. If not—"

"If not, yeah."

"Hey, I speak kifish real good, Chanur. I'll turn 'round and hail 'em all. Got a message?"

"Luck to you. *Luck,* Tahar, hear?"

"Same to you."

Moon Rising cut communications. Dur Tahar had her hands full, with her own crew doing well to be working at all.

She dropped her head against a shaking hand and drew a deep breath and tried to get herself in order.

Gods and thunders, the best we got—the ones I could trust—The best and the only friends we got except Jik—that gods-be pirate—and Vrossaru with her. Gods, don't let us lose 'em now.

I'll go religious, I swear I will, get 'em through jump with us!

"Coming up on mark," Haral said, while com crackled and sputtered with advisements from the rest of the group: *Moon Rising* had to be subtracted out of jump equations all the way down the run, a contingency that was all too close to happening. From his own limited board, Skkukuk rattled off a string of kifish exhortations and instructions, something about his captain; the *hakkikt,* praise to whom; and their destination.

Another thought froze her heart. "Tully. Has Tully got his drugs?"

"He's got them," Hilfy said. "He just reported on com; Chur's under; we got clear from all our passengers, in and secure."

Ten thousand things to come undone, ten thousand ways the whole business can go wrong—

The scan-projections were a shifting mix of color, Geran and Sif Tauran working feverishly to keep some semblance of accuracy in ship actions, with system scan blank and tc'a popping in at high-V: they had only their own knowledge, passive-scan; and their long-established, dopplered realscan; passive-scan and longscan leapfrogged, projection and factual report, older and older as their time-packet left the arena.

It was riot back there. Other ships appeared out of system fringes. The *hakkikt* had not fallen into the trap, had not sat there nose to station in the safe interval he might have thought he had before outbound ships could have faked a jump, braked beyond system edge and turned around.

Bastard has the luck.

Gods help the stsho.

"Ten to mark," Haral said, seeming unperturbed. "You want to take it on otherside, captain, or take her out?"

"I'll take it otherside." That meant mind in order. A precise knowledge of the coordinates and the parameters for error. "Eggs'll get you pearls we don't get system scan at Urtur either."

"Huh. *Akkhtimakt's* been through there, not too certain we even got a station there. If he ever got there. If *he* didn't short-jump and turn. That's eight to mark."

"Secure for jump," Hilfy's voice rang out over general com. The warning sounded early. For the strangers.

"We couldn't hope for that much," Haral commented.

"Seven."

"How's *Moon Rising?* What's their status?"

"They're not talking," Hilfy said. "'Ker Fiar's trying to raise them."

"Gods," she said. "Ha—"

"Priority!" Geran screamed across the bridge.

Instruments broke up. Cleared in wild retreating doppler. Com wailed in the earpiece. Pyanfar yelled to drown the sound and the pain as *something* passed them at C-fractional inbound, ran right down on them and whisked away into system. Her heart all but stopped; and lurched into action again in heavy thumps as someone sent the com-output to her.

It sang, it wailed, it moaned and howled up and down the scale like a lunatic; and its retreating image showed the perilous yellow of knnn-ID.

O my gods—

"Mark!" Haral cried.

And flung them. . . .

   . . . .outsystem. . . .

     . . . .into jump. . . .

       . . . .tranquility. . . .

     . . . .returning. . . .

   . . . .*down* again. . . .

. . . .*emergency*. . . .

Chapter Nine

. . . .emergency. . . .

. . . .emergency. . . .

. . . .Siren shrieking, auto-alarm from scan. . . .

Pyanfar reached, rolled her head to get view of the chrono and blinked to clear her eyes on the display. It was not at fault. They were on mark. On schedule. Urtur arrival.

. . . "Message," Hilfy mumbled, "message . . . kifish. . . ."

It came blasting out over the com, general. *"Proceed!"* came a kifish voice from Pyanfar's own back, their interpreter, live and with them. *"Our escort ships are laying down a pattern of fire, they are proceeding on!"*

"We stay on auto!" Pyanfar yelled at Haral. "We got ships at our tail—" Lest old habit take over.

Slow down and they had ships racing up their backside. They kept on, hurtling into Urtur system with all its debris of dust. . . .

. . . a star more like a black-stained, broken egg, sullen yellow at system heart, all bound up in a black, flat mist of dust and rock through which a couple of distant gas giants and a host of moonlets plowed rings. It was a scientific wonder. . . .

. . . a hellhole for inbound ships, where dust and rock could break down a starship's defensive bubble and strip away its *V*. Hit

the thick of it at their present velocity and they would make a UV glow, particles accelerated by the contact with virtual particles they brought with them, exotics shooting off in richochet fashion and creating an accelerated maelstrom of reactions that would bleed away their energy. Ships had to dump when they reached a gravity well; but a cloud like Urtur's had ways of doing it for a ship. . . .

. . . getting through the V shield, chewing away bit by bit in pyrotechnic decay, until it got to vulnerable realspace metal and quasimetals, and got the vital vane-surfaces, and gnawed away at the hull till it began to glow. . . .

Not yet for *The Pride*. Instruments jumped and flared as dust and larger debris met the bowshock of particles they carried with them and flared and came apart to join the stream and fly off in discharges at collision with still other particles.

They were a cometary fluorescence, if any living eye could track them, if any ship moving at that V dared be close to any other ship doing the same or had the time to look to anything but their own survival.

The trailing ships would be popping into system and running into their backturned message and the kif's as Hilfy relayed it on: *We're here, so are the kif, keep going, stay on auto.* And wide of their entry point, three kif launched precautionary fire before enemies could get organized, plowing through the medium as an irregular flutter of telemetry out of the maelstrom they were meeting, creating more hard radiation trails with the passage of their fire.

Their escort was not going to stop. It had to blow a hole for them through anything that might be in the way and keep going, they had agreed that much. But the kif had their own idea what precaution meant.

It was not saying that a contrary-coursed enemy could not come flaring bow-on toward them, to unintended collision.

Or that there might not be one of Urtur's rocks out there too big for their shields.

"We're not getting buoy telemetry," Haral murmured; and Pyanfar swallowed hard against the upwelling of nausea in her throat and fought the blurring of her eyes. Her hands were numb. It was the brace that held her right hand near controls; she shoved with a heave of her shoulder and swung it woodenly over, pushing Confirm to comp's automatic warning that they were blind.

"Bad habit hereabouts," she said between her teeth. And tried to remember what to do next, which was to read the advisements comp was programmed to hand her, data and detail matches to check against the autos.

Enemies might peg them by sheerest luck. A rock was more likely to do it for them. Sikkukkut's earliest ships had come through here and gods knew what had become of them, whether they still existed, whether they had not gone on to a kifish rendezvous at Kita or Kshshti.

—a knnn had grazed past them, otherside.

—hallucination?

Gods, no, it was real, it had been real—attack pouring into Meetpoint off several vectors, including Urtur . . . Sikkukkut's enemies had come out of Urtur and Tt'av'a'o and Hoas and V'n'n'u vectors—or space corresponding to those points—

Realtime months ago.

Your doing, Jik? Your gods-be contacts with the tc'a? Gods, gods, have you ever told the truth in your life? What have you done?

Had it been Goldtooth coming in at Meetpoint? Could he marshal methane-breathers to his aid—along with humans?

Could anyone guarantee the methane-folk?

Whatever had begun to happen at Meetpoint had played itself out already, while they existed only as a probability in the gods' intentions, an arc in hyperspace, a bubble with a slender stem to Somewhere shooting along in Nowhere Reasonable on the whim of V and vector and the dimples stars made with their mass—while they did that, ships had battered away at each other, and ships which might have been at Urtur might well have leapt out again days ago, with the kind of hyperspace arc hunter-ships could cut—sleek, power-wasting hunter-ships who could cut days off a freighter's time—

—but not *The Pride*'s, except they were encumbered with a handful of freighters who had to make it through to give them a chance at all where they were going.

—*Moon Rising,* o gods, where?

System buoy gave them nothing. *Industry* existed back there in that timelag; and *Starwind* and *Hope;* and *Lightweaver* to bring up the rear, unless *Moon Rising* made it on some miracle—

There was a sick feeling at her gut that had nothing to do with the after-jump queasiness. The numbers ticked away; warnings flashed all over the board, approaching mark, have to make it on schedule or lose it all—

"Coming up on dump," she said. And let the autos take them, as instruments blipped and flashed hazard warning.

—*Easy then to drift away, give it up, quit trying after the figures that glowed ghostly green just beyond her reach, just out of focus. Survival was in those numbers. It was just inconveniently far, everyone so godsforsaken tired and home so far and so fraught with disasters—*

Wake up, Pyanfar Chanur, focus, make the fingers feel, the hand move, the mind work—

—*long way home. Someone else's job. She was already there, the pale golden dust, the deeper gold of grainfields and the fleet herds that raced and bounded and soared for the sheer exuberance of running, sharp hooves and sharper horns—*

Blood and hani hide. No uruus was calved that could get a horn into Kohan Chanur, except for young Hilfy's mistake, wide-eyed youngster caught right in the path of one that should have gone the other way.

"It's all right," Kohan said. *And sat down, plump, right where he stood, with his hand pressed to his ribs and his nose gone pale. "It's quite all right."*

While Hilfy stood there in horror, only then catching up to what had happened, when all the rest of them had reached their peak of panic when na Kohan had, and moved; but Kohan was nearer, saw young Hilfy's danger, and hit the uruus like a projectile. It lay dead, its quickness and its beauty all still in the dust; he sat there with blood leaking through his fingers and a sick look on his face that was none of it for himself, only for what could have happened. And the rest of them, chagrined and self-disgusted that he had had to do what he had done, a skilled hunter caught like that, and none of them in position to help when a young girl's mistake near killed herself and her lord. Hilfy stood there thinking, they knew later, that she had killed him, killed her father, her lord she should have died for, the dearest thing in all her protected young life. She had never taken a scar. Never did.

Till a dockside brawl on Meetpoint; till the kif laid hands on her; till she was their prisoner for much too long—

Kohan would not know his daughter.

She's grown up, brother. She's not a girl anymore. Not anything you can understand anymore, your pretty Hilfy; you, tied to the world; her, a spacer, with a spacer's ways, like Haral, like Tirun, like me.

I don't want your world.

I've ruined her for it, taken her out of it, changed her in ways I wouldn't have chosen, brother; but I couldn't keep her prisoner myself; couldn't hold her, wouldn't try.

I hate it. I've always hated it. Not the fields, not the feel of the sun. It's the confinement. One world. One place. A horizon too small.

Minds too small to understand me.

I'd rather go anywhere than home. Rather die for anything than fat old women and empty-headed men who love their walls and their wealth and their privilege and never know what's out there—

Khym knows. Maybe you almost do. But I'm coming back for them. Hilfy and I. So gods-be many have bled for you. Or frozen cold in space. Or gone to particles, not even enough to find. You don't know the ways you can die out here.

I don't want to get there. Don't want to see the look on your face.

But by the gods I won't leave you to Ehrran and the scavengers.

—Aren't we coming out of it? Has something malfunctioned? Are there red lights? Gods, do you ever stop thinking when you lose it and the ship doesn't come down again, do you just go on—

—out again, and back to realspace, with V lower and the telemetry flicking past numbers in mechanical agony, red lights flaring—

"I got it, I got it," she mumbled to save Haral the effort. Not malfunction lights: it was gas out there, thick enough to glow and flare off their shields. The shield-depletion curve was rising, fluctuating as they swept up gas and hit a bare spot, where the shield recovered a little strength. The kifish escort was far away now. On auto, relying on numbers alone and not even in direct control, they achieved a kind of tranquility. Warning lights flickered, reminding them of laws and lanes they overrode. Haral swore and disabled them for the duration of Urtur passage, to be rid of the beep.

She fumbled after the nutrients packet, bit a hole in it and drank it down—and Tully, Tully was alone belowdecks, his poor teeth always had trouble with the packets and there was no one to help him, alone because the gods-be Tauran were too squeamish—

—behind her Skkukuk would be seeing to his own meal. Her stomach heaved at the thought. But his kifish voice came through now and again, delivering some information to Hilfy and Fiar at com, translating off those kifish ships up front.

Kifish transmissions everywhere; and *Chakkuf* and *Nekekkt* and *Sukk* were doing their job, the point of a spear that had to drive straight into Urtur before it stopped, re-vectored, and ran up the V sufficient for a jump out of this hell. That was the worst of it, that dead-relative-stop they had to do to line up that next jump, or slew through hyperspace askew from their target and depending on the next star to pull them in, loss of realspace-time, loss of everything if they miscalculated. . . .

Those hunter-ships were aware of their schedule, were able to make up that time and distance on sheer power, and rendezvous again, elsewhere. They claimed. It was their idea. A merchant pilot would have laughed, disbelieved it: and suffered a chill up the back at the thought of ships that could do that, knnn-like, as far off their capacity as they were off that of an insystemer.

She had no doubts. Clearly the kif would not have shown them everything they had.

And, gods, she would have given anything to find that fire answered, Akkhtimakt *in* Urtur system, resisting. He was not. That meant he was elsewhere. The terror reasserted itself, habitual and consuming.

"Chur," she heard Hilfy say. "Time you woke up. Chur—"

Persistently. She cut in on that channel herself. "Chur, gods rot it, answer, we're coming up on braking."

No answer.

"Geran," Pyanfar snapped. "You got backup, we're stable; get back there."

There was a snap from a released restraint. She did not look around to see. Did not try to talk to Khym, had no doubts of his safety, or Tully's. They were no different from other crew, probably had reported in to com monitoring, as the Tauran would report, from crew quarters, going through frantic prep for shift change while they had this small inertial stretch for the generation systems to recharge. The machine was keeping Chur quiet. That was what it was. It was supposed to. That was all it was.

"No gods-be hope of Akkhtimakt being here," she muttered to Haral.

"We ever expect it? Hope to all the gods those first ships of Sikkukkut's cut 'em good. We got station output, no buoy, no ship-com. No tc'a, f'godssakes, tc'a miners don't notice kif stuff. They're not talking either. Something big's been through here like thunder. Something that bothered *them.*"

"And a knnn comes in at Meetpoint. I want out of here. I want out of here real bad." Pyanfar took another swallow at the bag, another listen at com off Chur's cabin. There was the sound of the door opening. Geran's voice desperately calling Chur's name. She swept an eye over scan. All the ships behind them had dumped down. "We're all on. How're you doing, Haral?"

"I'm holding up." The voice was hoarse as her own.

Then: *"Chur's coming out of it,"* Geran said over com. *"Tell the captain."*

"I got that," Pyanfar said, punching in. "How is she?"

"Weak," the answer came back, which was not the answer she had wanted, not with what they had coming.

If Geran admitted that much, it was bad back there.

Pyanfar took another drink, emptied the noxious liquid into her mouth and swallowed hard. She threw com wide to all-ship. "We're stable. We're doing all right, high over the soup. If the two kif have jumped past us back to Sikkukkut, he's welcome to 'em. . . ." She cut it off. "Gods," she said to Haral. "Gods, I hope. What in a mahen hell's keeping our backup crew? Query 'em." The weakness came and went in waves. Her muscles had no strength left. They had awhile yet to run before they reached their turn point. *The Pride* would query for a Confirm; but if it got no Abort it would make that final dump on its own, reorient, find its own reference star and head out to Kura, would do it if they were all dead or incapacitated, taking its log records and everything it had into hani space, to brake at Anuurn and wait to be boarded . . . by hani, pray the gods. The chance that the automatics could do all that flawlessly was about fifty-fifty; but it was their third-backup, failsafe to feeble living muscle and overtired brains. Haral had run all that calc, even had it plugged into one contingency courseplot for Kshshti to Maing Tol; and one for Tt'a'va'o as well, all while she had been tied up with the kif. Brain-bending, meticulous checks, run fast and by the gods accurately. And Haral like the rest of the crew, like Geran back there trying to keep her sister alive, had far overrun her physical limits.

"Tully's on his way up," Hilfy said. Internal-com was not her proper assignment; but it was a fair bet Sifeny had not understood him. *"Na Khym's up and headed out upper sec. Tauran crew is on its way."*

"Thank gods," Pyanfar murmured. Things started to sort out. She could just about hold on that long. "Skkukuk."

"Hakt'."

"You're offduty." *No, gods, no, can't send him down the lift with Tauran crew coming up, they might shoot him.* "Soon's Tauran crew hits the bridge, you can go to quarters. See you at Kura."

"Kkkkt. Yes, hakt." Exhausted as the rest of them. "Hakt', there is not adequate resistance here. *Chakkuf* has advised subordinates of this. Akkhtimakt has gone elsewhere. The two advance ships will have gone on. I queried regarding those courses. Our escort does not know."

"Thanks," she said. Calmly. There was no course but what they were following. It was academic information. That was all.

While all the agreements that held the Compact together had been shattered.

"On the other hand there's a possibility both may have turned and gone for Kita," said Skkukuk. "Akkhtimakt, defilement on his name, might circle back to Akkht. If he had Akkht he would be formidable again. Homeworld could not stand against him if it were not aware that he is severely challenged."

"And not to Kura? Leave Akkhtimakt free to go to Kura?"

"*We* are that contingency, *mekt-hakt'*. Certainly the *hakkikt* has sent a message to Akkht. But that we are not aware of the course of these ships indicates that they are not part of our business."

"Or, of course, that our escort has separate orders."

"Assuredly. Should I have mentioned that? The *mekt-hakt'* is no fool."

She tasted bile. Her heart labored and skipped like something moribund, on its last strength. The lift-door light reflected in the monitor at her right hand. A group of figures exited, shadows in a dimly-reflected corridor. *Tauran, thank the gods. And where in a mahen hell's Tully?* She was not mentally fit for problems. She knew that. *For godssakes get up here, Tauran, I can't handle anything, I'm not sure I can walk across the floor.* Her chest was hurting again, a persistent pain. She violated her own rule, powering her chair about on a working station. But Tauran was there, Sirany and all the rest of her crew, and—dull shock —Tully was with them, Tully had ridden the lift up with strangers and gotten out unscathed, points to that crew's nerves and decency.

She unbuckled her restraints and groped after the chair arm. She was in that kind of condition. She heaved herself to her feet as Tully went off the back way to the galley, on duty; and Sirany Tauran and her crew headed for their change-off. "We got it easy," Pyanfar said, though opscom had been open for monitor the while. "Escort's been laying down fire ahead of us, we got no sound out of Urtur station, we got no sound out of kif insystem. We got an hour to run before we hit our last dump and turn. We're still missing Tahar and Vrossaru. They didn't make the jump."

"Understood," Sirany said. "I've been on your com feed since before we dropped. Knnn. Knnn, for godssakes."

"Knnn and trouble of some kind back there at Meetpoint. Whether that's good news or bad for Tahar or for the kif I don't know. I hope to all the gods it's Goldtooth's bunch, but they weren't running IDs." She passed a glance aside as Skkukuk unbuckled. "Kkkt," Skkukuk murmured, and got up to his full, if unsteady, height. *"Hakt'."* That was only one captain he saluted; he bowed and turned and walked off the bridge, bound below, while Tauran crew took the briefings, the critical situations, from Chanur crew on the last of their strength.

Pyanfar straightened her shoulders and looked at Sirany. "You got a real good crew," she said of Sif and Fiar.

"Yeah," Sirany said, but the flick of the ears said immensely pleased. And said something else she could not read. "We got it, go."

Time then to step out of her way and let another captain to *The Pride*'s boards, the codes stripped to master-unlock, even the log and their private files. Fire-codes, data-codes, the whole ship. "All open," she said to Sirany, and turned and collected Haral, who left the boards like she was leaving a lover, with a second and a third look. She put a hand on Haral's shoulder and shoved her galleyward, paused to shepherd Hilfy through, and Fiar too, offshift with Chanur crew; but Sif Tauran went to hang over the back of Sirany's seat at the main boards and deliver a quiet report.

My compatriot. My maybe-enemies and allies of necessity. My crew of men and aliens and reluctant, ambiguous hani. Clans were more absolute in the old days; the hani tongue had nothing native to express halfway loyalties. A hani had to come to the deep wide black to find it. Among kif and mahendo'sat. And humans. "Tirun," she said out loud, and gave an irritated jerk of the chin at Tirun, who delayed with her opposite number, on her feet and physically clinging to the seat. "Come on, gods rot it, cousin, time's running."

Tirun came. Geran arrived from down the corridor, blear-eyed and staggering. "We're relieved," Pyanfar said. "Come on. How's Chur?"

"Alive," Geran said, and her mouth went hard shut, as if that was the only word that was going to get out. But: "Going to get something down her," Geran muttered in passing. "Going to sleep there this trip."

"Huh," Pyanfar said, venturing no more than that. The two of them crowded into the same bed, that was what Geran meant: there was nowhere else in that lifesupport-crowded cabin. She said nothing about it, tried not to think of anything at all, but the bridge and the galley corridor went strange in her sight, all near and far at once.

Dark and stars and the monstrous shape of a knnn ship bearing down on them as if they were a minnow in the deep.

Kif ships putting down a steady barrage of fire into nothing at all, because there might be something out there. (But there might equally be helpless bystanders. Mahendo'sat. Hani. Tc'a.)

Strangers with their hands on *The Pride*'s controls, delving into Chanur records—

Kef'k docks, all lit in fire—

Three hundred thousand stsho dying in sudden vacuum, delicate, gossamer-robed bodies frozen and drifting, with horror on their faces.

Human shapes, tall and mahen-like, pouring by the thousands into a hallway, Tully times infinity, armed and hostile—

"Captain—" Tirun had her arm. Held onto her, as the hall went dark in her sight and the wall suddenly ended up in the way of her shoulder.

"I'm all right," she snarled, and shoved the hand off.

"Aye," Tirun said, in the tone it deserved.

She made it as far as the galley, dropped into a seat as her sight went dark again. Someone shoved a cup of gfi into her hands and her vision cleared on it; she got it to her mouth and forced a nauseating swallow down. Grimaced then and nearly heaved. A sandwich arrived in front of her, in a hairless human hand, Tully and Khym in better shape than any of them who had been on duty since Kef'k. But the mingled stink of them all was enough to turn a kif's stomach. It was more than enough for a hani's, and mixed with the godsawful smell of gfi and food and the ammonia-stink that had somehow gotten onto all of them. She had always run a clean ship, an immaculate ship. Now this.

While the Compact was trying to come undone, and, gods—

"I'm worried about the kif that went out of here," she said. "Sikkukkut's. Not just Akkhtimakt's lot. The pair of Sikkukkut's that went out on this heading before he came into station—" Remember. Remember it. Mind did strange things when jump shook it and set it down again. There had been such kif. She and Skkukuk had discussed it. There had been methane-breathers. There had been Jik, on their bridge, spilling an incredible sequence of evidence into their computer. She forced a mouthful down. "I got to tell you, *ker* Fiar, and you can tell your cousins, we got a Situation aboard: we can't always say what we'd like to say. Skkukuk's real stable, but we don't tell him we're not the *hak-kikt's* loyal friends. Wouldn't bother him in some ways. But he'd think we were crazy. Kif thinks you're crazy, he won't do what you say. So we just don't fill him in on everything. You got to understand him—"

"Aye," Fiar murmured in a guarded tone, because, perhaps, it seemed incumbent on her to say something to that insanity, surrounded as she was by Chanur and Chanur's odd crew. Khym attracted as much of her attention as Tully did, little nervous moves of her ears, following sounds. They came desperately forward. "You think one of those lead ships went on to Anuurn, captain?"

"Could have," she said, and Haral:

"Our escort's in a way to cover anything they choose to cover. Emissions all over the godsforsaken system. No telling what's here. But *they* know what they found before they churned it all up. That's for sure, whatever they've cut out of what they send us."

"You're not working for them."

"Gods, no," Pyanfar said. Maybe Tauran clan had believed her assurances from the start but Fiar wanted to be reassured in words she could hear. "Skkukuk was a present. One I didn't choose. But I get the feeling his alternative was worse. Kif serve the ship they're on and he's on this one. Fight for us like a maniac, he would. And has."

"He any trouble?"

From a young and worried hani who was about to bed down and sleep on lowerdecks, with a kif down the corridor. Humans, Fiar seemed more able to take in stride. Even one handling the food she ate. But her shoulders were bristled.

"He gives you any, tell him I'll skin him. With a kif that's literal." Gods, when had she gotten so callous? Another gulp of sandwich, on a stomach that was taking it better. Little talk. Little problems. What about the kif, captain, he going to go crazy and cut our throats? What about the human, captain? What kind of thing is it, your husband and this alien rubbing shoulders and making nothing of it, and this human handling the food we got to eat? "We're going *home,* Fiar Aurhen. Home and gods know what else waiting for us. Got no passengers here."

"I heard—" Fiar said, and whatever she had heard waited when Sif Tauran showed up late and edged her way past Khym in the little galley. Not without a look.

"Heard what?" Pyanfar asked.

Fiar swallowed a choking bite. Her ears went back, her eyes blinked, watered, and fixed on hers dead-on and wide. "Word is—what happened at Meetpoint last year, how you came in there and took it apart

214 • C. J. Cherryh

when they got—particular. Captain. How you set to with the Immune. How you had a run-in with the kif and that mahen hunter. Whole Compact has the rumor the humans are coming in and you're involved in it." Her voice went hardly audible. "To get trade, maybe. Maybe something else."

"Who said?"

"I don't know who said. It's all over. And the treaty and the *han*— What're we going to *do* when we get to Anuurn, *ker* Pyanfar?"

An edge of panic there. Of outright fright.

I don't blame you, kid. Not at all.

"Mahendo'sat are moving to cut this off," Pyanfar muttered. "We got the plot on it. This is one godsforsaken mess. But we got that hope. Fact is the kif that moved on Meetpoint is about as worried as we are—that's what we were working on. That's all that got us out of that port."

"Does our captain know this?" Fiar asked.

"About the mahendo'sat? Dunno."

"No," Haral said. "I briefed *ker* Sirany on ops and course and the fact we and the kif aren't cozy. Mahen business I didn't say."

That was right. It had been in the report. Otherside of jump. She was losing things. She stuffed more sandwich in her mouth. Waved a hand at Haral, who took that signal and started spilling what else she knew; Tauran ears sagged, flagged, flattened. And:

"You talk to your captain," Pyanfar said, to Fiar, to Sif Tauran, "before you head below. Tell you another thing. You're on my crew shift. Tully here's crew. Shares quarters on this shift. My orders."

"Work," Tully objected. "I wake, work."

"Shut up. You're on my shift and you stay that way. Give me trouble I'll bed you with Skkukuk." She swallowed another mouthful of gfi and shuddered. "I got no time, we got no time." While Geran staggered off with a pair of cups Khym had given her, for herself and Chur. "We got to get there, is what. Our guns may be all Anuurn's got, you hear me?"

Tauran ears pricked and half-flattened again in dismay. And maybe, maybe an increasing bit of belief.

One of their number was lost already. *Moon Rising* arriving late or in any condition was a sight she would give a great deal to see. And there was less and less hope of it.

She shoved herself away from the table, shoved sandwich wrapper and empty cup into the disposal. She was working on autopilot, same as *The Pride*. Programmed stuff. Lower brain functions.

In the same way she turned and wandered through the bridge, where foreign crew sat working, as strange to see there as if they were mahen. Or human. Sirany Tauran acknowledged her presence, and Pyanfar flicked her ears back and nodded in return, before she wandered out and down the corridor.

Nothing else was wrong. If it were, Sirany would have said. Tauran crew was going to do something about intership communications, try to relay a coded do-watch on mahen ships. Or whatever they might manage to get across of their situation. While *Aja Jin* rode beside them.

She paused at Chur's open door. Geran was there, at the bedside. " 'Lo," she said, and was not sure if Chur responded; her eyes were blurring out on her. "Hey, we about got the hard part, cousin, just hang on, huh? We're all right. We'll make it."

She got into her own room, made one trip to the head, fell face-down into bed and coordinated herself enough to jab the bedside console and power the safety rig over, never forget that, gods, never forget, an old spacer never lost that reflex, move down the corridors right smart, stay out of open areas, get to safe small places in case the ship had to move. Broken bones and smashed skulls else. Spacers died of bad luck like that, a ship moving to save its steel hide and some poor bastard of a spacer smashed to pulp down a corridor become a three-story drop—epitaph on many an acquaintance: *the luck ran out.* On a ten-ring spacer it could happen—

Luck out on Tahar and Vrossaru. Gods help 'em.

After a dark space the restraint hummed, a large and warm weight settled onto the same mattress and a warmth settled about her. "We're about to brake," Khym said; and woke her up just enough to feel a drunken panic.

"Restraint," she said. "I've got it," he said, and she opened her eyes blearily on dim light and the arch of the safety web going over them, on a familiar face, a large arm going over her like the arch of the safety, a huge body shaping itself to hers, awful and stinking as they both were, straight out of jump and headed in again without respite. She hugged him back, hard.

The vanes cycled again, blowing velocity in a dizzying pulse of neither here nor there, right down to the lowest energy they could reasonably achieve. It was a hunter-ship maneuver. Honest freighter never had the reason to do a thing like that.

Urtur dust screamed over the hull, shields downed during the low-V of their turn and reacquisition, dust abrading the vanes. The whole ship wailed and keened in sound that hurt the ears.

Gods let Tahar make it after all, gods save the rest of us, where's the kif?

"Unnnh." Khym clenched his fist in her mane. "Claws, Py, gods—"

Realspace acceleration started up, the unsettling *G*-shift of rollover.

"We're going," she said, "we're going all right." Which might or might not be true. There might be enemies after all. Or a big rock the shields would fail on. It was all Tauran's problem now. Not hers. Not hers.

The dust wailed away, changing pitch.

"Py—"

He burrowed in closer, arm stretched above her. "I'm holding on," he said; and did: his weight kept her steady and comfortable, so that her groping reach after the handgrip became too much effort. He stayed like that forever, in a position that could not be comfortable for him. She tried again to move and get a foot braced against the safety-rim. "I've got it," he said again, "it's all right, Py."

"Sprain your gods-be shoulder," she muttered.

He breathed into her ear and tongued the inside of it, like in the dark of off-watch, like the two of them twenty and brand new again. "Good gods." She caught her breath and lost it again. "Not now, Khym."

"Think of a better time?"

He couldn't, under the strain they were under. But he amused himself. While they hurtled on toward oblivion and it was clear he was in pain.

"Gods be fool man," she said. "Love you like my sister." It sounded stupid. It was the only way she knew to say it to him, in hani, so he would know what she meant. "Always have."

"Man's got no brother," he said. He was breathing hard. Strain was in his voice, while the scream of the ship went on and he kept up his lackadaisical attentions. "Man's alone. Man never even knows what I've got exists at all. Not alone anymore. Never alone anymore. You were right. You were always right."

"Gods, I wish I were." *I wish I was right about what I'm doing, what I've done. We're going to jump and they haven't got that gods-be com on, they cut the gods-be com, we don't know when—*

She hazed out. She came to and realized *G*-stress had shifted and Khym had come down on her limp as a dead man, breathing hard. That was no matter. He was warm, and without him she would shiver; she felt it.

"Mark," a sudden voice came over com, not Haral's, stranger-voice. *"We're outbound."*

—into jump.

    —falling.

"Hello," said the young man, sitting on the rock, beneath blue sky, above a golden valley; and she took him for a Wanderer, up to no good on Chanur land. She set her jaw and drew a deep breath and made herself as tall as she could: No nonsense, man, take a look at the spacer rings and figure you're not dealing with any young fool; I'll shred your ears for you.

"Hello," she said, on her way up from Chanur lands, on the road. She had chosen to walk, when she might have made a landing here, created a little stir, coming in like that. But she was romantical in her youth.

What it got her was a young bandit, that was what. Real trouble, if he was also crazy. And worse trouble if he carried a knife. Some did.

"You're on Chanur land," she said. *"Wise if you'd move along."*

"You're Pyanfar," he said. And, gods, he was beautiful, his eyes large and gold-amber, his mane thick and wide. He stepped off his rock and landed on his feet in her path. *"Are you?"*

"Last I checked. Who in a mahen hell are you?"

"Khym Mahn," he said. *"Your husband."*

    —down.

        —alive. By the gods alive.

            —and where? Gods, where? Kura. Kura. Got to get up, get to the bridge—

No. First dump. Got—remember interval.

"We all right?" Khym murmured. His weight hurt her, hurt her all the way to her bones. She was smothering. "We at Kura?"

"Move," she said, gasped. Gasped again when he tried, and fought and moaned her way to the edge of the bed, reaching for the console, involved in the edge of the safety net. "This is Pyanfar. We all right? Where's that gods-be com? Give us com, hear?"

There was delay. *"Aye, captain,"* a strange voice said. And waited, by the gods *waited* during some on-bridge clearance, while a rag-eared bastard of a Tauran com officer asked *her* captain for clearance to report, that was what was going on.

"Gods-be—"

Khym moaned in that way he had when he was about to be sick. And rolled over to the other side of the bed.

Com came through, a busy crackle of voices.

Khym was not sick. But she did not bother him either. She lay there listening to the data-chatter and the heavy machine-sounds of the ship.

"We're not getting buoy-output, from Kura," someone said. And sent icewater flowing through her gut.

Someone swore over com.

"Standby number two dump," a voice said then.

And the ship cycled down again, a lurch half into hyperspace—

—no buoy at Kura.

—in hani space.

"I came here to wait," Khym said, *on that path, beside the way she would have had to take. Perhaps someone had just phoned. He was perhaps another romantical fool, having come this long trek to sit alone and wait on a prospective wife. His face had a kind of wistful vulnerability: she had not known it then, but when she remembered that look afterward, she knew what it was, of experience. It was hope. It was Khym's gentle and earnest self, open to everything, entranced with her.*

And he had escaped his sisters and his wives and gotten away alone. Or they did not care for him the way they ought: that had been her first thought when she believed he was who he claimed to be:

"You alone?" *Anything might have happened to him. Some bandit might have attacked him. Some Chanur hunter might have taken him for a bandit and asked questions later. Or he might have fallen in with a group of Chanur herders who might have taken a fancy to him, and precious much they would have believed his claims to be their neighbor. A lord never got out in public. Except at challenge. And Chanur and Mahn, old allies, would never challenge each other. In those days.*

Gods, *she had thought atop it all,* I'm betrothed to a fool in a house of rump-sitting fools who can't keep track of their own lord.

"It isn't far," he said, *pointing back toward Mahn land.*

Gods if I don't keep you better, *she had thought; and then knew she could indeed do no better. Home was not a place she stayed. She had to trust the other wives and his sisters and his female cousins, who clearly could not handle him.*

I'll have to knock heads in this house. Do I really want to get into this? If I weren't a fool I'd go home right now and leave him out here.

Gods, he's good-looking, isn't he?

But so're a dozen more I could find in the bushes.

"I don't do this all the time," he said earnestly. *"I told them—"* A gesture back toward the heart of Mahn land. *"—I was going to the garden. I guess no one's looked. I wanted to see you—"*

He knew he was in the wrong. He knew he had made a bad impression. He knew he had even made a dangerous mistake, if she had a notion to take offense and go back to her clan, figuring a fool of a man was an easy mark for her lord; then he might die a young fool, and Mahn was in danger, if she were either unscrupulous or truly outraged. He knew this and he worried, now, when it was too late. Break her neck, he might, if he could get his hands on her. But it was not likely that he could. She was fast, in those days, and looked it; and might have a knife or even a gun (she had); and had the advantage of her clan, who could kill him under any circumstances for being where he was, but under felony charges, could dispossess his sisters and his kin and send them out homeless. He knew all of this. ("I thought you would go back," he had said to her in after years. "I thought if you did I would have to challenge. And you would hate me. And so I couldn't do that either. I'd spend all my life trying to get you back.")

She set hands on hips and looked him up and down. Here in this isolated place where only they knew what might happen. And flattened her ears at him and slowly pricked them up again when his drooped. "Huh," she said. "Well, you got your border wrong." Even a man would know where that was. The flick of his ears showed he had indeed known. And deliberately trespassed, by the difference of two hills. The one in Chanur land just happened to have better vantage. And she came up close to him and up next to him and laid hands on him, which only his wives and his sisters could do without offense.

They were husband and wife before she walked him home. Out there on the border of Chanur land, as if she were some landless scoundrel and he some equally landless lad with hopes. She knew what she had married before she got there. A romantic, who, gods help her, asked her ten thousand questions, what was it like in space, where did she go, how long was she staying, would she come to see him every time she came back to the world?

He was ingenuous and reckless and a veritable encyclopedia of trivialities and natural science. He loved poking about under logs and into ponds, as devoted to hunting out curiosities as he ever was in hunting the game in which Mahn hills were rich; he could study a flower for whole minutes. Or the color of her eyes. She was not sure she liked being studied, there under Anuurn summer skies. She had come up to Mahn after a husband for politics, for finance, because they had dealt with him indirectly and believed his sister, that he was a decent domestic administrator and a man with some legal sense and no disposition to quarrel with

Chanur; a fast few days in Mahn, a satisfaction of certain urges that were about to come on her, and which were misery on shipboard—and she ended up with a shy-smiling young man who did a fool thing like trespass and let himself be led off into the bushes and who spent whole minutes telling her how unusual her eyes were and (being Khym) what the statistical frequency of gold-and-bronze was with her ancestry.

She had known then she had gotten herself an odd one.

> *—aren't we coming out?*

> *—Gods and mahen devils, what are they doing up there? Is that the drop?*

It was. *The Pride* came down with a vengeance; Khym moaned; and she did; and heard the curses over com about the inlaid program in Nav, about the fools who had laid it in and the condition of Tauran stomachs.

Got to get up there. Second dump, I got to.

They had laid in food stores in the room, pinned to the console. She groped after them, packets the same as they used on the bridge. Dared not retract the net. Not till she got an all-clear.

Then over com: *"Gods fry it to a mahen hell! What is that thing?"*

She jabbed the com button, fighting with the net. "What is it? What's going on up there? This is Pyanfar Chanur, gods rot it, what's going on?"

Delay.

"Gods blast you, don't you give me authorizations on my own ship! Give me Sirany! What in a mahen hell's going on up there?"

"Chanur. We're stable. Proceed with crew change."

"Gods be." She retracted the safety restraint, rolled over and got her stiffened legs off the edge and hauled her sore torso upright. "Oh, gods." *Never, never make love in jump, oh my ribs, my back, o gods.* She got herself upright, swallowed down a rush of nausea and reeled and staggered, limping, toward the door.

A black streak shot down the hall, about ankle-high, squealing as it went.

"Gods and thunders!"

The Dinner was loose again.

She came reeling and limping her way onto the bridge with the crew-call sounding out over the general address, and grabbed the back of observer-two seat to steady herself while she got a look at the monitors, at scan, at a situation that looked tranquil enough, except for the kif running silently ahead of them. No firing here. No output from station either.

They were in hani space, and Kura, the second-largest station in that space, was dead silent at least as far as buoy output went.

"Kif've tripped a warning," she surmised suddenly, and staggered her way toward Sirany Tauran, grabbing the back of her seat to hold herself steady. "That's where buoy went. Shut itself up the moment it got kifish ID. *Which* kifish ID it got and how long ago, that worries me. Has our escort made it in? Did they overjump us?"

"Neat and sweet, they did, about two hours' worth. Got plenty of power on those ships, and their emissions trail's strong and clear. Covering up everything."

"Have we got a message going out? I auto'ed a message for Kura."

"Aye, captain," the com officer said. "We're three minutes out of response time."

"It tells Kura what we can. Advising any ships here to get home. Fast."

"Same I sent," Sirany said. "Same all the others been sending, their own ships' wrap on it. The mahe's been transmitting coded stuff, long burst just before we left Urtur."

"Huh." More than *huh*. But not with Sirany. Worry broke out all over again. *Jik's still with us. Still on our side.* She scanned the monitors and saw the positioning of ships, the still-broken pattern, the hole where Tahar ought to be and was not. "No sign of Tahar."

"No sign."

She gnawed her mustaches and waited, eye on the chrono. "We get any response?"

"Negative."

"We got some godsrotted vermin run through here," Sirany said.

"I know it. We cleaned it out once. Skkukuk's gods-cursed food supply. Something's got loose again."

"F'godssakes. What are the things eating?"

"The ventilation filters."

"Lifesupport?"

"We got an electrical screen on the main systems from last time. We got it covered. Don't worry about it. The problem's in our watch. Just a stray, more'n likely. We'll get it."

"You thought of sabotage? That gods-be kif—"

"Is crew."

"Not in my watch, captain. That door of his is locked from the boards."

Question my judgment! On my bridge, in my chair, rot your hide! It was also a sane and reasonable suspicion. She restrained herself and got her voice quiet. "That kif," she said, "is our translator. *Protocol* officer and a gods-be decent one. Crew." It half-choked her. *Get your backside out of my chair, Tauran.* "He takes orders. Takes 'em fine. He's had a lot of chances to kill one or the other of us. Saved my hide back at Kef'k." *And I don't let him loose either, but he's not risking his neck in those corridors hunting vermin.* "Shift. I'll spell you, work with yours and spell 'em off as mine come in. You did a marvel, Tauran, got us here through that soup, real fine job and strange boards—" *Compliment the graynosed bastard. Keep us friendly. It* was *a good job. We're alive. We still got all our ships behind us, Jik and Harun and the rest, and all three kif out to front, and she's trying real hard to be polite, isn't she, Pyanfar Chanur? More suspicious than young Fiar. Wiser and harder and she has to be. She's got to push me a little. Got to keep her eyes clear and play the hardnose and try to get at truth, that's what she's after. She didn't fail us. Hasn't failed us.*

"Fancy stuff," Sirany said, still sitting. "Mahen-make. Real fancy. That comp's a wonder."

What'd you pay for it, Chanur? What buys equipment like this, state of the art, class one stuff, when Chanur's broke and bankrupt and all space knows it?

What's this we hear about you and mahendo'sat and the Meetpoint stsho?

Before we go to sleep again—what kind of ship are we on?

"We got our tail shot up. Emergency patch at Kshshti. The mahendo'sat wanted us out of there real bad. It's this passenger of ours."

"The kif or the human or the mahendo'sat?"

Pushing hard now. Her pulse hammered and her ears flattened as Sirany turned in her seat to look up at her.

Out in the dark places too long, maybe, Chanur?

"I'll argue that in the *han*," Pyanfar said. "But our records are unlocked. Had a look, have you?"

"I've been busy," Sirany said. "Real busy." Her ears were flat. "Interesting stuff. But the important thing's still to get home, isn't it? We do it your way. Your rules. You want that kif in on com, that's fine. We got two more jumps to go. You want us to bed down with the gods-be kif, if you want to vouch for his manners, I'll take your word on it."

"Listen. I mean this. Don't expect him to be hani___
hand off if he thinks you're pushing me. Tully's quiete___
of you and he's got troubles you don't know about; le___
husband—let me tell you, *ker* Sirany, since you've said not a w___
let me tell you: my husband's steady as anybody at the boards, and gods
help him, you won't shock him, not after this trip, he knows what ship
life is; he knows how to take orders, and you don't have to worry about
him. Or Tully. They work together in galley. No problem with tempers.
They *like* each other."

Sirany's ears went down and struggled bravely erect. "I saw the
ring."

"Didn't win it in a fight. Won it sitting the boards doing his job while
Haral Araun had her finger on a destruct button. And he'll take your
orders, or mine, or any senior's. That's how it is. I want your help, *ker*
Sirany. It's *good* we've got someone aboard who doubts us. And every
word in that log is true. You understand me?"

Sirany's ears went half-flat. White showed at the corners of her eyes
and her jaw was hard. Then the ears came up. "We'll worry about that
when we're through this alive."

"I'm fighting for the *han.* They'll call me a traitor. They'll put that on
my tomb if I get one. You understand me yet? It's one thing to be a
gods-be hero. If we get through this alive, I want someone, I want one
hani else to know this crew's not what they'll say we are."

Fear showed in Sirany's face. Undisguised. "What do you want, *company?*"

"I want your influence. We got two fights. *One's* in space. The other's
with that fool Ehrran and all her ilk. The *han* tucks its collective head
down and the kif have got the axe hanging over it. You hear me,
Tauran? I'll do whatever I have to. If you see what I see, you'll be with
me. Whatever else you think about me."

"You're a lunatic!"

"I'm doing something. What in a mahen hell has the *han* done right
lately? What has anybody done about it?" A claw popped through the
seat-leather as her hand clenched tighter. A second. "Tauran, how long
do you think we can sit still while the Compact's blown to a mahen
hell? Humanity's coming in on us. Mahendo'sat've done something stupid, they've done something that's touched off humans and got something started that they don't understand and I'm not sure the humans
do: Tully's witness to that, and he warned us. Jik's tried to do something to save us all, and it's cost him. He at least knows his people've

'm fools. Like the stsho. Like hani. *And* the kif. And maybe the tc'a, gods save us. And even the humans may know by now. Most of 'em are fools by doing something. Ehrran just got *us* a brand-new treaty with the stsho, did you know that? And look where they are. Look what we're into. The kif just took 'em. We got kif backing into hani space. We got Kura not answering here. We got Akkhtimakt in such a mess that hani space is the only thing left he can get to, because Sikkukkut's sent out ships to every jump-point in reach and blocked his other routes. Meanwhile there's a major mahendo'sat push coming down out of Kshshti, which if Akkhtimakt's spies are worth anything, he knows and Sikkukkut doesn't—*he's* been at Kita and up by Kshshti. That bastard's going to let Sikkukkut take the hit from the mahendo'sat while he pulls off into hani space and comes up again at the mahen underbelly, straight up at Iji. You *know* the mahendo'sat, you know they'll fragment if the Personage goes out. They won't have a defense. And humanity's going to be right in the middle of mahen territory with a whole lot of ships, ships that can jump short, just like our friends the mahendo'sat and just like the kif, ships that can shorten the time between strikes like nothing we want to imagine. But we won't worry about it. We'll be lucky to have a world left. And we'll belong to whoever wins. With nothing to say about it. If we survive at all. We got *one* of our men in space. One, and you know how safe this ship is, with half the kif in the universe hunting us and the other half about to. The whole rest of our species is on Anuurn. And it takes one big rock, Sirany Tauran, one *C*-charged rock, and we're all widows and brotherless. Forever. You hear me? You know what I'm saying?"

Tauran said nothing. The ship hurtled on, crossing planetary diameters in every few heartbeats. In silence, all about them, inside the ship, inside the space between them.

"Tauran."

"I hear you. This is all crazy."

"Tauran's a spacing clan. Three generations. You know what I'm talking about. That mess you got into at Meetpoint. Could you even explain to those old old women in the *han* why you couldn't take out running? What chances you had getting up to *V* or what those distances are like? How many of 'em *understand* a stsho?"

"*Who* understands a stsho?"

"How do they formulate policy with them, make a treaty with them, tell *us* who live out here that we're supposed to stand off the kif, do I guess—that they expect us to dispose of the kifish problem, because it's going to take them ten, twenty years to change their concept of the way kif behave, or what the mahendo'sat are likely to do, and gods save us when they start dealing with the humans and their three governments, all fighting each other? What in a mahen hell are they going to do right now when Akkhtimakt comes into system? Order the Llun to bar them from station? Put hegemony sanctions on them? *Study* the problem?"

"It's too much—"

"I'm asking another clan to damn itself. With me. I'm asking all the rest of you. I'm asking those who know what I'm talking about to do something about it. We're not dealing with scattered pirates anymore. Hani out here'll do the right thing. I'm betting all we've got on that. Traders'll have stripped down, some go home, some scatter like seeds on a high wind. Everywhere. They're warned. But it won't save us from a rock. It won't protect us if some kif decides to take our species out. I can't get to the *han* to tell them what I'm telling you. I can't explain what happened at Meetpoint—gods *know* what's happened at Meetpoint. Or what's going to follow us. Or when. If Sikkukkut sent a ship out we don't know about, and some bastard's tailing us, they might pick up our directional transmissions. We can't do anything but what we've done."

"I read your running orders. I got your message from Sif. And I'm not a fool."

"I never took you for one. I got that impression early on. And I've got to go on walking the track I've been walking. Inside. Same as Jik's done. Till we've got Akkhtimakt stopped. There aren't enough hani ships in all space to do what we have to do, against hunter-ships and gods know what. We *need* the kif's firepower, even at the risk we're running. That's the game I'm playing, Tauran, and you know what I'll hear from the *han* if I can even get to 'em. *Illegal contacts. Violation of treaties. Illegal personnel for the eternal gods' sake, on my ship.* If somehow we live through this and the *han*'s still operating, they'll probably hit us both with a charge of *registry* violations. That's how much they understand. You *know* who we're dealing with. Those old women are up with every twitch and power shift in the insystem markets, they know who's leaning where in the vote, they know every move and current in Anuurn affairs, and every dustup in history between the River Hegemony and the Amphictiony of Pesh and every other gods-be particle of past history that isn't going to matter a whole lot, Tauran, if one incoming rock kills every living thing on the planet back to the bugs and the worms, is it? A whole lot of expertise that's by the gods *useless* in the only question that matters, which is what are we going to by the gods *do,* Tauran, with what we know and where we are, and what we got behind us and ahead of us that we know about and they don't?"

"I'm hearing you," Sirany said. There had been a quiet stir about. Chanur crew was up. Tauran crew was still in place. But it was very quiet now. "I'm hearing you. I'm agreeing with you. But I've still got to think about this, Chanur."

"Think all the way to Kura Point. I'm going to send you Sifeny and Fiar back to your shift; let you all work it out. Take my own back to the boards. Human and my husband and the kif and all. With my thanks, *ker* Sirany. They're good. I don't like to mess with teams that work. Yours or mine. And we need some crew rested full. For contingencies."

"You got it." Sirany released restraints and climbed out of the chair. "Get you a sandwich back here," she said then, and gathered up her crew, galleyward bound. Pyanfar stared at her retreating back, still hanging onto the seat. In case. The way any spacer held onto things in a moving ship. She looked at her own crew, at sober faces of Chanur who had arrived around her.

Ears lifted. "Good," Haral said.

"I hope," she said, and slid a glance Geran's way, at a face that showed trouble. "How is she?"

Geran shrugged. The woman had gone so gaunt herself that her ribs showed. Her worry was tautly held, made a darker spot above her nose, an indentation in her brow that had gotten to be part of her expression.

"You're a mess yourself. We need you. Get in there with Sirany's crew, get some food down you; Tully'll run some back to Chur. Don't argue with me, gods rot it, I'll have your ears. Chur'll have mine if I get her there without you. Hilfy, get the rest of us up here." The assigned crew was all there, all settling in as Hilfy's voice began calling Tully and Khym and Skkukuk on the general speakers.

"Mess," Pyanfar said, and flung herself into her chair. Haral was beside her, already in control of things. "No sign of *Moon Rising.*"

There had been a chance. There was less and less. It was four months back at Meetpoint, as hyperlight ran down the starlanes, but not by the way they traveled; whatever had happened there was four, five months old and about to get older.

"Long time back," she said, while the data flowed past her.

"Kura's alive," Haral said. "Just not talking. Kif's scared them plenty. They shut down everything. They got no ships here or they're all lying silent."

They had been a long time away from home. And far from the *han.*
"Gods know what the stsho taught us, huh?"

Years the way homeworld saw it. That was the way of spacers. To
stay young while the worlds aged, and groundlings connived and con-
trived their little worldly plots and made their gains in the intervals
when spacers were strung out between the stars, lost in dreams.

"Kif's not having any trouble out there. Real fine piece of navigation,
that."

"We got troubles, Skkukuk's gods-be dinner's loose again. Got careless with his door open."

"Or we missed a couple of 'em."

"What's it eating, that's what Sirany wanted to know. That's what *I*
want to know."

"Maybe it's gotten *acclimated* to electric shock," Hilfy said, breaking
in on station-to-station. *"Adaptive,* Skkukuk said they were. Akkhtish
life."

She looked straight across at Haral with a sinking feeling about her
stomach.

"Lifesupport," Haral said.

"Check it. Those godsforsaken things eat plastics."

"We'll get it." Haral was out of her seat and headed. "Hilfy, get the
menfolk on it. Get Skkukuk!"

"We can't leave our gods-be schedule. Can't. We got no way to recalc
this thing and get word to all the ships back there fast enough. Gods rot
it—" They were off auto-pilot see-and-evade while crew was coming up.
It put the ship at some risk of damage. Not doing it was worse in terms
of fragile flesh and bone. They had lives at stake back there. She
punched a button to usurp com. *"Ker* Sirany, we're staying stable a
good half hour. I'm taking your advice on the vermin. We're trying to
track them down."

"Understood," Sirany's voice came back, clear above the quiet of
other voices in the galley. And, politic, not one other word.

Second jab of keys tied into com. "Skkukuk, this is the captain speaking, you hear me, son? Your gods-be dinner's loose again, I want 'em
counted, I want to know where it is, I want it out of our way, or I'll
have your hide for a wallhanging, you hear me?"

"Kkkkt," the answer came back, dopplered from pickup to pickup.
"Hakt', I let nothing escape, this is not my doing, not my doing, mekt-
hakt'—*I am on my way, at once, at once—Fools, fools, hold the lift!"*

He doubtless believed it about the wallhanging. She ducked her head between her hands and raked her claws through her mane. Tell the Tauran they were sane and this cut loose. It was ludicrous. It was deadly serious. No telling what systems the things could take out. The whole ship was infested. She had lost her reputation already. She stank, the whole ship stank, was acrawl with kifish vermin and gods knew what else, the whole clean, well-ordered universe was turned inside out and the vermin were the last, grotesque insult. The gods' own dark humor, that was what it was; just a final, ugly joke on the species. Take out the ship that might save them, with a mucked-up lifesupport, filters ruined, gods knew where they could get in and short something out with their wickedly sharp little teeth.

How many of them?

Breeding during jump? Something that lived so gods-be fast it just went on living and breeding even in hyperspace, generations upon nasty, squealing little generations?

Nothing could do that. Most animals did well to breed at all on shipboard, with all the noise and the clatter and clank that kept them upset; *nothing* could shift its metabolism like that and live realtime in hyperspace.

Even kif couldn't.

Could they?

She stared at the situation on the screens in front of her, she kept the ship on course while one crew had its necessary meal in the galley; and Geran came back to tell her she had just reassigned Khym and Tully from galley to the hunt and she was, by the captain's leave, taking a cup of soup to her sister, by the captain's leave. Please. In spite of her specific orders.

"Gods. Yes." Pyanfar took another desperate swipe at her disordered mane and part of it came out on her claws, the way a body always shed during jump, but no one on ship had had a bath in over four realspace months and six or so subjective days. "How is she?"

"Just real still. Says—says there's a trouble at home. Says there's kif going there. Says *Moon Rising*'s behind us. Akkhtimakt's ten days up on us. She says."

A chill went up Pyanfar's spine, and right down again to the gut. "She could be right." For a moment she had a conviction Chur could well be right: crack scan tech and sometime navigator, Chur *knew* how much time determined hunter ships could gain on a band of freighters. Then she saw it the way Geran had to see it. Chur was a practical woman. And she was babbling prophecies across lightyears. Jump could do that to a mind. There were casualties who never came in out of the dark. She had seen them, sitting in the sun at hospital, with Anuurn's blue sky above them forever and not a realization in the world where they were.

They were everywhere, that was their delusion. They would always be everywhere. If there was anything mystical about it, the thing that was themselves had just reached infinity and stayed there, like a machine with a broken cutoff switch.

"She wants to work," Geran said.

"Tell her—" Pyanfar drew a breath. *"Can* she?"

"No."

"Get her fed. We got an hour insystem here. I'm taking you offshift; you stay with her."

"No." Geran's ears went flat. "No, captain."

"You want one of the Tauran? Tully, f'godssakes? You do it. We got Tirun to take scan. We can run this one short or I can haul Sif back in. *Stay* there."

Geran's face went hard and desperate. Ears flicked and struggled up again. "Tully," she said. "I mean, he's not going to *do* anything, is he? Sleeps with us below. They're friends. Aren't they?"

"Yeah." Less said on that the better. "The good of the ship. Good of —a whole lot of people. Yes. I want you on the boards if you got your mind there."

"It'll be there," Geran said. "Do her good. She can't argue with Tully. I'll feel better about it." And she went, with a solid purpose in her stride.

Pyanfar settled into her place, listened to the chatter insystem, ran checks, took a cup of gfi when Fiar came bringing cups round. Charity. Out of their own galley.

The hunt went on, upper decks and lower. And the system they were running through stayed far quieter than it ought to be.

"They got the upperdecks filter changed out," Hilfy said. "Caught three of those things. Skkukuk swears they didn't slip from his collection. Old stuff, he says. They're coming from somewhere."

"Great. Wonderful." She clicked through changes on the comp. "That's fine news." *Ought not to snap. Crew has enough on their minds.* "Sorry."

"Aye, captain."

You've grown a lot, Hilfy Chanur. Can't tell you that. Grown woman never wants to hear that. Can't tell you anything anymore.

"First escort's jumped," Tirun said. "We're on—"

The fifteen-minute warning sounded, a double pulse. *"That's fifteen,"* Hilfy's voice rang out through the halls.

Pyanfar punched in on the same channel. "Leave it, whatever it is. Give us an easy trip, get yourselves to stations and quarters, wherever they are, forget the gods-be mess, I want you where you're going on the five. Tully, you go to Chur's room. Now."

"Got," that lone human voice came back. And other acknowledgments. Perhaps no one had broken it to Tully until now where he was spending the jump.

He would not object. He understood. Would do anything for Chur. *Friend,* he would say.

What Chur would say about Tully in her bed was another matter.

Annoy her. Make her mad. Get her mind *back.* That was what might work. Of a sudden she saw Geran's logic, clear and plain.

"He's what?" Chur murmured, and blinked at her sister, and at Tully standing all diffident at the foot of her bed.

"Taking care of you," Geran said. "Mind your manners. You take advantage of him the captain'll skin you. Hear?"

Chur blinked again, deciding finally that this was funny. The worried look on Tully's face was funny. There was a time she would have worried. Had been a time—yesterday, it seemed—when she had wanted no more of anything but hani. It was strange how all that had washed away, as if jump had left it behind, left her washed out, new, all things and everywhere. A god would feel this strange sensation, as if all space was her body and her brain, the stars so many particles. She might be a god. She laughed at them both, and flexed the fingers on the arm so long stiff it had gone beyond pain. Machinery ticked away. She had learned how to cheat it, how to keep her heart quiet and not trigger its anesthetizing flood through the tubes. She felt the pulse increase and settled it down again, deliberately.

"Brought me a handsome lover, have you? I must be better. C'mon, Tully. It's all right. They got one hand out of operation."

"I stay with," he said. Innocent of everything.

He stank. Everyone did. She did. There was no help for it, though Geran tried to keep her clean. That was all right too. Geran went off and left them together, Tully standing there lost-looking, and the com crackling with reports.

The reports confused her. They had hunted the black things out at— wherever they had been.

They were back again at Kura. Little slinking evils. A god might have worse things to deal with. They were only nuisance-nightmares.

"Go soon," Tully said, and sat on the edge of her bed. "I be with you." He patted her knee under the blankets. That hurt a little. All her joints ached. "You be fine, Chur."

It was nice to be told that by someone other than Geran, who was biased. She drew a larger breath.

"We go to Anuurn," he said, and held up two slender, agile fingers. "Two jump. We got—" Another rearrangement of the fingers. "Nine ship. Make safe."

"Against the kif?" For a moment space went inside and out. "No. Tell the captain—tell the captain—trouble. They'll be waiting off Tyar."

"Geran tell," Tully said. "She tell, all right?"

"Logic," Chur said, and waved the free hand, a loose, limp failure of a gesture. "Logic—position. The geometry of the thing—" She stared at him in despair. Geran had looked at her as if she were crazed. Tully simply blinked, beyond his vocabulary.

"Danger," she said. *"Danger,* gods rot it."

"Understand," he said. And looked at her with fear. With Geran's look.

Crew returned. Pyanfar ran the checks. They were still on the mark. They had no communication with the other ships excepting the necessary crosschecks of position and exchange of navigational data. It was not politic or wise, considering possibility of spies overhearing them, to do more than they had done. Their messages would be reported, as often as they were detected, and some they had sent were already pushing the limits of prudence.

Hakkikt, she would say, such arguments were necessary. They won us allies. Isn't that the point?

If she got the chance.

The five-minute warning sounded. The ship started procedures. Data started coming up. Tauran crew and their mahen passengers reported themselves secure.

"Sukk just made jump," Geran said.

"Coming up on mark," Haral said.

They left behind a scrap of message, to persist after them. *Danger to Anuurn. Assist.*

Chapter Ten

... Down. ...
     ... one more time. ...
        ... *"Kura Point, Pyanfar."*

She was young. Back in Urarun's day. Green kid on her first trip back home again. Looking forward to Anuurn and swaggering about the estate.

See me. Ring and all. Got this scratch dockside at Meetpoint, I did. Difference of opinion, me and a Jesur crewwoman.

Gods bless. What were we fighting about?

No matter. We healed fast in those days.

"Meet you at the door, Hal." With a slow and heavy-lidded look, while a graynosed spacer (that was the name: Pura Jesur) Pura Jesur thought she could push a couple of Chanur kids and have a bit of fun. Herself and Haral, insubordinate and full of young arrogance toward a rival ship's crew. And drunk. That too.

Gods save us.

Urarun Chanur being the captain on the old Golden Sun. *She retired as captain two voyages after. Chanur clan took the ship out of service, sold it finally to Thusar, where it ran under the name of Thusar's Merit, a little ship. A lot of ship, for a little clan like Thusar, new to spacefaring. Chanur retired the shipname. Transferred the crew eventually, as many together as they could, to the newbuilt* Pride. *Urarun Chanur died in her sleep one night planetside.*

. . . "Captain."

"I got it, we're on, aren't we?"

"We're running smooth."

How's Chur? Calm down, she won't answer yet. Can't answer. Gods-be drugs. No. Tully's with her. "Tully. Report. How is Chur?"

A long pause. Muzzy human. Tully was always hard to rouse after jump.

"Tully? How's Chur, Tully?" *Is she alive, Tully? F'godssakes, answer back there.*

"She sleep."

"Are you sure? Is she all right?" With Geran listening. But it was what Geran had to know.

"She sleep," Tully's voice came back again.

"We've got acquisition on our escort," Geran said, dead calm, onto business. "We're still doing fine, captain."

I have no nerves, captain. The job gets done. For the ship and all of us.

"No buoy here, either," Haral muttered.

"No sign of anything." She drank down the concentrates. Her hand shook. She wadded up the foil packet and thrust it into the bin after, and wiped her face. An appalling lot of hair came away. Teeth were sore, when she pushed them with her tongue. One felt loose. That more than any wound she had ever suffered made her afraid; not of dying. Of time. Of the inevitable wall that said this far for a body and no further, courage and wit and skill notwithstanding.

Where are we? Is what I remember true?

Gods, how did I get here? Get this old?

Kif. Kif out in front of us. It's all true. No hallucination. Gods, if it were a hallucination, if I was back there with Urarun all this time, if I never knew these things, if these friends, this ship, this terrible mess— were all illusion—

Earflick. A weighty number of rings chimed and rang against each other.

Old graynose. Yourself, Pyanfar. Here. In this gods-be mess. Wake up. Come back. You're fuzzed and drifting. . . .

. . . *when did I get old?*

Haral beside her. A flash and flicker of monitors at her board. Scan information vanished for a checklist, one critical moment. Reappeared again. Haral had missed a switch and changed all the priorities in a rippling flicker of screens. *Haral* had missed. That never happened.

"You on?"

"I got it, cap'n. Sorry. That's confirm on *Aja Jin.* They're in on schedule."

Vermin. Little vermin.

drop again. . . .

. . . *reform.*

". . . got us stable."

"Hilfy. Relay that. Tell our relief we're looking for 'em up here fast as they can do it. Skkukuk, you're discharged. Get some rest."

"*Hakt',* I should check the filter traps."

"Do it fast, then. Go to it."

"Yes, *hakt'.*"

Long hour till jump-out.

And still days down. She did not want to know how many. The figures were lost in her jump-mazed brain.

Akkhtimakt's ships were indisputably in front of them, already gone, in transit toward Anuurn. Of the two missing probes, nothing. Their own escort was there, that was all.

She forced another nutrients-packet down. Swallowed and listened to an eerily deserted nowhere, the dark mass of Kura Point, its little beacon extinguished. Not a place hani had ever found it economical to put a station, it was just an astronomical oddity, Kura Point Mass, a lump of rock that just incidentally made hani an independent species—making a route to Meetpoint and other species through *hani* space only, and not through mahen Ajir, to the sure annoyance of the mahendo'sat.

An accident of nature that had cut four months off the Anuurn-Kura run and saved the whole hani species from becoming a dependency of the mahendo'sat.

It just sat there radiating away, dead and quiet. A chancy, spooky place where hani met and hailed each other, glad of another voice in the tomblike silences. Have a breakdown here and a ship just sat and waited for rescue. Which might bankrupt a running ship. Weeks waiting on help and months getting a repair crew out from Anuurn or Kura star.

She made the count on those coming in behind them. "Send," she said to Hilfy. "*The Pride of Chanur* to all ships. Status check."

Because the silence oppressed her, because of a sudden, this last, this perilous last jump, she wanted a voice or two out of the dark. She wanted Jik's most of all, wanted it to come across the way she was used to hearing it, deep and humorous and reservedly friendly.

Crazy. Crazy impulse. Why him? Ought to want his ears, I should, I ought.

Lying bastard that he is. He's not suffering on that ship of his. Got enough crew to rotate shifts with no pain at all.

They're built *for this kind of run. A ship like* Lightweaver, *or* Starwind, *back there, they're going to be feeling it near as bad as we are, gods help 'em.*

Kifish advisements came in, cold and exact. No pain there either. *We are running well,* one sent. *Glory to the* hakkikt.

Hani ships: *"We're hanging on."*—Harun's Industry.

"We got one system on backup."—Pauran's Lightweaver.

"We counting? We got four." That was *Shaurnurn's Hope,* a youngish voice. *"We're patching, this lay-through."*

"We're doing all right. We've got a few red-light conditions. We're seeing to them." Munur Faha, on *Starwind*.

And last of all: *"We all time good condition, friend. I be here, no worry. What you 'spect, a?"*

Hilfy made acknowledgments, passed advisements, in a wan, tired voice.

And from Geran, quietly, speaking to someone: "How is she?"

"Geran. You want to get back there? That's an order, cousin."

"Aye."

No argument this time. Tirun signaled she was covering that station. A belt clicked, and Pyanfar gnawed her mustaches and fought the hypnosis of the blinking lights, the wash of green on the board—*Going to lose her,* was the thought that wanted through, and she would not let it.

Bone and muscle. Vital organs. Nutrients. Steel and plastics could last the trip. Living bodies needed time to rebuild, and there was no recovery in their schedule.

Do kif suffer this?

Image of a black bundle of rags, Skkukuk collapsing in her arms, virtually moribund in the first jump they had made.

Image of black, ravenous lengths of fur and muscle and sharp little teeth gnawing away at *The Pride's* vitals, fatal, voracious stupidity destroying the vessel which kept them from the cold of space.

Like the *han* and the stsho.

We learned the lesson: the kif must have learned it. The law of controlled predation: neither predator nor prey can survive alone. Intelligent predators manage their resources.

Do you recall that lesson, Sikkukkut?

Burn the land? Lay waste whole ecosystems?

Suicide, *na* kif. Kill the stsho and you will die. Take out hani and mahendo'sat and the economy the stsho live on collapses, same result.

A predator needs his rivals as much as he needs his prey. Ecosystems interlock. One predator, one prey, can never sustain itself.

Her eyes hazed out. She knew the signs. Forced herself back again, arched her shoulders. Withdrew her arm from the brace and hissed at the pain.

"You all right?" Haral asked.

"Gods," she said, short of breath from the hurt. *Old age, cousin. It's old age for sure. You and me. It's not fair this should happen to us. We were immortal. Weren't we?* "We got one more jump to make. One more." That reassurance was for herself. *Not that much more to go, Pyanfar, not that far. Done it time after time, haven't you, lived days while Anuurn lives a month. Two months out and back.*

But the gods of the Wide Dark gave time with one hand and took it with the other. Wore a spacer out from the inside, strained the heart, took the steadiness from the hands. Kohan was graying, last she saw him. Graying in earnest. But he sat on his cushions in the stability his wives provided him in Chanur's lands, and hunted his preserves and had the best of care. He never knew hunger, only a lunch delayed in the field, his wives and daughters and nieces and cousins and juvenile sons all slogging along with the makings of a small feast. Rough living, the groundlings thought. A hunt burned off the fat and quickened the blood and a little hunger put an edge on a body.

O gods, Kohan. Late lunch. A tragedy.

Never been jump-stretched, never had your fur falling out so thick it left a shimmer of bare skin beneath it, never had your backside hurt because the bones hit the seat, never wake up from jump and find the bones and tendons all prominent, your hand like a stranger's at the end of your arm, your teeth sore and your joints aching like the stab of a knife between the bones.

Another food packet. Something on the stomach.

"What in a mahen hell's keeping Tauran?"

"They're in the lift," Hilfy said. About the time the lift door opened, bright and spreading reflection in the right-hand monitor, and dark figures came down the hall, resolving themselves into hani silhouettes and hani presence.

She turned the chair around and saw Sirany Tauran, saw her face change and her ears flatten in dismay at what she saw. Like looking in a mirror. *Am I that bad?*

She reckoned that she was.

"We're stable, everything clear," she said to Sirany. And levered herself up from the chair, caught herself on the arm and on Sirany's suddenly offered hand. She had a close view of Sirany's face then, wide, shocked eyes. She shoved herself upright and tried to find equilibrium.

"*Ker* Pyanfar—"

"Want to rest," she said.

"Go to it," Sirany said. "We'll bring you something. You, your whole crew. Get to bed."

Pity, Tauran?

She resented that. Resented it with an irrational touchiness and knew that it was irrational. It was concern the Tauran offered her. Was belief in them. Was what she had been trying to rouse in Tauran in this long alternate life-death they were locked in.

How long? Months on months now.

How long have the kif had to do harm at Anuurn?

Gods, were they gone from Urtur long before us? Was the force at Meetpoint only a part of what they have? Were they already weeks ahead of us?

Are we running into a trap meant for Sikkukkut?

Chur seeing visions.

Black vermin in the ducts.

"Pyanfar—"

A hard grip settled onto her right shoulder. Claws bit. She stared into lambent, hani eyes. "I let Jik go," she mumbled, knowing she was rambling, but suddenly it seemed to matter, it seemed something that Tauran had to know, part of the puzzle, the jagged pieces that resulted when someone dropped the universe and it shattered, scattered, made new patterns that a ship had to navigate. "It's important." But that was not enough to say. "The mahendo'sat are the key. Neither predator nor prey. They're important. Always prying into things. Like Tully. The humans are like them. Both predator and prey. Be careful. The mahendo'sat didn't know that. Humans are trouble. They'll confound us like the mahendo'sat. Like the methane-breathers. The kif know that. Even the *han* had instinct on their side in that one. We were right."

"Captain," Haral said. Haral's face this time, displacing the other. "Captain, here's *here*. Watch the time, cap'n."

She blinked. Jolted back to physical motion again instead of all-movement, particle-dance and star motions. Blinked again. "Yeah," she said. Blinked a third time and things hurt again. Her legs felt unsteady. "I'm going."

("Is she all right?" someone asked, not a Chanur voice. Young voice. Fiar.)

Pyanfar turned around, flattened her ears, fixed the young tech with a stare. "She's *fine,* youngster." She drew a larger breath, continued the sweep of her eyes on back to Sirany. "I've preset us to drop close in. May have been a mistake. We do the best we can."

Doubt. Plain and clear on Sirany's face. *This is what we've got to rely on, is it? Woman's been through too much. Too long, too far. We're bound to sit duty on this leg and we have to hand off the ship at Anuurn to a lunatic. With all that may be at stake.*

"Sirany, if you think I'm not tracking right, you're mistaken."

"Didn't say that." Not a bristle at the familiarity of first names. Not a twitch of irritation. It *was* pity. The ship crossed planetary diameters at a breath or two, and a fool wanted long arguments on the bridge, distracting the crew from their business.

"Get to work," Pyanfar said. "Eyes on those boards!" Ordering the wrong crew. *"Somebody* get their eyes on those boards. I don't care which." *So much for inattention, Sirany Tauran. Which of us is wit-wandering?* "I'm telling you," she said, trying to dredge gnosis up from the free-association where it was wandering. Dark territory. Nowhere. Numbers and lines spread wide through the Compact. "Jik is the best we've got. Rely on him and his First. And I want com through to allship this time. The kif too. We can't afford to come out the other side wondering where we are."

No, Pyanfar Chanur, we certainly can't afford that. Still the doubt. Below the surface now, like a fish gone into deep waters. Surface smooth, a relief to have the proprieties back again. But the doubt was still cruising along down there, all sleek and dark and quiet.

To flare up at the wrong moment, and turn and bite you, yes, Pyanfar Chanur.

"We're still on auto?" Sirany asked. *"Still?"*

"Good computer," Pyanfar said. "Good crew. I told you those nav figures are *right.* I'm not a liar, *ker* Sirany."

"No," Sirany said, quiet against her heat, "I really don't think you are."

"What I was talking about. Think on it, you said. *Think* on it." *See, I remember. Do you, Tauran? Your mind that clear? Or do you still think I'm crazy?* "I'm asking again. Here and now. Before we get make drop at Anuurn."

"Join you?"

"That's what I'm asking. You're supposed to give the rest of the captains out there some kind of report before then, aren't you? Sure you are. But you haven't, yet. Jik would have reported it to us. Unless you coded it real clever." She leaned hard on the chair back, eased the weight on her legs. "What are you going to tell them?"

Long hesitation. "That you're no pirate. That we're convinced of that."

She stood there a moment. Blinked, trying to run it through her brain. "But not that we're right."

Sirany's ears went down. Not anger. Profound distress. "I'm still figuring that out for myself."

"How long are you going to think about it, huh?" Her pulse thumped in her ears. The bridge fuzzed in one long smear of lights both white and green. "We got no gods-be time left when we come out. You understand that?"

"You've set the comp that way. I know."

Black closed in. Cleared again. "I set it," she said carefully, "to get us in there as close in the well as we could get. We got one lousy lot of Akkhtimakt's kif in our way. We're not going to have time to sit and talk about it. We don't have the guns to hammer our way clear across system from far out. We aren't fit for a long fight. This ship has *seen* fighting like that before, at Gaohn, captain, and I don't want to do it again. Odds get up to you, fast."

A hand descended on her shoulder, ever so gently. "Cap'n. Time."

"I'm onto it, Haral, I'm gods-be onto it." She drew herself up on a deep breath. "We're one ship down, we're up to our noses in kif, and I am not, by the gods greater and lesser, *ker* Sirany Tauran, a raving lunatic." A second breath, speech clear and spaced this time. No shouting, no hysteria. "I am giving you my sane assessment of the situation: we're aiming one set of kif at the other set and hoping to the gods we have enough left to push them outsystem. If we don't, we are going to die there, collectively and gods hope, without seeing what else will happen. And I am not having my plans tampered with and my commu-

nications setup interfered with and myself and my crew deprived of necessary information *or of control of this ship at the last moment* do we understand each other, *ker* Sirany? I'm going to take controls at Anuurn. My shift. That's the way I set it up, that's the way it's going to be, don't play hero with me. You want to fight, you'll get your share. Not on the drop!"

Sirany's ears were down. Not anger. That fright-doubt expression again. They lifted and twitched and flattened and lifted again. *And what will you do about it, you and your crew, none of you fit to stand?*

Someone moved. More than one someone out of a chair.

Khym's gusting breath. Khym looming like a shadow over in the peripheries of her vision.

Male and crazy. It was in the sudden nervous flick of Sirany's eyes.

"He's on our side," Pyanfar said hoarsely. She was disarmed by that threatening move of his. There was nothing left to say. Sirany doubted her husband's sanity if not her own and they had just lost all hope of reason. Clock was running. The ship was headed for jump and they had crew to take care of. She made a despairing wave of her hand, not sure she could find equilibrium if she let go of the chair. Everything swam in a blur. "See you otherside, *ker* Sirany. Gods hope." She let go, resisted the urge to grab Khym's arm, managed to keep the deck stable and the exit steady in her vision.

"Pyanfar." Sirany's voice, name unadorned.

She managed to turn around. Steadied herself, Khym's shadow to her left, Hilfy and Tirun over there somewhere. Haral still beyond.

"It's concern, understand," Sirany said. "It's not—doubt, *ker* Pyanfar."

"I'm going to fall on my face," she said calmly, rationally. And stared as much at the level line of the control boards beyond Sirany's back, to keep something level in her vision. The bridge was trying to tilt. "Send us something to eat for godssakes and let us go, *ker* Sirany."

She managed to turn, still keeping the counters level in her sight, walked out without the use of her internal equilibrium. One foot in front of the other. Khym was behind her. Others were. Chur's door was shut as she passed it. Where Geran was—she could not remember, whether Geran had gone to the galley, whether she had heard her pass that corridor.

She reached the door of her own quarters. Fumbled after the lock and got it, and staggered in and fell into bed.

"I'm going after food," Khym said in a voice hoarse and deep.

"They'll do it."

"Me," he said. "I make sure it gets done. We're time-critical."

And came back out of a confusing darkness and shook at her till she sat up and wrapped her hands around the cup he gave her. Whole jug of the stuff with him. Awful. Full of sickly spices. Tofi. "Gods, you got to put that stuff in?"

"Way I cook. Shut up and drink it. It's got calories."

She drank it, drank another cup because he insisted. Ate the dried stuff. Her hands just fell away limp and dropped the packets. He fell in beside her. Out of some terrible reverberating tunnel the intercom was ringing with strange hani voices: *"Rig for jump."* Operations noises. Strange crew. The words echoed and twisted in and out of her brain, losing focus. She felt after the security of the restraint webbing, found it, and all the while the room kept coming and going.

Khym had remembered the safeties. Half conscious as he was, he had remembered that.

"They're all right," some real voice said from the doorway. "Excuse me, captain."

It confused her to a mahen hell. The door shut. Tauran security check.

They had had a door open.

Black things. Might *feed* on a body while it was helpless.

Kifish life, active in jump, when they lay inert and unable to move, to feel pain. Might wake up with fingers gone. Bleed to death. Gnawed to a rack of bones, aswarm with slinking vermin.

A siren went.

"We're going," Khym mumbled against her shoulder.

She grabbed him and held tight. Trust their lives to Tauran. And her programming and the Nav-comp, and the lock on that door.

"Last jump," Hilfy murmured, in her bunk beside Haral's and Tri-un's and Geran's, down in crew quarters. Two beds were empty. Chur's and Tully's. She clenched her claws into the mattress, counting breaths. Tully had stayed topside with Chur. She had been shocked when Geran showed up to join them. But: "I got to work otherside," Geran had said. As if she had turned all emotion off. Their lives and more than their lives rode on Geran, otherside. That was true. And Geran came down to rest with them, face cold and set, leaving her sister to Tully's care a second time. "He's good with her," Geran had said. "She wanted him."

And sent you away? Perhaps Chur had done that. Gods *knew* what Chur's condition was. Geran kept her mouth shut.

"How is she?" Haral had the nerve to ask. The same question. Forever the same question, as if it was going to have some better answer.

"Holding," Geran said. "Holding." No optimism. Geran had stayed up there a long time and come down at the last moment of stability, with the alarms ringing.

"She able to eat?" Tirun was merciless. Trod right in where even Haral did not dare.

Long silence out of Geran. Then: "Yeah. Did pretty well." In a flat and hopeless voice.

Last jump.

"I programmed that son to take us right in close to Anuurn," Haral said between her teeth. "Forty-five and eight by six. Lay you odds we get it inside point five."

"We'll string it a bit," Tirun said, all matter-of-fact calculating the drag and push of entering and already-arrived ships on the gravity slope. Deformation calc. Keeping the mind busy.

It was Geran and Chur who always laid the bets. Even that was offkey. Geran refused to take the bait. She remained in dire silence. It was not money Tirun and Haral were betting. It was drinks in the nearest bar.

Hilfy stared at the overhead. Terrified.

We're not going to make it, we're not going to make it, we're too few and the kif too many, we can't push them. Sikkukkut's ships are a throwaway—we're all throwaways.

What's a kif care, how many ships he loses?

Cheap annoyance to his enemies.

And we were pushing him too hard.

"Otherside," Pyanfar murmured, "we got to move. We'll run stable right after the first cycle-down. You got to count. First pulse, then get up and go even if we got an alarm going. I don't know if Tauran's going to call us. I don't trust that."

"First pulse," Khym said against her ear, all indistinct. "Right. Got it."

"Got to—"

—*down.*

—*the wide dark again.*

She struggled to remember her own name. It was important to recall. She lay with an alien snuggled tight against her, his strange smooth hand holding hers ever so loosely. He had drugged himself before this, and lay helpless, as his kind had to be, in order to face the deep.

Chur, the name was. She stayed, tied by that loose grip on her essence. She could not have left him alone.

Left my son. Lost him. Never find him again, never know.

Not leave my friend out here helpless. No.

She was aware. It was not normal to be this hyper-stretched. She knew this. She had time, in this long waking of subjective days, to sort through things, not in the waking dream of time-stretch, the dim haze with which minds got through the deep, slower than bodies, but wide-awake in the twisting dark. She stretched out like the ship, and ran calculations in her head with one part of her brain, and kept the tether of that strange, fine-boned hand.

Not leave him. She thought of Tully and remembered *why* they were here, remembered aliens, and the ship, and the situation, Situation, the captain would call it. She forgot about time with Geran, Geran being forever, like the stars and the movement of the worlds. But Tully came from elsewhere; was more lost than she was. Tully had period and limit. There was a time when she had not known him. There was never a time but this that she had lain so close to him. She tried to tell Geran this, explaining why she wanted Tully to stay. "Get out," it came out of her mouth. Not the way she had meant it, but speaking with her mind that full was a surreal experience. Calculations. Numbers. One could spill out too much. "Gods rot it, get. Go. I don't want you here. Him. He's enough. You got work, Gery. Get to it. You want to kill us at those boards?"

I'm sorry.

She wiped that scene. Built another. She sat in bed, propped with pillows.

"We got troubles," she said, which was what she had meant to say. "Gery, I want my place back."

"You'll get it," Geran said, gently (she knew Geran would say exactly that thing, knew the precise cant of the ears, the pained look, the soft, quiet tone). "Come on now. We got relief aboard. Tauran. I told you that. You want to go to the galley, have a sit? Something to drink?"

"All right," she said; and let herself be led there, slowly. Seated, in familiar surroundings. Tully was there. He came and laid his hand on her arm.

"You scare me," he said.

"I'm sorry," she said. (Back in bed a moment. Tully lying there asleep, drugged senseless. Pretty mane he had. Prettiest thing about him. The gods could have fur like that, all sunlight. She scared him sometimes. But he snugged down against her: maybe she kept him warm. *Friend,* he had said just as he was going out. A little pat of his hand on her shoulder, a smoothing of her fur. Friend.)

They were all there, all the crew, at the galley table, which made no sense with things as they were, at risk. Only the captain was missing. And the kif. Someone put a cup in her hands. Geran shaped her hands around it and nudged them, helped her carry it to her mouth. It was hard to get back again. Hard. She was aware of heat in the liquid. It tasted of nothing at all. It was hard to focus small enough, to adjust her ears to hear the noise of their speech, to concentrate her mind to sort this kind of detail and not raw calculations of the sort she had been running.

She blinked at movement, at the captain's voice. Pyanfar had shown up, sitting between Haral and Tirun. Khym was meddling about in the cabinets, on galley duty again.

". . . I'm not easy about this," Pyanfar said. *"Some reason, I'm just not real easy about this next jump. We're going into it close to Anuurn as we can. I don't know what we're into. But it's been too quiet, all along the way. Kura had no time to get us a message. I wish we'd come closer to the station."*

Chur blinked. Blinked and found Jik there, when she had remembered only dimly why he was there at all. Their little galley table held more places than usual. Space folded itself. A lot of things fit.

"Push them out of the system," Chur said then. *"That's what we have to do. Cut them to ribbons on first encounter. The* han *knows they're coming. The mahendo'sat have told them. Haven't you, Jik?"*

"A," the mahendo'sat said, and shrugged.

"There was Banny Ayhar. Ayhar went on to Maing Tol. You gave them a message, Jik, when they shot me at Kshshti. I've figured their course home. That's where they'd have gone. Nothing would stop them. Not with what they knew. Not with what you gave them to carry. Isn't that so, Jik?"

"Good guess," Jik said, in better hani than he usually spoke. He leaned his elbows on the table. *"Bad luck at Kshshti dock. How you know 'bout Maing Tol?"*

"I told her," Geran said. *"Told her the message was all right. Gods,*

she got a hole in her gut defending it, you think I wouldn't tell her that? It was important, after all."

"Better be. I got a hole in my gut to prove it. You think I'm going to lose track of something like that? Banny Ayhar went on to Maing Tol and I know she went with something of yours. I know what I'd have done in Banny Ayhar's place. I'd have gotten out of there fast. I'd have run for home the safest, shortest way. And the Personage at Maing Tol would have a thing to say to the han *about then, wouldn't he, knowing he had to arrest that whole crew or let them go. Let them go with a message. Let them go with a whole mahen company to see them home."*

"I'm not at controls," Pyanfar said. "I've been thinking about something like that. I've hoped it was so. But this isn't my shift. Not my watch."

"I told you that," Geran said.

"Hey, you think I don't keep track of things? I'm better than that. I know where I am. I've known all this time. You think it's easy running calc in your head? I know where every ship could be. And how long. I know their mass and their cap. I know what their drop time is. I got gray hairs in this game. I know our competition, don't I? Not competition this time. Our help. All the help we got. Trust me, captain. I got it figured for you."

"Not my watch," Pyanfar said again.

And left the table. Was gone.

So did others. "I'm sorry," Jik said. "I'm not here."

Then she was alone with the crew again. Khym left. Then she did.

There was deathly quiet. Tully was anchor, in a long dark sea.

She reached out and carefully, in motion that took the better part of a day, perhaps, in timestretch, disconnected herself.

. . . down again.

. . . gravity slope.

It was hard to move at all. But Chur did that, levered herself to the side of the bed and remembered—she could have forgotten nothing—to put the safety back. For Tully's sake.

Longer still down the corridor, which reeled and snaked and kept going into the lighted bridge. Perhaps it took a day to walk it. Dark things skittered and moved, ran like black, rapid serpents in the corridors.

New logical track: moving and breeding. Feeding where they could. Insulation. Plastics. Ignoring barriers.

Akkht-bred. Like the kif.

Alert within jump.

   . . . down and still falling. . . .

She made it as far as the captain's place. And leaned there. "Captain," she said, perhaps another day in the saying of it: "The mahendo'sat. A message has gone to them. A message can have reached from Maing Tol to Iji. Ayhar of *Prosperity* will have come home. From Kirdu to Kita is one jump. A ship can have gone to Iji from there. From Kirdu to Ajir, one; from there to Anuurn. Our ships will have heard. They'll come home, captain. As we are, coming home at the earliest possible. The mahendo'sat will not have resisted this move. The quarry goes to the small valley, but hunters cross the hill. That is only reasonable." Words slurred. She watched the slow twitch of a listening ear. *Not* her captain, but this stranger. Tauran. She knew that too.

"Believe us," she said to that captain. "Believe what we've told you."

Other calculations. The solar system danced in her memory, swung through two years of positional changes. Lanes threaded like moving spirals of color through this maze of rock, converging on Anuurn.

Cover a ship with mass and emissions-noise, a gravity well it could stay in, concealed in dancing fragments, in the thunderous emissions of a gas giant. Akkhtimakt *knew* there would be attack coming in at him. He had had time to plan and research the moves he hoped to make, and attack could not possibly take him by utter surprise.

She crossed to the com board, reached the slack hand of a Tauran crewwoman, punched in a channel. "Kif. Do you hear me?"

"Kkkt," the voice came back, slow and slurred. *"Who calls? Who is this?"*

She reached—it was terrible effort—to the board. Sat down in a vacant chair. Tully's. Between two Tauran crewwomen. She freed up armaments from that master board and set her hand on that control, preprogramming fire on the Tyar vector from their entry point.

Black things ran and squealed. There were red lights on boards, systems failures. She went to the main board and carefully switched to backups, system after system, where automation had failed.

   . . . down again. She staggered, held to the board, blinked with the jolting *here* of the bridge about her, where she spent her life. The crewwoman beside her was turning her head in confusion, the whole of the bridge was real for the moment before it began to darken.

"My gods," someone said. As *The Pride* fired on its own.

The dark folded round again, but it was only a dimming of the light;

and there was pain, the bite of the strap against her sagging body. She pushed herself upright again. She reached for the com-switch again, threw it on wide. "Captain. This is Chur. Get up here. Emergency, emergency."

"How in a mahen hell'd she *do* it?" a young voice cried; and another: *"Captain!"*

As space sorted itself into sanity, as alarms wailed, advising of systems gone backup; as they ran into a wavefront of information that said ANUURN, ANUURN, ANUURN—

"My *gods!*" someone yelled, seeing something.

And their own ship answered, automatic: *The Pride of Chanur.*

They were well into system. *Close* to the star. To the sun that had warmed their backs as children and beaconed them home trip after trip.

Anuurn buoy was out. No help for that. "Watch out for Tyar," she said to the scan operator by her, tried to say. As *The Pride*'s weapons fired again.

Pyanfar ran. She had never moved so hard, straight out of jump. She hit the door with her whole body, triggered the lock and staggered into the hall and ran it with the thud and thump of Khym running behind her. A blurred figure came out of Chur's room and collided with her, embraced her, stink of human, half-naked and all but falling. "Chur—" Tully said, but she sorted out from him, already on her way, and left him to obstruct Khym's path.

Bridge loomed, lit and swimming in and out of focus. She grabbed the doorframe, safetywise hand-over-handed toward the nearest console and lurched for the next, heading for the captain's seat, grabbed the back of it and hung there. "I'm here," she gasped, and Sirany twisted in the seat and began to get out of it. "Get to observer one. Too far to go below."

"We're still firing," a youngish voice said. "Do I stop?"

"Priority, we got no buoy here."

"What are we firing at?" Sirany snapped. "Gods and thunders, what are we doing? My gods, we're high-*V*—those guns—"

"Not sure," that one said; and: "She's fainted—" Another voice. As Pyanfar grabbed Sirany's seatback. *"Out!"* she yelled at the Tauran; and Sirany cleared it as she threw herself into it, a collision of bodies. "Tyar vector," someone said; and: "Stay your posts," Pyanfar snapped, blinking at a blur of lights, and felt blind after the general hail:

"Chanur, get your backsides up here! Run for it! Tauran, cancel fire, cancel."

"My door, my door! Fools!"

"Unlock the kif," she said to the Tauran copilot/switcher. Confusion behind as Tully and Khym tried to ascertain Chur's state. "Khym! Get her to the galley, emergency secure. Get liquid down her if you can." They had run that drill, galley-secure, smallest fore-aft space next the bridge. Close the corridor-access and hit the padded benches, collapse the table to use for auxiliary brace, and belt in and tie down. In the tail of her vision they took Chur out that way. Sirany moved and came on over intercom from the seat Chur had left. "I'll aux switch, Chanur."

"You got it," she said, ripped a nutrients packet loose and downed it, her eye to the chrono and the red numbers flashing on the screen. "Gods—" Into the general com: "Make that lift, gods rot you, *run,* we got thirty seconds to dump, *run, run, run!* Ride it out in the lift!"

"We'll make it!" Haral's voice. Dopplered and moving, from the com. *"Let it go!"*

Images got to her screen. She jammed a com plug into her right ear and listened with one ear to that flow, kifish jabber.

Fifteen seconds. Noise from the intercom, wide open from both ends. Shouts and curses at a recalcitrant door. *"Open the gods-be lift!"*

Then: *"We're in.* Different speaker. Tirun this time. And: *"Wait, wait, wait! Kkkkt-kkt-kt! Wait!"*

"Hurry!"

"Kkkkkkkkkkkkkk—"

Dump.

   —down. Velocity drop.

      —red lights. Breaking out like plague.

O my gods, don't let us lose it here.

Not now. Not now.

Normal space. Anuurn and kif. She swallowed down sickness and flicked switches while the Tauran switcher next to her fed her images.

"Position, position, where in a mahen hell are we?" Not Haral beside her. Fire was going on out there, their kifish escort hammering away at something forty five degrees off and low. Haze blossomed on the scan as it cleared. They had no clear way to know *what* the kif were firing on. "Com, gods rot it, where's ID on those ships?"

"No ID," the young voice answered. "I'm not getting ID."

"Captain, we got hits out there, Tyar vector!"

"Targeting."

"We don't know who we're shooting at," Sirany objected.

"Targeting, gods rot it, did I say fire? Get us a gods-be lock on it!"

"Gods rot yourself, did I say I *wasn't?*"

Not a crew up here. A collection. Left and right hand tangling. In the monitor a light-reflection showed, widened. Lift door opening. She looked at the time and saw fifty seconds to next dump. *"Fifty to dump, clear those seats, number two, three, five, seven—Chanur crew's in upper main, we got a fast shift, bail out and go, move it!"*

"Get!" Sirany yelled at her own crew. "You heard her. *Galley!"*

Every regulation in the book was fractured. Crew bailed out and fled in mid-ops, a scramble for the galley corridor. Running footsteps hit the bridge deck and seats sighed and hummed and belts clicked, new crew in. New voices reported over com.

"Your sister's all right," Pyanfar said.

As the chrono ticked over and they went down again—

—programmed dump.

More red. Red, red, red.

O gods, not the main boards—

Lifesupport out.

Gods fry those slinking things!

Over to backup on three more systems. Final backup on another.

Out again, with telemetry coming in, Chanur voices delivering information.

"Affirmative: Akkhtimakt. Tyar vector, breaking for nadir."

"Fire."

As another disruption streaked past them, disrupting scan.

"That was Jik!" Geran said.

"Go for 'em!" Tirun cried, and: "Kkkt! Sgot sotikkut pukkukt'!" from Skkukuk.

More disruptions. A welter of high-V projectiles, passing by them.

They added their own, lower-V, and a burst of beamfire from their small bow projector. Hydraulics whined and thumped, reloading the chambers on the launcher, tracking. The source of the fire was off— gods, in the ecliptic. A chill went up her back. Chur and premonitions. The first fire they had thrown out was the most damaging kind, high-velocity, aimed blind.

Someone had keyed the guns.

Whump and groan. Another missile round off. More loading.

"Stand by braking." *Gods hope the systems hold.* As she threw them into rollover, the guns still tracking and firing under auto.

She threw the mains in. Her hand was shaking on the board, even with her arm thrust through the stress brace. Her vision fuzzed under the strain, and something small and black flew past her head and hit the forward bulkhead beyond her panel, squealing and yelping. Three story drop, where it had come from. "Gods!" she yelled in revulsion: it ran right back over the boards and chittered and squealed as it went, tiny claws scrabbling as it climbed against the *G*-force and ran right over the counter along the bulkhead, the course of least resistance.

Then colors blossomed all across the scan.

"We got company!" Geran yelled, and pounded the board. "Gods, o gods, they're ours, hani IDs—hani ships lying off-system ecliptic, they're coming in!"

Chapter Eleven

"Hani ships!" Hilfy cried. "Waiting—O gods, someone got 'em the word! They're coming in on our escorts' wavefront!"

"Ayhar," Pyanfar said. Her heart again. It was a good hurt. As if the universe itself were not large enough to hold it. "Gods look on her, Banny Ayhar got through!"

While *The Pride* hammered down its *V* and Akkhtimakt's kif picked theirs up, faster and faster shifts. Comp subtracted their *V*-drop out of that relative *V* increase and still came up with a plus. "The bastards are running!" Haral exclaimed. "They're getting out of here; they got Ajir for an outbound—"

"They got Jik on their tail," Tirun exclaimed. While on com, Sif was trying to explain it all to the crew in the galley. A cheer racketed out of that section, weak and wobbly in the strain of decel, but a cheer all the same.

"They are lost!" Skkukuk cried, and a string of something else in kifish.

His former associates. Akkhtimakt and all his minions, and Skkukuk was not with them in their debacle, but in the lead ship of the winning side. It was surely a sweet moment to a kif, all his maneuvers justified. He chittered and hissed and all but chortled. "Give me a channel," he cried. "Hakt', give me a channel, praise to my captain, *mekt-hakt'*, they will not turn, they dare not turn, give me a channel!"

"Affirm," she said. It seemed little enough to keep a kif content. And having gotten it he sent out a steady burst of clicking main-kifish.

Fools, was the burden of it. *Join my captain, join us in success, turn and rend the doomed and hapless fools who lead you!*

"Com," Hilfy said. *"Harun's Industry* says their compliments and they're wanting instructions."

"Come about and stay after them and for the gods' sweet sake let the comp do the shooting, we got too many allies out there that look like the other side."

"Kifish signal," Hilfy snapped. "Skkukuk."

"Notiktkt has begun to fire on its fellows!" Skkukuk cried. "It signals its loyalty, *mekt-hakt'!"*

O my gods.

She stared, appalled, listened as Skkukuk rattled off more and more names. As kif hindmost in the whole retreating force began to add their fire to the attack on their own forces, and hani ships swept in like a wave, hammering at the ships that were attempting to flee.

Hammer and anvil. More and more kifish defections, and the Ajir vector, the only way out at their velocity and on that heading—barriered suddenly with yet another wave.

"My gods, what's *that?"*

More breakout of plague on the com, this time nadir, ships lying emissions-silent suddenly having picked up velocity and started to run.

Howling out mahen IDs.

"My gods, we *got* 'em," Haral yelled. And laughed aloud and pounded the console. "You hear that? That's the mahendo'sat! We got the kif between us, Akkhtimakt's forces are defecting right and left, they're chewing each other to bloody rags!"

Pyanfar stared at it with her mouth open. With bits and pieces of things sorting themselves into vague order, as they had been ordered for longer than she had wanted to look at them.

She did not cheer. There was an obscenity in what was happening in front of them. And yet not obscene or unfit. No more than the little vermin that had multiplied and succeeded against all odds.

It was kif out there, surviving again.

Doing the best they knew to do.

Murder is possible here. Ours, committed against kif innocent by their own lights.

In one stroke, I can order it, clear our system of kifish ships till we can get organized in defense. Wipe the aliens out of home system.

It's prudent to do. It's only prudent.

But gods help me, I'm not a butcher.

"Send: *The Pride of Chanur* to all ships. Cease fire, cease fire on all kifish IDs that signal surrender."

Then com reached her down the other vector, backflung from Jik.

Requesting that same message that she had anticipated and just sent.

Braking continued. Fighting diminished. There were still casualties. Solid mass became drifting clouds. Scan attempted to track misaimed projectile-fire and confused itself with the sheer magnitude of the problem till Geran gave it a Disregard on non-intersect-potentials.

They reached lower and lower *V.* "Take it," Pyanfar said, and Haral slewed *The Pride* around to use the mains on acquisition in a new vector.

Headed for Anuurn.

Vid came up. Haral had been too busy for that till now. The homestar, Ahr, shone brilliant yellow. Lifebearer. Hearthfire to the species. And the paler, nearer, light that was Anuurn.

Home again.

With a straggle of battered, stress-damaged merchant ships slewing about in disordered break out of the rigid formation they had kept so long and so far, Harun and little Faha, Pauran, and last and limping, Shaurnurn, reporting damages, talking to each other over com.

"This is Sirany Tauran." Sirany had gotten herself an output channel. *"Affirmative on the linkup, inquiry affirmative, all ships. They're all right. Chanur's clean and clear. Thank the gods."*

"Gods look on us all. Here and otherwise." Harun was talking, Harun always the leader in that group.

"We've got that," Faha said, and other acknowledgments came in.

While the slaughter went on, while a hard burn shoved at them and made breathing difficult, and a lightspeed message proliferated through ship relays.

"We've got contact with Gaohn," Hilfy said. "They ask for a report."

"They know by now," Pyanfar muttered. "But answer them. Send: *The Pride of Chanur* to Gaohn. We claim navigational priority. Clan business. End message. Put a call through to Kohan. Ask him how things are down there."

On Anuurn. At home. On that small shining sphere in all the wide dark.

It would take a long time. Question and answer went slow at this range. Conversations were all one-sided.

"Where in a mahen hell is *Vigilance?* Did we pick up Ehrran's ID anywhere?"

"Affirmative. Affirmative," Geran said, all business. "Five ships are putting out from Gaohn. We got a pickup on Ehrran. They're moving now. Make that six ships. They're not talking."

"I'll bet she's not. Where's Ayhar? Gods rot it, where's Banny Ayhar and *Prosperity?*"

The burn stopped. Her vision cleared, her voice no longer had to force its way out of her throat. A wave of giddiness came on her. Depletion. Fight-flight reflexes let go and the body had dues to pay. She clamped her jaws against nausea and fumbled after a packet, dropped one and got another. Bit down on it and swallowed and swallowed, which was the only thing else she could do but retch. *Going to faint. O gods. I don't do this.* "Haral—Sirany. I'm not—"

"Cap'n? *Cap'n?*"

She drifted. Lay still under a ceiling which was not the overhead of the bridge. Blinked at it and at Khym's anxious face.

"You fainted," he said.

"Gods rot." She drew her hands up to locate her head, which seemed drifting loose and all fuzzed. "Who's running the ship?"

"Ker Sirany. We're inbound for Gaohn. It's all right, Py. We did it." "Jik. . . ."

"The kif jumped, such as could. A lot surrendered. They've attached to the other kif. To *Chakkuf.* Skkukuk's been talking to them, telling them—Hilfy says—that they'll do well to hold still."

"Where's Jik?" Fear set her heart to hammering. *"Did he jump, gods rot it, did he jump out?"*

"We aren't tracking him. It got—pretty confused, Py. Not Geran's fault. Sirany says so. We—lost some ships. His ID just cut out."

"He's lying. Gods-be, that bastard's pulling another one." There was an obstruction in her throat. She wanted to break something. Anything. There was dark around her vision, a pain all through her gut. "We need him." All quiet and hard to get past that knot. *Oh, Jik, Jik. Another gods-be doublecross.*

What do I do now? What am I going to do?

"Cap'n?"

It was not a voice she expected to hear. Not loose and wandering around in places like her cabin. She lifted her spinning head and looked at the worn, wan hani clinging to the doorframe. "Chur? F'gods-sakes—"

"I'm doing all right," Chur said.

"Huh," she said. "Huh." And fell back into the pillows. It was all she could manage at the moment. The whole cabin was going into slow rotation. It felt like tricks with the *G* force, a little acceleration this way and that way, but if she asked was that going on she would look the fool. It was her head. Her equilibrium.

Gods. Sikkukkut. Where? When?

A weight depressed the end of her bed. A hand touched her leg. "Cap'n." Haral's voice, ragged with fatigue. "We got a little rest now. *Ker* Sirany's arguing with Gaohn, telling 'em we got right of way and they can by the gods quit quibbling. She's all right, captain. Swear she is. Never shot at anything in her life, her and her crew, I think they're a little shook. Us—we're falling-down and gone away. Whole crew. Thank gods for the Tauran, thank gods, I say."

"I say too," she murmured. Felt a touch across her brow, her ears. Khym's hand. She opened her eyes and stared at the uninformative ceiling. "Was that Chur in here?"

"Not walking too good, but she's put on weight. Turned a corner somewhen and started storing it up instead of burning it. Skkukuk's having lunch—"

"O gods." Her stomach heaved.

"We got to get those things cleared out somehow. *Skkukuk* says Chur got to the bridge in jump, went into some kind of hyperdrive, started telling the Tauran what to do when they came out, got us all waked up— Cap'n, *somebody* threw a bunch of relays on manual, got us over on backup systems, or we wouldn't have made it: those gods-be black devils had got into the works, chewed stuff up good. And somebody aimed the guns. Chur doesn't remember, but I got my guess who did it. Or we'd be on the long trip for sure."

She blinked and absorbed that. Remembered bailing out of bed and running the corridor. Was not too clear on how she had gotten into her own seat. Or how anything had happened. The mind did not function well on the trailing edge of jump.

Did not function well after too many jumps, either.

"Call to home," she remembered. "We on response-time yet?"

"Gaohn refuses to relay."

"Gods and thunders, *politics,* politics and we got a system full of kif—"

"They've got Ayhar under arrest, cap'n. We're still on course. We got *Vigilance* in our way and we got three other big freighters just hanging off and not doing anything. They'll have fire position on us if we keep coming. They warned us. Have to ask you what you want to do."

She lay there and breathed quietly a moment, ran that situation through her aching skull once and twice and a third time.

Vigilance positioning itself where it could go head on with them or strike at their tail if they docked.

You gods-be fool, *I got thirty, forty kif out there!*

Bring kif against the han? *O my gods, my gods. That fool's going to call bets and I can't bluff, those kif back there don't know where to stop and I can't hold them else. I can't bluff, Ehrran! Don't try to call it.*

"Mahendo'sat. Where are they?"

"They're braking. Holding steady relative to the kif. Keeping an eye on 'em."

"And no sign of Jik." That pain was back again. It hurt to blinding. "Gods *rot* the luck." *He's got to be alive. Out there somewhere. Preserving his options. Saving his own people. He has no choice. And I did it, I, I gave it to him.* "Ayhar arrested."

"Aye, cap'n. We inquired. We got a communication from Llun, onstation. They're real sorry, they got no choice."

Old friends, the keepers of Gaohn station. Old allies. Under a lot of pressure. "That all they said?"

"Says plenty, doesn't it, cap'n?"

There was a time they were Py and Hal and Tirun. Across every accessible dock in the Compact. Here they were, graynosed and at wits' end and Haral was sticking by formalities. Haral had held that line ever since the day she got set upstairs, command post, being heir to Chanur; and Haral, equally qualified, being sub-sept, got the second seat. It was the System.

"Captain?"

"Yeah. It says plenty. It says every godsrotted thing *wrong* with us." She shoved herself up on her hand and an elbow, flung her feet for the side of the bed. Blood was moving in her veins again. Her vision cleared. "I'll have Ehrran's ears, b'gods if I don't. My own hands. In the condition I'm in, I could take that blackbreeched prig! I'll kill her!"

"We got other word," Haral said, and braced her back, setting her down with both hands. Held onto her. "Rhean sent on com—says

Chanur's fallen. Kohan's exiled. Mahn's got the estate. Rhean's broken with the blockade out there. She and Anfy—coming in hard behind us with *Fortune* and *Light.* Pyruun—Pyrunn got Kohan to safety somewhere. They swear that. So it's not all lost onworld, and we got help on the way if we just hold and wait. Sirany's up there trying to keep the thing from blowing to a—"

"Mahn." She shook her head, blinked. Tried to focus on it. *"My godsrotted conniving son?"*

"Our godsrotted conniving son," Khym said at her back, his voice a low rumble. "And our twice conniving daughter."

"With *Ehrran!*"

"With their own interests, Py, when were they ever anything wider?"

"Gods. *Gods!*" She flung off Haral's hands and slapped Khym's interference aside. Hit the floor with both feet wide and swayed there till she had shaken the fog out of her eyes. Then she headed for the door.

The corridor.

The bridge, where Tauran crew filled the seats.

"Give me com," she snarled, coming up over Sif Tauran's shoulder. Sif hesitated, throwing a startled glance her way.

"Captain—"

"Give it to her," Sirany said. *"Ker* Pyanfar, I'll give you your chair."

"Keep it. We got troubles." She slipped into the vacant post between Sif and Fiar. "Get me Gaohn station. Are armaments still live?"

"We're shut down, captain." Nasany Tauran, down at Tirun's post. "Reactivate?"

"Do it." The com light signaled available and she punched in on the frequency.

"Pride of Chanur hailing the station," Sif was saying. Trying to raise a response. Another light was blinking, another channel active. Sif punched it in, on a momentary pause. "That's a call from *Vigilance,* captain. They advise us we're under arrest."

"Tell Ehrran there's a threat to Gaohn and we're not it. Stand by. That's all."

The message went.

"Gaohn station," she said on her own. "This is Pyanfar Chanur, *The Pride of Chanur.* Stand by to record and relay." Gaohn was hearing: that was beyond doubt: every official on that vulnerable and threatened station would be prioritized onto their transmissions. "Llun, you've just seen the first and smallest wave of our assault on Akkhtimakt's ships. The next one is incoming. Naur, there's no time for your politics. Your treaty with the stsho may have destroyed the whole species, hear me? Your relations with the mahendo'sat are tottering. Attack on our own world is possible and imminent. It is possible that no life will survive on Anuurn surface. I appeal to you, I *beg* you, anyone who can get their menfolk offworld right now, *do* it, get us a chance, for the gods' own sake, get to shuttles and get to shelters. There are still three large groups of ships unaccounted for and one of them has threatened attack on Anuurn itself."

Static. Sputter. *"Pyanfar Chanur, retreat from this course."*

"Is that Ehrran? Gods rot you, is that Rhif Ehrran?"

Static and squeal. *"This is Rhif Ehrran, Chanur. Take your kif and go deal with your owner."*

"Is that what you're going to tell the next attack that comes rolling in here? Are you going to arrest it? *You absolute and total lunatic, get that ship out there on Kura-incoming where it can do some good and stay out of my way before I blow you out of space! Deny my crew medical attention! Turn tail and run at Kefk! What do you write in those gods-be reports of yours? By the gods nowhere near not the whole story, not the part where you take stsho bribes and connive with the kif against the* han! *Get that ship out where it belongs!"*

No response. From anyone. Not Ehrran, not Gaohn Station. Not from Anuurn itself, while lagtime ran on.

"They're Immune," Sirany said, a low voice from her other side. "You're challenging an Immune, Chanur."

"Arm. Target."

"Ker Pyanfar, they're hani!"

"They've arrested Banny Ayhar. They've arrested the courier that just risked her by the gods neck and Ayhar clan's whole livelihood getting word to the mahendo'sat and getting word back here again, bringing back the captains and the crews from Maing Tol all the way home—*Where do you think those ships out there with the mahendo'sat came from? They've swept in out of mahen space, that's where! With* the mahendo'sat! We got the gods-be *hakkikt* coming in here, we got this blackbreeched prig quoting rules from Naur and all their gods-cursed pets downworld—"

Sirany spun the command chair about, facing her. "I said I'd surrender this. I'll do it. I don't agree with what they're doing. But let me talk to Harun. Give Ehrran a chance to back up, for godssakes, Chanur, back off! Give 'em time to react, they have to have a way to save something!"

She clenched her hands on the leather of the chair arm, hit the control and turned it to face Sirany. *No.* Muscle reaction jerked her mouth. Stopped breath. Put a black ring around Sirany's taut figure. *Time, for the gods' sakes, the godscursed fool, the fatherforsaking bastard—Pride, pride above the* han, *Ehrran's precious face—* A breath then. A sane breath. "All right." Another. "All right. Let's talk to the *spacing* clans. Let's talk to Harun and Pauran and Shaurnurn and my sisters out of Chanur, and all the ships back there. They've arrested Banny Ayhar. The ships back there—they know what got them home. Tell them about Ayhar, tell them the rest of it, b'gods, we got it for them, the whole gods-be thing!" She spun the chair about, activated comp at that station and exhumed a log record. Accurately, first try. No one on *The Pride* was going to forget that date, that hour, that time.

Kshshti station: Ehrran trying to take Tully by force, kifish attack coming from two sides on the station docks, Akkhtimakt and Sikkukkut, Banny Ayhar's dispatch to Maing Tol carrying a message from a threesided conference: herself, Jik, Rhif Ehrran.

Ehrran agreeing to go with them into kifish territory.

Second log segment: another date, another moment: exchange between *The Pride* and *Ehrran's Vigilance*, kin-request for medical aid, denied, made contingent on surrender of Tahar crew from Chanur sanctuary. Granted when they logged a false emergency and got in touch with *Aja Jin.*

"Capsule it," she told Sif. "Every hani ship out here. Then capsule the whole gods-be log and shoot it over to Gaohn hard afterward. Tell them beam it down to Anuurn archives. File petition for Ayhar's release. Let's see if for once, one time, the *han* can understand what's going on out here. Put our wrap on that log transmission. There's a lot we can't say in front of kifish witnesses, but there's by the gods enough there to hang that fool. Brake to standby reply."

"B'gods there is," Sirany said. "Sif. Send: *Industry* and all the rest. Slow to standby. Transmission follows."

Alarm rang. The take-hold. *The Pride* prepared itself for braking. Other bodies hit the seats, Chanur crew, Haral and Khym and Geran, on upper decks and close enough to make it to vacancies. Blind-tired. Gods, yes. Her own head was too heavy to hold up. Her hands shook on the boards. There was not a critical control she would trust herself to handle.

Thank gods for Tauran.

"Captain." Tirun from the com, voice strained by the decel. *"Give us a window, we'll get up there."*

"Negative, negative, stay down there. You want scan on monitor down there you got it. I want you rested. Hear?"

"Captain—"

"Do it, Tirun. Don't fight me. Trank out if you got to. I need you later, hear me?"

Delay.

"Trank. I mean it, Tirun. I got to come down there?"

"No, cap'n. Loud and clear. We don't need the trank, though. Can I ask—"

"Gods help me." Her voice faded and breath all but failed her. "Get off the com, f'godssakes, cousin, give me a rest."

"Out, cap'n." Short and quiet and off the com. Instantly.

She ducked her head into her hands. *Was I short? I didn't mean to be short. Call 'em back. Tell 'em—O gods. Tell 'em what?*

Brain won't work. That's all. I can't think. Call 'em back, they'll know I'm off.

That'd make 'em rest real easy, wouldn't it, Pyanfar?

Professionals down below there. Not kids. Not stationsiders. Tirun knows what I mean. She'll trank if she has to. Professional.

Got to sit on Hilfy and Tully. My young fools. My devoted young fools. Where's Chur? Where's Chur in this shaking-about?

"Geran, is somebody with Chur?"

Dip of the ears. "They took her downside. Crew quarters."

Safe, then, and not alone. One detail not on my shoulders.

Then:

"Transmission from *Vigilance,*" Sif murmured. Data flowed onto her number one screen. Wordage abundant.

It was what she expected. Selected log entries. Two ships firing log segments back and forth like beamfire. Truth and counter-truth. "Godsbe fool," she murmured. Some of it was potentially explosive with the kif.

"We got that interview with Sikkukkut," Haral said.

"Save it," she said. "We got kifish ears out there. If Sikkukkut loses face here, we may have troubles we can't handle."

"Sfik," Khym said. "It's *Chakkuf* we have to worry about, isn't it? That's the leader."

"You got it." A chill and a warmth went through her. Her husband, on target and calm and having picked up more on the way than she gave him credit for, the way he always did. On the bridge, in a seat beside Tauran crew, and no Tauran twitching an ear at it. *Do you know what you're hearing, Tauran? It's change. It's power tilting and sliding. And there's one way in all the universe I can out-do that bastard over there commanding* Chakkuf. *Take and hold. Grab with both hands.*

A kif well understands this exchange of messages.

A kif understands what I'm asking the spacer clans to do, and he understands Ehrran's position, that it's eroding, fast. The kif aren't meddling in this, thank the gods, they know this is a situation they can foul up if they lay a hand on it and they don't want to do anything. They're waiting for me. Of course they're waiting for me. Thanks, husband.

"Message: priority." Data leapt from Sif's monitoring to monitor one, a flood of mahen log output, off a ship named *Hasene*.

Mahendo'sat. My gods. They're affirming Ayhar's story.

"*Priority, priority.*"

Color-shift had begun on certain ships on far-scan, positions relayed and matrixed via continuous dopplered interlink from ships in position to pick them up. Certain ships were disentangling themselves from that welter of dots out there where the kif-kif-hani battle had wound down to stasis.

Stasis no longer.

"Priority."

Six of the spacing clans were moving. Coming in behind *Chanur's Fortune* and *Chanur's Light*. Faha kin and Harun clan were among them.

"Inbound," Haral murmured. "Gods hope they're on our side."

"Stand by armaments. We don't know what that lunatic Ehrran's going to do."

"That's spacers at Ehrran's back," Haral muttered. "Those five ships out from station behind her. I'd worry, in Ehrran's place. I'd worry right fast."

"Priority! That's a burn, Ehrran's maneuvering—"

Unmistakable on the passive-scan, the little flicker of the directionals; then mains cutting in, a deluge of energy from *Vigilance*, while the ships behind her stayed still.

Ehrran kept on with the burn, accelerating on an insystem vector, while information continued to shoot this way and that through the system. Then Ehrran shut down to inertial: they were leaving, but not at any great pace. *Vigilance* still had plenty of option to turn around. Or roll and fire.

"Bastard," Geran hissed.

Still dangerous. Very.

Sudden, heart-stopping flares showed from one of Ehrran's backers. But that was rollover, turning nose toward Gaohn and home, the same direction as the incoming ships.

"That's *Raurn's Ascendant,*" the Tauran First said.

Flares from the others, one and the other, and the next and the next. Rollover in each case.

Pyanfar clenched her hands and flexed the claws and gnawed her mustaches. *I haven't got the strength to stay on the bridge. I can't do this. I can't last it. My gods, what am I going to do?*

When it was most critical. When hani existence rode on it.

"Medkit," she said, fighting down a wave of nausea. "Fiar. Get me the medkit. Stimulant. I'd better have it."

"Captain," Haral said hoarsely, in hardly better shape.

"Don't. Don't. Get me the stuff, get me a sandwich. I got to, Hal."

"You got it," Haral said. While Fiar was off at the cabinet getting the kit.

"I'll get the sandwich," Khym said. "Gfi. Whatever you want."

His cooking. Gods. Not the tofi. She turned a dull and helpless glance his way. "Thanks. Hold the gods-be sweet stuff, huh? Just make it fast and simple."

"Fast and simple." He got out of his seat, grabbed the seat back for balance and headed up toward the galley, about the time Fiar came back with the kit, laid it out on the counter and pulled a syringe out.

She held out an arm. Held it there while the needle went in, while Sirany's voice whispered out of the distance, talking to other ships.

"You can't do this twice," Haral was saying. "Hear me. I'll put you out, cap'n."

She gave Haral a bleak stare. It was an honest threat, meant to save her life. The stimulant hit with a wave of giddiness, sending her heart thudding. For a moment her own pulse was all she could hear, and if she moved she would drift free off the floor, disoriented.

Harder and harder pulse. She drew a great breath. A second. "I'm all right," she said. And knew she had better not get up. The bridge spun and swung as if ship rotation had gone totally erratic.

Food arrived. Sandwich first. Cup of water. Fiar ran courier. The water went down best. She forced a single bite of the sandwich.

"Worse shape than Chur," Haral muttered at her side. "Gods, go off, we got running time, take it."

"Get some food yourselves. You. Geran. Get. We got everything covered. Get, hear. Want a tour with the kif?"

Haral's ears flattened. Old threat. Old joke. Not a joke, nowadays. She cleared the chair and took hold of Geran's arm when Geran got up and staggered. Both of them were out on their feet.

And leagues and leagues to go for Anuurn's sake.

It was a knifing pain when she let her mind shift to home, and Kohan, and a refuge which did not exist any longer. The bright blue world was there. Chanur was not. Dissolved. The estate legally in the hands of her son Kara Mahn.

And her son firmly under the influence of her daughter Tahy, who was groundling to the depths of her short-sighted, narrow heart.

I never knew you! Tahy's voice, Tahy's face, nose wrinkled in anger. *That ship, always that ship—*

And Kara, big lad, inheriting height from both Khym and herself. *And brains from neither.*

The gfi arrived, in Fiar's careful hand. She sipped it. It was overstrong. It hit her stomach like acid. But the warmth comforted. That much.

"Send to Gaohn," she said. "Pyanfar Chanur to the Llun. We call on Gaohn station to release the Ayhar ship and crew. The ships out here constitute sufficient of the *han* to make a temporary quorum. You have that authority. Officers of the *han* will respect this order or deliver themselves to the protection of Llun Immunity. We take possession of the station in the name of the *han*. End message. List the clans out here. Put all of them signatory to it."

It was a drunken, arrogant move. It was also fast, and it gave the downworld *han* no time to organize or decree.

"Good bet the *han's* in session," Sirany said. "Down there."

"They would be. Yes. Let 'em debate what to do. Let 'em debate till the sun freezes. Dither and stew and argue. We've got an emergency out here. Send my apologies to the other ships for using them on signature, we got no time for transmission lag. We're operating under stress out here. Ask them to send a confirm and back me. Tell them we've got to get into Gaohn and get Banny Ayhar out of there.

"We're already getting confirms on that quorum call," Sif said.

It hit slowly. Like a wave of cold and heat. *My gods, it's going to work. What do I do?*

Jik! gods rot you, Jik, what do I do?

264 • C. J. Cherryh

"Call the clans in front of us. Ask them would they return to Gaohn and secure Ayhar's safe release."

"Aye," Sif said. "Sending." And a moment later: "Llun responds. Ayhar crew is in process of release already. *Prosperity* is being serviced. Llun sends its compliments, *ker* Pyanfar, and asks what about the kif, quote, *What are we facing?* End quote."

The relief was giddy. She probed it a moment, replayed the statement that echoed in her skull, whether it was real or stim-induced hallucination. *Good news, my gods, it's still working.*

"We're coming in. Tell them that. Tell them I'm coming in for conference and if any of the *han* downworld want to get themselves up on the next shuttle, they're welcome. Tell them no danger from forces with me, repeat, *with* me. End message. Just that way, *ker* Sifeny."

"Understood. Re-request on order to the ships in front of us?"

"Tell them stand by. Does Llun need help onstation? Query them that while you're at it." *I'm muddling. Not thinking of things. I'm dangerous up here.* "*Ker* Sirany. I'm resigning operationals. Policy I'll handle. Refer to yourself and the other captains—all other—" She gave a desperate wave of her hand. "—stuff." And fumbled after the belt and tried to stand up.

"Help, cap'n?" Sif reached and grabbed her arm. "*Ker* Haral!"

I'm doing quite all right, thank you.

And the whole bridge went gray and dark.

Operations chatter. Quiet stuff. She got to her feet hanging onto the chair and held to the back of it.

All in gray. Dark a moment. And the blood rushing in her ears.

Someone got to her. Someone held onto her. "You want to walk," Haral said.

"I'm walking." Legs insensate as dead meat. Equilibrium gone. Haral had one side, Khym had the other.

It was a long, long walk to her quarters. The corridor lights writhed like the spine of a glowing snake.

"Just gone too far," Haral said. "Knew her like this once at Ajir."

Liar. I was drunk then. I'm scared, Hal. I haven't got anything left and they need me.

"I got her." When the whole universe did a sharp and sudden tilt. Khym hauled her along with an arm about her. Might as well have been flying, upside down and sideways.

Bed then. Mattress. Sheets. Pillow.

"Chur's room," Geran's voice said, hoarse and panting and utterly exhausted. "Haral, tell 'em. We can fall in there."

A body landed beside her. Thump. The safety restraint hummed and clicked.

Dark then.

Till the gravity shifted and she came awake with a reflexive clench of the claws into what was not mattress, but her husband; he hissed and shifted and jerked as he came awake weighing less than he ought and with gravity not where it ought to be.

"Uuuh!"

"Docking. It's all right, it's all right, we're at Gaohn." Mumble. Even that was not sufficient goad to get the body moving. The brain dimmed down again, with too great a load to push. More *G*-shifts. Clang and thump. Not safe to stand, in the condition she was. Prudent just to lie there and catch the few extra moments of drowse she could. Before the clangs and thumps of contact told her the grapples were secure. Then was time to get on her feet and clean up.

Safety hummed into retraction. It was Fiar standing over them, with a tray in her hands and an ears-back worried look on her face. The ship was miraculously stable and quiet. "Captain. M'lord. You want to try to eat something?"

We aborted dock? Backed off?

I slept through the grapple-noise? The connects? Gods, we're not on rotation.

She levered herself up on her arms. Khym stayed unconscious beside her. The place smelled. They did. Everything did. Her eyes were sticky and her mouth felt awful. "Situation," she said.

"We're in, captain. Berth thirteen. Got a solid line of our ships out there beyond us. Just everybody sitting, except us, except our lot—Harun and Pauran and Faha and all, we're in dock right together. So's *ker* Rhean and *Chanur's Fortune.* Ehrran too. Anfy Chanur held 'em under her guns on the way to dock, she's still got *Light* standing out right nearby, but Ehrran's still talking for Naur and them, but spacers are mad, captain, they're not having any of it. They want to see you. We told 'em you were in no fit condition. But my captain asks, she says maybe you should get up there and see 'em soon as you can, captain—we got a whole lot of kif and a whole lot of hani eyeball-on out there around Tyar; but she wants you to have a breakfast and take it slow, her word, captain."

"Gods." She shut her eyes with force and opened them again, trying to focus. Fiar looked exhausted, ears flagging in a curious, lopsided way that made her look younger than she was. Stable at dock. Other ships having had time to make it in. Anfy and Ehrran in standoff. She reached and took the offered cup. Biggest they had. Full of savory soup, steam going up like a wish to the gods. "Unnnhh." She took a sip. Blinked the kid back into focus. "Ayhar. Where in a mahen hell's Ayhar?"

The ears sank. "They still got them hostage, captain."

"Where?"

"Up in station. *Ker* Rhean and Harun and my captain, they're working on it, but there's some holdup, and they got fighting at the shuttle-ports downworld, some on our side and some on theirs, and they can't launch, except a couple got away—The Llun are mediating that, captain says, trying to get the shuttles clear to launch, and some of the Immunes onworld, they're trying to negotiate—"

"A mahen hell with that."

"Meanwhile your crew is coming on, captain said they should take their orders from *ker* Haral, and *ker* Haral said—"

"The kif. Where's the kif?"

"They're just staying out there. That kif Skkukuk wanted to talk to them. My captain said no. *Ker* Haral said no."

"No," she said, and took a careful mouthful of soup as Khym moaned and rolled over and lifted himself on his elbows. "Food," she said. "Khym." The soup was hot as Ahr's fires. Instant stuff. Wonderful stuff. They were still alive and the cabin was staying still and the worst things were far from as bad as they might be. No major confrontations. Kif staying where they belonged. Everybody where they belonged. Excepting Ehrran and a set-to at the shuttle-dock. And Ayhar; and gods knew where Sikkukkut was. Alarm bells kept going off all down her nerves. *That bastard Sikkukkut pulled a surprise arrival at Meetpoint. Does he need originality?* She shivered convulsively, blinked and guarded herself as Khym shook the mattress getting himself propped up. "Here." She gave him her cup and took the other, the tray more convenient for her, then glanced up at Fiar's anxious, dutiful face. "Llun's fending rocks, is she?"

"Lots of rocks," Fiar said. And dipped her ears in nervous respect. Embarrassed, now that Khym was awake. She was young. "But my captain told them on station lines, about the kif, about the methane-breather we saw. About all those stations shut down. About the humans and the mahendo'sat. Everything. Figuring they might not have had time to sort the log out, they better know."

"Good. Thank her. I'll be there fast as I can."

"Yes, captain. You want anything—"

"You want to turn that monitor there on, on your way?"

"Aye, captain." Fiar hugged her tray under her arm, flipped the switch on the wall monitor mounted next the bath and dived out again. The door shut.

"Uhhhn," Khym moaned around a swallow of soup.

The system schema on the monitor showed what the young spacer had said: a lot of hani ships within spit of Gaohn station and a lot of kif and hani and a scatter of mahendo'sat staring at each other farther out on the fringes. All at relative stop.

No Jik. Not showing himself. He wouldn't.

Not dead, not dead, gods rot it. He jumped and got himself after those bastards or he's out there calling the moves and waiting for Sikkukkut. Has to be. We got too many mahendo'sat in this system just sitting there cooperating. He's going to use my whole by the gods solar system for a mahen battlezone.

She reached to the console and punched the com. The tick and chatter of bridge operations invaded the cabin. Quiet talk. Reassuring in its monotony. Llun clan was in charge of the station, fair and sane: trouble in the corridors, but Llun had central, and sanity was making progress out there. Against Ehrran's best efforts.

"We're all right," she said.

All right. My gods, Pyanfar. Where's Kohan? What's happening out on dock, onworld, what are we going to do?

"Uhhn," Khym said again. Drinking soup in constant little sips as if it was going straight to the veins, direct transfusion. They had both shed all over the sheets. Fright. Exhaustion. Depletion.

"Bath," she said. It was the thing she wanted most, more than food, more than sleep. She set the cup down on the table console, crawled out of bed and left her breeches on the floor on her way.

Straight into the shower cabinet and on with the water and the soap. Lots of soap. A deluge of soap and hot water.

A shadow showed up against the transparent door, tall and wide and hani. She opened the door and let him in.

Both of them then, soaked, soaped, and by the gods clean, just standing propped against each other under the warm water jets until she found her eyes shut. Falling asleep again. "Gods. We got to go, husband."

"Uhhhn." Like mornings downworld. Incoherent for half an hour at best.

She got out, cleaned her teeth, dodging sore spots, dried halfheartedly with a towel and hunted up the last pair of clean breeches in the drawer.

And the pocket pistol. Gods, yes, that.

Out into the chill of the corridor still tying the cords, the deck cold under her feet.

"Captain," she said.

Sirany was still at her post, on a mostly deserted bridge, just herself and her First. The place smelled of unwashed hani. And Sirany's face as she swung the chair about, was marked with fatigue and strain. "Ker Pyanfar." The voice was hoarse. "We're doing all right, but we have a lot of questions backed up. Whole lot of people want to talk to you. I want to talk to you. What do we expect?"

"We expect another wave of kif in here. Meanwhile I'm wondering where in a mahen hell a certain pair of mahen hunter ships have got to and where we misplaced about half a hundred human ships that are doubtless armed and meaning things we don't want to think about."

It was maybe more than Sirany wanted to think about. Her face had that kind of look.

"Yeah," she said. "I've been wondering these things. Maybe I've been hoping you didn't. But in a way I wish you did."

"Different truth once we got to dock, once we threw Akkhtimakt on to the mahen side of the line?"

"I don't mean I thought you were lying." Ears lowered in apology and rolled flatter as the jaw took on a harder line. "That's a lie. I still don't know. But I don't think so. I'm betting everything on it. But what choice have I got? There aren't any sure things out here. I tell you something, ker Pyanfar. They tell all kinds of stories about you. Since Gaohn. Since you took out the way you did and kept—" Ear-twitch. "—kept na Khym and all. And wouldn't lickfoot to the han. I heard a lot more stories on Meetpoint, while we were stuck there. Stsho are scared of you. They call you changeable, the stsho do."

"They'll call me worse than that. I figured a crew that had the nerve to come aboard this ship had the nerve to handle the boards under fire. Way we'll have to yet, maybe. Even against hani, if you had to. I'm telling you the truth now. I'm working only our side. The mahendo'sat have doublecrossed us so many times you need a chart to track it. But they're the best allies we've got all the same, and I'm hoping that conniving friend of mine is still alive out there beyond system edge."

"Waiting for the rest of the kif?"

"I think b'gods sure he is. That ship's equipped. *Lots* of com equipment. I've never been onto that bridge, but I got the idea it's not a small place. *Lot* of crew and techs. Ability to short-jump. Goldtooth's *Mahijiru* has a lot more facilities, but I don't think it gives much to *Aja Jin* in abilities. We lost track of more than one ship in that flurry out there, and I'm not sure any of 'em are dead. Kif have this concept. *Pukkukkta.* Revenge. Destruction. That kif Sikkukkut has launched ships down all the lanes. Into all sorts of space. He's prepared to take civilization out. He says. He gives the impression it's no use to him. I think otherwise and I think he knows it, but I don't want to put it to the proof. We've lost track of kifish ships too and it worries me. I want a count if anyone can get it."

"Maybe they met each other out there. Maybe that's where *Aja Jin* is."

"If we were lucky." She tightened her mouth. Headache still bothered her. "If we were real lucky. But whatever happens we've got to handle what's coming in from Meetpoint, whoever survived that set-to back there. If it's the kif we're dealing with it's got to be one voice talking here. One."

"I understand you." Sirany's hand trembled on the arm of the chair, jerked in a small tic. She gripped the chair arm till the tendons stood out.

"You want to bring the captains aboard?"

"We got no room in dock. Have to stack 'em in lower main. No. I'm going outside and hope to all the gods I live through this. I'd be expensive to lose. Real expensive. *I* can talk to that kif. My kif can talk to those bastards out there. Where is he?"

"Lowerdecks. Well-fed, I might add. I wonder he can move."

"Gods." She walked over to the com console and punched in the number. "Skkukuk. What's this you want to tell those kif out there?"

"Is this you, *hakt*'?"

Hani voices. Different voices. "Godsrotted sure it is, *skku* of mine."

"Kkkkt! I am delighted!"

"Worried about me, were you?" Gods, a change of captains aboard, possibility of mutiny in the air, the kif like a lit fuse and she had never

picked it up. "I told you hani are a peculiar lot. You asked contact with the kif out there. What were you going to do, in particular?"

"Call them in, *hakt',* to take this ship."

Gods, gods, and gods. Perfectly logical. Her own crew exhausted, in his eyes perhaps acquiescing to this threatening change of authority on the bridge. Ships were moving and threatening everywhere. And here was one little constant light of kifish loyalty, a kif who knew no other hani would tolerate him and who planned to serve her interests through his.

"I'm in command here. No problems. What do you think ought to be done, regarding those kif out there?"

"Kkkt. Put me in command over them. That is your best action, *hakt'.* I am a formidable ally."

"Skkukuk. What rank did you hold? Is it proper to ask that?"

"Kkkkt. Kkkkt."

"Not proper. All right. Let me point out something to you, Skkukuk. Sikkukkut is a bastard, a real bastard, with a sense of humor. I think if he ever did get his hands on you again you might never get out with a whole hide. Despite your cleverness. *He's* too clever not to know you're clever. Do you understand me?"

"Hakt', you are completely correct. What will you do?"

"Why, I'm going to give you all those kifish ships out there, and a treaty with the mahendo'sat and the hani, *skku* of mine, and tell you that if you will take my orders very closely you may fare very well. But first you have to take those ships and hold them."

"You will see, you will see, *mekt-hakt'."*

She leaned over the First's panel and unlocked doors. "There you are. You can just go down to ops, down to the auxiliary command right down the corridor to your left, and you can use com in there. You call yourself one of those ships for transport, and you pack up your Dinner and any weapons you think you need, and you get yourself out there and remember how far you are from kifish territory, and who your *friends* are. Hear me?"

"Kkkkt. Kkkkt. I will give you Sikkukkut's heart!"

"You take orders! Hear me?"

"What you will, what you will, Chanur-*hakkikt."*

Promoted, by the gods.

There was a deep, gnawing cold at her gut. Raw terror.

Just made my will and testament. To Sikkukkut, should some fool stationer pick me off out there. To my beloved enemy: a new and kifish *problem.*

Enjoy it, bastard.

She looked at Sirany, who was staring at her in dismay. "One thing about the kif. When they're on your side they're on it. And they're on it as long as they're profiting by it. That's a real happy kif down there."

"I hope to the gods you know what you're doing."

"I'll tell you. If something happens to me, if you have to take charge of this mess, rely on my crew and threaten Skkukuk within fear of death, then turn him loose. Best insurance in the world. He'll respect you for it." She had an impulse toward the weapons locker, for one of the APs, remembered it was Gaohn out there, civilized, home; and then went and did it anyway, pulled the heavy piece out and belted it on. "Tell my crew meet me belowdecks. Tell the captains I'll see them in dock offices."

Off the open docks, out of the way of snipers. She had gotten wary in her new profession. *Learned the hard way, like any fool.* "Khym stays aboard. So does Chur. You can tell them that in the appropriate quarters, too. Tell 'em it's an order. Skkukuk's calling a kifish ship in. We don't want any more hani ships sitting at dock than we can help."

"Relay that," Sirany said to her First. And glanced back again. "Take care, for godssakes."

"Huh." She leaned over the com console, punched in on station. "Llun. Want to talk to you."

"Chanur. Pyanfar." The station-Immune's voice was calm and quiet. "It's a trap, *Pyanfar, it's a—*"

Something hit the mike at the other end. And silence, then.

Sirany rose from her seat. The First turned in hers.

She stood there paralyzed a moment, then turned and started punching codes. "Rhean! *Fortune,* are you hearing me?"

"Com's dead," the First said; she could see that, the telltale not lit: the dockside com relay was cut off. Pyanfar half-knelt in the seat, reached and put in the ship-to-ship as her incoming com board lit and the First started taking calls. Other ships had gotten that sudden cutoff. *"Pride of Chanur* to *Chanur's Fortune, Chanur's Light, Harun's Industry*—all ships relay: trouble in central com, we've got troubles—"

"Pyanfar!" A familiar voice, her own sister's, out of two years' absence. *"This is Rhean, they got somebody into central, that's what they've done, they've cut Llun off—"*

"I know that! Bail out of there! Get 'em out!"

And in the same heartbeat: *Gods, the kif. Pull off, Pyanfar, let the station stew in its own troubles, deal with it later, we got kif incoming.*

No, gods, no, if there's no control here, Sikkukkut will take it himself, he'll come in shooting. We've got to get Gaohn in hand, get our ships repositioned if we can.

"Pyanfar." It was another voice, coming from the speakers, deep enough to shake the speakers. A male voice. Off *Chanur's Fortune.*

"Kohan? My gods! Is that Kohan?"

"Pyruun sent me. Llun just called Immune Sanction, did she not? I distinctly heard it."

Hani answers. Hani mutters. From a voice she had never looked to hear again.

"My gods."

"Pyanfar?"

"Immune Sanction. Yes. By gods, yes. Tell Rhean I'll see her out there."

"Ehhran," said Tauran's First, impeccably and crisis-wise serene at her post, "has just called Sanction from her side against Chanur and taken possession of the station in the name of the *han.* She says we are all under arrest. They have taken Llun clan under Ehrran protection."

"In a mahen hell they have! Message: transmit: *Spacer-clans!* Get to the docks and get to central! Arm and out!"

Acknowledgments came back, some mere static sputter. Gods knew how many were following. Or who would.

"Pyanfar," came another voice, clear and familiar and cold. *"Anfy, on the* Light: *we're positioning ourselves over station zenith: any ship fires, we'll blow it to blazes. Go for 'em!"*

"We're going!" she said back, and grabbed Tauran's First by the shoulder, cast a desperate look at Sirany Tauran's dazed face. "Take care of my ship, hear me!"

And dazed and aching as she was, she ran for it.

Chapter Twelve

She was wobbling when she reached belowdecks, staggering with the weight of the gun; she ran face-on into the others as she came off the lift and into the corridor—regular crew, with Tully and Khym. "I sent orders," she said to them both. *"No. Stay here."*

"It's changed out there," Khym said. "Py, for godssakes—"

Panic set in, facing that obdurate desperation, that look in his eyes, which met hers and asked, O gods, with a desperate pleading for his own place. If she never got him back alive . . . if she lost him out here; if, if, and if. She saw all the crew in the same mind, all thin-furred and haunted-looking, ghosts of themselves, but with weapons in hand and ears pricked up and eyes alive though flesh was fading.

"We've got to hit fast," she said, and saw Chur come round the corner from crew quarters, leaning against the wall for support, Chur with a rifle slung at her side. "You—" she said, meaning Chur. "And *you,*" meaning Tully, who was provocation to any hani xenophobe and a class one target. "You—"

"Tully and I hold the airlock and cover the rest of you, right." Chur's voice was a hoarse whisper, befitting a ghost. "Got it, cap'n. Go on."

That was the way Chur worked, conspiracy and wit: Chur cheated at dice. So would Geran. For cause. Pyanfar drew a ragged breath, threw a desperate look at Geran Anify and got no help: silence again, now that

Chur was back in business. "Then for godssakes keep Tully with you," she said, and jabbed Tully with a forefinger. "Stay on the ship. Help Chur. Take Chur's orders. Got?"

"Got." With that kind of Tully-look that meant he would argue to go with them if he thought he could. Language-barrier worked on her side this time. "Be careful."

"Gods-be sure. Come on," she said to the others, and shoved off the wall she was using to lean on for a moment, and trotted for the airlock.

Alert began to sound, *The Pride*'s crew call: not their business, though muscles tensed as if that alert were wired to Chanur nervous systems. There was the thunder of steps in the corridors, additional crew running to the lift behind them as they reached the airlock corridor. More footsteps behind. She looked back. Skkukuk appeared, coming from the other direction. "Orders!" she yelled at him, *get!*" and he vanished in the next blink of the eye. Then: *"Sirany!"* she yelled at the intercom pickup, her voice all hoarse, "open that lock—" because it was not Haral up there, Haral was beside her; and she had to depend on strangers to get their signals straight.

The airlock hatch opened. She threw the safety off the illegal AP, and inhaled the air as a wind whipped into their faces: *The Pride*'s pressurization was a shade off; and that wind out of Gaohn smelled of things forgotten. Of hani. Of cold and hazard, too, and the chill reek of space-chilled machinery. She jogged through the lock and into the passageway, yellow plastics of the access tube and steel jointed plating, and sucked up a second wide gulp of the air her physiology was born for. Something set into her like the stim, a second wind, a preternatural clarity of things in which the whole tumble of events began to go at an acceptable speed.

"These are hani," she said, drymouthed and panting as they ran along the tube, trusting her crew around her as she trusted her own reflexes, knowing where each would dispose themselves, that Chur was where she had said she would be, that she had Tully under control, that Tirun, hindmost with her lameness, would be watching everything they were too shortfocussed to see up front, that Haral was at her side like another right hand and Hilfy and Geran were with Khym in the middle, Khym being the worst shot in the lot, and not the fastest runner, but able to lay down barrage fire with any of them if it got to that. *Hani,* she reminded them as she came off that ramp and headed aside for cover of the gantry rig and the consoles. Down the row another crew was hitting the docks about as fast: that was Harun. And Sif Tauran arrived: Pyanfar spun around to stare at Sif in some confusion, saw Fiar coming at a dead run down the ramp. "We're offshift," Sif panted. "Captain says get out here and help."

"Come on," she said, seeing Fiar's youth, the grudging frown on Sif —sent along for Tauran's honor, then. Another Battle for Gaohn. Everyone wanted in on it.

Fool, Sirany, this is hani against hani, don't you see it? No glory here—

There were others arriving on the docks and running up the curved flooring toward them. Some of Shaurnurn, a trio each of Faha and Harun, not whole crews, but parts and pieces. That meant that those ships were still crewed, enough hands aboard to get them away if the kif came in; enough to make them a visual threat if nothing more. She had not ordered that. Perhaps Harun or Sifeny Tauran had. It was sane. It was prudent. She still wished she had the extra personnel on dockside, with their firepower. No other crew had the APs or even rifles: it was all legal stuff. Most of them that had run the long course from Meetpoint looked exhausted already; it showed in their faces, in the dullness of coats and the set of the ears. And Harun and the rest had only come from four jumps back.

But others were coming to join them, glossy of coat and in crisp blues; in vivid green; in skycolored silk: crews and captains of other ships from farther down the docks, ships which had run their own Long Course getting in, perhaps, but which were at least clear-eyed and fresh from their time on blockade. Banny Ayhar's contingents. The ships in from mahen space. Pyanfar drew a breath, blinked against dizziness and an insufficiency of blood and in a second hazed glance at that one in sky-blue, recognized her own sister. Rhean Chanur, looking much as Rhean had looked two years ago; with a tall figure coming up behind Rhean amongst the girders and hoses and machinery of the dock, a male figure conspicuous amid that large crew of Chanur cousins and nieces. The man had too much gray on him to be her brother, but no, they were indisputably Kohan's features, it was Kohan's look about him, and he wore a gun at his hip, a pistol, which gods knew if he even knew how to use—

His Faha wife was with him, Huran, Hilfy's mother. So were others of his wives: Akify Llun was one, on his side and Chanur's and not with her own kin. "Pyanfar," Kohan said when they came to close range. They stared at one another a moment, before Kohan blinked in shock at what else he saw, the thin, scarred woman his favorite daughter had become, Hilfy Chanur *par* Faha, who came across to him and offered her left hand to touch, because she was carrying a black and illegal AP in the other. Hilfy Chanur touched his hand and her mother Huran Faha's, giving them and her aunt Rhean and her cousins the nod of courtesy she might give any comrade-under-fire, with a quick word and an instant attention back to other of her surroundings, taking up guard with crewmates who shadowed her: she signed Geran one view toward the open docks and took another herself, all while everything was in motion, crews were taking positions of vantage, so there was no time to say anything, no time at all. Kohan looked stricken, Huran dismayed. Khym coughed, a nervous sound, somewhere behind her.

"We've got to get through to central," Pyanfar said. "Get Banny Ayhar out of there, get the Llun free—"

My gods, they don't know what to do, they're looking at me, at us to do something, as if none of them had fought here before this, as if they didn't know Gaohn station.

There was a time and a rhythm in leading the helpless and the morally confused; a moment to snatch up souls before they fell to wrangling or wondering or asking too keen questions.

"Come on," she yelled at them, at all the lunatic mass of hani spacers that was persistently trying to group round her like the most willing target in all the Compact; and yelled off instructions, corridors, crews, her voice cracking and her legs shaking under her as she started everyone into motion—in the next moment she could not remember what she had sent, where, when, as if her mind had wandered somewhere back into hyperspace and she had the overview of things but not the fine focus. . . .

. . . .battles fought at ports and in countrysides on a little blue pearl of a world where foolish hani thought to prevent a determined universe from encroaching on their business. . . .

. . . .Pyruun bundling Kohan onto a shuttle, smuggling him aloft to Rhean, gods knew how they had managed it or at what risk; but, then, mahendo'sat had once smuggled a human in a grain bin, right through a stsho warehouse. . . .

. . . .Banny Ayhar racing home with a message which proliferated itself across all of mahen space, sweeping up hani as she fled homeward: and alerting mahendo'sat as well, from Maing Tol to the mahen homeworld of Iji, so it could not then be taken by surprise by any kifish attack, try as Sikkukkut would. The incoming and outgoing ranges of solar systems would be minced: the mahendo'sat would have had time for that laborious action, especially up near Iji and Maing Tol, so nothing could have gotten in the back door. They *would* have done that, while hani ships were moving home like birds before the storm. Mahendo'sat would have pulled every spare ship borderward in defense and offense, set in motion agreements with the tc'a, so that the elaborate timetable of mahen ship movements would have functioned as a spreading communications net, news streaking from jump to jump and spreading wide with every meeting of affected ships. . . .

. . . .even to hunter captains far removed from the inner reaches, captains like Goldtooth, no longer operating on their own discretion, but receiving information and reinforcements. . . .

. . . .Goldtooth had been vexed beyond measure when *Aja Jin* had violated the timetable by showing up at Kefk; *that* had been his anger, that, the reason of his fury at Jik, *that* the reason why Goldtooth had rushed away: his orders had dictated it. And what might he have told to Rhif Ehrran to send her kiting out of there with a message for homeworld? Look out, he must surely have told her: beware the consequences when the push *he* knew was coming rammed the kif right down hani throats. He had sent Ehrran where *The Pride* was supposed to be, and where Banny Ayhar was already headed, Jik would have told him, in a much slower ship but with a message he had given *her,* if she had lived to get to Maing Tol. Goldtooth's plan had worked till *The Pride* blew a vane coming out of Urtur and had to go in for repair, til Sikkukkut stole Hilfy and Tully and lured *The Pride* off to Mkks and then (Jik following his opportunity and a hani's desperation, and seeing only one way to make his schedule *and* keep his position on the inside of things) to Kefk, where things went even more grievously awry; where hani proved intractable and divided by bloodfeud, and Chur lay dying, preventing *The Pride* from making that critical dash homeward by the Kura route, to warn of disaster at Meetpoint. . . .

. . . .Goldtooth had given them that med equipment to make a long run possible, gave it to them the way mahendo'sat had spent millions upping *The Pride*'s running capacity, last-ditch try at sending updated information on to Anuurn and spacer hani. . . .

. . . .because no ship could get through the kifish blockade at Kita; and in the end they had to rely on the slim hope of Banny Ayhar's ship. Jik had failed to convince Ehrran to veer from her stshoward course and *The Pride* had involved itself deeper and deeper in the heart of Jik's schemes; Ehrran had not budged till Goldtooth confronted her with more truth than Jik had yet told any of them.

Pyanfar blinked, brought up against a brace and hung there while the dock spun in her vision. Her brain wanted to work for a change, and the white light and gray perspectives of the dock were chasing visions of dark and stars and tiny ships in wheeling succession. Her AP was in her fist. Steps thundered past her as others secured the other corner and the neighboring corridor turned up empty of everything but scattered paper and a closed windowed door that said DOCKSEAL in large letters. KEY ENTRY ONLY.

"Gods rot them all!" She fired. Thoughtlessly, because an AP was as good a key as any; and fired again through the smoke and the deafening thunder as shrapnel off her own shot peppered her hide. "Gods-be *fools!*"

The door was never armored to withstand that kind of blast. The window-seal went. She was not up to running, just walked behind the fleetfooted youngsters and the foolhardy who went racing up to step gingerly through the shattered pressure-seal window.

She stepped through: her own crew stayed about her, and Rhean's lot, as if it were a walk up a troubled dockside, back in the days when a winebottle was the most fearsome missile and an irate taverner the greatest hazard a hani crew on dockside had to deal with. She trod on something sharp, winced and flinched, walking into a corridor her followers had already taken possession of: Fiar and Sif jogged out to the fore.

"Slow down!" she yelled. "Rhean, hold it back!" —As the whole thing became a faster and faster rush forward; she could not keep up, had no wish to keep up there with the young and the energetic. They had to take the stairwells beyond this long corridor, they had to go up the hard way, not trusting the lifts that could be controlled from the main boards: Gaohn was too big to take quickly, except by overwhelming force. And time was on other sides. Time was, O gods, on the side of Sikkukkut. . . .

. . . .who arrived at Meetpoint to drive his kifish opposition against the anvil of mahen territory, knowing that there were limited routes Akkhtimakt could take: down the line into stsho territory was one, where there would be no resistance—but Goldtooth and the humans had sealed that route.

. . . .the second to methane-breather territory, but that was a deadly trap: *no* one wanted to contest the knnn.

. . . .the third course lay past Sikkukkut to Kefk, which would have put Akkhtimakt at psychological disadvantage, though ironically not a positional one: there was no worse place for a kif on the retreat to come, than into kifish territory, a wounded fish into an ocean of razor jaws. . . .

Think, Pyanfar, it's late to think. The enemy either has one choice more than you've thought of, or one fewer than they need.

Sikkukkut knew that some message had gone with Banny Ayhar—knew that someone would have carried it, and where mahen forces would come—he had used the mahen push, anvil and hammer, but he never trusted the mahendo'sat, not Jik, manifestly not Goldtooth. He obviously didn't stop Ayhar.

Or he didn't try because he wanted it to happen.

Gods, could Jik have told him? No. No. He surely wouldn't. Not to someone that smart and that canny. They cooperated with limits. It was convenient for both sides. For separate reasons.

But why did Sikkukkut value me from the beginning? Why did he and the mahendo'sat both value me enough to keep us alive and set me here, with this much power?

Is Sikkukkut a fool? He was never a fool. Neither is Jik. Nor Goldtooth.

If Sikkukkut lost too many ships fighting for power, my gods, he'd find some other kif gnawing up his leg the moment he looked weak. That's what the mahendo'sat are doing to him, whittling away at him. It's the kif's chief weakness, that aggressiveness of theirs. Does Sikkukkut know that? Can a species see its own deficiencies?

Look about us at ours, at this pitiful spectacle, hani against hani, spears and arrows flying in the sun, banners aflutter—

I see what keeps us from being what we might be.

Can he?

Can—?

"Look OUT!" someone yelled; and fire spattered from the end of the corridor.

"Any word?" Chur asked. She had left the rifle in lowerdecks. To carry the thing was more strength than she had, and there was no enemy aboard. She arrived on the bridge with Tully close behind her and clung to a seat at her regular post. It was a strange captain who turned a worried face toward her. "I'm taking orders," Chur breathed, to settle that, and clung to the chair with her claws, the whole scene wavering in and out of gray in her vision, her heart going like a motor on overload. "Any word on them?"

"Ehrran's threatening to back out of dock and blow us all. *Light*'s threatening to blow *Vigilance* where she sits. We're supposed to have a kifish ship in here picking up—that. Skkukuk. I've told him that's all we want it to do." There was a fine-held edge to Sirany's voice, an experienced captain at the edge of her own limits. "Handle the kif."

"Aye," Chur said, and crawled into the vacant chair between scan and com and livened the aux com panel. With Tauran crew on either side of her. Tully sat one seat down. Other seats were vacant. Fiar's and Sif's.

Handle the kif. Indeed.

Skkukuk thought of himself as crew. He was loyal. Geran had said that much with a grimace. And Chur had gotten her own captain's instructions to the kif on open com. That and the encounter belowdecks was all she had to go on, while the kif waited below in lowerdeck ops, for transfer arrangements to be finalized. But she had been in the deep too long to panic over the unusual or the outré.

One of the black things skittered through the bridge and vanished like a persistent nightmare, long, furred, and moving like a streak.

On scan, one of the kifish ships nearest had just flared with vector shift.

Skkukuk's tight-beamed request for transport had had time to be heard and was evidently being honored.

"Tully," she said, leaning to look down the board where he had settled in. "We don't know when the humans come, right? You record message: *record,* understand? We send it to system edge, wide as we can, and constant—" She remembered in dismay she was not dealing with Pyanfar. "Your permission, cap'n."

"What?" the snapped answer came back. She had to explain it all again. In more detail. And: "Do it," Sirany said. "Just keep us advised *what* you do. You got whatever you want."

She drew a larger breath, activated com output and set about explanations, alternately to kif and to human and to *The Pride*'s interim captain. Then there was the matter of communicating with their mahen allies out there, whose disposition and intentions were another question: not many of the mahendo'sat ships had stayed insystem, but such as had were out there face-to-face with the kif, and nominally linked to the hani freighters who were also holding position out there in that stand-off. So far they were letting the kifish ship move out where a kifish message with *The Pride*'s wrap on it had indicated it should go.

Blind acquiescence was asking a lot, of both mahendo'sat and hani. And even of the kif.

But things had to stay stable. More, they had to sort themselves out into some kind of defense, both internal and external. The next large group of ships to come in, at any given moment, could be Akkhtimakt's kif in a second strike, which would swing the whole kifish allegiance in the other direction; or it might be Sikkukkut, having disposed of Goldtooth; or Goldtooth and the humans. Or either without the other. Gods knew what else. Panicked stsho, for all they knew. Or tc'a.

Far better that whatever-it-was should meet an already existing wavefront of information designed to provoke discussion instead of indiscriminate fire.

Handle the kif, the woman said.

She sent it wide. In half a dozen languages and amplified via whatever ships would relay it, to all reaches of the system, continuously, since Gaohn station relays and apparently those of the second outsystem station and both buoys were not cooperating. She was talking to more than those insystem and those arriving; she was talking also to a certain mahen hunter, who had lost himself and gone invisible.

Chanur is taking Gaohn Station. This solar system is under control of Chanur and its allies and its subordinates. You are entering a controlled space. Identify yourselves.

"Hold fire!" Pyanfar yelled, turning, her back to the sidewall, the AP up in both hands where it bore on a flat-eared, white-round-the-eyes cluster of hani blackbreeches, Immunes, who were framed in the corridor opening and vulnerable as stsho in a hailstorm. A shot popped past her, high; one streaked back. *"Hold!"* Khym yelled, and: *"Hold it!"* Kohan Chanur echoed, two male voices that rumbled and rattled off the corridor walls in one frozen and terrible instant where slaughter looked likely.

But they were kids who had run up on them. Mere kids. Their ears were back in fright. None of them was armed except with tasers and they were staring down the barrels of APs that could take the deck out. They thought they were going to die there. It was in the look on their faces.

"Don't shoot!" one cried, with more presence of mind than the rest, and held her little pistol wide.

"Are you Ehrran?" Pyanfar yelled back at them, and one of them bolted and ran.

The others stayed still, eyes wide upon the leveled guns.

Prisoners we don't need.

Gods-be groundling fools.

"Get out of here!" she yelled at the rest of them. *"Out,* rot your hides!"

They ran, scrambling, colliding with each other as they cleared that hall, no shot fired.

She turned again, saw weary faces, bewildered faces, saw dread in Rhean Chanur and the rest, spacers who had come home to fight against kif and ended up fighting hani kids. That was the kind of resistance there was. That was what they had come down to, trying to take their station back from lunatics who threw beardless children at them.

"Gods save us," she said, and drew a ragged breath and shook her head and winced at the thump of explosion, which was Haral with their allies blasting their way through another pressure door that had been, with hani persistence, replaced with another windowed door after the *last* armed taking of Gaohn Station. Nothing bad would ever happen twice, of course. Not at civilized Gaohn. Not to hani, who had no wish to become involved in foreign affairs. Gaohn Station prized its staid ways, its internal peace, maintained by ceremonies of challenge and duel.

"Gods curse Naur," she said aloud. "Gods curse the *han.*" And shocked her brother, and surely shocked *ker* Huran Faha, whose shoulder-scar was from downworld hunting, who knew little more of kif than she knew of hyperspace equations. Pyanfar shoved off from the wall and kept going, stepping through the ruined doorway.

"Stop," the intercom said from overhead. *"You are in violation of the law. Citizens are empowered to prevent you."*

There were no citizens in sight. Everyone with sense had gotten out of the section. Those on Gaohn that were not spacers outright, excepting folk like Kohan and Huran, and red-maned Akify who had lived so long downworld with Chanur she had forgotten she was Llun, were all stationers, who knew the fragility of docksides, and knew there was a Chanur ship and a flock of kif and mahendo'sat looming over them. There was a way to slow station intruders down. Anyone in Central might have sealed and vented the whole area under attack, had they been prepared. Had Gaohn station ever been set up for such a defense. But no, the necessary modifications had been debated once, after the first taking of Gaohn, but never carried through: the Llun themselves had argued passionately against it.

There would never, of course, the Llun had thought, never in a thousand lifetimes come another invasion. The very thought of it disturbed hani tranquility, the acknowledgment of such a calamity was against hani principle: plan for an event and it might well create itself. To prepare Gaohn for defense might create a bellicose appearance that might cause it to need that defense. To provide Gaohn corridors with windowed pressure doors (which permitted visual communication between seal-zones in some contamination or fire emergency) was a safety measure and a moral statement: there would never come the day that the station would have to take extreme measures.

So it had fallen to Ehrran quite simply.

And the foreign forces that were coming in had never heard of such philosophy, and cared less. How could one even translate such a mindset to a kifish *hakkikt?*

How could a kif who planned across lightyears comprehend the Llun, let alone the groundling Naur, and the mind of the *han,* which decreed all on its own that hani would be let alone?

. . . .a kif who planned. . . .

. . . .a kif who let loose a mahen hunter ship and a hani force to accomplish a task for him which he—

—could not do himself?

—did a kif ever believe force insufficient?

Could a kif be so subtle?

Gods-rotted right a kif could be subtle. But not down any hani track. A kif wanted power, wanted adherents, wanted territory—

—Sikkukkut knew, by the gods, that Goldtooth was not done, and being capable of tricks like short-jumping himself, he knew what Goldtooth might have done at Meetpoint, a trick that *she* had only discovered when they pinned Jik down and wormed it out of him.

Knnn and gods-knew what had come in on Sikkukkut at Meetpoint, and what would Sikkukkut have done back there? Stayed to contest it? Run home to Kef'k and Mkks, or Akkt?

One wished.

But that was not Sikkukkut's style. The wily bastard would have put more and more of the mahen puzzle together, the same as they, Jik's determined silence notwithstanding. Since Kef'k, there was less and less left that Sikkukkut had to know.

That intrusion which had nearly run them over on their outbound course had been attack coming in again at Meetpoint, that was what it had to be, with the methane-breathers coming in the Out range as methane-breathers were crazy enough to do; and right before Sikkukkut launched his own pet hani toward Anuurn, he had been couriering messages right and left to other ships. . . .

. . . .Sikkukkut was planning something, and *he* had that babbling traitor Stle stles stlen aboard: the stsho would have told him anything and everything about Goldtooth he knew to tell.

Small black creatures stayed active during jump. They were from the kifish homeworld. So could the kif? Were they plotting and planning all the way, was that the secret to kifish daring and fierceness in their strikes, that they came out of hyperspace clearheaded and focused, revising plans such as hani and mahendo'sat and humans and anyone else would have to make well beforehand?

My gods, my gods.

She slogged along after the others, her own group lagging farther and farther back. Flesh had its limits. Even Hilfy flagged. Her pulse racketed in her ears like the laboring of some failing machine. There was that pain in her chest again, her eyes were blurred.

We may not have even this time. We shouldn't be here. I should turn this back, get back to the ship, prepare to defend us—

—with what, fool? This vast armament you have?

—turn kif on kif? Can you lead such creatures as that, can you even keep a hold on Skkukuk if you can't get control of Gaohn?

Jik, gods rot you, where are you?

Another doorway. An AP shell took it out, just blew the window out, leaving jagged edges of plex. The youngsters and then the rest waded on through the wreckage that loomed in her vision like an insurmountable barrier, the gun weighing heavier and heavier in her hand. Kohan had gone ahead with Rhean. Khym was still with her. So were all her own crew. "Looks like we got rearguard," Haral gasped, a voice hardly recognizable. "Gods-be fools not watching their own backsides. Groundlings and kids."

"Yeah," she murmured, and got herself through the door, walked on and wobbled in her tracks. A big hand steadied her. Khym's.

The PA sputtered. *"Cease, go back to your ships immediately. Vigilance has armaments to enforce the decree of the* han. *It stands ready to use them. Do not endanger this station."*

"Ker gods-be Rhif's safe on her ship," Geran said.

"Patience, we got the *Light* up there over her head, she's not going anywhere."

"We got a kifish ship coming into dock," Haral said. *"There's* trouble when it comes. Gods know what that fool Ehrran will do."

Another agonizing stretch of hallway. The first of them had gained the stairwell. There was much yelling of encouragement, inexperienced hani screwing up their courage before a long climb that meant head-on confrontation with an armed opposition.

They were out of range of the pocket-coms. Too much of the station's mass was between them and the ships at dock.

"M'gods." Footfalls came up at their backs, a thundering horde of runners. Pyanfar spun, on the same motion as the rest of the crew, on a straggle of hani in merchants' brights, with a crowd behind them all the way down the corridor, a crowd a lot of which was blackbreeches, strung out down the hall as they filtered through the obstacles of the shattered pressure doors. *"Over their heads!"* She popped off a shot into the overhead, and plastic panels near the shattered door disintegrated into flying bits and smoke and a thundering hail of ceiling panels that fell and bounced and paved the corridor in front of the onrush.

"Stop, stop!" the cry came back, with waving of hands, some of the merchants in full retreat coming up against the press behind, and a dogged few coming through, holding their hands in plain view. "Sfauryn!" one cried, naming her clan, which was a stationer clan: merchants, indeed, and nothing to do with Ehrran.

"We're Chanur!" Tirun yelled back at them, rifle leveled. "Stay put!"

The press had stalled behind, tide meeting tide in the hallway, those trying to advance through the broken doors and those in panic retreat. The few up front hesitated in the last doorway, facing the guns.

"Ehrran has Central!" the Sfauryn cried.

"You want to do something about it?" Pyanfar yelled back.

"We're trying to help! Gods, who're you aiming at? People all over the stations are trying to get in there!"

"Gods-be about time!" Her pulse hammered away, the blood hazed in gray and red through her vision. "If you can get the phones to work, get word to the other levels!"

"Llun's with us—Llun've got portable com, they got some rifles— It's Llun back there behind us, Chanur. They don't want to get shot by mistake!"

"Bring 'em on," she cried. Gods, what days they had come on, when Immune blacks meant target in a fight. She leaned on the wall and lowered the rifle. Blinked against the haze. Rest here awhile. Rest here till they had the reinforcements organized. Llun! honest as sunrise and, thank the gods, self-starting. They had been doing something all the while, one could have depended on that.

But they could still get shot, coming up behind the spacers up front. Someone in spacer blues had to get up there and warn the others in the stairwell that what was coming on their tail was friendly. "Who of us has a run left in her?" she asked, and scanned a weary cluster of Chanur faces, ears flagged, fur standing in sweaty points and bloodied from the flying splinters.

"Me," Hilfy gasped, "me, I got it."

"Got your chance to be a gods-be fool. Go. Get. *Be careful!*"

To a departing back, flattened ears, a lithe young woman flying down that corridor while the shouting reinforcements got themselves organized and came on.

The tide oozed its way through the shattered door, over the rattling sheets of cream plastics that had been the ceiling. It swept on, past a bedraggled handful of heavy-armed hani that hugged the wall and waved them past.

"Time was," Pyanfar said, and hunkered down again as the last of them passed, the heavy gun between her knees, Haral and Geran and Khym already down, Tirun leaning heavily against the wall and slowly sliding down to her haunches, "time was, I'd've run that corridor."

"Hey," Khym said, tongue lolling. He licked his mouth and gasped. "With age comes smart, huh?"

"Yeah," Haral said, and cast a worried look down the corridor, the way Hilfy had gone. Hilfy with a ring in her ear and a gods-awful lot of scars, and a good deal more sense than the imp had ever had in her sheltered life. Hilfy the veteran of Kef'k docks and *Harukk*'s bowels. Of Meetpoint and all the systems in between and the circle that led home.

"Kid'll handle it," Pyanfar said. "We hold this place awhile. Hold their backsides. Got to think. We got *Vigilance* out there. We got kif to worry about."

Station poured out a series of conflicting bulletins. Events were too chaotic for Ehrran to coordinate its lies. "They're still threatening to destroy the boards up there," Chur said. And: "Unnn," from Sirany Tauran. There was nothing for them to do about it. But there *was* a steady pickup of information from Llun scattered throughout the station, static-ridden, but decipherable. It gave out a name. "They've met up with the cap'n," Chur cried suddenly, on a wave of relief, and pressed the com-plug tighter into her ear to try to determine where that meeting was, but Llun was being cagey and giving out no positions.

"They're saying they've linked up with Chanur and the rest and they're headed with that group."

There was a murmured cheer for that. ("Good?" Tully asked, leaning forward to catch Chur's eye. "Good?" "Gods-be good," Chur said back. "The captain's found help.") While Tauran crew stayed busy all about them, stations monitoring scan and outside movements, keeping Tully's recorded output and her own going out on as wide and rapid a sweep of the sphere as they and *Chanur's Light* could achieve in coordination, snugged against a rotating station, and sending with as much power as they could throw into the signal. Especially they kept an eye on *Vigilance* at its dock, *Vigilance*'s image relayed to them by *Light,* as a kifish ship headed for them, conspicuous now among all the others and coming the way a hunter-ship could, by the gods *fast*. While on a link all his own from belowdecks ops, and without a need to sweep the available sphere, Skkukuk maintained communications with his fellow kif.

"Chanur-hakkikt skkutotik sotkku sothogkkt," his news bulletin went out, and Chur winced. *"Sfitktokku fikkrit koghkt hanurikktu makt."* Other hani ships were picking that up, and there were spacers enough out there who knew main-kifish: *The Chanur* hakkikt *has subordinated other clans.* Something more about hani and a sea or tides or something the translator had fouled up. Skkukuk was being coded or poetic, was talking away down there, making his own kifish sense out of bulletins he got. She considered cutting him off. She thought of going down there and shooting him in lieu of ten thousand kif she could not get her hands on.

But the captain had given her orders. Pyanfar Chanur had asked it, and asked it with all sanity to the contrary, which meant it was one of the captain's dearly held notions, and *that* meant Pyanfar Chanur intended her crew to keep their hands off that kif and let him do what Pyanfar had said he should do.

This kif had saved the captain's life. Geran had told her so.

This kif was Pyanfar's kifish lieutenant. Pyanfar herself had told her so.

For Pyanfar's reasons. If they were to go down, as well be on the captain's orders, where they had lived forty years, onworld and off. If Pyanfar Chanur said jump the ship they jumped; if it was on course for the heart of a sun, they objected the fact once to be sure and then they jumped it.

It was a catching sickness. The Tauran captain was doing much the same, obeying orders she doubted.

While one of *The Pride*'s black, verminous inhabitants boldly sat on its haunches in the aisle by the start of the galley corridor and stared in wonder at the fools who ran the ship.

Up the stairs, up and up until the bones ached and the brain pounded for want of air. Hilfy Chanur had gotten herself up to the fore of the band, *after* dispersing parts of the Llun contingent down every available corridor as they ascended, to round up other stationers and get them moving down other corridors. There was one advantage to holding the heart of a city-sized space station, which was that one had all the controls to heat and light and air under one's hands.

The Ehrran had that.

But there was also an outstanding disadvantage to holding Central: that it was *one* small area, and that a city-sized space station had a lot of inhabitants, all of whom were converging on that point from all corridors, all passages, every clan on the station furiously determined to put the Llun *back* in control of systems the Llun understood and the Ehrran interlopers patently did not.

If there were Llun working systems up there at gunpoint, they were doing it all most unwillingly, and Ehrran had only the Llun's word for it just *what* they were doing with those controls.

Fools, aunt Pyanfar would say. A space station was a good deal different than a starship's controls; if there were even experienced spacers in the Ehrran contingent up there. Mostly it had to be groundling Ehrran, blackbreeches whose primary job was trade offices and lickfooting to Naur and others of the Old Rich and the New.

Aunt Rhean was beside her as they climbed. Her father was just behind, grayed and older by the years *The Pride* had been away. And somewhere they had picked up two other men, young Llun, who had come in somewhere around level five and charged in among them in a camaraderie quite unlike men of the common clans—Immunes, free from challenge all their lives and having not a hope in the world of succeeding their own lord except by seniority, they came rushing in, stopped in a moment of recognition, likely neither one having known the other was coming, and surely daunted by Kohan's senior and downworld presence. Then: "Come ahead, rot you!" Kohan had yelled at them. And they had paired up with a great deal of shouting and bravado like two adolescents on a hunt. There were Llun women, armed and experienced in the last desperate battle for Gaohn. And it was all headed right into Ehrran's laps.

If the captive Llun up in control had been willing, they could at least have killed the lights and put the station reliant on the flashlights the Llun and the station merchants and some of the spacers had had the foresight to bring with them. They could have vented whole sections of the docks, with enormous loss of life. They could have fired the station stabilization jets and affected the gravity. They could have thrown the solar panels off their tracking and used some of the big mirrors to make it uncomfortable for *Chanur's Light*. Perhaps the Ehrran urged them to these things at gunpoint.

But none of them had happened.

The level twelve doorway was in front of them. Locked. Of course that was locked. One of the Ehrran had probably done that on manual. They surely held the corridors up here, between invaders and Central.

"Back," Hilfy yelled, and those in front of her cleared back and ducked down as best they could on the stairs, covering themselves. An AP threw things when it hit. And this door went like the others—the window was down, when she opened her eyes, her face and arms and body stung and bleeding with particles. The broken doorway let in a swirl of smoke, and a red barrage of laser fire lit the gray, exploding little holes off the stairwell wall up there.

For the first time panic hit her, real fear. This was the hero-stuff, being number one charging up the stairs into that mess. It was where her rashness and the possession of that illegal AP had put her.

"Hyyaaaah!" she yelled in raw terror, and rushed the stairs, because running screaming the other way was too humiliating. She fired one more time and got plastic-spatter all over her as the shell blew in the corridor and ceiling tiles hailed down in front of her. For a terrifying moment she was alone going through that doorway, and then she felt others at her back, blinked her burned eyes wider and saw black-breeched hani lying in the corridor, some moving, some not; saw laser fire scatter in the smoke and aimed another shell that way.

There were screams. She flinched.

They were hani. They were downworlders. They had no experience of APs or what it was like to have a body blown apart or walls caving in with the percussion of shells. The survivors scrambled and fled and left guns lying in their disgrace, while outraged Llun charged after that lot, the two stationer-lads yelling as they went.

"Door," Rhean said, having arrived beside her, and she pointed to where the Llun were already headed.

"No problem," Hilfy gasped. She was cold all over. Her hand clenched about the grip of the gun as if it was welded there: she had lost all distinction between herself and the weapon, had lost a great deal of feeling all over her splinter-perforated skin. She cast a look back to see how many of their own had made it through, and it was a sea of their own forces in that corridor.

She walked now, over the littered floor, past the dead, where the others had run; and up to the sealed door their charge had secured, near where a shocked handful of Ehrran prisoners huddled under guard. It was the last door, the one that led into Central. "I'll blow it," she said. "You got to take it the hard way—" remembering only then that it was a senior captain she was telling how to do things. It was so simple a matter. It was hurtfully simple. Near Rhean Chanur, near her father, were hani who surely knew. There was Munur Faha, for one. And the Harun. They had to charge in there hand to hand against guns that might destroy fragile controls and kill fifty, sixty thousand helpless people.

Fools. She could have wept over the things she saw. *Poor fools. My people. Do you see now? Do you see what we've done to ourselves, what a plagued thing we've let in, because we tried to keep everything the old way?*

There was information coming in, finally, scattered reports booming out over the PA as Llun portable com began supplanting the reports out of Central: *"Ehrran is in violation of Immune law,"* one such repeated. *"Llun has appealed to all clans to enforce its lawful order for Ehrran withdrawal from station offices and enjoins Ehrran to signal its intent to comply."*

That announcement was becoming tiresome, dinning down from the overhead. Pyanfar wiped her bleeding face and flicked her ears and looked up at the wreckage of the speaker, which gave the advisories a rattling vibration and garbled the words.

"I'd like to shoot that thing," Geran muttered. Which was her own irritated thought.

"Gods-be little good we're doing here," Pyanfar said. "That's sure." Her throat was sore. Her limbs ached. She put effort into getting onto her feet. "Hilfy can take care of herself. Whole station's in on it. Better to get back to the ship, get Chur off her feet."

"Not putting her in any station hospital," Geran muttered. "Safer on the ship."

Which was what Geran thought of Gaohn's present chances, with kif incoming. Or Geran echoed Chur's wishes, if they all went to vacuum and there was no real difference.

"Yeah," she said, noncommittal, and pushed herself off the wall she had braced on. "Gods. What'd I do to stiffen the arm up?" The AP weighed like sin. The debris in the hall was an obstacle course, stuff that stuck in the feet, up in the sensitive arch of the toes. Broken plastics and bits of metal mingled indiscriminately on the deckplates. The mob that had come through had left bloody footprints, but they had seemed crazy enough not to feel it much. Pyanfar limped and winced her way over the stuff, the crew doing the same.

"We got that kif incoming," Tirun said.

"Gods, yes. Llun's not going to like that much." It was about the first thing the Llun partisans were going to learn when they got back into contact with whatever Llun personnel were keeping the station going under Ehrran guns. *Crazy Chanur's bringing kif in.* And Llun at that point had to wonder what side Chanur was on. So did the others, up there with Hilfy.

It was a fair question.

She caught her breath, wiped her nose, seeing a red smear across her thumb. No wonder she was snuffling. And how had *that* happened?

Down the corridor, past one and another of the shattered doorways, over debris of broken plastics, the stench of explosion and burned plastics still hanging in the air, cleaned somewhat by the fans: things were still working.

And Pyanfar was in a sudden fever, now she had begun, to get back to *The Pride* and get out to space again, to deal with the kif she had in hand before she suddenly had more kif than she could deal with.

They reached the corridor end, where the last shattered pressure door let out on the open dock. She stepped over the frame, swung the AP in a perfunctory and automatic sweep about the visible dock, right along with the glance of her eye, which had gotten to be habit.

An AP thumped: her brain identified it as one of that category of dreadful sounds it knew; knew it intimately, right down to the precise sound an AP made when it was aimed dead on: and the twitch went right on to the muscles, which asked no questions. She sprawled and rolled as the world blew up around her; rolled all the way over and let off a shot with both her hands on the AP, in the maelstrom of her crew shouting and shots going off.

My gods, into the doorway, thing hit us dead center—O my gods!

Second shot, off into the cover of the girders.

"You all right?" she yelled back at her crew, at her husband. "You all right back there?"

"Get back here!" Khym's voice, deep and angry.

Third shot. *"Are you all right, gods rot it?"*

A shot came back, hit the wall. She made herself a part of the deck. "Py!"

"Get out of the gods-be door!"

"Chanur!" a voice came over a loudhailer. *"Leave the weapons and come clear of there. You want your crew alive, we have you pinned! We have women coming down that corridor at your backs—"*

"Ehrran?" she yelled out, still belly-down. "Is that Ehrran?"

"This is Rhif Ehrran, Chanur. We have crew behind you. Give up!"

"She's the same gods-be fool she ever was." Haral's voice, somewhere behind her, something in the way of it. Door rim, Pyanfar earnestly hoped.

"You got to match her, Hal? F'godssakes, get out of that door!"

"Hey, she just told us we got company to the rear. You want us to go handle 'em, or you want help out there to fore, cap'n? She's a godsawful lousy shot."

"Chanur!"

"I'm thinking!" she shouted back. And to Haral: "Is everyone all right back there?"

"Na Khym caught a bit in the leg, not too bad. You want to back up, or you want us to come out there?"

She looked out toward that line-of-sight where structural supports gave cover. And up. Where a gantry joined that area, with its couplings and its huge hoses and cables. A grin rumpled her nose and bared her teeth. "It'll be for'ard." As Ehrran yelled again over the loudhailer. *"Chanurrr!"*

"You gods-be fool." She flipped up the sights, aimed, and sent the shell right into the center of the skein. That blew some of the huge hoses in two and blew the ligatures and dropped the whole ungainly snaking mass down behind Ehrran's position, hose thick as a hani's leg and long as a ship ramp dropping in from the exploded gantry skein, hitting, bouncing and snaking this way and that with perverse life of its own. Pumps screamed, air howled and safeties boomed; and blackbreeched figures scattered for very life, in every direction the bouncing hoses left open.

She scrambled up. "Come on," she yelled to her own crew, to get them clear in the confusion, out of that exposed position; and: "Captain!" Tirun yelled.

She whirled toward the targets, got off one shot toward the one figure who had stopped in the clear and lifted a gun. It was not the only shot. APs and rifles went off in a volley from the door behind her, and there was just not a hani at all where that figure had stood. The shock of it numbed her to the heart.

"Still a fool," Geran said, without a qualm in her voice.

And Haral: "Couldn't rightly say who hit her, cap'n, all this shooting going on."

"Move it!" she snarled then, and shoved the nearest shoulder, Geran's. The rest of them moved, covering as they went, Khym limping along and losing blood, but not overmuch of it. *The Pride* was a short run away, *Ehrran's Vigilance* out of sight around the station rim; it was *Harun's Industry* that might well have taken damage in that hit on the gantry lines, if its pumps had been on the draw. Still spaceworthy, gods knew, the pumps were a long way from a starship's heart. They ran across the edge of a spreading puddle of water and mixed volatiles: the toxics, thank gods, ran their skein separately, in the docking probe in space: *those* were not loose, or they would have been dead.

They could all still be dead if *Vigilance's* second-in-command decided to rip her ship loose and start shooting. That little stretch of dock loomed like intergalactic distance, passed in a dizzy, nightmare effort, feet splashing across the deck in liquid that burned in cuts and stung the eyes to tears, that got into the lungs and set them all to coughing. Pumps had cut off. On both sides of the station wall. Gods hope no one set off a spark.

"Chur!" That was Geran's strangled voice, yelling at a pocketcom. "Chur, we're coming in, get that gods-be hatch open!"

They reached the ramp. She grabbed Khym's arm as he faltered, blood soaking his leg. She hauled at him and he at her as he struggled up the climb, into the safety of the gateway.

Then they could slow to a struggling upward jog, where at least no shot could reach them, and the hatch was in reach. She trusted Chur's experience, *The Pride's* own adaptations: exterior camera and precautions meant no ambushes—

"We got that way clear?" Haral was asking on com.

"Clear," Chur's welcome voice came back. "You all right out there?"

All right. My gods!

"Yeah," Haral said. "Few cuts and scrapes."

A numbness insulated her mind. Even with eyes open on the ribbed yellow passage, even with the shock of space-chilled air to jolt the senses, there was this drifting sense of nowhere, as if right and wrong had gotten lost.

A hani that sold us out. A hani like that. A kif like that gods-be son Skkukuk. Which is worth more to the universe?

I shot her. We all did. Crew did it for me. Why'd I do it?

Hearth and blood, Ehrran.

For Chur. But that wasn't why.

For our lives, because we have to survive, because a fool can't be let loose in this. We have to do it, got to do something to stop this, play every gods-be throw we got and cheat into the bargain. Got to live. Long enough.

What will they say about us then?

That's nothing in the balances. That there's someone left to remember at all—that's what matters.

Chapter Thirteen

The lock shot open and it was Tully on the other side, Tully alone and armed and out of breath, his lively pale eyes widening when he saw them, shock and worry at once. He holstered the gun and reached for Khym as he limped over the threshold, and got a snarl for his trouble: "Let be," Tirun said; and: "I'm all right, gods rot it!" from Khym. "Gods! Let me alone!" And: "Shut up," from Tirun. "I got a lame leg from that kind of stuff. Down to the lab and move it."

While Tully shoved a bit of paper at her. "Chur send. Kif ship come send take our kif gods-be quick now. Got Central fine. Now got ask question from station hani what we do. Lot worry. Sirany captain got smart, let Chur do."

More human babble, mingled good and bad news. *Urgent,* Chur's message said: *Courier* Nekekkt *is braking. Lighter is enroute to pick up Skkukuk back at E-lock. I have transcript of all his communications to the kif. They seem clean. Communications from station indicate Ehrran holed up in Central, attack ongoing; no mention from Llun regarding kif;* Vigilance *applying to* han *for instructions, captain's whereabouts unknown. . . .*

That was a message a few moments old. Long as it took for Tully to run down the topside corridor and down the lift and down another passage to meet them. There was more than that happening. *I am trans-*

mitting messages to system edge, Tully assisting; Tauran cooperation excellent—

Thank the gods for Chur Anify. And everyone else involved.

"Come on." She swept Tully up, Tirun having snatched Khym on through; Geran and Haral limped along with her.

Was altruism possible? Had Ehrran come at her in defense of the station itself, tried to arrest Chanur crew in hope of seizing control of the situation, knowing that kifish ship was incoming?

Sorry about it if that's so. Real sorry. All I got time to be. She hurt everywhere. Her eyes blurred with particulate dust and her nose still bled. She stank of sweat and volatiles.

There was no time to wonder about it. She headed for the lift.

Two of Sifeny's crew and one of her own were still out there in the shooting. And her husband was down in sickbay to let an exhausted, shaking spacer hunt a piece of shrapnel out of him.

Those were the things she wanted to worry about, the things a hani could somehow manage.

It was not what was waiting for her topside.

There were casualties. One dead. Three likely to be. The dead one was one of the lads from Llun; and Hilfy stood over him and looked down at a boyish, simple face. Nothing much. A boy who had been too brave and a little foolish. Playing at hero.

Gods. Gods. He never knew it was real.

Did he? This boy? Could he imagine Harruk's black gut? A kifish dockside?

Or did he have to?

A hand touched her shoulder. Her father, sweaty and bloody and breathing hard. And safe. She looked up at Kohan Chanur: he towered, huge and kind and perhaps no longer or ever as innocent as she had always thought him.

She looked at him and saw he was also hunting someone who no longer existed. His daughter. The unscarred one. Perhaps he wanted her to show some emotion. That made her saddest of all, that if she softened it would be a lie. Sadness was all she could muster. She only looked at him.

Her mother was more practical. Huran Faha stood by, with perhaps a little amazement, a hard and reckoning look between them when she turned away, a warning look, because there were Llun taking back this control center as Ehrran clanswomen were rounded up and led away. It had not been that hard at the last. Poor groundling fools who melted away in hand-to-hand so fast it was over in a couple of shots and a tangle of bodies, Ehrran struggling up close and intimate with spacers who learned their infighting in dockside bars. Not a chance in a mahen hell, after that. Easy stuff.

Only the boy, who had never dodged. Who just plunged ahead in his simple bravery because that was what men were supposed to do, wasn't it?

"Gods blast 'em!" Suddenly the anger was too much, and there was nowhere to spend it. She had no wish to stay and answer close questions from the Llun.

She was not known the way her aunt Pyanfar was. She was only another spacer, thin and scarred and unremarkable, except that she had stood for a moment with Chanur clan, except for a moment the lord of Chanur—*ex-lord! O gods!*—had laid his hand on her shoulder. It was time to be gone back to her ship. She gave a look to Fiar and Sif, caught their eye in one sweep and slanted an ear toward the door. Time to be out indeed, before Llun caught on to who she was, and what crew she belonged to.

But a brusque presence swept into the center, graynosed and haggard and accompanied by a band of hani in hardly better shape—the look, Hilfy had gotten to know it, of spacers off a brutally hard run. Dulled fur, thinned patches. She knew them, had seen this lot last on a Meetpoint dockside with police closing in on all of them.

Banny Ayhar and her crew filled the doorway, blinked, and stared at her closer than a chance encounter warranted. "Is that young Chanur?" Banny asked. "Is that Hilfy Chanur?"

Hilfy's jaw refused to work. The wits that had done quite well up to that point, turned to butter.

"Chanur for sure!" Banny drew a deep breath, and her ears slanted back and up again. "They told me what you did." Down again. "Got us free, b'gods! Gods-be fools! But what's this with you and the kif?"

There was profound silence at her back, and profoundest attention to the question.

"Chanur," another voice said at her back. *"Ker* Hilfy."

She started out, past Banny. But that obstacle was not moving.

"Kif," Banny Ayhar said. "That's what I want to know. What's going on?"

It was stop or fight. A fight now could do Chanur no particular good.

She glared at Banny Ayhar with flattened ears and the power of the AP in her fist which was right now worth nothing at all.

My gods, I can lose it all. Everything. If they get wind of what we're doing, they'll throw it wide and high and we'll all die, the whole world will die for it. O Banny Ayhar, you godscursed fool, you're about to throw away everything you won.

"You got the message here," she said to Banny, quiet and urgent, ears up now. "You want to lose it all? Or you want to stand with me here?"

She was talking to a captain; and a hardnosed one; and flatly forgot the *ker* and the respects: she threw her whole life and self into it.

Banny's ears twitched this way and that in the deep hush. Everyone in the whole center must have heard that appeal, as if Ayhar and *Prosperity* were part of all that tainted Chanur. There was Harun back there. And Munur Faha. She was *not* alone. Even in the matter with the kif. There were senior captains to rely on. There stood Fiar and Sif, co-conspirators off the same bridge.

She saw a sudden guardedness in Banny Ayhar's eyes, the look of an old trader and an old hand in rough places. The old woman knew when she had gotten a high sign, by the gods she caught it up; and it was suddenly spacers and stationers in the control center, spacers and Them, which was only slightly less foreign than the kif.

"Chanur," that Llun voice behind her said, a woman's voice of some age and authority.

But before she turned, Ayhar lifted her chin in that way that from Anuurn docks to Meetpoint, said *Ally, till I find out different.*

"Cap'n, they got into Central, they got it."

Pyanfar crossed the bridge in the wake of a cheer from both crews, to lean on Chur's seatback. "Clear?"

"Not officially confirmed yet." Chur did not look around. Her ears backslanted as she flicked switches and punched buttons. "Gaohn station, this is *The Pride of Chanur,* we got an incoming lighter, we'll handle that. Appreciate word on casualties at your earliest." Pause. Flick of the ears. "Captain, we got a general announcement: *Remain calm. Llun has retaken Central.*"

"They'll have every clan in reach of there asking casualties. We've got to sit and wait, I'm guessing."

"I'd like it better if they got some operators on output. We just got that same message cycling over and over. Nobody's handling anything.

We got what we got from a ship-to-ship off a Moura freighter. *Somebody's* got com in there."

Pyanfar gnawed at her mustaches, spat and gnawed again. "We got no favors coming. Those with bad news get it first, that's the way of it. They're all right. Just keep after 'em."

While Tauran crew methodically handled the approach of the kifish lighter, which was coming in toward the docking boom aft. And a certain kif was standing there with bags and Dinner packed. One hoped.

("Skkukuk," she had said lately, over com. "This is the captain. Just want you to know I'm back and we're quite well in control.")

("I had absolutely no doubts," the kifish voice came back to her, tinny the way E-deck pickup always sounded. *"I will give you the hearts of your enemies.")*

Literally. It was not a thing she wanted to contemplate at the moment, with the possibility of casualties up in Central and the dire memory of Ehrran out there on the docks. She flinched from that every time the image came back to her, and it came time and again.

Nothing left. Nothing, O gods.

An Immune. With all the trouble she was, she was still an Immune.

She listened while the sorting-out of com and the docking of a kifish lighter proceeded.

"You want your chair," Sirany offered her a second time.

Meaning: command of this situation. Everything that went with it. She looked at the Tauran, saw the exhaustion and the anxiousness of a woman who feared every moment she sat there and feared equally to abdicate that chair and turn it back to Chanur.

"I'll take it," Pyanfar said. "I want to get my second up here; you mind to sit observer? Fit both our crews in here and galley: we got need of all the expertise we got."

"I'll sit it," Sirany said, and hauled herself out of the number one place. "Two minute break and I'm back here."

"We have touch imminent," the Tauran working that docking said, never pausing: the interface between crews went through smooth as the shift of a few bodies, and never a missed beat.

Not a jolt as the kifish lighter made its contact with the boom. Retraction whined away, a moan throughout the ship as the boom swung down and dragged lock and lock into contact.

A hani might wish to say goodbye. Even to a kif. It was not the way of kif. The presence quit *The Pride* with never a word and never a report, just the abrupt communication from the lighter pilot that they were ready for undock.

Then the lighter took off, rolled and left with all the speed it could muster, a little sputter of its engines against *The Pride*'s hull.

That was, she reckoned, another ambitious kif, the captain of that so-quickly moving ship out there, the one which had appropriated the responsibility for picking up the hani's kif.

Not the foremost among the ships out there. She knew that much by now. It was about the third-subordinate, not in contention for primacy in Sikkukkut's favor; so it was taking a calculated risk, maybe to do in its passenger, maybe to listen to him, depending on how things developed. And right now there were probably some very worried captains on the number one and two kifish ships. There were worried captains *everywhere* among the kif out there, Sikkukkut's highest captains sweating sudden adjustments in hierarchy: they had just gained a lot of Akkhtimakt's ships.

Good luck, my skulking shadow. Good luck. To both of us.

She drew a deep breath and flipped switches.

"We pulling out?" Haral wondered, beside her.

It was what she ached to do, get *The Pride* out of station, away from dock where it was less a target. "Want to get our people back." There was a cold lump at her gut. *I want to hear something out of Central, gods rot it. What kind of a hash have they got going up there? Station's stable. No damage alarms. They can't have shot it up too bad.*

Kohan's too reckless. Gods, don't let him have rushed in there.

Hilfy, now, Hilfy can cover herself.

"I don't credit that answer," the Llun said quietly. *"Not tip off our enemies.* I don't see any enemies here, *ker* Hilfy Chanur. I see alien ships moving out there, I see this station in jeopardy, I hear talk about a threat to the planet. I'm wondering where it comes from. I'm wondering what else we don't know about."

Hilfy kept her ears up, let them dip a bit in displeasure, brought them up again. Kohan was there, Kohan stripped of his title and his courtesies, the whole clan—gods, the whole clan must have deserted Kara Mahn's takeover and exiled themselves with their lord rather than submit to the Mahn and his sister. The powers of Chanur were most likely here: like Rhean. Like Jofan, who must have connived at getting herself and Kohan and the rest up to Rhean.

She was never prouder of her clan and her kin. *"Ker* Llun," she said, quietly, steadily, "I can tell you this. It's not numbers that'll win this one. We can't match numbers with what's out there. We haven't got the ships or the guns. Best thing we've got on our side right now is a mahendo'sat we've lost track of out there and the deep-spacers. My aunts are three of them. Ayhar here. Harun and Faha and Shaurnurn and Pauran and Tauran. And all the rest. Whatever men and kids are onstation, we'd be safer to get them off, out of here: every ship that hasn't got the guns to fight—take the men and the kids far as they can run into mahen space, and we just hope to the gods they'll get the word in a few months that Anuurn's still here. If it's not—there'll still be hani. That's what we're fighting for. The worst place in the whole system to be right now is one of our armed ships; second worst is the space stations; third is the world down there. You've got to turn the spacers loose, *ker* Llun, it's not Chanur I'm talking about, I'm not asking favors; I'm asking you turn the spacers *loose* and let us have a chance." She held out an arm, turned a shoulder, where kif had left scars that would last all her life. "That's the kind of treatment kifish guests get. Never mind what they do to the ones who aren't hostages."

"Are you," the Llun asked in a slow and level voice, "are you that now, Hilfy Chanur?"

"Hearth and blood, Llun. We're our own."

"We're on that ship." A young voice, talking out where seniors were silent. It wavered and all but died. Then Fiar Aurhen *par* Tauran edged her way past two captains and faced the Authority of Llun, flat-eared and with her voice pitched too high. "They're r-right. They ran clear from Kshshti—"

To station-bound Llun, Kshshti was only a place on a map, remote from all experience. Mkks was beyond their imagining. For a moment Hilfy felt a profound terror, the gulf between them uncrossable.

"We got a mess out there," Banny Ayhar said in her rumbling voice, and sniffed and hitched her pants up before she flung an arm out to gesture. "F'godssakes, you got your house afire you ask them as have buckets, Shan Llun! You don't lock 'em up and call 'em traitors! To a mahen hell with the gods-be *han* deputies and the notebooks and that trash! You can't call any referendum from the kif and they don't have any study committee! You godsforsaken fools, you listen to the likes of Ehrran till they take your station over and you *don't* listen to them that's had their shoulders to the dike. Look at 'em, you say! They got mud on 'em, must be they brought the flood! And you never seeing they've been propping up the gods-be timbers!"

There was profound silence. The Llun's ears flickered minutely in restraint. The eyes were gold and large and black-centered.

She waved a hand at the Llun who was taking furious notes.

"Record that a quorum voted. The Llun have heard the vote. The Llun call civil emergency: the amphictiony is space-wide." The hand fell. "Which captain do you want in charge?"

The silence went on several breaths. "Pyanfar Chanur," Kauryfy Harun said.

"Banny Ayhar," another said.

"Gods and thunders, not me," Banny said. "Pick someone who's got some idea what's out there. Chanur's stayed alive this far. I'd go with their knowhow."

Quiet mutters then. "Chanur," Munur Faha said. And: "Chanur," from Shaurnurn and Pauran and a scatter of others.

"Chanur," the Llun said, with another wave of her hand. "Implement the orders. Tanury: evacuation operations. Nis: communications interface. Parshai: spacer logistics. Open the boards. Get it moving."

Hilfy stood there with her muscles cold and uncooperative. It had all changed course. She was free. The ships were. She cast a grateful look Banny Ayhar's way, but Ayhar was already moving; and beyond that consideration she knew where she belonged. Fast.

She was into the rush for the door and collected Fiar and Sif before she recalled she owed some glance toward her father and her mother, some apology for having set herself forward: but the Llun had cornered her, they had wanted *her* answers, and Rhean had stood there in the silence an accused clan had to maintain. With dignity. The little dignity that Chanur had left, with its land gone.

I'm sorry, she wanted to say. But the rush carried her through the door and there was no time to spend on goodbyes and regrets.

Gods hope they talked Kohan into going refugee with the other men. Gods hope.

She doubted that they could.

Where are the rest of us, the old aunts, the kids, my sisters and cousins?

On Fortune *and* Light? *How many could they get aloft?*

If that's so, if we lose those ships, Chanur will die here.

She did not wait for the lift. There were too many waiting. She joined the impatient ones that ran the stairs, all the way down again to dockside.

* * *

"... *earnestly hope,*" the voice out of Gaohn Central Control said, precise and patient, "*you will remember the lives on this station; but we realize that this is not the greatest priority under the threat that exists. Therefore we do not encumber you with instructions of any sort. Take what actions you see fit. The citizens of this station are carrying out all domestic safety precautions. We will not issue any further order to you until this emergency is past. Gods defend us. You'll have other priorities. End statement.*"

"Thank you, Llun." Pyanfar kept the voice cool, the hand steady over the contact. "We'll be putting out as quickly as possible. Can we have all dock crews on line?"

Gods, where had she learned such short courtesy? The kif? She got the acknowledgment and punched out of the contact. But there were no promises that meant anything. There was nothing she wanted to say, that might not get to one of the other ships and have one of those captains second-guessing her. That was not kifish manners: it was hani good sense, hani levelheadedness. So the whole gods-be system defense was in her lap. So they were sending men and children out to the far quarters of mahen space, to be sure something of the species survived. It was what the Llun ought to have done days ago, instead of waiting till disaster came in on them. Rage boiled up in her and shortened her breaths as she kept the pre-launch checks going, one and the other switches, while Haral ran those on Tirun's board. Armaments.

There was another ship coming into Gaohn's traffic control, up from the world itself: shuttle-launch, out of Syrsyn. The information trickled out of Central to *Light*'s query: an unauthorized lift. An escape. A junior pilot and a single flight tech. The story came in from a ground station: the little Syrsyn Amphictiony had heard the warning out of space, and gotten the menfolk and the teenaged boys and girls of at least six clans all onto a commandeered shuttle, the men and the boys all drugged beyond argument, and that whole fragile, precious package presently climbing out of Anuurn's atmosphere.

That terrified her more than Gaohn's danger. Syrsyn was taking the monumental risk of an action she had asked them to take. And it was so small a ship, and so helpless, and a fool thing to do, under-crewed and gods knew, with no flight plan but up. Use the engines, get course *after* they were in space, trust someone would take them in: lifesupport adequate for—gods, what kind of figure? how many on that ship? Six clans'

304 • C. J. Cherryh

kids, the menfolk, a couple of women to handle the emergencies and keep down panic—

Four, five hundred lives?

How many of Chanur were still ground-bound?

Gods, get us away from this dock. Give us a chance.

Let us get at least to system edge.

There were no mines laid, gods-be nothing done, to forestall invasion. The *han* directed: the *han* had no grasp of mahen tactics, gods help them, no *knowledge* what the universe was shaped like above their day-sky, how ships and objects incoming and dropping out of hyperspace went missilelike to a sun, and coincidentally the near planets, of the habitable kind, at velocities that made them undetectable until they arrived. And the farther out from the system center the defense was set, to prevent such strikes, the larger the sphere of defense, and the wider the gaps in it, even if a body was reasonably sure what jump point it was coming from, and whether it was sticking to standards like system zenith entry, or whether the cant of the local star and the origin-well permitted something like a nadir arrival. It was a good guess where anything incoming from Meetpoint might arrive via Kura. Which was, gods knew, the shortest route.

But it was a lot of space. And if the kifish bastard did some fancy maneuvering at Kura they might just come in nadir.

Or they might already *be* there, having short-jumped. That thought set the hair on end all down her back: Sikkukkut or gods-knew-who might be out there and by now inbound, well knowing the position of everything in the system.

"Take the count. Mark."

"Mark." Haral started the clock running. "Tirun. *Na* Khym. We're on the count."

"We're on our way," Tirun's voice came up from lowerdecks.

Put Khym in his cabin? It was where he belonged.

No. *Give him that. We're not going to get out of this one the same as we got in. The last time, husband. I think this crew knows it.*

"Hilfy's just called," Geran said. "She's on her way to the ramp. With Sif and Fiar. Not a scratch on 'em."

"Got that." A muted murmur of relief across the bridge. The lost were found. Hydraulics sounded below, as Haral opened up the lock from the board.

I ought to wish she missed the ship. I wish she had. Gaohn's got a better chance than we have.

The airlock sealed again. *The Pride* took back its own.

"We're on count," Geran advised the new arrivals. "Get up here."

Six minutes.

"Captain—" From the Tauran comtech. "We got contact with *Ehrran's Vigilance.*"

"Give it here." Pyanfar punched the button when it lit; and her gut knotted. "This is Pyanfar Chanur."

"Captain." The voice that came back was cold and neutral. *"This is Jusary Ehrran. Acting captain. Vote has been taken on this ship. We will act in system defense. We will go to Kura vector."*

She looked aside at Haral, at a flat-eared scowl.

"Gods-be earless bastard," Haral muttered. Bloodfeud: there was no doubt of that. With an Immune clan. They could not decline that, or their offer of help. "Covering their gods-be ass."

"We got no graceful way, have we? You want to leave 'em docked at Gaohn?"

"Captain—" The tech again. "Ayhar's on. *Prosperity.* They're aboard."

Bad news and good, like opposite swings of the pendulum. The whole universe was confounded. She punched in on the indicator, the first one still blinking. "This is Pyanfar Chanur. Banny, I owe you a drink."

"You owe my whole crew drinks, you notch-eared old dockcrawler, first we get back to port."

"You got it, Banny. Take care, huh? I'll get you sequence in a minute here." She cut out and punched the other. While quietly, a little murmur among the crew, the rest of them arrived, Tirun and Khym, Hilfy and Fiar and Sif. There was sorting-out going on, Chanur crew prioritied to seats. "He's got ob-2," she heard, Geran's voice. Definitively. A murmur from Khym. A Tauran voice, quietly. And Tully and Hilfy. It was all getting arranged over there. "We got a prelim sequence here," Haral was saying, likely to her sister Tirun. "Central's passed control over to us, we got the say." And into the microphone: *"Vigilance,"* Pyanfar said. "This is Pyanfar Chanur. Stand by your sequence."

"Understood," the acknowledgment came back. And: *hearth and blood,* she heard unsaid, under the chill, precise voice. *Later, Chanur.*

"We'll cover you same as the rest," Pyanfar said.

A small delay. *"We appreciate that, Chanur."* Grace for grace. The woman had some positive qualities. Then: *"This is your fault, Chanur."*

"We'll see you in the *han,* Ehrran."

The com-telltale went out.

306 • C. J. Cherryh

The power came up, the undocking sequence initiated. Familiar sounds. There was a great cold in her gut and an ache in her side. A sequencing flicked up on number one screen. She keyed affirm, and it flicked off: flashed out to all the ships via Central.

Fortune and *Light* were going wide out on either side of their formation; her own group contained the ships she had come with: *Industry* and *Shaurnurn's Hope, Starwind* and *Pauran's Lightweaver.* And ships that had run with *Fortune* and those that adhered to *Ayhar's Prosperity* each to those captains' discretion—a great number to *Prosperity,* with more on the way. *Ehrran's Vigilance* took farthest sweep, nadir. Not the hottest spot. The catcher-point. The one to take the strays.

It was the second time for some of these crews, the second time they had ever uncapped the red switches on the few armaments a freighter carried. Two years ago. Or whatever year it was, currently. Gods. She had lost track. Four? More than that? Kohan's face flashed to mind, Kohan grayed and time-touched. The world changed. More of the people she had known in her youth onworld would have died. Of old age.

How old am I? How many years did we lose out there?

The month, two-month jumps added up to years fast, with so little dock time between. She suddenly tried to think what her son and her daughter might look like, Kara Mahn and Tahy, down there ruling Chanur land, sitting in the *han,* for the gods' sake, *Tahy* senior enough to sit in the *han* and talk for Mahn, and vote against Chanur interests. Of a sudden the baby faces leapt to adolescence, to adulthood, to broad-faced maturity, Kara's sullen, broadnosed face gone more sullen still, Tahy's furtive look gone to something pinched and unpleasant—a smallish teenager become a smallish, surly woman whose ears were always flicking about as if she suspected conspiracy. A mother's imagination painted these things and touched her children's manes with gray. Kara's ears would be notched up right proper. Kohan had gotten the ears the first time Kara made a try for Chanur land: it was a good guess Kohan had gotten him again. In return for his own scars. *Gods. So fast. Life's so fast. How much of it I've missed.*

Grapples withdrew. Undocking jets eased them out, under Haral's careful hand. Com babble came to her, three operators at once, on their separate channels, each dealing with procedures some of which went to Tirun back there at the aux panel.

She used her own comp, sorting the data that sifted past Tirun. *The Pride* backed hard; and something black and furred and angry shrieked and scrabbled across the decking, crack! against the bottom of the panel. It squealed in rage and scrambled sideways under the acceleration.

"Gods and thunders." She kicked at it, hardly sparing attention for the little bastard. Figures were more important. What it had done to systems back aft, gods only knew. It escaped, off galleyward. "Have to purge the ship to hard vacuum to get rid of those things."

"I'm not sure," Haral muttered, "that *that*'d do it. Standby rollover."

The Pride rolled, *G*-shift and re-shift; and six of the mains cut in, a moral shock this close to Gaohn. Laws and regulations were fractured. But Gaohn was under disaster-rigging, population snugged to the inmost sections. They made speed. They passed the zone where the aux-engines were permitted and slammed the mains in full.

They were free. Moving. Bound for the system rim.

Gods knew what was already out there, inbound.

"Communication from *Mahaar's Favor*," Chur said, "bearing off Tyar. They're AOS on our earlier transmission and say they're holding position."

Standing nose to nose with the kif.

She cast a wary eye at scan, where a dot that was a kifish ship stood all too close to Gaohn with the lighter-ship in its gut.

Too gods-be close to Gaohn and Anuurn.

It's a mistake. I'm a fool. They'll kill Skkukuk, poor bastard. They'll take him apart and they're in position to take the station out.

Fire on 'em? Gods-be kif hunters bury their personnel sections deep inside, got twenty feet of stuff to blast through to get a hit on the things, godsforsaken missiles we got won't dent it that deep without us throwing 'em at V and we're near sitting still even yet. Fool, Pyanfar, fool.

While acceleration went on. There was a stuffiness about the air. An unpleasant taint, like chemicals. Like dust in the air. Ozone. Filters were out. They had a redlight condition on the lifesupport board. They ignored it.

She blinked her eyes. For a moment it was *Harukk*'s dark gut, the flare of sodium light. Dark-robed kif and the smell of incense and ammonia.

Kifish ships at dock at Kefk, lean and wicked and massive-vaned bristling with guns. Like that thing out there.

"Priority," Hilfy said, and froze her heart. "Captain, it's *Nekkekt*. They're asking instructions."

Gods, of course *it won't turn now. Things are too uncertain. It's in crisis they kill their officers.*

And their allies.

"Have 'em put Skkukuk on."

A pause. While the mains blasted away, squaring the *V* and bringing them at an angle to the kif. Kif could fire from any angle. *The Pride* and the rest of the freighters had their limits.

It's godsblessed suicide. Bluff from one end to the other.

"They're sending for him," Hilfy said. "Captain, there's a Situation over there. That was the captain who asked instructions, I think, by their comtech."

"I think you got it," she muttered. *Push the bastard. Make him get your own skku to the mike. Gods. What're the han doing, what are they thinking, the ships out there? Chanur's talking to the kif, we got a kif right into Gaohn, we got kifish and human transmission going out of this ship. . . .*

It's Harun and the rest they're watching. The ships that came with me. Spacers. That's what they're taking their cue from—they know Chanur could be crazy, but not Chanur and five other clans and the mahendo'sat. They're holding steady so far—gods, they know *the kif, they know this whole mess is unstable.*

If they knew how much—

"Skkukuk to your com one," Haral said. A light blinked.

She punched it. *"Skku of mine. We're taking Kura vector. See to it."*

There was a pause. *Is he on? Gods, let's not have a mistake.*

"Chanur-hakkikt." In a voice cold and clear and clipped.

Skkukuk? Is that Skkukuk?

"Pukkukt' on your enemies, hakkikt. I will give them to you."

"Skkukuk?"

A pause. *"Of course, hakkikt-mekt. Skkukuk."* An edge to the voice. The tone was different. *"Pukkukt' on* all *your enemies. Rely on me."*

What in the gods' name is he up to? Is that him? What's going on with him?

Is this some gods-help-us kifish test?

Or a kif gone important?

"Get those gods-be ships into line and get it organized. First one makes a wrong move, take it out!"

"Yes."

The light went out. Like that. A little chill went down her back.

"What've we created? Migods, what've we created out, huh?"

Haral looked her way. Mirrorlike. *"Mekt-hakkikt, was it?"*

She blinked. The chill got no better. And no questions came through com from hani ships. Or station. Or the few mahendo'sat keeping their post out there with the kif Skkukuk had just appropriated.

Not a word from Sirany Tauran, sitting a duty post like crew.

It's out of control.

Crew's not talking. Stations are too quiet. What are they thinking, for godssakes?

Last run we make, and we know it, don't we? It's not what we used to be. None of us are that.

She coughed. "We got one of those gods-be black things loose somewhere up here, gods know where it'll land when we maneuver, just want you to know that."

"Gods," someone muttered. And it was as if the whole crew drew a collective breath and loosened collective muscles. "What say?" Tully asked plaintively, lost as usual. "What say?"

"Captain said—" Khym began.

"Movement on *Nekkekt,*" Geran said monotone, deliberate monotone. As Haral prioritied scan up. No emergency. That was where it had to be.

"Transmission," Hilfy said. "Skkukuk's passing your orders to the kif. Ordering the clans and the mahendo'sat to clear out of their way."

"Confirm that to our allies."

A pause. A longer-than-one-breath pause. Then: "Aye." And compliance, rapid pushing of buttons.

"Captain." Chur's voice, quiet, very quiet. Strain was in it. "I got this idea—"

"Spill it."

"The kif. They know their enemy. They turned round here. Akkhtimakt's ships—" The voice faded out, restored itself. "They knew it was sprung, the trap— They've been here—how long? Jik went on—but there's others—"

"Timetables. Gods. The mahendo'sat know there's a second wave, they knew it. Hilfy. Transmit: *Hasano-ma.* My gods, we've been sitting on that code program—Jik's letter. Run the coded parts through. Spit it on at them. Send it out on the Ajir vector. Put our wrap on it and get the mahendo'sat—gods, gods, gods, the man gives us a key and a coder and we sit on it."

"That'll worry the kif some."

"Good! They love it. Jik. Jik, gods rot it—no, he hasn't gone on. He doesn't have to jump all the way to Ajir, b'gods, he can *stop* out there, stop, turn, and get back here, and the kif know it, they know it, *that's* why they're stalled. Akkhtimakt's run into a trap, and his ships saw it coming, by gods, he was already pinned here thanks to Ayhar—We came in and his ships panicked; and defected; and now they don't know what to do."

"Kill their captains," Haral said grimly. *"That's* what they're doing, you want to lay odds to it? One place they're not going is back to Akkhtimakt. That bastard's gone. Run to the deep for sure, and his crew will kill him and turn that ship around if they can stop fighting mahendo'sat long enough: they'll be out of there and back through here like a shot if they get half a chance."

"Tirun. What's the mahen AOS?"

"Good eight minutes."

She gnawed at her mustaches. A good hour Light to the nadir range. Maybe two out, if there was a mahen force out there lurking.

Gods blast you, Jik—throw the hani at it again, do you? Use us for a decoy. Set us up. Unless you're already on your way. And you won't be, will you? It's a trap the kif understand. The lurking kind. That's why the *kif flinched, why I've got me a dozen kif out there trying to figure out whether to listen to me now and turn on me later—*

They don't know what might come through out there first. Anything *could. If it's Goldtooth they better have joined me. If it's Sikkukkut they better not have. Poor bastards. What's a kif to do but stall?*

And Skkukuk, that gods-be conniving son is out there risking his neck because it's logical. He's mine. He senses I'm against the hakkikt *and Sikkukkut's going to kill him right along with the rest of us, that's what's going on in that earless head of his—he's taking all he's got and charging the bastards headon with the widest bluff he can run—*

Gods, can you call a kif brave?

"We got a—"

Priority!" Geran cried. "Blip's in, bearing zenith ten, twenty two, ten. . . ."

The scan image flashed red-rimmed, flashed red on the newly arrived blip—

"Knnn!" Hilfy said. "That's knnn output—"

"Vector, vector—"

A line popped onto the course diagrams, the whole perspective shifted, rotated, showed it passing through system on a trajectory right past them, while the dopplered image flashed to yellow: "Going right through system fringes," Geran said, "passing within—Tyri orbit to nadir range."

"Gods, I don't like this." That was Sirany. Quietly.

"All sorts of strange fish," Pyanfar muttered. "Goldtooth. They ran right before Goldtooth at—"

"Priority, priority, we got another one—"

"It's here," Haral said. As the scan image acquired another blip that blinked and came ahead. The knnn kept dopplering, the image rotating to show relative position: comp had the hazard warning blinking all round the edges. "Same course."

"Not knnn," Pyanfar said. "That thing's might not be knnn, I got this terrible feeling—"

"Fake a knnn ID?"

"Who'd dare fire on it? Put the armaments on track. Warning to all ships: Hilfy."

"Aye."

"Armaments locked," Tirun said. "And tracking."

"It's just gone kifish; it's *Harukk!"*

"Gods *rot*—To all ships. Inertial!"

"Slow him down?" Haral was mind-reading again. *The Pride*'s mains cut out abruptly, an abrupt feeling that *down* was no longer aft, bodies were suddenly *not* lying flat on backs but attracted weakly seatward under the slight rotation—the whole board went blurred a moment in her eyes and a feeling of vertigo and panic came over her—

"We've got—got to play it step by step. Hope to gods Sikkukkut's being smart again, smart'll hang him—*no*body understands the *han."* A screen flashed change. More kif were dropping into system. IDs multiplied. *Harukk. Ikkhoitr.* Others of the old association.

It was very quiet for a moment. Just ship after ship dropping out of hyperspace.

And hani ships biding in prudent silence. Even Ehrran. No moves but the cutting of thrust, instant and undisputed. Keep the formation. They were still ripping along at more speed than insystem navigation rules permitted.

Think, fool. That kif's either fired or talked out there, the other side of Light. Do one or the other.

"Com to my board." The readylight flashed link to com one. *Gods, they got our message wavefront out there, everything Chur's sent out, kifish and human: and they can't crack the human stuff.* "Get scan relayed out there, give 'em everything we know. Fast." She punched the mike in. *"Harukk,* welcome to Anuurn: this is Pyanfar Chanur, aboard

The Pride of Chanur. Akkhtimakt is defeated, his ships have defected, praise to the *hakkikt.* If enemies follow you we are ready."

"*That's* by the gods sure," Haral said under her breath, when she punched out. Haral's ears were flat. Pyanfar found her left hand clenched on the seat, claws right through the leather.

So what's he done? Fired or talked?

Farther and farther.

"*They're dumping!*" Geran yelled, and a yell and a collective breath and a gasp went through the bridge. "Thank gods," someone said. Tully muttered something humanish and faint.

"Keep transmitting that message," Pyanfar ordered. "Repeat, repeat."

"We've got it going," Hilfy said.

Five ships. Five, six ships in the system now. *Harukk* and *Ikkhoitr.* And another one. Seven.

How many? Gods, how many? Did he get away free? Run early and save his ships?

He's got to have lost some. At Meetpoint. At Kura, if the mahendo'sat got there from Ajir. They've got to have done that. Run them through that gauntlet and peel a bit more flesh off them. Give us some help, for godssakes!

Eight now. Nine and ten, widely separated.

"Priority," Hilfy said, "from *Harukk*-com: gods, it's code, we got some kind of code, it's for those ships back there. . . ."

"Keep our transmission going."

The ache grew around her heart, grew and grew. The blood pounded in her temples. Not a sound from the ships around them, nothing from the ships behind, yet . . . yet. Light had a little lagtime for them.

"*Nekekkt's* answering," Hilfy said. "All code."

So what are you doing, Skkukuk? What are you up to? Who's in charge on that ship?

Twelve. Thirteen ships. Fourteen.

"*Priority.*" Com came through direct to her earplug. "*Instruction from the* hakkikt, *praise to him. Restore buoy output to our ships. Surrender this system and all its ships instantly. It will exist under the authority of my* skku *Pyanfar Chanur, whose orders come from me. Cease all hostilities. You are dealing with the* mekt-hakkikt *Sikkukkut an'nikktukkktin, who allots the rule of this system and its adjuncts to his vassal Chanur.*"

She let the breath hiss softly. *Gods-be, what must they think now,*

Rhean and Anfy and Harun and Banny and the rest—what in a mahen hell do the kif back behind me think, and what kind of a move have I made with Skkukuk?

Then: *Gods help me, I've got it, I've got it all, everything in my hands to protect, my people, my allies. He's not shooting.*

Now what do I do?

"Reply: Pyanfar Chanur to the *mekt-hakkikt* Sikkukkut an'nikk-tukktin, praise to his foresight, his enemies are under my hand."

Ambiguity. *Gods save us all.*

Haral had looked her way. And there was that little black thing slinking back from the galley, in a hurry, as if Tauran crew in there had done something violent.

"Smart is all we got," she said to Haral. "I remember what Gold-tooth said. We get this situation calmed down a little and then I go for a little visit to *Harukk*. That's what. We take Goldtooth's suggestion. Snuggle up to this kif and get him."

"The two of us," Haral said.

"No. *You* got a ship to run. Get our *V* and *Harukk*'s matched, that's what we got to do. I'd hit him now if we had the angle and his *V* to use, but we can't break through those shields, slow as we are."

Haral kept looking at her. She was talking about suicide. Haral knew it. Haral also knew the other plain fact, that their armaments were nothing against hunter-ship armor—unless one or the other in the encounter had *C*-fractional velocity to add to the impact, virtually head-on. And Sikkukkut, praise to his wily kifish heart, was not obliging them.

" 'Bout the only thing we can do, don't you think?"

"You mean just board and shoot him pointblank."

"Hey, they never have been too fussy about us carrying weapons. Kifish etiquette's on our side, isn't it?"

"Yeah," Haral said.

"He'll ask me aboard. You wait and see. I get my chance, and then you blow his vanes if you can. I don't have to tell you. You know what you're doing." A look aside at Haral. Old partner. Old friend. The one who just as well could have captained *The Pride* a long, long time ago. Who right now looked at her with that stolid calm behind which was a great deal of pain. "Long time."

"Yeah," Haral said again. "Watch out for *Ikkhoitr*, that's what I got to do. But that's not your job in there right now. No one but you's got the credentials, hear me?"

"Nobody *else* can get close to the gods-be kif—"

"He's going to be expecting a move like this. That's *why* no one else can get close to him. This is why it doesn't work for the kif. No percentage in it. You do it, Py, and we got ourselves a kif ball-up right here in the system."

"We just got to get me inside there, that's what we got."

"We got those mahendo'sat hanging off system. We still don't know where Goldtooth is—he could come tearing through here any minute, f'godssakes, him and the whole clutch of humans. We got that message going out to the mahendo'sat. Jik's coming in here—don't do it. Don't throw yourself into that mess. We just stay tight here, we talk to that bastard as long as he wants to talk, we got to hold our *nerve,* captain, that's what we got to do. We got to just bide our time and hope to—"

"Captain," Hilfy said. "We got a query from *Vigilance*. Query, query, query, quote. That's all they say."

"Gods *rot* that nest of lunatics. Tell 'em shut it down. My gods, they'll blow this up yet. Tell 'em—No. Tell 'em what I said. Shut it up. Next ship transmits out of turn I'll have some ears for it, say that. Tell *Harukk* again the system is stable and his enemies are in retreat. Say that we have a contingent of mahendo'sat insystem in support of Jik, who's gone on in pursuit of Akkhtimakt. Say that we're ready to meet and arrange things."

Eighteen ships in. The range out there was a confusion of ship IDs and colors as ships downshifted their *V* and others kept arriving.

"Aye," Hilfy said.

"Captain," Tully said. "Wrong. Ship wrong."

"Gods." Geran's voice. "No ID on that last ship. It's not outputting. We got an anomaly out there."

Her heart sped. "Track and target. Get me vector on it."

"Working," Sif said.

It was behind the others. The line popped up, projecting course right with the rest of the mass.

Chapter Fourteen

It kept coming, a ship on which ID squeal had malfunctioned.

But that kind of malfunction was a kifish trick.

A pirate trick.

"My gods. It's not theirs. It's not theirs, they know it—stand by, stand by armaments!" Pyanfar shoved her arm into the brace and gulped air in starkest panic. "Haral! Control to me!"

"Aye," Haral said on the instant, went over to switcher-one while Tirun busied herself with the tracking of the armaments.

"What *is* it?" Sirany wondered from her vantage.

"A stray," Pyanfar said. "It's a godsforsaken stray, Goldtooth's or—"

"Priority!" Geran yelled, but it was already clear on the screen: the interloper had not dumped, and something else had come out from it: missile fire, projectiles launched *C*-fractional at ships that were relativistically stationary targets dead ahead of it.

"Priority!" Hilfy cried. "It's Tahar! That's *Moon Rising!* My gods, she's going to run right through them!"

"Track on *Harukk!*" Pyanfar yelled, and slammed the mains in. "All ships, fire at will—tell 'em that's an ally coming through!"

The armaments were tracking. Missiles launched with a thump and a

316 • C. J. Cherryh

shock against their own substance. Dead against *Harukk,* everything they owned to throw, hard as they could throw it.

"*Ikkhoitr!*" Pyanfar yelled over the whine of reloading. "Tirun, get their vanes. Never gods-be mind the others! Hilfy, give me output!"

"You got it," Haral said. "Tully, output! Talk to humans, got it?"

In the case there was anything back there to talk *to.* All kinds of com ready-lighted, human channel, mahendo'sat, kif, hani, while that dopplering ghost that was *Tahar's Moon Rising* came ahead pouring fire at a single target, savvy and deliberate.

"This is the *mekt-hakkikt* Pyanfar Chanur: Akkhtimakt is fallen and Sikkukkut has run here pursued by a thousand enemies who are my allies, hammered between mahen forces and the unity of *han.* In this *pukkukta* I give you a chance, *Chakkuf, Nekekkt!* You've served us well on this voyage. You have my favor now! Hani ships and mahendo'sat, be sure of your targets! *Harukk* is your target, and any other ship which fires in our direction! Make no mistakes! Kifish ships, run from this system and my agents will hunt you down even to Akkht! Join us in this hunt and become among the first of my *skkukun,* all of you strong enough to maintain your place! Hani, fire your loads and scatter!"

This while *The Pride* belched out all the missiles and all the fire it had; while a deluge of fire converged from the ships in formation. Something came over com, overhead, general address: a hani voice, a familiar voice:

"*Here's from us, you godsforsaken motherless son of a nightwalker! Hearth and blood! from me and my crew!*"

"Tahar!" Pyanfar cried. "Gods rot you, *I forgive you!*"

A timelag off in messages. The kif had only limited fire-sweep aft, because of its own vanes, and it had to track a ship whose missiles were only scantly lagged behind its comwave, the difference between real-space *V* and lightspeed. Tahar's missiles hit: others were still incoming from all points of the sphere.

"*Chanur,* mekt-hakkikt!" another voice came blasting into her ear. "*I am here, behind you, praise your foresight! Our ships are coming!*"

"Whose in a mahen hell is that? Is that *Skkukuk?*"

"It's coming from *Nekekkt,*" Hilfy said.

"Time to get out of here," Pyanfar cried, "transmit, hani ships: Scatter, scatter." She reached and rang the collision warning for the Tauran crew off in the galley, kicked *The Pride* bow-nadir and threw in the mains with all they had.

It was all they could do to evade return fire, some ships rising, some going wide, some diving systemwise, like the blooming of some vast flower, each as they finished their load of missiles and got down to the beam guns. Tirun kept the guns tracking as they dived, firing for all they were worth.

It was still forward motion they made; but it was angular, kiting along skewed and hurling all the energy the mains had to give to that slew toward nadir.

Gods grant—

"Hai!" The whole ship banged and slewed violently, so that the course was different than it had been— "What'd we lose?" she yelled. "Gods rot it, what blew?"

"Vanes—" Tirun started to say.

Second impact, like the loudest thunder that ever cracked: the ship jumped sideways and a whole panel started flashing red. A small black body went hurtling and hit the wall, a black blur till it hit: it scrabbled right across the top of the control panel and Pyanfar swallowed and spat a red spatter that shocked her as much as the sound, only then feeling what her teeth had done to the inside of her mouth. "Gods *fry* that kif bastard—you all right?" The cursed black thing was as terrified as the rest of them, fellow in misfortune. It ran and screamed in rage: she did not even hit at it when she had the chance. There were too many switches for two hands, too many systems over to backup and third backup and past. *"Damage report, gods rot it!"*

"Chur," Tully's anxious voice came. "Chur!"

"We lost the whole vane, I think it slewed down into the mains." Tirun's voice, hoarse and breathless. And the firing of the guns resumed, re-aligned to the new track, while gods knew where they were going.

"Priority," Geran said, "we got fire over us—our kif are moving, the mahendo'sat are moving—we're clear of it—"

"Industry's bad hit," Hilfy reported. "Khym—Chur—"

"I'm with you." Chur's own voice, weak as it was.

"Cease fire, cease fire."

While the mains slammed away at them. Then it was a matter of finding their bearings, getting the skewed *V* shaved down. She got a screenful of garble out of Tracking, reoriented to bring the dishes and receptors to optimum—no matter which direction *The Pride* was physically headed: coherent data started coming up.

And camera image, an area of flares in the battle zone as *The Pride* began rollover to brake.

She looked round at her own bridge, still swallowing blood, saw all the stations still working. Wiped her mouth and glanced back again at the images Haral sent her way.

It was still happening out there. But more slowly. There were ships in wreckage out there, blown in those flares. She earnestly hoped one of them was *Harukk*.

She remembered Stle stles stlen. And felt a chill as she hit the com-button, the contact still live. "This is the *mekt-hakkikt* Pyanfar Chanur. Report."

"*Praise to the* hakkikt," a kifish voice came back eventually. "*We give you your enemies.*"

And others began, a flood of ship names, *Nekkekt. Chakkuf. Ikkhoitr* itself, declaring fervent loyalty.

Not a hani voice. Not a one.

Or a mahendo'sat.

"This is *The Pride of Chanur* to all hani ships: acknowledge status; hold other transmissions pending. Thank you."

She sat there staring after. And shaking, little tremors which had nothing to do with the stench of dead air in the ship and the ozone and the fact that the bridge fans had stopped working. Or that there was a periodic and rhythmic shock against the hull which was some piece of debris trailing and still in motion while the mains hammered away at their drift.

Just the bridge sounds and the distant thunder of the mains. And a great loneliness.

"Everyone all right? Is everyone all right?"

"I got a patch on it." Khym's voice. "It's all right."

"Galley." Sirany's voice on general com. "You all right in there?"

"I think I got a broken rib," the answer came back. "But we're all right, how's it going, captain?"

"Going to go stable in a while, hold on."

Stable. My gods, they're killing each other up there. Kif are butchering each other in the corridors of those ships out there, kif are doing what kif do when they win and others lose, and how many ships have we lost out here? What do we do, hit the kif now while they're confused?

The kif would. If they had our options. Poor naive sons. They don't understand what's all round them. They don't understand what hani are capable of.

Fire on them—and change us forever.

Do that—and be sure there is a forever.

"You want me to trim us up?" Haral asked, while several channels of com talked away, getting damage reports out of other ships, ascertaining casualties. *Fortune* reported minimal damage. *Light* was going to have to limp into dock. There were others. The information came up on the screens.

Ayhar's Prosperity: damage: no casualties.

Harun's Industry: heavy damage: braking and maneuvering positive. Casualties: four.

Faha's Starwind: heavy damage: casualties: two.

Pauran's Lightweaver: vane gone: casualties: minor.

Ehrran's Vigilance: no damage: no casualties.

Nirasun's Melody: minor damage: no casualties.

Shaurnurn's Hope: lost.

Tahar's Moon Rising: out of contact.

Suranun's Fairwind: out of contact.

The list went on. More and more names. They blurred in her sight. As *The Pride* braked, and the stress hammered away at them.

Then: "Priority, priority," Geran exclaimed. As scan started blinking furiously. "Breakout zenith."

Ships were coming in. A lot of them. One; and three more. And five.

"O my gods," Sirany breathed.

"If it's Akkhtimakt—"

Then the ID started flashing. Mahendo'sat.

Mahijiru.

"Goldtooth," Pyanfar muttered, and slammed her fist down on the console rim. "Goldtooth, gods rot him—*Now* he shows up. Now, by the gods, now he comes chasing in here, comes in here with by the gods bastard frigging *mahen* interests, to sweep up the poor godsforsaken hani they've done it to *again,* b'gods greater and lesser, one more frigging time we bleed for them, their godscursed meddling selfish gods-be-feathered interests! *Tully!*"

"Aye, cap'n!"

"Get on that com, hear, *com!* Fast. Tell the humans no shooting, understand, *don't shoot!*"

"Don't shoot, I got, I got, cap'n!"

It started going out.

And hard on it: "*Mahijiru,* this is *The Pride of Chanur.* Cease fire, cease fire. These are allied ships. Dump and brake and hold off. Do not transit the system. Other mahen ships hold the approach to Ajir: nothing passed here beyond their capacity to deal with and mahen authorities in that direction are forewarned. Repeat: the Ajir approach is defended by mahen ships. Stay where you are. All mahen ships anywhere receiving: this is Pyanfar Chanur on *The Pride of Chanur*: cease all hostilities. End. Repeat that." She slumped back then, at the end of her energies. "Till response."

"We have a transmission from *Vigilance*. They register protest."

"Tell 'em—tell 'em we note it. Tell them—" It was easier and easier to think in kifish mode. "Stand in line, gods rot it. And consider where they are."

There were more and more ships arriving in the range. It was nightmare. If it had been an hour earlier it would have been a rescue.

By that much, you cursed bastard. By that much you missed it.

By that much Tahar was almost with us. Across all that space. Goldtooth must have held Sikkukkut—must have pinned them down good. The kif must have thrown something at him again at Kura. Must have— gods know what they did. Keeping Sikkukkut from overjumping us. When he came in here he was desperate. Needing me, for godssakes. He couldn't fire on me, I was the last hope he had.

We got ships out there—needing help.

"Human ship!" Tully cried. And talked to someone a steady stream of babble, as if they were on the same timeline. It was Tully's old message those incoming ships must have picked up. It was the old message they had responded to.

The same as Goldtooth must have gotten their own former chatter, and known well what ships were out to meet the enemy. She cut the mains, let them go inertial on what they still had, on the rotational *G.*

While Tully poured out something, rapid and urgent. And went on saying it. One assumed it was friendly. One assumed nothing nowadays.

She felt a hundred years older. And turned herself and her chair and looked over the bridge, at a crew worn and tired beyond clear sense, at more gray hair than she recalled a few weeks ago. Or maybe it was the stark lighting. Or maybe it was that they all looked older, thinner, abraded away by distances and a load they had carried too long.

I want to see Chanur again.

But Chanur land was Mahn territory. Nothing could change that, unless Kohan could take Kara Mahn; and the weary, grayed man who had met her on Gaohn docks had not the strength left. The wit, yes; the wit and the will and the canny good sense that had been more than figurehead in Chanur these many hard years. A real power. A mind and an insight shrewder than many a woman's. But time bore down on Kohan, that was all. The only hope was Hilfy Chanur, who might find herself a man to take care of Kara Mahn: there was nothing Pyanfar Chanur or Rhean or any of the former powers could do about it any longer.

She saw Hilfy sitting there, talking to someone, likeliest one of the nearby hani. *Up to you, kid. It all is, from now on. Our time is done. You think you've grown up. You're Chanur now, have you figured it out? I don't envy you.*

Except your youth. I wish I'd known you and you'd known me forty years ago. They looked like rough years then. But the years you've got ahead—I can't see into them. Like there was something in the way of me and this ship, like a curtain I can't see past.

I always used to know where I was going. And now all I can see is aliens. And all I can think of is the mistakes I've made; and how to get this straight somehow.

Her eyes drifted to Tully. To him. The alien among them.

It's an enemy at his back, isn't it?

I got to be, Tully, poor Tully, I got no choice. You warned me, and I see it clear, I see everything down that way with no trouble at all, and I'm going to do you hurt, I can't turn back from that.

You gods-be knew it, didn't you? Knew it from the time you came to us. Always thinking, never talking. Afraid of me and not afraid. For two good reasons.

What'll they do to you when I'm through? Where'll you go?

My friend.

"Hilfy. Get me Banny."

"I got *Prosperity* right now. You want Banny in person?"

"I want her." She turned the chair back square to the board and punched in. "Banny. Banny, you hear me?"

"Such as it is, Chanur. It looks like we got help out there."

"I don't know how much the mahendo'sat told you, Banny, but we got some other visitors out there and I can't talk about it real clear just now: we got politics here. I'm asking hani ships to form up; I'm going to ask the kif to do the same and they're going to do it, Banny, they're going to do it. Then we're going to have to do some talking—you want to take charge of the hani ships for me, just keep it kind of quiet and trust me. We're not out of this yet. We got a real problem here. A real problem. Banny."

There was prolonged silence.

"Banny. Haurosa naimur f'fhain'haur murannarrhm'ha chaihen."
Ambush in the trees, Banny. . . .

More of the long silence. "Accepted."

That was the first thing.

The next was harder.

"Message, Hilfy: tell the kifish ships to put themselves in order and stand by for instruction. Stop all forward drift."

"Aye."

"Chur: transmission to *Mahijiru.* Quote: This is Pyanfar Chanur. Hold your ships where they are. Your Personage is aware of the kifish advance; mahen ships were in position to prevent escape by the Ajir corridor. Ajir corridor, repeat, is secure. We ask you dump all *V* and wait. This situation insystem is still extremely volatile. The kif remaining here are under my personal direction and within *han* jurisdiction. I ask you instruct your allies to total dump and recall all other mahen ships to your group immediately. Cease all hostile operations. All ships are in *han* jurisdiction. Repeat, request immediate total dump and hold pattern. Endit and repeat at intervals. Transmission to *Nekkekt:* This is the *mekt-hakkikt* in person. Permit withdrawal of mahen ships from center system. Continue to reduce all *V:* cease all drift toward mahen position. Take no action against mahendo'sat. Wait orders. Endit." She slumped back in the chair. Waited with her claws clenched.

"That's a dump," Geran said finally. And she began to breathe freely again. More when they saw the second one.

But attacking ships might do as much.

Then *Mahijiru* took the third dump, coming down to insystem velocities.

"Thank gods, thank gods," she muttered. And over com: "Banny, we're gaining on it. We got it stopped." Out on that channel. "Hilfy. Get me Goldtooth."

"Working. Lagtime 10.9."

Twenty-two on the roundtrip of messages. Far out in the range still. But Goldtooth had to be AOS on the initial message now. Ten minutes ago. Other ships incoming were observing the same sequence; and that was all but certain to be pre-arrangement.

Humans, migods, humans drug themselves senseless. We got doped-up pilots out there. Robotics. Gods know what.

They have to stop with the mahendo'sat. Stop and get their bearings. Or plan to blow the system to a mahen hell.

They wouldn't. Couldn't. Gods save us. They have to take Goldtooth's lead till they figure things out.

It's not over.

She drew a shaky breath. "We're going stable," she said on bridgecom. "Free to move about, arrange your own covers, five minutes, maybe longer: maybe ten, fifteen gods-be *days* out here, I dunno." She lifted shaking hands to her face, just shut out the sight of things if not the sound, and rested. Quietly some of the crew saw to themselves. "I'm all right," she heard Khym's low complaint. "Gods rot it, I can get to the gods-be head."

From her husband. Who had a hole in his leg and a plasm patch, a deep wound that had to be swollen and hurting if it was not worse than that. *She* wanted a trip to the head. Desperately. She decided to take the chance and unbuckled.

"Captain," Hilfy said. *"Nekkekt:* stand by replay."

"Uhhhhn." *It starts. Kif have sorted out. Who am I dealing with?*

And from the earplug. "Mekt-hakkikt, I have all these ships in my hand, praise to you. We will strike at your order."

"Who am I talking to?"

"Mekt-hakkikt, *to your faithful Skkukuk. I have carried out all your orders. I will deal with all your enemies. Name them to me."*

"Right now, Skkukuk, I'm just real glad to hear from you. You keep those ships of yours under control and you don't make a move without my direct order. Hear me?"

"I will give you your enemies' heads and hearts."

"I'm real fond of you too, Skkukuk. Just do what I said. You get your com linked up to mine and you stay in constant touch. Anyone twitches, I want to know about it. These hani with me are allies. They won't cause any trouble."

"And these mahendo'sat and these invaders?"

"Wait for my orders. That's all." She punched the contact out. She was trembling. She set her elbows on the counter and dropped her head a second time into her hands, wiped her mane back. Haral was still by her. Someone else was moving about. It was all distant. She had no wish to talk to anyone.

"Captain." It was Nifeny Tauran holding out a sandwich and a container of something liquid with a null-cap. The sight of it turned her stomach and attracted her shaking hand. Gfi. She took a sip of it, and felt another urge unbearably strong.

"I got to take a break," she said to Haral. "We got the gods-be kif, don't we?"

"Go," Haral said.

She spun the chair about and took her own way to the galley corridor and the head. The air everywhere seemed stagnant. *Three days and we'll have the whole gods-be lifesupport in a mess. We can't go that long. Crew's got to get that system up.*

She passed Tauran crew in the galley, one with wrapped ribs, sitting white-nosed at the table, the other capping up food as fast as she could. "We got a while stable. Get the slinkers out of the godsforsaken filters, get that lifesupport up."

"Aye," the Tauran said, a distracted, exhausted look till she realized who was talking to her. Then the ears came up. "Aye, cap'n."

She made the trip, into the closet of a head, came out and shouldered past Tirun on the same mission.

"Captain," sounded in the com-plug in her ear. *"We got Mahijiru. They're indicating that they want us to pull back to Gaohn. They're waiting for reply."*

"In a mahen hell," she muttered, and went through the galley, down the corridor with a hand to either wall, onto the bridge where she had sight of Hilfy and the rest. "Tell them hold that perimeter. We'll accept *Mahijiru* only. That ship can come in for conference, and we'll draw back to Gaohn. We're not having any others."

"Aye," Hilfy said. "We've got query from *Vigilance,*" Sirany said. "Ayhar is telling them shut it down."

It was one more thing than she wanted to know. She hand-over-handed herself back to her own post, fell into it and sat drinking at the gfi in minute sips that did not agitate her stomach.

It was a long wait for messages. Goldtooth and the humans were a long distance out.

She drank. She wiped her blurring eyes and leaned back against the seat in as much relaxation as she could take. While *The Pride* slewed on, inertial. The hani formation was spreading itself around the kif. *Vigilance* was far to nadir now and out of her way. Ayhar was considerably off to sunward and beginning to take some of the way off. So were others of the merchants, trimming up. Kifish ships were in hard decel, those going in both directions until they could take the speed off and achieve a coherent pattern.

But *The Pride* was going where it belonged. Out into the open. Where it formed no part of any group.

One of the calls Chur had handled, listed on monitor three: from Rhean: *Do you need assistance?* Reply: *Negative: fully operational; thanks.*

Another, from Ehrran: *Query, query, query.* Reply from Fiar: *All queries deferred. Your patience appreciated.*

One more, from Ehrran. *Protest lodged.* Reply from Hilfy: *Sink it in your own datafile; advise you kifish allies are monitoring your transmissions and misunderstandings are possible. For your own safety and safety of those near you maintain com silence.*

Tully's, through the translator: *This is # # Tully # # # call # # # # do not # # this is # # hani # # with # #.* . . . No reply listed.

From *Shanan's Glory,* far to the rear of the combat: *Shall we come in or hold position?* From Banny Ayhar, monitored: *Hold relative position. Maintain full-sphere surveillance.*

From Gaohn Station: *This is Gaohn Central: general inquiry.* From Banny Ayhar, monitored: *Firing has stopped. Situation uncertain but improved.* Harun's Industry *will be making return to Gaohn with casualties for medical assistance and will courier details. Possibility of strike in your vicinity still exists but is less probable. Reserve other inquiry for* Industry. *Chanur remains in contact with various allied ships. Ayhar is directing hani ships in the zone of contact.* . . .

From Ayhar: *We have computed trajectory on missing ships. All vessels along these lines be alert to evade or assist as needed.* . . .

"Captain," Hilfy said. "Message from *Mahijiru."*

It had already hit the screen: *Ana Ismehanan-min advise you we got talk number one urgent.*

"Reply: Quote: *Mahijiru* is welcome alone. All other mahen and foreign ships must hold position. We will not support violation of our system borders by any agency however friendly. The approach of *Mahijiru* is clear and velocity should not exceed normal limits. Please convey to all your ships our thanks for their support, and proceed without escort to a point where we may conference without appreciable timelag. There is no urgency. I repeat the earlier advisement: few ships passed our system borders and there were more than adequate mahen forces on the outgoing vector to have handled the problem. Akkhtimakt is finished. Sikkukkut likewise. End. Repeat that at five till acknowledgment."

"Aye," Hilfy said.

She rested a moment then. Just rested, eyes shut, head against the seat back. It was all the rest they were going to get.

While around her, crew moved carefully about on necessary errands or took a chance to stretch. Chur Anify and Khym went offshift to the galley, their two walking wounded, while a pair of exhausted Tauran risked their necks trying to clean the lifesupport filters. Fans went on, highspeed, shut down again. Went on yet again, with a decided ozone smell in the air.

"*Mahijiru*'s moving," Tirun said finally, on cover for Geran. "*Priority, priority,* we've got a general movement all along their formation."

It was already on monitor, a sudden and ominous blinking all along the mahen front that sent her heart speeding. "Message? Gods rot it, is he *saying* anything?"—while crew, away from seats, in the galley, wherever they had strayed to, came scrambling unordered: in-ear coms, and a fine sense of disaster when it started.

"Negative. He's just started to move. All of them—We got—got an inquiry from *Nekkekt*, quote: *Shall we attack?* Advisories—"

Other crew hit the seats, low murmur of exchanged information, the passing of duties, briefings in two words and a key punch that logged in: Geran, Hilfy. Others were already there. "I tell human stop," Tully protested. "Give com."

"General output," Pyanfar snapped, as Haral hit the seat beside her and logged on. "Hold steady. Message to *Mahijiru:* Hold position. Keep your ships back. We will not be bluffed. Reply to query at once and brake. Endit and repeat. What's our lagtime?"

"Fourteen nine," Tirun said; and a hani message turned up on channel two. "*Chanur, this is Ayhar. What in a mahen hell is going on?*"

"Ayhar. Hold firm. Hold firm."

"*Hold firm! We got a half a hundred ships gone stark lunatic! What do they think they're doing?*"

"They think they're getting through, they're pushing us, that's what they think they're doing. Those are human ships out there. Stand firm—"

"Mahijiru," a voice broke in on her into her left ear. "*Same Goldtooth. H'lo, Pyanfar, old friend!*" Cheerful as any dockside. "*Good hear you voice, same good find you one piece. Long time chase, damn good job stop these bastard. Got you number one message, good news. You number one fine, a? Same. Plenty ship. Same you tell these fine kif they stand by, we make deal 'bout how they get home.*"

"Mekt-hakkikt!" Into the right ear. "*We are tracking this advance.*

Give us the order! We are your allies! This mahendo'sat is a devious and a ruthless liar! Take him!"

"Goldtooth, I got a real anxious kif here. Now it's seven-odd minutes ago, and if I don't see those ships of yours start braking in thirty seconds from the time you get this, I'm going to take some serious measures. I'll clip you good, friend. *Your* ship. Now you stop, and you get ready to talk this out, you don't push your way here. You want an incident, you want trouble that's going to echo all the way to Iji, I got to serve you notice these hani ships aren't moving. I'm timing this real close. I know you, old friend. If I call your bluff like this, you'll shoot if I don't. So you better be doing what I say by now, because if you aren't, you got a fight coming. Endit. No repeat. *Time* that bastard. *Skkukuk!* You keep those ships of yours in line."

"*Yes.*"

"Jik!" Hilfy's voice, between two beats of a panicked heart. "Jik's transmitting, incoming—"

"Negative scan," Geran said.

Lightspeed wavefront, inbound, the buoys not reporting and no one in position to pick him up.

"*Pyanfar—*" the thin voice reached her. "*We follow you fast we can, damn, you not engage, not engage—*"

He was talking about the kif. She realized that finally. He was that far away. Hours out.

Hours ago, when he had fired off that message, he had known Sikkukkut incoming and that a few fool hani were in a lot of trouble.

About his own partner, he could not know.

Nor could Goldtooth know that he was there. For seven more minutes.

"Goldtooth. I'm in contact with your partner now. Ismehanan-min. My friend. There's a lot of data you don't have. Critical information. It's Iji at stake. It's your border. We've got a kifish *hakkikt* here willing to talk borders. What we've got left at Meetpoint you know and I don't. But I've got a passenger, an old mutual acquaintance, who has some real important information. And I'm not talking to a fool, Goldtooth. I want a face to face meeting. You, me, a few old friends."

"One minute," Tirun said, timekeeping.

"At Gaohn. Dockside."

Chapter Fifteen

The docks at Gaohn were deserted, with the profound chill that came of seals cutting off the air circulation, the deckplates so cold they burned the feet; and Pyanfar limped a bit—had been limping since she rolled out of bed stiff and sore and knowing what there was yet to face.

There had been a little leisure, on the way back to Gaohn, a little time for *The Pride* to run at a decent, safe rate; for aching crew to tend their own needs and the ship's, and to catch a nap and a hot meal.

She went in spacer's blues. It was all she had left, and that was borrowed. She went with her own crew about her, and left *The Pride* in Sirany's capable hands.

Another lostling had turned up. Dur Tahar had quietly showed up on-scope, blinking in with an ID signal and turning out not to be a piece of hurtling wreckage. "Friggin' hell," Tahar had said when they got her on com: "you don't think I'm going to run my ID, *us,* while we got you standing off half the Compact and most every hani ship out here ready to blow us to dust and gone. I'm not coming in yet, Chanur. I'll meet with you or one of your ships, I'll let Vrossaru and her crew off, but I'm not going to go in to dock . . . not this old hunter. I'll just watch awhile."

"You running with Goldtooth? Or Sikkukkut?"

"Me? Gods upside down, Chanur, you got an exaggerated idea how fast we are. I got out on your tail, been following your emissions trail like a highway clear from Meetpoint, trying like hell to catch you up, but I blew two more systems making that gods-be Urtur shift: sorry if you had any fondness for that kif. Me, I owed him. Plenty."

"You godsforsaken lunatic! You could have blown us all."

This during two hours of timelagged exchange. And after a longer than usual pause, in which she had thought Tahar might have quit talking: "Chanur, if you ever trusted that kif, you got something yet to learn. He made you too powerful, haven't you got it yet? So did the mahendo'sat. Do I have to tell you?"

She had sat there then, after Dur Tahar had in fact quit talking, a decisive signoff. She sat there receiving the information from Gaohn that a half dozen little light-armed freighters had scattered down the Ajir route with a precious cargo of hani lives, the men and children of the Syrsyn clans.

Seeds on a stellar wind.

And she looked Khym's way, her husband sitting backup duty at a quieter time on the bridge, taking his time at scan while exhausted senior crew took theirs at washup and rest. He did not notice that glance: his face, dyed with the light from the scope, was intent on business.

Whatever we lose here, she had thought then. *For all we failed in, one thing we did.*

There was one other man there on the bridge. And he did look her way. She thought she had seen every expression Tully's alien face had to offer. But this, that all the life seemed to have left him, no more of fight, as if something in him had broken and died. Except that the eyes lighted a moment, glistened that way they did in profoundest sorrow; and looked—O gods—straight at her. While Hilfy, leaving the bridge, paused to put her hand on his shoulder. For comfort. For—

"Come on," Hilfy had said. "Tully."

You know, don't you? Pyanfar had thought then. *You know she'll leave you now. Her own kind, Tully. She's Chanur now. The Chanur. And you're ours; even when you go back, your people won't forget that, will they? Ever.*

Gods help you, Tully. Whatever your name really is. Whatever you think you are and wherever you go now.

Like Tahar. They don't ever quite forget.

I'm no fool, that look of his said back to her. *Neither of us are. We're friends.*

And perhaps some other human, unfathomably complicated strangeness she could not puzzle out.

Tully came with them onto the docks this time. It was the second time for him onto Gaohn station, among staring and mistrustful hani, in a confrontation where he was a showpiece, an exhibit, a pawn. They gave him weapons. The same as themselves. So he would know another important thing in a way the sputtering translator could not relay.

Last of all she had caught hold of him in the airlock, taken him by the arm and made sure he was listening: "Tully. You can go with the human ships. You're free, you understand that. You know *free?*"

"I know free," he had said. And just looked at her with that gentle, too-wise expression of his.

Down the docks where a line of grim-looking Llun had set the perimeters of this meeting, the towering section seals in place on either end of this dock. There were stationer clanswomen, spacer clans. And a delegation from the *han* had come thundering up from the world, only just arrived. There were weapons enough. And Llun guards enough to discourage anything some hani lunatic might try.

The Llun marshals were no protection against the hunter-ships which had come in, snugged their deadly sleek noses up into Gaohn's vulnerable docking facilities, and disgorged their own guards and their own very different personnel. Three mahendo'sat, a human ship, and a trio of kif: besides *The Pride* and *Harun's Industry:* that was the final agreement. *Aja Jin, Mahijiru,* then one other mahen ship named *Pasarimu,* that had come in after Jik; *Nekkekt, Chakkuf, Maktakkt,* and finally something unpronounceable that Tully said for them three times and they still could not manage. The Human Ship, they called it by default.

The gathering on the dock was very quiet, and all too careful. Even Jik, who had on a dark cloak and kilt so unlike his usual gaud it took a second look to know it was Jik. Only a single collar, a solitary bracelet. An AP on his hip and a knife beside it. That was usual. Soje Kesurinan was there, brighter-dressed and no less armed. And with them some Personage walked with the captain of *Pasarimi,* complete with Voice, with all the appropriate badges. Official, yes. Indisputably.

There was Goldtooth, in the same dark formality. And his own escort. Not a flicker of communication passed between him and his partner.

Harun and Llun, a tired crew in spacer-blues, with Kauryfy herself in green and the Llun all in Immune black.

Another lot came in black: a mass of shadow drifted out from the perimeters, all alike in their robes, their hoods, their utter sameness to hani eyes, all bristling with weapons. One of them would be Skkukuk, but she could not find him by the clues she knew, the gait, the small gestures. There was a tall kif evidently in charge, one the others evidently gave place to.

Who is that? Is it my *kif?*

She feared it was altogether another. In one sense or another.

And the humans, from whatever-it-was. She had seen the like once before: different kinds of humans; different shapes; any species had that. But these varied wildly, some handsome in a Tully-way; some just strange. They all wore dark gray, all glittered with silver and plastics, body-fitting, skin-covering suits: even the hands covered. Not one was armed with anything that looked like a weapon. Com equipment. Plenty of that. They remained an enigma. And stopped, at about the distance everyone else had stopped, like points of a star.

Fear grew thick on this dockside: it was evident in the set of hani ears, in the way kif and mahendo'sat moved. In the way that Tully stayed right at their side, and no human advanced beyond the mahen perimeter.

There was another thing in the system. There was a very real knnn and a tc'a out there, singing to each other in harmonics of which the computer-translators which were supposed to handle such things, made no sense but positional data. It was significant and ominous that the matrix of the harmonics had the position of Gaohn station in it.

The knnn were interested. That was more than enough to account for the fear.

But the representatives from downworld would hardly comprehend that much: they would, most likely, be getting their first look at a mahendo'sat, let alone kif or humans. And perhaps they had a resolution in their hands; or perhaps the debating was still going on, and Naur and Tahy Mahn *par* Chanur and others of that worldbound mindset were still arguing protocols and policies. Gods knew. If she let herself think about it she grew cold, killing mad.

They had set out a huge table, for godsake, a table and chairs there on dockside, the Llun's council furniture moved out, that was what it was, hani council furniture, as if all these factions could be gotten together, as if in all the chaos and amid ships moving in with major damage and injured, some fool (from Anuurn surface most likely) had time to insist on tables and chairs which would hardly even accommodate the anatomy of some of the invaders. With knnn running around the neighborhood, and ships still at standoff out there in the zenith range, over fifty of them determined to force an issue and get passage through, others determined to move kif who would literally die of the shame, and kif who were as doggedly determined to resist.

Gods-cursed groundling fools. If that knnn out there comes calling, we won't survive it. Do your resolutions understand that?

Humans have fired on them. Tully says.

Jik's played politics with the tc'a. Gods! does he know *what that is out there, is it something that's come for* him, *for the mahendo'sat?*

Tables. My gods, we're lucky to get these species within shouting distance of each other! The kif never do anything without the scent of advantage, they're here *on a thread, on the least thread of a suspicion that I'm their best way out.*

And Jik and Goldtooth aren't talking, they're not looking at each other, the crews don't mix—and who in their own hell is the Personage Pasurimi *came in with?*

Came in with the ships out of mahen space, not the Kura route. Came in, my gods, from Iji, that's where he's from. That's someone from the homeworld.

That's Authority. That, with the Voice and the badges and the robes. And he hasn't introduced himself. The Voice hasn't spoken a word. The han*'s been insulted and they don't even know it.*

They're frozen. No one's not moving. It's the kif they distrust.

"Skkukuk," she guessed, taking the risk. And the foremost kif lifted his face the least degree, then lowered it, belligerence and manners in two breaths. Even amiability. For a kif.

"Mekt-hakkikt," that one said. So she knew it *was* Skkukuk. But he took it for a summons, and a panic seized on her, instinctive aversion as that band of kif crossed the deck plating and got between her and the mahendo'sat and the humans. And swung their weapons into line as they went.

"Weapons *down,* for godssake." The panic made her voice sharp. Skkukuk instantly hissed and clicked an order to his company. Weapons lowered. She grabbed the chance two-handed. "There's not going to be any shooting. On *any* side." One of the Llun came too close and she flattened her ears and rumpled her nose. "Get back, gods rot it." But the mahendo'sat had come closer too. Suddenly there were a great many guns, her own crew with their own rifles slung conspicuously toward level. "Back off!" Haral snapped at a graynosed hani who moved in with foolhardy authority. And shoved with the gunbutt.

"Chanur!" that hani shouted.

And faced three kifish rifles.

"Hold it! Sgokkun!" Her heart all but stopped. She physically struck a kifish rifle up, out of line; and that kif got back and stood clicking and gnashing its inner teeth, its fellows likewise confused.

"Mekt-hakkiktu sotoghotk kefikkun nakt!" Skkukuk snapped; there was quick silence.

Quiet then. Even the downworld hani had it figured how precarious it was.

"We don't need any shooting," Pyanfar said, her own heart lurching and thumping and her knees shaking. Her voice gathered itself somewhere at the bottom of her gut. Khym was by her, *close* by her; between her and the hani, thank gods for his wits and his instincts. She waved a hand to clear the kif back and get a view of where the humans were, where the various mahendo'sat had gotten to; and the humans had stayed where they were, a good distance back. Goldtooth and his armed group had followed up all too close and Jik maneuvered to the side, both of them between the kif and the Personage. "Use your gods-be heads! Skkukuk, just stand there. Just stand. Goldtooth. Ana. We're all right here. You're not going to be using those guns; let's just all calm down, can we?"

"We come here talk. Same settle this mess." Goldtooth's dark brow was knit. He waved a hand indicating the perimeters. "We got knnn out there all upset. You got lousy mess, Pyanfar. Now I talk with you, you make big mistake."

"Yeah. I found out about that. Nice of you to tell me what you were doing. Nice of you to tell Jik, too."

"Jik got no choice. Got important hani, got human, all same mess at Kefk. Try to pull you out. You got go pull Tahar out, we don't 'spect same. Bad surprise, Pyanfar. Bad surprise. All same come out. We got Sikkukkut, got Akkhtimakt, both. We got no more worry with kif, a? So you let these fine kif go back to ship. They want go home, we let go. Best deal they got."

"Have no dealings with this person," Skkukuk said, beside her. "Our ships are the defense of this system. We are faithful, *mekt-hakkikt.*"

No threats, no untoward move. The hair prickled down her back. It was not subservience in this kif. Just quiet. The intimation of power, but not quite enough power: the kif was here, talking. It was a move Sik-

334 • C. J. Cherryh

kukkut exceled at, but this kif was smoother, and Goldtooth was giving good advice, O gods, if there were a power that could shove the kif back to their borders and keep them there.

That power was standing right in front of her. A mahen-human association.

If she did not know what she knew, from Tully, about what humans stood to gain. About human powers currently at each others' throats, and spread over an area that would, could! (a single look at the starcharts told that) dwarf the Compact.

"I have to know," she said, quietly, reasonably, to Goldtooth, "what happened to the stsho." Like it was gentle concern. It was desperation. It was suddenly their bulwark on that side, their trading-point. Without them—

Does he see? Does he suspect why I ask? He's no fool, was never a fool, O gods, this is one of half a dozen minds that rules the whole godshelpus Compact, he always was, he's one of those the mahendo'sat just turn loose to do things on the borders, things that echo years across civilized space. He still is. Even with a Personage here.

"We do fine." An unlooked-for voice. Jik had pulled out one of his abominable smokes and was in the process of lighting it, as if those dark eyes of his were not alert to every twitch from hani and kif. "Ana tell me he get there number one fine, three, four day fight. Chew up Sikkukkut good. Fine for us here. Our friend Sikkukkut—" He capped the lighter and drew in a second lungful of smoke. "He know then damn sure he got trouble. We owe damn lot to Banny Ayhar. Same you, friend. Same all hani come spread alarm."

"The stsho—"

"Little damage. Lot confuse. Methane-folk take care real good." A gesture with the back of the hand with the smokestick, vaguely outward. "Same knnn. Offi-cial, a? With tc'a interpreter. Same be tc'a been long time with."

"The same from Mkks?"

"A. Same all way from Kshshti. Tt'om'm'mu been real co-operative."

"Then it *is* your agent."

A wave of the fingers, amid a hani and a kifish murmuring. "Same talk lot people, a? I tell you, Ana—shoshi na hamuru-ta ma shosu-shinai musai hasan shanar shismenanpri ghashanuru-ma shesheh men chephettri nanursai sopri sai."

Dialect, thick and impenetrable. It had as well be coded. But

Goldtooth's face went guarded, his eyes darker, with the least small shift toward the left.

Toward Tully. Just that little twitch.

It was a guess what Jik had said. Or how much. A second shift of the eyes, that little degree that showed a white edge around the brown. Back to her this time. "Nao'sheshen?"

"Meshi-meshan." Jik tilted his head back, a gesture behind him. "Meshi nai sohhephrasi Chanuru-sfik, a?"

It did not please Goldtooth, whatever it was. "Shemasu. We talk. We talk plenty. We tell Personage. You tell these kif go. Now. We deal with methane-folk. You fix stuff here."

"Fix stuff!" She caught her breath and her wits in the same gulp after air, saw backs stiffen left and right and lowered her voice instantly. The *han* was back there. The Llun. There was a deafening silence.

"Kkkt," Skkukuk said. "Kk-kkt. This mahe does not dictate here. There will be *no* escort. There will be *no* mahen ships in our territory. Do not be deceived."

"We talk later," Goldtooth said, and got one step.

Weapons came up. In one move. So did mahen weapons.

"Hold it!" Pyanfar yelled, and shoved a rifle barrel. A kif's. It was momentarily safer.

"Chanur," a hani voice began.

"Shut *up,"* Tirun said.

"Let us begin it here," Skkukuk said. While Jik put himself between the kif and Goldtooth. Carefully.

"Let's not." Out of the peripheries of her vision she saw a human movement, a quiet melting away of certain of that group toward cover. "Tully! Stop them."

Tully shouted out, instant and shockingly alien and fluent. With an uplifted hand. And that motion stopped.

"Cease this!" the Voice snapped, and said something else in mahensi, too fast and too accented to follow.

"Withdraw them," a hani said. Downworlder, graynosed. Elderly and overweight. *My gods, Rhynan Naur. That gray, that old.* The voice rang with something of its old authority in the *han.* "We will not have our space violated. We will not countenance—"

Skkukuk's rifle swung that way. "Don't," Pyanfar said sharply. "Gods rot it—shut up, Naur. Everybody. Don't anybody move."

"You Personage," Jik said at her left, at Skkukuk's. "You want stop, *you* got stop. Shemtisi hani manara-to hefar ma nefuraishe'ha me kif."

"Trust that we will do that," Skkukuk said, all hard and with jaw lifted ominously. "We do not intend to take any voyage in your company."

"We got solution." Jik winced and pinched out the smokestick that had burned down to his fingers. "Pasuru nasur. Kephri na shshemura, Ana-he. Meshi."

"Meshi ne'asur?"

"Lot better. Same I say." Jik looked her way. "We got *spacer* hani, same. Sikkukkut be damn fool doublecross you, a? Damn fool. All time I say you lot smart. Got whole lot *sfik,* whole lot stuff, Pyanfar Chanur —same like I say. Same Ana here find you, same Sikkukkut want you— damn good. Now you got say like Personage, you got make decide."

"Decide, *decide,* f'godssakes, there's no *decide.* We got you and the kif trying to blow each other to the hereafter all through our solar system—"

"You Personage. You got kif. You want deal for the *han?*"

"I don't deal for the *han!* I'm telling you, me, Pyanfar, you talk to your Personage and tell him what Tully told us."

"I do." Jik looked at her in a strange and maddening way. "You not be *han.* You be Personage. Send *hakkikt* back to kif—how you guarantee, a? Stoheshe, Ana." With a glance at Goldtooth. And back again. "The *han* decide this, decide that. You do what you want with *han.* But the *han* be for Anuurn. You be Personage for hani, Personage for kif, same Tt'om'm'mu want save you life. You got the Person-thing. Born with. You understand this?"

"What are you talking about, for godssakes?"

"You no damn fool. You see. You see clear. Sikkukkut get power by create little *hakkikt* and take what they got. Let them do work. He lot smart kif. Till he make you *hakkikt* and try take what you got. You got the Person-thing. He think he got more, he damn lot mistake. We don't mistake. This kif here don't mistake. You got whole thing in you hands. Me, *I* recognize. Same like this kif. Long time."

"No. My gods, no!" She waved her hand, cast a look at the hani behind her, at her crew and back again.

"War, friend. What I tell you happen? Not war like ground war. War like new kind thing. Like crazy thing."

"Then send your gods-be human friends home! *Out!* Turn those ships around, restore the balance, for godssake!"

"How you guarantee Anuurn be safe, a? How you heal stsho? How you 'splain these human we got change mind? How you deal with knnn, a?"

A sense of panic closed in on her. Not alone because it was all logical, and the pieces were there. She looked around again at the hani lines, at her own people, at some faces gone hard and ears gone flat. At others, spacers, who just looked worried. Like her crew.

Like Goldtooth.

And not a sound from the kif.

The politicians would hang her, eventually, when all the furor died down. It was the last shred of Chanur's reputation they asked for.

"Yeah," she said. "Well, it's clear, isn't it? We just tell these humans they have to leave. That you consulted with some high Personage and there's a lot of trouble and they just have to turn those ships around and get back the other side of that border. Which we can do, can't we? It just might give Skkukuk here a good chance to go home in style, number one fine—a whole shift in policy, a new *mekt-hakkikt*, a new directive. I'm not real interested in going *into* kifish space, Skkukuk my friend: I'm just real pleased for you to be *hakkikt* over all the kif you can get your hands on. And all you have to do is hold that border tight once the humans cross it outbound."

"Kkkt." Skkukuk drew in a hissing breath. *"Mekt-hakkikt,* you justify my faith in you."

"You won't cross into mahen territory."

"They won't cross into ours."

"They won't." Looking at Jik. And Goldtooth. Goldtooth lowered his small ears and bowed his head slowly, with reluctance.

"I hear," he said quietly. And made the same gesture to Jik, and to the Personage as he turned away.

Something's wrong with him. Something mahen and crazy, and something I don't know: I've done something to him. I've beaten him.

Two plans. Two treaties. The mahendo'sat rise and fall on their successes; and they disown the failures.

"If I've got to run this business for a while," she said to Jik, "I want him. What would he think about it?"

Jik's eyes flickered and something lightened there. "He tell you you got damn fine fellow."

"This Personage of yours—" She tilted a careful ear toward the robed mahe with the Voice. "Iji?"

"Same. I talk for him. He don't got good pidgin. Same his Voice. He also Personage, see you got same Person-thing, lot strong. He say—God make Personage. He—" Jik gave a helpless gesture. "He say God make lot peculiar experiment."

She laid her ears back, trying to put that on one side or the other. "Tell him—gods, just tell him I'll do what I have to. First thing—" She put her hands in the waist of her trousers. They were icy; her feet were numb from the decking. And it was still raw fear. "Tully."

"Captain?"

The humans were first. She kept her shoulder to the *han* representatives and to the Llun; and felt a dull shock to find Skkukuk's armed presence a positive comfort on her left, where it regarded breaking that news.

"What we do, we talk a little trade, talk up all the trouble they got to watch out for. I figure maybe they've seen enough to worry about. Maybe we just tell them it gets *worse* up ahead."

"They go," Tully said finally, coming out of that small fluorescent-lit room on Gaohn dockside, where mahendo'sat and kif and humans and hani argued. Armed. Every one of them, since the kif were worse without their weapons at hand than with. And they went at it in shifts, till Tully came out in a waft of that godsawful multispecies stale air, and leaned against the doorframe. "They go." He looked drowned. Sweat stuck his hair to his forehead and his eyes looked bruised. After three days at this back-and-forth, herself out of the room for clean air and a new grip on her temper, agreement was like the floor going away.

"Go? Leave? They say yes?"

Gods, who threatened them? What happened? What went wrong? Belligerence was not the strategy she chose. Discouragement was. She had hammered this home with Skkukuk until the deviousness and the advantage of the tactic slowly blossomed in his narrow kifish skull, and his red-rimmed eyes showed a distinctive interest, which, gods help them all, might turn up as something new in kifish strategy.

"They say yes," Tully said, and made a ship-going motion with his flat hand. "Go way home. Kif and mahendo'sat go with. First mahendo'sat, then kif, with few hani. You got find hani ship go. Make passage 'long kif territory."

"That bastard." Meaning Skkukuk, who had ulterior motives in running a parade of exiting humans right through kifish territory. It was also the shortest route. And Tully just hung there against the wall blinking in his own sweat and smelling godsawful no matter how much perfume he dosed himself with. He picked it up off the others. They all did. But overheated human still had its own distinctive aroma.

"Good?" he asked.

"Gods." She drew a deep breath and took him by the shoulder on her way to the door. He had to go back in. They still needed him. The mechanical translators were a disaster. And he looked all but out on his feet. "Yes. Good. Thank gods. Can you go a little longer? Another hour?"

"I do." Hoarse and desperate-sounding.

"Tully. You can go with them. You understand. Go home."

He blinked at her. Shook his head. He had that gesture back. "Here. *The Pride.*"

"Tully. You don't understand. We got trouble. We're all right now. After this—I can't say. I don't know that Chanur won't be arrested. Or worse than that. I have enemies, Tully. Lot of enemies. And if something happens to me and Chanur you'd be alone. Bad mess. You understand that? I can't say you'll be safe. I can't even say that for myself or the crew."

He did not understand. The words, maybe. But not the way the *han* paid off people like Ayhar, like Tahar, who was still not in a mood to come in. Gods knew what they reserved for Chanur.

"I friend."

"Friend. Gods. They owe you plenty, Tully. But you got to get out of here with somebody."

His mobile eyes shifted toward the door, the same as a hani slanting an ear. *They.* "Not good I go with."

It made sense then. Too much. "They got the *han*'s way of saying thanks, huh? Same you, same me with the hani. Gods-rotted mess, Tully."

He just looked at her.

And they went in one after the other. To get down to charts and precise routes.

Across the table from a tired, surly lot of humans.

Tully talked again, from his seat halfway down the table. In a quiet, colorless tone.

What came back sounded heated. But not when Tully rendered it. Simply: "They go. Want us come home with."

"No," the Llun said, before the mahen Personage got a word in. Skkukuk just sat and clicked to himself.

"This isn't a good time," Pyanfar said. Being an old trader. Tully rendered that in some fashion. "Knnn out there." And he rendered that, which got surlier frowns.

"Kkkkt," Skkukuk said, lifting his jaw, which they probably failed to understand.

Tully said something. It was probable that Tully *did* understand.

They were disposed to go to their ships after that.

"We've got it," she said to the Llun, after, herself and Tully outside in the corridor again with the Llun guard, when it was all adjourning. They were somewhat kin, she and the Llun senior. They kept it remote: the Immunes cherished their neutrality.

"We expect," the Llun said, "that the mahendo'sat may come up with some reparations."

Pyanfar's ears went down. Her jaw dropped. "My gods, we just *got* the kif and the mahendo'sat settled—"

"You have a peculiar position."

She went on staring at the Llun.

"Unique influence," the Llun said.

Trading instincts took over. In a blinding flash. *My gods. They* need *something, don't they?*

Gods save us. The mahendo'sat.

I can get The Pride *running again. Maybe get clear of this port. Bluff them out of arresting us.*

"It occurs to the *han* and the Immunes collectively," the Llun said, "that if you can do this, you can do other things. You have an extreme influence with the mahendo'sat."

My gods, my gods, they don't see yet! The mahendo'sat, the mahendo'sat are all they can see. The stsho and the mahendo'sat. Their precious trading interests. She walked away, stared off down the corridor where her own multispecies escort waited, rattling with weapons. Like the knnn and the tc'a out there, which Jik and Goldtooth swore was a tolerably friendly presence. And a pirate ship which was lying very quiet, but assuredly listening. She knew Tahar, that she would go on listening till she knew it was time to run for it. *I'm dangerous. I'm a plague and a danger to them. But they're mistaken what the danger is.*

"Chanur. The *han* is offering you your land back."

She turned around, blinked and stared at the Immune. "You mean my son is giving it up. Surrendering the land? Or the *han* is just confiscating it?"

"They'll work something out. They're disposed to work something out."

"Gods-be greedy eggsucking bastards! What are they asking? What are they buying? *Who in a mahen hell do they think they're trading with?*"

"I don't think they know either. I don't think they imagine. *I* do. The spacer clans do. They're saying they'll fight if the *han* lays a hand on you. They know what it would mean with the kif and the mahendo'sat. I know."

"They're crazy!"

"You're in a position. What will happen if you aren't? Tell me that."

Skkukuk being what Sikkukkut wanted to be. Jik discredited. Shake-ups in the mahen government. More craziness.

It was not what she wanted to think of. It lay there day and night in her gut like something indigestible.

So did the solution.

"So the *han* just wants me to come down there and play politics and pay the bar tab, huh? Cozy up with the Naur."

"I didn't say that. I don't say the Naur won't try." The Llun looked as if she had something sour in her mouth. "I don't say you'll have to listen to them. You've got friends. That's what I'm trying to say. Unofficially."

"Because I won in there."

"I'll be honest. Some clans would have stood by you. The Llun couldn't have. We have other considerations. I'm not talking to a political novice. I'm not one either."

"Meaning you know what I *could* do."

"You're hani. You came back here. You came back here like Ayhar did. Like all the rest. That's some assurance what you'll do."

"The land's the rest, is it?"

"Some accommodation can be worked out."

Her heart hurt. Acutely. It took several breaths to dispel enough of the pain to talk. "I'm too honest, Llun. I'm too gods-be honest to take that deal. I'm too honest to do that to the *han,* and I mean *us,* not what sits on its broad backside down in that marble mausoleum and tries to play politics in a universe it doesn't by the gods *understand.* I'm the best education they're ever likely to get. You're right. You and your guards don't lay a hand on me or mine. You *know* what it would set off."

The Llun's ears had gone flat. "Is that a threat? Is that what I take it for?"

"Don't worry about me. I'm not Ehrran. Or Naur. I don't keep notebooks. And I'm going to be a lousy houseguest. You understand that? I can't drag that kind of politics into the *han*. I can't sit in the *han* and handle the kif. Or the mahendo'sat. Or the stsho. That isn't what the kif and the mahendo'sat created. I don't have any kin anymore. I can't have. I can't pay those kinds of debts. Come on, Tully."

She walked past the Llun, away from her and down the corridor without a backward look. She hurt inside. There were only foreigners waiting for her. And the crew she had to face. And explain to.

"Wrong?" Tully asked.

"No." She felt better, having said that. Having decided it. She laid a hand on his shoulder as they walked. "Friend," she said, and discovered that felt better too.

"Pyanfar." He stopped, faced her, pulling something from his hand and, taking hers palm up, pressed that something into it. She opened her fingers. It was the little gold ring. The one from lost *Ijir*. From some other friend of his. "You take." He reached out and touched the side of her ear. "So."

It was the most precious thing he owned, the only thing he really owned, the only link he had with his dead. "My gods, Tully—"

"Take."

She clenched her hand on it. He seemed pleased at that, even relieved, as if he had let something go that had been too heavy to carry.

"You want to stay or go? Tully?"

"Stay. With *The Pride*. With you. With crew."

"It's not the same! It won't be the same! Gods rot it, Tully, I can't make you understand what you're walking into. The crew may leave. Hilfy will have to. I don't know where we'll be. I don't know how long this will last before it gets worse."

"Need me."

She opened her mouth and shut it. Of all the crew she reckoned might be steadiest, she had never even reckoned him. Like the ring, it was too profound a gift.

"Come on," she said.

"We're doing all right," she said, on a full stomach, in the crowded galley—the Tauran had gone, with Vrossaru, aboard *Mahijiru*, trailing the humans out. There was a matter of getting back to Meetpoint and picking up their ships and cargoes. *Ayhar's Prosperity* had a guaranteed run in that direction too, with a full hold, which Meetpoint might direly need. And, good or bad news, one never knew, the knnn had disappeared with the tc'a, off on a vector which ought to get it lost in limbo, if it were not a knnn, and capable of making jumps that other ships could not. Toward stsho space, it looked like. At best guess.

"We got word from Tahar," Haral said. "They got the message."

"What'd they say about it?"

"Said thanks. They said they'll believe in a *han* amnesty when they get it engraved, but they say they plan to shadow us awhile. Till the word gets around."

"Huh." It was prudent. Dur Tahar was that. She let go a small sigh. "*We* got some business at Meetpoint too, soon as they get our tail put back together." She took a sip of gfi. There was a vacancy at table. Hilfy was off doing Chanur business. Which was the way it had to be. Married, within the year: that was what Hilfy had to do, find herself some young man strong enough to take her cousin Kara and pitch him clear back to Mahn territory.

In that choice she had burned to give advice; but what was between her and Hilfy had gotten too remote for that, too businesslike. It was her own hardheaded, closemouthed pride. She saw it like a mirror. Hilfy knew everything; more than Hilfy might ever know when she was a hundred.

Then: "Hey," Hilfy had said to her when she left, not captain-crew formal, but a level, adult look eye to eye. "I'm not going hunting round in Hermitage. I'm just putting the word out I'm looking. Me. Heir to Chanur. And the winner gets a shuttle ticket up to Gaohn. I don't care if he's handsome. But he's by the gods going to have to have the nerve to come up here and meet my father."

"Huh," she had said to that. Since she had resolved to disentangle herself from clan business as long as the Personage business persisted. She did not, likewise, offer advice to Rhean or Anfy or any of the others.

"I'm telling you," she said now, to the crew, to her cousins, her husband, and a human, "you don't have to go out on this one. You want some ground time, gods know you've got it coming." With a look under her brows at Chur, who had it coming doubly. "Or station. Or discharge. To *Fortune;* to *Light.* Anywhere. I'm the gods-be Personage of Anuurn, I can get you any post you want, it ought to let me do *some* things I want to do."

Long silence. "No," Haral said. And: "No," like an echo from Tirun.

"World's not safe," Chur said, and shrugged uncomfortably. "But I met this Llun fellow. Immune. Quiet. Real quiet."

"You want your discharge. Or just some leave time?"

Chur sighed, a heave of her shoulders. "Gods, I want till we get the tail fixed, that's all."

Geran had looked worried. Terrified for a moment. The shadow passed.

Khym looked Chur's way. And back to her, with a quiet and considerate expression. Sometimes the thoughts went through his eyes so plain she could read them. After all these years.

Epilog

The docks reeked of foreignness, of metal and oil and machinery, and they echoed with announcements and the snarls of monstrous machines; it was a frightening place for a boy from a land of blue sky and golden grass. Hallan heard the PA thundering advisements the cavernous gray spaces swallowed and gave back garbled in echo. He looked about him and saw groups of black-trousered Immunes moving down the docks in a cordon across the whole dockside: what little he did catch from the PA was alarming, snatches of advisories to clear some area, but he had no idea what section four green was or why the lights were flashing blue down there and red where he was.

It was a confusing arrival for a downworld lad, laboring along with his pass and all his worldly possessions in a brand new spacer's duffel. He had spent two bewildered hours in immigration, then taken what turned out to be the wrong lift up from the shuttle dock; then into an administrative office for directions, and down another lift, then, which went sideways as often as it went down and came to dead stop on the main docks, resisting all his attempts to get it to go up. So he had ventured out into the docks of Anuurn, which dazed him with echoes and its true size and its reality after so many dreams. It was a dangerous place, his sisters had warned him; it was wonderful; it overloaded his senses with its noise and its echoes and its foreign smells. It was too huge a place, its few people too hurried or too rough-looking to bother with a newcomer's foolish questions. The docks ran all the circumference of the station: he was sure of that, and surely, if he started walking in the up-numbers direction, section four could not be too far from the section seven he was hunting. He walked along where there was no traffic at all, in the shadow of the gantries, and went from berth 14 where he had come in to berth 15; 16 was a working berth, all its lights lit with a glitter which stirred his sense of the beautiful—white and gold, a hundred lights to shine on the lines and the gantry and the whole surrounds. The ramp access looked to be open. The dockers were driving their vehicles away, and no one noticed if a boy kept walking, so he might pass by as close to his dreams as he had ever come in his life.

But now—*CLEAR THE AREA* the speaker overhead said while he panted along at the foot of the towering machinery, there by the lights. *CLEAR THE AREA,* and something more that he could not hear in the garble. He looked around desperately and saw the Immunes moving and the docks suddenly deserted. His heart began to beat in panic: he wondered was it a decompression warning, whether something had gone dangerously wrong on this dock or somewhere near—he had heard horror tales from the war years.

But in his casting about for direction he spied a spacer, a graynosed woman whose ears had, gods, a whole fistful of voyage-rings, who sat on the skirt of some huge piece of machinery, just sitting, observing the whole furor, arm around one knee, her ears backslanted in the racket; suddenly she was looking straight at him.

He dropped his ears at once in politeness: and in outright awe at the spacer rings and the easy assurance of this veteran who was everything he was not and longed with all his heart to be. He would never have come her way on his own; but she was staring at him as if he were somehow more interesting than the chaos and the goings-on with the Immunes. He thought he detected an invitation, a summons in the twitch of a many-ringed ear: and he hitched up his duffel and all the courage of his seventeen years.

"H'lo," he said, walking up—his smile and his friendliness had won him a great deal in his life, and he relied on it now, when he was afraid, slanting an ear toward the commotion behind him. "Lot of noise, isn't it?"

The spacer nodded.

Not a word. Not the least ear-twitch of friendliness. He was left a fool, twice desperate. His blue breeches were brand new. His ears were ringless. His duffel still had package-creases and he swung it back behind him and dropped it where it was less conspicuous, figuring he had mistaken her invitation: he was suddenly anxious only to get his directions and go, before he found himself in something he could not handle.

The eyes raked him and down in lazy ease, flickered with some kind of interest. "Wrong side of that line, you know."

He cleared his throat, looked nervously over his shoulder. "What are they doing down there?"

"What are you doing up here?"

"I—" He looked back again full into the spacer's lazy stare, that stripped him down to the bones and the truth; there was not even a lie he knew how to tell. "I'm new here," he said; and dropped his ears in deference when her mouth pursed in dour amusement. "What's all the commotion down there?"

"The Pride's in port."

He could not help himself; he looked back again toward the distant lines and drew a large breath. The *station,* for godsakes, he had truly come to the station, where fantastical species came and went; where fabled ship-names were ordinary on the freighting lists, and many-ringed spacers sat about ordinary as could be. And on the very day he came up from the world, *The Pride of Chanur* just happened in, with no advance notice in the newsservices, nothing at all to tell the world it was coming. He saw nothing for his looking but a solid line of black-breeched Immunes in the distance, practically no one on the docks there or near at hand; and nothing at all of the ship-boards down there: gantries obscured the view. He looked back and tried to catch his breath. "Gods, I'd like to see it."

"You don't *see* a ship, son, they stay out there." She was laughing at him, all dour-faced. "But you could go up to the observation lounge, the cameras'll give you a view."

"I want to see *them.*"

"Who?"

"Them."

"The Personage? Gods-rotted lot of nonsense."

He caught a quick breath. His ears went flat. *Nonsense. My gods!*

"Nonsense," the spacer said again. "No different than you and me. What d'you think, boy? Blackbreeches scurrying around like chi in a fire, shut down the whole gods-be dockside—"

"Well, oughtn't they?" He was indignant. *One of the old ones, this, one of the surly old-timers, just blowing off. She doesn't like a boy being up here, doesn't like me being on any ship, ever. Walk off, that's what I ought to do. She probably has a knife somewhere, even a gun in that pocket, gods know what.* "I'm going to go have a look." He grabbed up his duffel again.

But the spacer patted the machine-skirt. "Tssss. You won't get anywhere through that line. Just a lot of trouble. Have a seat, boy. All bright-eyed and new, are you?"

He was off his stride. He delayed. And knew himself a fool when the old spacer took on a friendlier, amused look. Turn about for his pretense of being what he was not, that was what she had given him. Fair and fair.

"Sit. Crew's going to be down here in a bit. What ship are you going to?"

"Not to a ship. Yet. School. I'm Meras. Hallan Meras. From Syrsyn." Confession once started, tumbled out in the old spacer's unchanging stare, and his ears burned with embarrassment; she had known even when she asked, but she did not ridicule him. "I *want* to be a spacer." It was his dearest dream. He saw it coming true and she did not laugh when he said that either. *One of the old ones.* "Have you—" He cast another look down the dock, leaning forward, and saw nothing of ship names at this angle either. "Have you ever seen the Personage?"

"Lots of times."

He looked back in awe. "Are you a friend of hers?"

"What's the matter with you, boy, what do they teach you nowadays, all this fuss to see some Personage, what's *seeing* do, anyway? Makes me worry, that's what. Hani I knew'd spit in the eye of somebody that wanted all that bowing and guarding. You ought to."

He understood then. "She got me here," he said. And when the old spacer blinked: "That's why I want to see that ship. I wouldn't *be* here without her, without what she did. That's why."

"Huh," the old spacer said. "Huh." And: "Uhhnnn—" With a gesture outward, toward the sudden flashing of a strobe light and the arrival of several official cars. "Llun."

"Are we in trouble?" Hallan got anxiously to his feet as his spacer companion stood up. He snatched up his duffel and held onto it. Immune officials and weapon-bearing marshals were getting out of the car, coming their way, while suddenly, adding to the confusion, there were other spacers coming down the ramp out of the ship, one of them a man, one of them—"O my gods," Hallan said, having seen humans in old pictures, and having seen a picture of this one.

"Cap'n," one of the spacers said, scar-nosed and broad-faced; and coming their way. "My gods, you going like that?"

"Too much fuss," the old spacer said, and dusted off her trousers. "Drives me berserk, this whole business. They want a decree, I'll give 'em a decree. Haral, meet a nice kid. Hallan Meras, meet Haral Araun. Sorry we can't stay and talk right now. Luck to you."

She walked off with the crew from the ship, the human Tully and all. And *na* Khym *nef* Mahn, who was the first man in space.

One of the crew lingered a moment, a small woman who looked him up and down with eyes that for a moment seemed to see—gods, inside him and around him with a force that left him all but shaking. Chur Anify. The strange one. She was the one that had charted the new Points off beyond Minar, and probes had found them, a bridge to other stars. She was almost as famous as the Personage.

"Who is this boy?" A Llun officer asked, all hard and threatening.

"He has a right to be there," Chur Anify said, and the officer looked at her and dropped her ears and let him alone.

"Are you some relative?" that officer asked when the cars had left the dockside and grim Llun marshals stood double guard outside *The Pride of Chanur*'s ramp access. "Are you Chanur?"

"No," he said, holding his baggage and still dazed as if all the stars in space spun about him. That had been the Personage, the *mekt-hakkikt* of the kif, the Director . . . there were as many names as there were species in the Compact. She had talked with him, this power that could move a thousand ships and mediate affairs among species.

With him, as if he were truly someone who mattered.

Or as if he might be that someone, someday.